WHEN
SPARKS
IGNITE

ERIN RIHA

Cover design by Ashley Ruggirello

Book design by Ashley Ruggirello

Map by Christopher Winkelaar

Hardcover ISBN: 978-1-942111-91-7

Paperback ISBN: 978-1-942111-92-4

eBook ISBN: 978-1-942111-89-4

REUTS Publications
www.REUTS.com

For Thelma Maye and Susan, the original badass women in my life.

CHAPTER ONE

*A*s a wave knocks into the ship, Neve curses in Espancian.

"I can do this, you know," Meredith says, hovering over my oldest friend like a mother hen.

"Can someone tell the captain to take it easy, already?" Neve hisses, lightly sweeping a feather-thin brush along the edges of my lashes.

"It's always like this when going from the Mittlesee to the bay," Meredith says.

"Well then perhaps the captain should be used to it by now? Or else give in to the fact that this is not his calling."

Another wave rocks the ship and Neve's brush darts dangerously close to my eye.

"Could we maybe wait just another minute until we're in smoother seas for you to poke at my eye?" I ask. Neve's expression is blank but she takes a step back. Meredith leans in, peering over Neve's shoulder and examining my face.

"How did you get that blend beneath her eyes? It's

always so dark, and I've never been able to find the right mix."

"There's aloe vera in my concealer," Neve says, the faintest hint of pride flashing in her hazel eyes.

"Really?" Meredith says, reaching for the tincture and putting just a little bit on the back of her hand. "Oh, there is! I would've never thought — "

"Of course you wouldn't," Neve says, "because you don't make your own products."

"I do," Meredith says. And with that, she fumbles through her bag for her magic cloths. Neve watches as Meredith wipes the cloth over her hand, and it comes away completely clean. Neve lifts her eyebrows, and now I need two hands to count the number of times I've seen her look impressed.

There's a knock at the door.

"Ladies?" Alvin calls through the door. All three of us roll our eyes at Declan's personal assistant. He's only about five years older than any of us, but acts like he knows more than we do and we're just idiot children.

"Yes, Sir Alvin?" Neve calls. Meredith and I stifle snort laughs. He hates when she calls him that, but hasn't actually gotten her to stop it yet.

"It's nearly time. Is Miss Arden ready?"

We roll our eyes again. Maybe some of the other girls would like being called "miss," but it sounds so odd and weird attached to my name. Especially on this ship. It's been very casual on ships for me until very recently. Nobody is listening in. Nobody is vying for prestige or some sort of honorarium. Not on a ship with not nearly enough showers.

"If your captain would stop running into tidal waves, we'd have been ready a long time ago," Neve responds.

Meredith playfully slaps Neve's arm, and I try to stifle a smile as Neve comes at me with her brush again.

I hear the door open, and Alvin harrumphs.

"She'll be ready in just a few minutes, sir," Meredith says. Meredith has to call him sir. He's higher on the imaginary hierarchy and, technically, her boss. Not that I'd ever let him fire her. But we can all hear the tinge of sarcasm when she says *sir*, and it makes us smile.

"Sir Declan has been waiting for—"

"And he'll wait as long as it takes if he wants a presentable bride," Neve says with a bite. Everyone goes still at that, and I feel the blood drain from my face. It's not exactly a secret that we're going to be married. But it's one that I've been trying not to think about.

"Yes, ma'am," Alvin says. I swear I hear him click his heels, and then the door shuts.

"You should go easier on him," I say, tugging on Neve's skirt as she blows on my eyelids, coaxing the liner to dry.

"Why would I do that?" she asks.

"I think he's fond of you," Meredith says, a teasing note in her voice.

"Open," Neve says, tapping my shoulder, ignoring her. I open my eyes, and both girls are staring at me. They blink once, twice, and then—in unison—smile and nod.

"Perfect," Meredith says. "I'll never know how you have such a steady hand."

Neve turns away from her, as if there's a clear answer to that. I still don't know what happened between when she left the peninsula and when I found her in Sudersberg at Irina's brothel. I've tried to ask, but it's clear she's not ready to talk about it. One thing is for sure: Meredith is right. Neve's hand is steady, and her eyeliner has gotten much more consistent than it ever was when we were beneficiaries together on the peninsula. I hope she'll tell me someday.

"Isn't it going to be too warm for this?" I ask, standing and pointing to my blue lambswool twinset sweaters and gray-and-white calf-length plaid skirt. "I thought Brandeissland had palm trees?"

"In the southern part of the country," Neve says, a note of bitterness on her tongue.

"It's winter everywhere, Arden," Meredith says, a little more kindly. "Though not too cold to wear flowers in your hair when the moment should arise . . ." My stomach tightens at her clear reference to being Declan's bride, and I look away. She turns and approaches with a beautiful white brocade coat. I slip my arms into it with her help and marvel at the way it hits at exactly the right length so that the skirt can just barely flare beneath it, giving the otherwise stiff jacket a touch of femininity. I tuck the compass I wear on a chain beneath my top.

"Right," I say, feeling stupid for not realizing that if it was winter in Nordania, it would be winter here too, even if it is along the southern coast of the Mittlesee. Neve obviously knew this. If I'd stayed at the institute, I might have known this too. Or maybe I should have known it anyway?

"Stop it," Neve snaps, handing me a slip of paper. The same slip of paper that Irina gave me on the pier before we left the Port of Pleasure.

"What?"

"You're getting flushed. I'm not adding any more makeup. That blend is perfect."

"Don't you mind her," Meredith says, adjusting the collar of the jacket just so. "The flush will only make Declan think you're happy to see him."

My cheeks stop heating. Neve snorts but says nothing.

It's been a strange two weeks since he arrived at the Port of Pleasure and rescued me and Neve from bounty hunters. We've been slow to return to Nordania, although even that has been an uncomfortable discussion.

Once we get back to Nordania, we are to be married.

And I don't want to get married. Not yet. Not while there's still so much uncertainty.

"Pop quiz," Neve says, pulling me out of my tangled web of uncomfortable thoughts. "The daughter of the Brandeiss emissary to Nordania is . . ."

"Amelia," I say. "She's nine years old and loves steeplechase."

"She does?" Meredith says, blinking in surprise.

My stomach tightens with doubt. She's right. What nine-year-old loves steeplechase? But I think it's correct.

"Yes?" I say.

Neve sighs, pinching the bridge of her nose. "Yes. She's a weirdo who loves steeplechase and sedimentary rocks. Some people are just odd. Even at nine."

"I wish I'd known you when you were nine," I say under my breath. She lifts her eyebrows, but doesn't say anything more. I know she came to Nordania from Espancia, but I don't know when. The things I don't know about Neve could fill the lower levels of this ship. Even the brig.

A mishmash of confusing emotions washes over me at the mere thought of the ship's jail—and its only occupant. I refocus my attention on an imagined wrinkle in my skirt.

Another knock at the door jolts me out of my battle against the woolen skirt, and I answer the door myself. I'm about to say something snappy to Alvin, but instead, it's Declan.

"Oh, hi," I say, stuffing my hand into the pocket of my jacket. The paper slip is warm and soft against my hand.

"Oh, hi," he says, a teasing glint in his gray eyes. He looks smart in his navy wool overcoat and charcoal gray suit. The cerulean tie somehow makes his eyes look even more gray. "You're ready?"

"I think so?" I say, responding to the question in his words.

"Oh," he says, realizing his gaffe. "I mean, you look ready. I mean —you look lovely. Beautiful."

"Thank you, " I say. Meredith and Neve stifle chuckles behind me, though not very well.

"Ladies," Declan says, turning his attention to them with a princely smile. "You both look lovely." Meredith blushes and curtsies. Neve follows suit, but there's no blush to her expression. Sometimes, I wonder what would have happened if they'd chosen Neve instead of me. Fiona would've probably wet the bed the first time she got on Neve's wrong side, for one. Neve is literally on my team, and she still scares the hell out of me.

"I'll try to have her back at a reasonable time," Declan says in a teasing voice. The girls laugh, the appropriate volume and the appropriate length. "Shall we?" He offers his elbow, and I take it.

We walk down the hallway toward the ship's stern. He has an easy confidence, and even though we don't agree on everything, even though I feel unsteady in this dynamic and this world, I feel safe on his arm. Maybe it's in his warmth, or his princely posture? Or maybe it's how, when I slip my hand into the crook of his elbow, he tightens his elbow just enough to know that he's not going to let me get swept away from him.

We stop at the door to the back deck. We've done this at every stop over the past two weeks. And there have been far more than I expected. His initial plan was to take me back to Nordania directly. Then a request for a visit came in from some dignitary in Sudersberg. Then another. This is the fifth or sixth — I've lost count — and it's the same dog and pony show every time. We stand on the stern of the ship as we come into port and wave like the happy couple the world expects to see. Then we disembark and go see a house, or a church, or a playground. Actually, I don't mind the playgrounds. There are always children there, and they don't know they're supposed to act a certain way around me.

Then we go have a meal of some sort, and I eat a "ladylike" portion, no matter what it is, and then Declan has port or sherry or whatever the local after-dinner liqueur habit is, while I have tea with the women, whoever they might be. Then, when there aren't any other ears, I ask the women if they know of any of the Embers — the graduates of the institute who have gone elsewhere. They're the only people whose support in our relationship might truly change the tide. So far, I've come up empty-handed. Which begs the question: where *are* the Embers?

"Are you ready?" Declan asks, gently squeezing my hand with his arm. I nod. Then he opens the door.

Right away, a smack of cold wind lashes my face, and I'm grateful Meredith braided the top half of my unruly hair back so I'm not eating my curls.

"Brisk," Declan says around a shiver. I laugh.

"It's like a kick to the teeth," I say. He laughs, loud and genuine. And gazes at me with adoration.

I love this version of us. I love the way he looks at me, and I've seen the pictures of the way I look at him. It's really beautiful. As we approach the railing, we see the photographers and wave. Just then, another blast of wind whips at us and my jacket flies open. Declan turns me toward him, taking hold of my lapels, and buttons it up to my chin, one pearly closure at a time. When he reaches the top one, he clucks my chin so that I'm looking up at him.

"Better?" he asks. He slips his other hand around my waist, tugging me close.

"Better," I say, forcing a natural-looking smile.

"I'm going to kiss you now," he says. It's not a romantic thing to say. It might look romantic. But between the two of us, it feels like he's asking to shake my hand. And yet, every time he asks, I swear I see a flicker of hope in his eyes. Like something different might happen.

"Okay," I say. His eyes dim, and he leans in and presses a chaste kiss to my lips, then the tip of my nose. He pulls me into his chest, and I hear him sigh against the quick beat of his heart. I can't help but think that I did this. I caused this disconnect.

"Declan," I say, as if needing to give him a reason why I haven't flirted, why I haven't invited him into my room, or why, in these two weeks, I haven't kissed him back.

"Come on," he says, with his practiced, handsome smile. "They'll be waiting for us."

With that, he offers me his ungloved hand. It's such a simple gesture. He's giving me his hand—no masks, no subterfuge, just him. And what have I given him in return? I reach for his hand and lace my fingers between his. Our hands are cold, and his knuckles feel tight around mine, but he glances up at me.

A soft, sad smile reaches his eyes as he lifts my knuckles to his lips.

I feel the paper burning a hole in my pocket. He's so open right now, and we're about to be surrounded by sycophants and suck-ups. We couldn't have a real conversation. Maybe this is as good a time as any to tell him about it—and to ask to find out where it goes, if it leads to Carmen and the rest of the Ember Network.

"Is there something on your mind?" Declan asks.

This is it. It's time to tell him. To ask if we can look for her.

Alvin clears his throat behind us.

Perhaps not.

"Let's go," I say. "Wouldn't want to make Alvin any more nervous." With an audience, a roguish smile crosses his face and he tugs me into his side.

"Oh, I can think of at least a dozen ways to make Alvin nervous."

Alvin blanches and averts his gaze.

Declan smiles as I slip my free hand into my pocket and let my fingers curl around the paper. The one with the code to get what I need:

Don't fuck this up, little girl.
43-15-12 S 124-49-23 E

CHAPTER TWO

"*L*adies and gentlemen, last questions," Alvin says into the microphone.

Press conferences are my least favorite part of this parade. They always ask the same questions, and only one or two are directed toward me. Even though Alvin promises they're always going to be "soft" questions, I still get nervous answering questions about whether I'm glad to be reunited with Declan, and whether I know how to make Nordanian Orange Cake—and do I make it with olive oil or butter?

The answers to those questions are always "Yes," and "Yes—with olive oil, of course!" Heaven forbid I might accidentally insult the olive oil council by showing preference for the dairy farmers of Espancia. And then I smile, and before anyone can ask anything more interesting, Alvin jumps in and redirects the questioning, or calls the conference to an end.

"Maria Jöstens, the Brandeiss Daily Caller," says a woman about halfway back, with dark hair and copper skin.

"Hello, Ms. Jöstens," Declan says in a perfect Brandeiss accent and practiced grin.

"What do you have to say about allegations from the Osterstanis that Nordania was involved in the latest explosion along the eastern corridor?" This isn't the first Osterstan question we've received. Honestly, I've been surprised by how many there are. Especially when I remember how fast Dean Edina shut me down when I asked her about Osterstan.

"I would first say that my thoughts and prayers are with the families impacted by that heinous crime. Then, I would yield the question to my father, who is the acting Prime Minister of Nordania and has far more insight into this tense situation than I do. But it is my understanding that Nordania has pledged two million dollars in relief aid to victims of the bombing."

Maria Jöstens doesn't look satisfied with that answer, but the rest of the reporters seem to be. Or at least, they want their questions answered instead.

Honestly, I don't know how he does it. Takes questions like these, day after day, and doesn't get frazzled or nervous, or frustrated.

"Benji Glastenberg, the Chronicle." A bald man in a suit stands from the second row, and Declan smiles in greeting. "Our readers were polled on their top two questions for you, so I'd like to ask both, if you don't mind."

"Not at all," Declan says with a grin.

"First, the slow down of copper imports from Nordania has been hitting our homeland industries hard. Do you have an explanation for this? Or an idea of when imports will return to normal levels?"

Declan's smile falters, only for a split second. I'm not sure anyone besides me and Alvin would notice, to be honest. But it does. Which makes me wonder—does he know about this?

"I'm sorry for the inconvenience to the Brandeiss citizens who have been impacted by this. My understanding is that there was a production issue several months ago, but that it has been addressed. Perhaps it will take a bit longer for the supply chain to catch up? Now, your second question?"

The reporter smiles indulgently, as if he knew Declan wasn't going to have a real answer for that question and merely wanted to get him on the record. This happens sometimes. That's why Alvin has insisted that I say as little as possible, because the last thing they want is someone like me—whatever that means—creating a scandal without realizing I've said something idiotic.

"Our second question is actually for Miss Thatcher," he says. Alvin motions for me to join Declan at the podium, but not without flashing me a tight smile that clearly says, *"Watch what you say."*

"Hello, Mr. Glastenburg," I say with a soft smile.

"Miss Thatcher, this may seem silly, but our readers want to know how Mr. Levington takes his tea."

The room laughs, and I feel my cheeks burn. Of course. Because I'm to be his wife, so I should know how he takes his tea. Alvin visibly relaxes, but when I look at Declan, he hasn't.

And then I realize why: I have no idea how Declan takes his tea.

I think back to Dean Edina and, before her, Headmistress Moyle. What would they tell me to do?

So I smile and decide to be honest, with a touch of charm.

"I'm sorry to say I don't know how Mr. Levington takes his tea. I've never made it for the prime minister before."

The room erupts in laughter, and Alvin shifts to cut us off, but the reporter interrupts.

"What about his son, then? What sort of tea should the housewives of the world be serving their husbands?"

"I honestly couldn't tell you. I prefer coffee, and Declan is a twenty-year-old man who makes his own tea. And quite well, I would imagine, as he's never asked for help."

The room is silent for the longest moment of my life. Then Declan cracks out in laughter—the belly-shaking kind of laughter that I haven't seen him do since before I left. It makes me laugh just as hard, feeling the pure joy radiating from him. And then it spills throughout the room. He presses a chaste kiss to my temple, and despite everything between us, I revel in the glow of his affection. I'm not ready to return it, not after the way my heart is still shattered, but the warmth feels good.

"Thank you, that will be all," Alvin says, cutting between us to the microphone. We wave as we're led off the stage and into a side room.

"Oh my god, Arden," Declan says, still laughing. He wraps his arms around me and pulls me into a hug, and I laugh as I hug him back.

"I'm glad you think this is funny," Alvin says. "You've just insulted both the institution of marriage and one of the largest exports of Brandeissland."

I stop laughing. Declan keeps chuckling.

"Come on, Alvin, it was a joke. People will understand it as such," Declan says.

"Doubtful. They take tea *very* seriously here, and you know it. How did you not know that? How could you be so—"

"Why don't you get us a tea service while we wait for our transport," Declan interrupts, his voice brokering no debate. It's very clear he didn't want me to hear whatever it was Alvin thinks of me. Although, I can think of a few choice words to fill that empty space. I've heard them all before.

"What kind of tea do you prefer?" Alvin asks, his dark eyes narrow and lethal—and directed at me.

"I'd prefer an orange pekoe, and bring coffee for Arden," Declan says.

"Are you sure that's wise?"

"Let's not make them think she's a liar," Declan says. Alvin nods and excuses himself. Then it's just the two of us. And we're still standing with our arms around each other.

"Did I screw up?" I ask.

"Yeah, probably," Declan says. But he sounds more amused than bothered.

"How badly?"

"It'll be fine. It'll blow over. They just might not love you here as much as they do in Swendenburg."

"You mean Sudersberg?" I say with a grin.

He rubs his forehead and laughs.

"It's been a day."

"Oh, they loved me there," I say, grinning at the memory of the chef at a dignitary's house bringing me a second game hen, and then offering a third. That was when the "ladylike portion" rule came into play.

"They love you in Nordania too," he says. His expression turns serious. Suddenly, it feels like we're too close. There's not enough space between us.

"Not everyone there does," I say.

"The tide has turned," he says, as I step away to adjust my heeled boots at the cafe table and chairs.

"Tides turn fast, I guess."

"Arden," he says, closing the distance between us. "We need to talk."

"Okay?"

"People do love you. I'm not joking. You're the first independent candidate in at least a generation. You came from nothing," he says, and I wince. He raises a placating palm, and I wait for him to continue. "And you're my choice. I'm not hiding behind that anymore. It's you. I couldn't be plainer. And then you were kidnapped."

"Declan," I say, my voice going soft as I sit.

"I know," he says, kneeling next to me. "I know. And we'll sort that all out. Although, it remains to be said that he deserves whatever punishment he would get for what he put you through."

I don't want to talk about Beck. I don't want to think about him or what he did. Because, while Declan can guess what happened — that Beck took money from Declan's mother to lure me away from Declan, and then to do whatever it took to keep me away, including manipulating me into falling in love with him — he doesn't know the full story. How real it was. He doesn't know just how much I fell for Beck, or how I gave myself to him in a way I never thought I'd be able to. In ways that I still wake up at night aching for him.

"I know this is painful. And I don't want to make things more painful for you. So, as soon as we can, as soon as you're my wife and protected by your position, we'll come clean about the deal we made with him, that he never kidnapped you, and then he'll be gone from our lives forever."

Everything he says should make me feel better. But it just digs the ache into my chest even more. Because Beck lied. He made me trust him, and then he lied to me, he lied to Declan. Despite everything, though, and as much as I hate to admit it, I can't quite imagine never seeing him again.

Declan puts his hand to my cheek. Instinctively, I lean

into his touch. I wish I didn't feel this pain, and that I could just forget about Beck. I wish I could lean into Declan completely and let him catch me. I blink up at him, and he's watching me, curious, patient. He's so patient. So careful and sensitive and giving. His lips are parted, and his thumb moves in slow arcs along my cheek.

Would it be so bad to love him? To kiss him? To marry him?

I lean closer, wanting to remember what it was like to kiss him, to taste him and inhale him and feel him in that way without so many prying eyes. His breath hitches. I feel the warmth of his breath against my skin.

"Orange pekoe for two!" Alvin announces behind us. I jerk backward, but Declan remains frozen, still not breathing. Alvin doesn't look repentant in the slightest.

"Thank you, Alvin," Declan says, finally exhaling. He rises to his feet and fixes a cup for himself. He adds milk, no sugar. I suppose I should know the answer for the next time someone asks a seemingly inane question. But another question nags at the back of my brain.

"Declan?"

"Arden," he says, stirring his tea. I hesitate. Look at Alvin. Declan waves a hand, and with a huff, Alvin is gone.

"I have to tell you something."

"Oh," he says, sitting upright. He always sits upright, but now, he sits even more upright.

"Not a bad thing, just a . . . thing."

"Okay."

I reach into my pocket and palm the piece of paper I've carried with me ever since Neve delivered it. I pass it across the table to him, but I don't let go.

"Irina gave this to me."

"Irina? The woman in charge at the Port of Pleasure?" he says with a frown.

"Yes," I say, even though that is hardly enough to describe the woman who runs an entirely woman-run conglomerate on the side of a mountain—the woman who was Beck's first love.

"May I look at it?" he says.

"Yes . . ." I say, but I don't let go of the paper. "You know I met Emlyn, right?"

He blinks at the mention of the former candidate he once fell in love with—so sharply, it's almost a flinch. But then he nods.

"Yes, I know you met Emlyn." Then he frowns. "Is this about her?"

"Not exactly," I say. Then I push the paper to him. He opens it, reads it, and the frown lines cut deeper into his face.

"These look like coordinates."

"I believe they are."

"If I'm remembering my coordinates correctly, these look like a location within Sudersberg."

"I think they might be," I say.

"Arden," he says, leaning into the table with a serious expression, "what has she asked you not to fuck up?"

I laugh. I don't think I've ever heard that word come out of Declan's mouth, and it sounds so awkward that it's almost charming. The corner of his mouth lifts, and for a moment, there's a lightness between us.

"There's a woman there. A former graduate."

He leans back. He wasn't expecting this.

"A former graduate? What does she want with a former graduate?"

"Nothing," I say quickly. I lean onto my forearms over the table. "I believe this woman could help me."

"Help . . . you?"

"Yes."

"Do you need help?" He looks confused, and if I'm not mistaken, a little hurt.

I'm not sure how much to tell him. I do believe that Declan is on my side. Or that he wants to be on my side. But he is still an integral part of the Nordanian government. What if he changes his mind about me, and then I've told him about the Ember Network? Could he use it against me? My heart is telling me he would never. But my brain is telling me to tread with caution.

"She can vote," I say, carefully. "At the assembly—at graduation."

"As can all the other graduates," he says, shaking his head. "It doesn't mean they will."

"Yes, but that's the thing," I say, forcing him to meet my gaze. "I think that if I could talk to her, tell her what I plan to do, then maybe she would—"

"What you plan to do?"

Oh. Right. We haven't renewed this conversation since I first got on this boat.

"Declan, it's important to me to make a difference. To change Nordania for the better."

"As it is to me."

"Great, then we're agreed."

"In theory, yes," he says. He reaches for my hand across the table, and as I watch his fingertips graze mine, it's like having an out-of-body experience. I see it happen. I feel his touch. But I don't *feel* it happening. It's a comforting sensation, but nothing more. Should I feel something more?

"What does that mean?"

"Well, in theory, we both want to make a difference. But it sounds like you have something less theoretical in mind."

I frown. What does *that* mean?

"I do."

"Well, tell me."

I chew on the inside of my cheek. Because that's all I have, theoretical ideas.

"I want to make things better . . . for the beneficiaries."

"Ah," he says, stiffening. "Right. I think that's a good idea."

"Okay," I say. "So if I brought something for consideration—"

"At the assembly?"

"Yes," I say, trying to temper my frustration. But he lets out a slow whistle.

"Arden, the assembly isn't just graduation and voting for popular bills. It's also for more mundane things like requesting funding for pet projects, carrying out votes for capital sentencing . . . people tend to lose interest and are less likely to vote for sweeping reforms because they just want to get to the banquets that follow."

"What are you saying?"

"There's no hurry. That's all."

"Maybe not for you, but there are so many girls out there who need us to move faster."

He lets out a heavy sigh. Then he sits back, taking his hand with him.

"Come up with a plan. And then let's talk about it."

"This is my plan," I say, pointing to the paper that sits on the table, unprotected.

"This is a location."

"I believe it's a person."

"Fine. Even if that's the case, it's one person." There's a knock at the door, and Alvin lets himself in.

"I believe you have a call coming in the next ten minutes, sir," Alvin says in his smooth, saccharine tenor. "And miss? Your transport is ready."

"Yes, thank you," Declan says, rising to his feet. Then

he looks back at me. "I'm not shoving this off," he says, as he literally shoves the paper back toward me. I take it and pocket it again, feeling defeated.

"Right. I understand," I say, standing. Then he grabs my wrist and tugs, keeping me in place.

"I won't forget," he says. Then he kisses my cheek, and he lingers. His lips are warm against my skin. It's more affection than he usually shows in private. His cheeks flush pink, as if he's just remembered, even though I almost kissed him earlier, before Alvin interrupted us once again. That man has terrible timing. I glance at him but he's paying us no attention. Which means he's listening in on every word.

"Mint and basil," I say.

Declan makes a funny face, and I lean into his ear. "It'll drive Alvin crazy to not know what that means."

"What does it mean?" His breath is warm against my cheek.

"It means mint and basil," I whisper. I kiss his cheek, and he laughs. I leave him laughing and shaking his head after me, with my coded goal tucked tight in my pocket.

CHAPTER THREE

"I don't know how you don't already know this," Neve says, daintily sipping from her teacup like she's been doing it that way her whole life. "This is basic stuff, Arden."

"It's basic for you," I say, crumbling the napkin next to my coffee. I tried her orange pekoe blend and had to gag it down. Tea is definitely not for me.

"It's your duty now to know the history of the country you're going to be representing." Neve has taken on the thankless task of filling in the gaps in my education, so that when I do get back to Nordania, whenever that may be, I won't be so egregiously behind the others. I need a leg to stand on to convince Declan that I should be allowed to sit for the graduation exam, and apparently, that leg is a pithy eighteen-year-old Espancian.

"Not to mention you should know how your future husband takes his tea. It should go without saying that, with a shameless flirt like Declan, if another woman knows how he takes his tea, it's just another opportunity for his eye to wander. Or for the press to infer that it has."

Would his eye wander? He's been so devoted, ever since the beginning. Well, other than the time I found him in the stairwell with Fiona. Or the time Molly revealed she kissed him. Or the time . . .

Neve arches an eyebrow, and I nod. I see her point.

"I know that," I grumble, tossing the napkin toward the middle of the table. She glares at it like it's offended her personally. With a huff, I pick it up and flatten out the wrinkles and creases, then fold it into a neat triangle and tuck it neatly alongside the saucer beneath my coffee cup.

"You want to change things for Nordanian women, correct?"

"Yes," I say, leaning forward.

"Then you need to know exactly what it is you're changing."

"I know what we're changing," I say, reaching for my notebook where I've been making notes on exactly what it is I want to propose. Ever since my talk with Declan, where he asked what I wanted to change and I came up empty, I've been thinking and taking notes. I'll need something much more than notes to have it ready for a vote at the assembly.

At the annual assembly, where the institute graduates its best and brightest, new legislation can be brought by any voting member. Once I've been sworn in as a voting member, I need to have something to present. Right now, all I have is a note to *"make things better."*

"Let me see that," she says. She takes the book from me a little more sharply than I expect, and my arm bumps into my cup, splattering lukewarm coffee on the white tablecloth. She lifts an arch brow, and I feel the shame of her disapproval deep in my chest.

Her eyes flicker over my notes, and to my relief, she doesn't immediately protest.

"This is interesting," she says, turning the page to continue reading. "It's crude, don't get me wrong —"

"Crude?" I ask, leaning forward to figure out what exactly she thinks is so unsavory.

"Shorthand, I mean," she says, flapping a hand at me as she keeps reading. Her eyes reach the bottom of the second page, and she lowers the notebook and looks at me. Just looks.

"You want to do away with the current beneficiary system?"

"Not do away with it. Just . . . regulate it. Better."

"Why do you think it's so bad? There are a lot of women who would never be able to access the heights you have without a benefactor." There's an edge to her voice that transcends the devil's advocate approach she prefers.

"What do you mean? I mean, yes. You're right, of course. But there are far more girls who never reach these heights. I wouldn't have if not for the fact that Conrad had no idea that CJ played that stupid joke —"

"So you stand to benefit in the greatest way possible from the failure of the current system, and you want to do away with it?" Neve glares at me. But she doesn't look angry. Just curious. Or amused. Or some cross section between the two that I don't understand.

"If you think for one moment that I wouldn't trade in safety for sitting on this damn boat —"

"Ship," Neve corrects.

My heart squeezes and flips. Nobody has corrected me like that in at least two weeks. Maybe a little more. I haven't been down to see Beck in that time. It wouldn't help, wouldn't make a damn bit of difference. And yet, there's part of me that aches to go back in time, to when I didn't know how he was going to deceive me — that he already was deceiving me. Neve is staring at me as if she pities me.

"I know what you're saying, Arden," Neve says, interrupting the gut-shredding spiral I'd fallen into. "But I'm not your audience."

I frown at her, and she sighs, passing the notebook back to me.

"If you present this, you need to be prepared to defend it. Not just on a personal note. You need to be able to speak to the general population of beneficiaries. To the general population of women who don't have the chance to better their station. The ones who see it as the best route for their own daughters. You need to represent them. And in order to do that, you need to understand where they're coming from, where they've been, and where they're going. Because if this doesn't pass," she says, pointing a perfectly manicured fingernail at the notebook that lays next to the coffee stain, "nothing will change, and you will have created a lot of powerful enemies."

"But that's why we need to find the other Embers—"

"I'm not arguing with you," Neve says. She sighs as if she's exhausted. "I think you're absolutely right."

"You do?" I lean back in my chair and nearly tip it over.

"Of course I do. This is smart and well-reasoned. It doesn't make any sense that benefactors, who may be bending the rules or worse, are responsible for hiring people to watch out for their beneficiaries' safekeeping. If the institute is the reason, and the government is responsible for the institute, then they should have a heavier hand in the safety and health and welfare of the women they purport to be the moral arm of the entire nation."

I stare at her. Her eyes are clear, and her tone

passionate. She would've been an amazing representative. Hell, she would've been an amazing First Family. I don't know what she's been through to get to this place with me. She still hasn't talked about it. Maybe I should push harder? As I look at the heaviness in her feathers, the way her eyes have aged her at least five years, I wonder whether not pushing has been a mistake.

"Neve—you would've . . . what I mean is, I'm—"

"Learn your history, Arden. It's not just your political career that depends on it."

I read until my eyes are crossed. First a book about Nordanian women's suffrage, and then another on women's political theory. I didn't realize that women in some parts of the country don't have access to the vote. Only women who can be vouched for by a voting member of the country can. Which, in most cases, means the male of the household. If the male chooses not to vouch for his wife or daughter, then that's that.

How did I not know this?

I find myself peeling an orange, wandering the halls of the ship, going deeper and deeper. It's not until I'm outside the brig that I realize this is where I was headed all along.

Neve's chastising comment may have been off the cuff, but it's stayed with me. Whenever things were too tough at the institute, in the classes or otherwise, I found myself going to Beck's cabin, and it helped clear my head. Even if it wasn't real.

And that's the thing I still can't get my head around. Because it felt so real. He really taught me to defend myself.

He really did teach me to navigate the Mittlesee, and to read the star maps. He taught me to embrace my mountains and make my trauma something that builds instead of breaks. My fingers press against my hip, over the tattoo he helped me get to cover CJ's scar. The memory of his lips pressed against that skin makes me flush hot, just as my chest squeezes and I have to work hard around the next breath.

"Miss?" I turn and see a guard standing at the door. "Should you be down here?"

It's a good question. The answer is obviously no. Of course I shouldn't. This man is a prisoner, though he isn't deserving of that label. He didn't kidnap me, not the way they think he did anyway. But he broke me in a way nobody, not even CJ, ever did. The cell is more for my heart than it is for anyone on board.

"Miss?" he asks again.

I look up, and I nod, stuffing the orange in my pocket. "I'd like to see him."

"Excuse me?"

"Give us a minute?" I ask. He doesn't look like he thinks this is wise. I press my hand to his forearm, and he looks at it. "I'll be okay. I just need a minute."

I don't know why he listens to me, but he does. He opens the door for me.

"Just tap the window when you're ready," he says. I nod and step inside.

My stomach tightens and anxiety flutters along my arms and legs like crickets in a cage of snakes. Beck is sitting on a cot, his back to the wall, eyes shut. He hasn't shaved, and his beard is thick but patchy. He still has the yellowish color of a healing black eye on the left side of his face, and his lips look chapped.

"Couldn't keep away, could yeh?" he says, still not opening his eyes.

I don't know what to say. I've thought about this moment more times than I would freely admit. And every single time, I say something far more powerful and potent than:

"Are you okay?"

I don't know why that's the first thing I say. But taking in the small, stark room with a small porthole, one light hanging overhead, a small sink and toilet at the end of his cot, I can't help myself. The corner of his mouth quirks, and even through his shrubby beard, I see a glimpse of my friend. Or the man who I thought was my friend.

"Come on, Arden," he says, and I flinch at the way he says my name. Not that I would want him to use that inane nickname. It never made any sense, and he never explained it. But it still reminds me that we're not friends. Maybe we never were. Even though his last words before he was taken were, *"Remember . . ."*

"Come on, what?" I ask. He opens his eyes, and they're more gold, less green. And a little bloodshot. Like he hasn't been sleeping. Not that I should care.

"Have a backbone."

I recoil. "Excuse me?"

"You know what I've done," he says, not moving except for the way his eyes take me in. "And the first thing you have to say to me is 'are you okay?'" He sputters and shakes his head. But he does it so slowly it's as if he's in pain. "I don't need your self-aggrandizing pity."

"Pardon me for caring," I say.

"You shouldn't."

"Well, you can't tell me what to do. Not anymore."

He tilts his head.

"Could I ever?" He sounds genuinely curious. I'm not going to answer his question, though. I think we both know the answer, but saying it out loud only gives him more power. Maybe he's right. I should stand up for myself a bit more.

I step into the small space and realize that if I take two more steps in any direction, I'm either at his cot or his toilet, neither of which I have any interest in touching. So instead, I lean back against the wall next to the door.

The ship rocks, and he grunts. As if he's truly in pain.

"Do you need a doctor?" I ask. He shakes his head.

"Tell the calumniating cozener steering this thing that he doesn't need to show off. We know he can drive the boat through a king tide."

"Ship," I say.

"I said what I said," he says. His mouth quirks, and his gaze meets mine. It's so familiar, like all those unspoken moments between us before. For a second, I forget that we're not on the same side.

"Have you met Neve?" I ask.

"Bossy broad with the eyes?"

"What eyes?" I say sharply. He lets out a wheezing laugh, and the way he stiffens, I can see that he is most definitely not okay.

"She sees everything."

"Yeah," I say. But I don't like it. It means she's been down here, and she hasn't told me. Of course, I'm the one who asked the question, so I proceed. "She's been helping me study."

"Bully for you."

"She doesn't think I'll be ready."

His gaze flickers back to mine and holds it for a long, painful moment. Then he shuts his eyes.

"You'll be ready." He folds his arms over his chest as if

he has all the time in the world to show me just how much he doesn't care.

"She doesn't think so."

"Since when do you care what she thinks?"

I shrug one shoulder. "I'm trying to write a motion. Like, a law. To protect other beneficiaries." He doesn't say anything, so I take out the orange and pick at the peel. It feels easier to talk if I have something in my hand, something to do. "It doesn't seem right that benefactors control so much. That even the people who are supposed to protect the beneficiaries—like Headmistress Moyle was supposed to protect me—are their staff. They report to the benefactors. It's no wonder there are so many of us who go through stuff."

"Stuff?" His voice is gruff, but I don't look up from the orange. I don't want to see what he's really thinking. He knows everything about me, even more than Neve, and I realize in this moment that this is why I'm here. I just need to talk to someone who knows me. Even if I don't really know him. I can't start over. Not yet.

"You know, the stuff with CJ and—"

"That wasn't *stuff*, Arden," he snaps. My throat is thick, and I have to swallow hard twice before I can speak again.

"You know what I mean."

He doesn't respond, so I continue.

"Neve doesn't think I believe in it enough. Or that I don't know how to defend it. That people are going to doubt my intentions or something." My fingernail finds purchase between the peel and the flesh of the orange, and I peel a long section. It's a good, thick section like the bitter ones Beck likes to chew on. I never understood that.

"Why do you like these so much?" I ask, holding it up. When I look up, his jaw is tense and his gaze is fierce.

"I like what I like," he says, his gaze unflinching. "Bitter and all." Then he looks down and shrugs. "It's just who I am, I guess."

"Turns out, I don't know who you are."

He looks away.

"Here, catch," I say, and I toss him the peel. But he doesn't move. The peel lands on his wrist. I wait for him to pick it up, but he doesn't even look at it.

His jaw feathers, and he looks down. Then he carefully, slowly picks it up and stuffs it in the side of his mouth. The whole time, he doesn't move his torso.

"Do they know how injured you are?" I ask.

"What are you doing here, Arden?" he asks.

For some reason, it's that question that tips me over the edge. I don't know what I'm doing. Maybe part of me wanted to see if it was all real. That the Beck I thought I knew was gone—that he never existed. Turns out, he is. But it doesn't feel any easier, and there's no sense of relief or closure. I feel the back of my eyes heat, and I have to blink quickly.

"I'll make sure a doctor comes down here."

"Don't bother," he says. I whirl on him.

"And don't be a fucking martyr," I snap. He lowers his hands, though there's a spark of amusement in his green eyes that pisses me off. He doesn't want me to bother with making sure his injuries—probably broken ribs—are attended to, but when I tell him to shut up, he's entertained.

"I'm not your problem anymore," he says.

"You never were my problem," I say. I turn back to the orange and break it in half before removing the rest of the peel. It's a stupid move. It wasn't ready to break open like that and juice runs down my thumb. I lick it up quickly, and then stuff the orange back in my pocket.

"Go," he says.

I look up and see him. Really see him. Gone is his bravado, whatever mask he's been wearing since I've been down here. His gaze lingers on my thumb. I can see the pain in his face, from his ribs or whatever, and he's not telling me to go—he's begging me. Even if I know he will never actually beg anyone for anything.

"If you want to send a doctor, fine. I can't help you with your exam or your measure—"

"Measure, that's the word," I interrupt. I feel my cheeks flush hot, but he doesn't react.

"Go marry Declan. That's what you're supposed to do. It's what you were always supposed to do. I was just the decoy."

There's a knock at the door.

"Miss Arden? Are you still okay?" the guard says through the door. I wipe my hand on my wool pant leg and nod, as if he can see me.

"Yes, I'm ready to go now," I say. He unlocks the door and opens it for me.

"See to it that this man is thoroughly examined by a doctor," I say before I pass through. "He has at least one broken rib, and I think there's something wrong with his mouth."

"My mouth?" Beck says.

"The stuff that comes out of it is truly horrifying."

As I pass through the door, I swear I hear the faintest wheeze of laughter.

CHAPTER FOUR

*A*s Declan and I stand on the stern of the ship and wave at onlookers in the port city of Stenson in Sudersberg, I wonder how close we are to Irina's coordinates. I want to ask Declan, but Alvin won't leave us alone. He's so close, I can feel the anxiety radiating off of him.

"He needs to calm down," I say through my teeth. Grinning and waving, always grinning and waving. Declan boops my nose.

"He's only doing his job," he says with a wide grin.

"Oh no, you didn't," I say, grinning and waving. "You did not just boop my nose."

"On the contrary," he says, tucking a stray curl behind my ear and leaning in, his breath tickling my ear. "I booped your nose, and then called you princess." Then he presses a kiss to my cheek, and we grin. And we wave.

"I'm going to get you back. Just you wait," I say through clenched teeth.

"Do you promise?" His grin turns a little sharper as he

tucks my hand back into the crook of his elbow. I roll my eyes at his flirting, but my stomach flips just the same.

The dockworker whistles up a signal, and Alvin waves for us to come back in so that we can exit properly portside.

"Before he can hear us," Declan says, slowing our pace and turning around to wave once more, "he's on edge because this is the first time we've been welcomed as a couple."

"Oh," I say. And it's only when he tugs on my hand that I realize I've stopped walking.

"Yes," he says, tugging a little harder. I pass through the door as he holds it for me. I don't know why this hits me as hard as it does. We've literally had meals together at every one of these stops before. I suppose I never stopped to think of how we were officially received.

Alvin is prattling on about something that I've tuned out just as Neve and Meredith approach to touch up my face and hair, respectively.

"What's he off about today?" Meredith asks.

"Apparently today, we're a couple," I say.

Both of them stand up and look at me, wide-eyed.

"Wow," Neve says, resuming touching up my cheeks with her largest brush.

"Is it wow?" I ask.

"It's definitely wow," Meredith confirms.

"For another country to recognize you as his official partner? Before the term at the institute is even over? That's a bold statement," Neve says.

"Do you think . . ." I say, and then stop, because the idea that just popped into my head—that Irina might have something to do with this, since the Port of Pleasure is also in Sudersberg—is so ridiculous it's not worth mentioning out loud. That woman hates me. Full stop. And one of the last things she told me was that I would be the death of Beck, and she pleaded with me to keep him safe. I haven't exactly kept my word.

"I'm not sure who else would have a hand in this," Neve mutters under her breath, just loud enough that I can hear as she steps in to pluck an eyelash off my cheek. "Make a wish," she says, holding the eyelash up to my lips. It's so unlike Neve that, once again, it makes me wonder where she's been and what she's been through.

"A wish for what?" I ask. She snorts and blows on it herself.

"Says the girl who has everything she's ever dreamed of," Neve says, but it doesn't sound kind.

It's a strange thought, that I can't think of a single thing to wish for. Even if I could wish on something as silly as an eyelash.

"Are you ready?" Declan asks, offering his elbow again. He looks handsome as always, and he has that aura about him that I've come to associate with only him. His hair isn't quite as golden as it was under the Nordanian sun, but it still has a hint of it, and his skin has a subtle glow. Perhaps that's it? But I think it's more likely his personality, the way he carries himself, and the way, when he asks me a question and waits for my answer, it's as if I'm the only person in the world.

A little fluttery flip thing happens to my chest, and I feel my cheeks heat. Is this what it feels like for infatuation to grow over time? I smile, a true one this time, instead of the grin-and-bear-it from the deck just moments ago, and I take his arm.

"Now, remember," Alvin says, his tall forehead shining with nervous sweat, "they really love chocolate here. Make sure, if you're given the opportunity to eat or compliment the chocolate, do *not* say you prefer nougat."

"Ah yes, I wouldn't want to play into the ancient chocolate-nougat rivalry," I say, deadpan.

"At least you know this time," Alvin says, not picking up on my joke. Declan covers his mouth with his hand, but I see the laugh he's concealing.

The whole day, we're never alone. Or at least, not long enough for me to ask whether we're near Irina's coordinates. But, that said, Stenson is beautiful. More beautiful than I was expecting. With white-walled cliffs and red-painted clapboard houses, it reminds me of New Covington in northern Nordania, where Beck and I stopped on our way to his family home. My chest tightens at the memory, but I try to refocus on the memory of seeing Declan there after long last. He told me he planned to marry me in New Covington. And this place has more than a passing resemblance.

We visit a church and a school. I don't care much about the church, although it is very pretty. It has a tall spire and lots of candles and incense to light at the front. Declan loves the churches we visit. He takes his time lighting three candles and saying his prayers. I say a prayer for the safety of our crew and the rest of the Embers. I light a candle for Zerah and say another little prayer that she is safe and happy, wherever she is.

The visit to the school is more fun. We join a group of children for story time, and then get to watch them sing a song. Declan is almost boyish in his joy listening to them. He is affectionate and, instead of offering his elbow, takes my hand. There are cameras, but something about the way I slip my fingers between his feels tentative and authentic.

Different than usual. Especially when he looks at me with shy eyes.

The weather cooperates, and we're able to make it to one last site before our planned dinner—a national park overlooking the Mittlesee. It's home to something like forty odd species of migratory birds who all nest in the cliffs overhanging the rough waters. By the time we return to the governor's mansion for dinner, we're windblown and famished.

It's a smallish dinner party, all things considered, with twenty people seated around one long table. Declan sits across from me at the end of the table, and when my table mate arrives, I'm pleased to see it's a woman who is not too much older than myself.

"You must be the woman of the hour," she says, her accent careful, but familiar. Almost Nordanian. Or as if she is trying to hide her Nordanian accent. My heart speeds.

"Yes," I say with a polite smile. "I'm Arden."

She nods and takes her napkin and sweeps it across her lap the same way Molly did on the first day of class.

"I'm Carmen," she says.

Everything around me skids to a stop. Not actually, but it may as well have. Because I think, perhaps, just maybe, I've finally landed exactly where I have wanted.

"Carmen?" I say. She smiles and leans closer.

"I used to be in your position," she says, carefully.

"You're a graduate?" I ask.

"Yes," she says with a nod. My heart races. I look around the table. Seatmates have paired off, deep in conversation, as expected. The clatter and treble of conversation fills the room, and I return to my own seatmate.

"And you knew Emlyn?" I ask softly. She stiffens ever

so slightly, then turns her head and looks at me, her expression entirely nonplussed.

"I hope you like chocolate," she says. "It's our local specialty. I believe it will appear in every course."

I nod, feeling the embarrassment of failure creeping up my neck into my cheeks in the form of hot. As the first course is served, creating added clatter, she leans closer as she raises her wine glass to her lips.

"We'll talk later."

I take the first bite of my steak frites in a bitter chocolate glacè, but it tastes far more sweet with the anticipation of knowing that, at long last, I'm on the right track.

CHAPTER FIVE

*D*inner moves at a glacial pace. If someone had told me six months ago that I would be irritated by a seven-course meal with no fish and chocolate in every dish, I wouldn't have believed it. But when the final course comes out —a dark chocolate liqueur the size of a single sip that I would normally pass on—I knock it back without a second thought. Declan lifts his eyebrows in surprise, and I try to play it off.

"It's so delicious," I demur, but I swear Carmen shakes her head in amusement.

Then the men retire to another room for brandy and cigars or something else manly. Most of the women move to another more suitable location—a parlor or conservatory or something feminine—for tea.

"I would love to show you the greenhouse," Carmen says as she stands. "I know it's unorthodox after such a heavy dinner, but I think you would enjoy seeing some of the plants I've cultivated."

"Oh, really?" I say, trying to sound casual. It occurs to me in this moment that I don't know how to be sneaky.

Whenever I've done anything sneaky, Beck has been by my side, telling me to keep it together or to stay quiet. This is the first time I have to do it on my own. It's not a pleasant thought. But I roll my shoulders and let out a low, steadying breath.

"That sounds lovely," I say with a soft, hopefully calmer, smile.

"Plants, huh?" Declan says, approaching where I stand from around the other side of the table.

"I like gardens," I say, and his smile reaches his eyes. It's sweet, and the truth is that whenever I think of gardens, I do think of him and his rooftop garden of herbs and vegetables.

"Just as long as you remember your favorite gardener," he says with a smirk. He's flirting with me. I'm immediately aware of the eyes of the room on us, looking to us for a sign that true love can still exist. Not just that, but that it's alive and well. But his expression is sincere, and I realize I can't tell the difference right now — is he playing at being the perfect partner? Or is this genuine?

"Of course," I say, realizing everyone is waiting for my response. Then I lift up on the tip of my toes to kiss his cheek. He curls his hand around my bicep and gives me a little squeeze, holding me against his cheek just a moment longer. And it feels real.

My face flushes hot, and I chew on the inside of my cheek as he and the other men leave, trying to keep my nerves in check.

"He's so sweet," Carmen says behind me. I nod and smile. It's what I'm best at, after all.

"The gardens?" I ask. She nods and motions for me to follow her.

She leads me through the hallways of the governor's

mansion as if she knows it intimately, which I suppose she would if she's been living here for however many years.

"Did you know Declan?" I ask. "I mean, when you were a candidate?"

She smiles and nods. "Yes, but he was younger. And much more awkward."

I laugh, because she has no idea how awkward he still is. If there's a way to be awkward, he and I have found it over the past few weeks.

"Tell me about him," I say, because it seems like the thing a doting almost-fiancée would want to know. But also, to my surprise, I want to know too.

"He was all arms and legs. He must've been thirteen? Maybe fourteen? Not any older than that. And his voice would crack whenever he greeted any of us."

I laugh, a little too loud, and it reverberates through the marble and glass hallway. I press my hand to my lips, embarrassed and apologetic, but she shakes her head, her dark eyes lighting up.

"It's okay. It was very sweet and often funny. He tried to be mature around us, detached and aloof, but always gentlemanly. If there's one thing to be said about him, it's that he has always been a true gentleman."

"I can't argue with that," I say. Although, I recall one time that word of him being a little less than a gentleman spread through the institute—mostly spread by Fiona herself. I wonder if that was actually true. He's only human, and Fiona is stunning, so I never doubted it.

"There was one time I was walking to class a little late. I knew Dean Edina would have my head for it"—she gives me a look, and I nod, knowing exactly what she means— "and he was in the hall. He stopped me and asked if he could escort me. I'm pretty sure he knew what would happen, but when he personally escorted me and apologized for making me tardy, all was forgotten and forgiven. He was just that kind of person."

I look down at the marble floor, at the way my satin shoes pop out from beneath my navy satin skirt. "He still is," I say. And even if she never understands the full extent to which he's still that person, I know she can hear the genuineness in my voice.

"Of course, he still snuck a kiss. Even at thirteen, he was a little flirt."

I laugh, because I can picture this version of Declan perfectly.

"Well, here we are," she says, opening one side of a set of glass double doors.

Right away, I'm hit with a wall of humid warmth. It feels gorgeously decadent, and the scent of wet earth and lush sunshine hits my nose. It's like being transported to the rooftop of the capital building. A massive domed glass roof curves overhead, melded into a grid with green metal beams. The space is organized with six rows of square wooden boxes, four deep. They're not quite as wide as Declan's, but just as impressive. Special lights hang over about half of them.

"You might enjoy this planter box," Carmen says, motioning for me to follow her to the far corner of the massive space. When I approach, I realize two things: Carmen knows far more about Declan than she's admitted, and she knows far more about me than she's admitted.

"Is this . . . ?" I start, plucking a small flat leaf. I hold it to my nose and inhale the fresh, minty scent.

"Nordanian mint," she says with not a small note of pride. "People don't think it's a big deal, but Nordanian mint is softer, more fragile, and its essence is more subtle and blends with other scents and flavors beautifully. Declan loved it. Does he still?" I nod, thinking back to the time we spent among his rooftop gardens at the capital building. The sweet scent on the warm breeze, the stolen kisses . . .

"You must miss your home," I say, trying to deflect from my warming cheeks. She shrugs.

"Of course, I have a fondness for where I grew up, anyone must," she says. It's an odd way to phrase it, and yet it feels like a coded message. Then she continues. "But I love my new life here. I feel like I am so useful, and have the potential to be even more useful in ways we haven't even imagined."

Her expression is clear: this is my opening. I clear my throat.

"I spoke with Emlyn—"

She clears her throat loud enough that I stop talking. As if names are too dangerous to use. I try again.

"I was at the Port of Pleasure," I say, and she nods, pruning the mint and moving on to the basil. I watch her twist the tiny white flower off a bud and have a flashback to when Declan and I did the same thing and I was stung by a bee. I can't imagine there are any bees here.

"How did you find it there?" she asks.

I huff. "It was unlike any place I've ever been."

"Was it?"

"Yes," I say, helping her pick the little flowers from the herb to make sure it doesn't stop blooming. "And I spoke with someone there who told me . . ."

"Told you what?"

"Pardon my language, but not to fuck it up."

She snorts.

"That's as good a code as anything," she says. I let out a breath. I didn't realize how tense I'd been until that moment. "Why are you here?"

I take a deep breath. "Because things need to change."

"What things?"

"I don't know how much you know about me . . ."

"I read the papers." She sounds disinterested, but her gaze is shrewd.

"Well, then you probably know more than enough. But just to be clear, I've not had it easy. My benefactor is not a good man. His son was worse."

"Understood," she says, rinsing the petals. They catch in the tide and swirl down the sink like moths in an updraft.

"But when I got to the institute, I realized I wasn't the only one. I mean, of course I wasn't. I must have known it on some level, but when you're in that situation, you can't think outside of that day."

Her eyes remain downcast as she continues rinsing the sink, as if trying to rid it of every trace of invisible pollen that it has collected.

"One of my classmates, she was bad off. I tried to help and, well, I made a mess of things. Now she's gone, and I don't know how to help her. But she had to be replaced."

"Let me guess, her benefactor deserved just compensation?"

Carmen's round face is plain and undisturbed. She knows this story. Perhaps she's lived part of it. For her sake, I hope not.

I nod in response. "I want to sponsor a bill to protect beneficiaries. And I want it to pass this year, at the annual assembly. I've done some math, and the potential power of the graduates of the institute is unstoppable. If I could find enough people, convince them to come back and vote for it—"

"I think what you're proposing is noble, but far more radical than may be practical."

She turns the dial on the water faucet to the hot side and steam begins to fill the sink. It's loud enough that it muffles some of our whispers.

"Radical how?"

"The men who take on the graduates? They're not progressive men. They believe in an old-fashioned system. They support it, and they want their lives to continue on in that same way. They won't be so easily convinced to let their wives return for such a radical vote."

"Well . . ." I say, thinking quickly, "what if the women don't tell them that's the reason for the return?"

"What would they tell them?"

"Could it be a celebration? That Declan has finally chosen a wife, and the next generation of the institute is ensured to continue as it always has?"

She smirks. "Is that what's happening here? You're going to marry him?"

It takes me aback. I nod, a little too late. She just smiles and shakes her head.

"That's the plan," I say.

"You don't have to convince me. You have to convince them."

"We can do that."

"We?" she says, shutting off the faucet and turning to lean her hip against the lip of the apron. "So he knows about this?"

"Yes," I say, simply. She flinches. As if she wasn't expecting that answer.

"Really?" She nods, looking down at her hands, examining a stubborn bit of dirt stuck beneath her fingernail.

"Yes, of course."

"And he's supportive?"

"Yes," I say. "Well, in theory."

"In theory?"

"I'm still working on a draft."

"This hasn't even been drafted yet?"

44

"It will be," I insist. She turns the water back on and soaps up her hands. The steam lifts, coating the windows directly in front of us.

"This isn't something that can be reused, or redone over and over again," she says.

"I understand that."

"And you need to find a way to offer protection to the rest of us."

My chest tightens. How had I not considered this? Of course, some of the graduates would be in bad situations. I'd been so focused on the younger girls that I hadn't taken the graduates into account. I don't know how to approach this, but there's only one way to answer this question.

"Yes, of course."

She nods.

"Moving forward, you should know that you'll need to use the code."

"The code?" I ask, keeping my voice low.

"*Lux altera*," she says, her dark gaze fixated on her soapy hands.

"*Lux altera*," I repeat.

"The next person you'll need to find won't say a word without that code. Roughly translated, it means, '*light the next.*'"

"The next person," I say. I know what she's talking about. It's the Ember Network. I will find her, and she will help me find the next graduate.

"I'll contact the next people on my list, and then I'll give you —"

A flash interrupts her. We're both momentarily blinded as we realize what happened.

"Is that —"

"A photographer," she says, her voice low. She turns off the water and wipes her hands on the front of her thick woolen skirt. She turns and moves quickly toward the door to the main house. I follow, feeling her nerves in her wake.

"What was that?" I ask.

"Someone has taken a photograph of the two of us alone together. That can't be a good thing," she says, holding the door open for me. A man in a jacket bearing the city crest strides toward us.

"Are you okay, madame?" he says.

"Yes," she says, her voice much more steady than only moments ago. "The perimeter appears to have been breached, Gareth. You'll want to—"

"Yes, we've been made aware. I was just coming to get you."

"Someone has taken a photograph of us. So check for cameras."

"Yes, madame," he says. "Might I escort you to the dining room where the others have gathered.

"Is this typical?" I ask, as he guides us back to the dining room.

"Yes, and no," she says. Gareth is obviously listening from behind us. "Officially, we're very safe here. Unofficially, there have been attacks."

"Attacks?" I ask, surprised.

"The messiness in eastern Osterstan has spread. Everyone is quick to point their finger, and those of us in public service are often the recipients."

"Do you feel safe?" I ask, softer. Gareth clears his throat, and I realize this is a loaded question—and one I won't get an honest answer to.

"Yes, of course," she says, a little sharply. We arrive at the dining room, and Gareth opens the door for us. I walk inside, and Declan is already there. He spots me and strides across the room in four paces, wrapping his arms around me.

"Are you okay, my love?" he asks. I nod into his chest and try not to think too hard about how good it feels to be held in his arms, or how it made my chest tighten to hear him call me *"my love."* But he's still holding on, not letting go, and it's getting a little warm. I push back, gently.

"I'm fine, Declan," I say with a soft smile. He cups my cheek and presses a kiss to my lips. Then seems to remember himself. My cheeks flush hot, and his go bright pink. Gentle laughter fills the room.

"Don't mind us," says Governor Flanders, Carmen's hand tucked stiffly into the crook of his elbow. "It's nice to see a young couple so enamored of one another. It gives the rest of us some hope in the world." Pleasant laughter fills the room.

Alvin arrives shortly after that and casts a disapproving look at the two of us, still holding on to one another. The route back to our ship has been cleared for safety. We say our goodbyes quickly and quietly, and Carmen and I exchange goodbyes. She leans in to press a kiss to my cheek and holds me tight, just a beat too long.

"Parth, Swendenland. The prefect's son's wife."

When she leans back, she's grinning as if she hasn't just relayed something akin to treason. Declan and I are quiet the whole way back, but we hold hands. I want to tell him, but Alvin is in the car.

"Everything all right, love?" he asks as we approach the dock. I nod and smile.

"Just tired."

"Not too tired, I hope," he says with a glint in his eye. A warm shiver flits along my neck. "Did you have a good conversation with Mrs. Flanders?" he asks. Again, I nod.

"It was perfect."

CHAPTER SIX

I should wait until morning light, I know this. But I can't.

Carmen is real and here, and now I know where to go and what needs to be done. But I'm not in control of this ship and Declan is. So, I wait up until he returns.

His room suite is surprisingly simple, and smaller than mine. It makes me feel a little embarrassed that I'm taking up so much space. But then, apparently I require a wardrobe four times the size of his and two assistants to apply said wardrobe.

His rooms are situated on the starboard side of the ship and consist of a bedroom, a bathroom, which appears to be small but well-appointed for a ship, and a sitting room with a table and chairs and a settee. That's where I'm sitting when he walks in the door.

He doesn't see me at first. He enters and turns to face the door, pressing it closed gently. Then he leans into the door, pressing his forehead against it, shoulders curved into the wall. It's such an intimate moment that it feels wrong for me not to announce myself.

48

It turns out I don't need to, because just then, he turns around and starts. His posture straightens, and his forehead smooths as if pulled on a string.

"Arden, what are you doing here? Have you been waiting all this time?"

"Yes," I say, standing—then, thinking better of it, sitting back down. He frowns, and I pat the seat next to me. "I need to tell you something."

He frowns harder and hesitates.

"Please, Declan," I say.

That appears to be enough. He approaches, taking the seat next to me.

"Is everything okay?" he asks.

"Yes, I'm fine," I say, but then I can't keep the smile off my face. "I'm more than fine. I know where we need to go next."

"Oh," he says, leaning back into the harsh, upright back of the blue velvet settee. He pinches the bridge of his nose. "About that—"

"Carmen is who I was looking for," I say, before he can say anything else. He slowly raises his chin, taking in my news.

"Carmen? You mean the coordinates?"

"Yes. And she told me where I need to go next."

"Where you need to—Arden, wait just a minute—"

"We need to go to Swendenland." He doesn't say anything, just looks at me, his expression unreadable. "She's going to help me contact the other graduates. But she can't contact them all. It would be too obvious. So she asked me to contact another graduate who is in Swendenland and—"

"Arden, we're going to Nordania."

"What?" I say. I laugh like it's a joke, but he doesn't join in. "No. No, we can't." I lean back, and I can't stop shaking my head.

"The call I had? It was my father."

"The prime minister called?" I ask.

"Yes," he says. "This little 'parade' that we've been on—his words, not mine—has cost a lot of goodwill within the legislature. People are getting antsy, especially those with the deepest pockets."

"They're threatening to pull their support if we don't return? I don't understand."

"As much as I've made my choice, and I'm happy we were recognized as a couple here in Sudersberg, it's not official in Nordania. Now that another nation has received us as an official couple, it's caused some headaches."

"What kind of headaches?" I ask. But I can see the way his mask fails at the edges. It's so subtle. The corners of his eyes falter, the creases between his eyebrows deepen, and his chin crinkles.

"We need to set a date to be married," he says. "And as much as you don't want this, I don't want to force you into it."

My chest tightens and cracks. Because yes, he's right: I'm not ready to marry him. He has been so good to me, so kind and patient and generous. Perhaps love could grow from that? I try to picture the ceremony. I haven't spent much time picturing my own wedding. I suppose I always assumed I wouldn't have much of a say in it. But to my own surprise, I can picture myself in a long dress, flowing in the breeze, rich with the scent of flowers in my hair.

"I don't want to hurt you," I say in a near-whisper.

He forces a smile, but won't meet my gaze. "I don't want to hurt you either."

I think for a long moment. Try to think of a way to express exactly what it is that I want in a way that will make sense to him—for us.

"I need good soil first," I say. He looks up at me, a confused, bemused curl to his expression.

"Arden, I don't—"

"We have the basics for it. You know? You respect me, and I respect you." He looks at me, his confusion giving way to understanding. He nods, as if telling me to go on. So I do. "I care for you, and I know you care for me. I want you to have great things in life and to do great things in the world—and I believe you can. And I think you feel the same way about me."

"Of course I do," he says. There's so much emotion in the way he says it that it makes my stomach flip.

"But I can't marry you if I can't vote. Because I can't set the sort of example that I want to set if I can't make a difference on that level."

He sighs. It's heavy and long. And then he nods.

"I completely agree."

I take a deep, full breath, and relief shifts into my face, my cheeks and forehead feel lighter. He smiles back.

"So then, we need to go to Swendenland."

He sighs and closes his eyes.

"Perhaps we can send someone else—"

"No," I say, feeling the opportunity slip from my fingers, "it has to be me."

"Arden, they're threatening to shut down the institute."

"What?" This is a shock.

"You've fled, and it appears I'm going to choose you. I mean, I *have* chosen you, but it's all about appearances. There is gossip about us sharing a room—a, uh . . ."—his cheeks pinken—"sharing a bed."

"Oh."

"Yes. Of course, it's just garbage gossip, but . . ."

"But that doesn't matter."

"It will color your reputation."

51

"I don't care about my reputation."

"You should."

I sigh. He's right. I laugh, but there's no joy.

"This is so stupid."

He laughs. Loudly and with his heart and gut in it. "I couldn't agree more."

"So, what? We pick some random date, and then it's done?"

He flinches. I've misspoken.

"Arden," he says, reaching tentatively for my hand. I let him take it, and he cups it in both of his. "If you don't want to marry me, we can come up with another plan. But I want to marry you, because I think . . ." He flushes again, his voice so soft I have to lean in to hear it. "I know we could be good together. But if you don't feel that way, then tell me now. Before things . . . progress beyond repair."

Oh.

I don't say it out loud, but behind the facade of planning and official announcements, I see exactly what this is: a boy asking a girl to love him.

My heart twinges in the most painful ache. Because I know exactly which part of my heart should sing for him, and that part is dead. It's black and silent and broken. And he deserves someone whose whole heart can sing for him.

But perhaps it's possible to mend a broken heart? Especially if that heart was led astray by lies and deceit?

"I want to be the woman you need me to be," I say, trying to choose my words carefully. "But I am who I am. And I've always been a little bit broken."

"You're not broken," he says, curling his hands around mine, protectively.

"Yeah," I say, feeling a hot lump rise in my throat. "I am. When you met me, I was broken in a different way than I am now, but—" I look up as a flash of hurt darkens his gaze. "But I think, with time, I can heal."

"Of course you can," he says.

"Perhaps, with the right soil," I say, returning to the metaphor that I think he'll understand, "something really beautiful can grow between us. And I wish I could tell you what that looks like, but I think that's the best I can offer right now."

He is quiet for a long moment, and I can't quite bring myself to look at him, to look up from our joined hands.

"I think that is reasonable."

"Okay," I say, then lean forward. "Then you understand why I need to go to Swendenland?"

He sighs. "Yes, of course. But it doesn't change the fact that this is a Nordanian ship, and I am the Nordanian heir and have to heel when called." He sounds bitter and disappointed. I'm not sure in whom. "Arden, I want to give you the world. I want to help you get this bill passed, but I still don't know what's in it, or what you're asking for, or how, if it is passed, it will be paid for."

"I told you, I'm working on it."

"And I believe you will bring it together in a way that is right. But what you're asking is a lot."

"I understand. And after talking to Carmen, I realize that we need to incorporate some sort of safety net for graduates who find themselves in trouble—"

"What?" He pulls his hands away. I sit, stunned at his reaction.

"We need to offer some protection for graduates or former candidates who have been placed outside Nordania and find themselves in trouble."

"Arden," he says, then he launches to his feet, rubbing at his forehead. "Whatever happened to small changes?"

"I imagine it will take some time to incorporate everything, but it's nothing that shouldn't already exist."

"I'm not arguing with that, but what you're asking is a complete rebuke of the way things have always been done. You're asking us to reach into the homes of private citizens in different countries. It's harsh and judgmental and—"

"The right thing," I hiss, rising to my feet.

"You will get no support from the coffers."

"I don't need support from the coffers if I have the Embers."

"The Embers?" he says. I've said too much.

"The graduates, I mean."

"Arden—"

"Declan, maybe this won't work. Maybe it is asking too much. But I have to try. If I don't try, then what am I doing? If we can't protect the most vulnerable among us— and those who are supposed to be the moral arm of—"

"Who have become private citizens of other countries."

"Are they the moral arm of Nordania or private citizens of other countries? You can't have it both ways."

Declan flinches, sputters, and looks genuinely confused.

"We have until the end of the week to return and set a wedding date, or else we have been instructed to elope before we return."

It's like a smack to the face.

"That's four days from now," I say.

"I know." He looks truly apologetic.

It's clear that this is a power move. Perhaps it wasn't just a rogue photographer who saw me and Carmen in the greenhouse.

"I want to vote."

"You need to graduate to do that," he says.

"I'm going to do that."

"If you don't, I won't be able to marry you," he says. "And then I won't be able to protect you."

I blink and stare at him.

"You don't think I can do this?"

He edges closer and reaches for me — but stops himself.

"I don't think there's a thing you can't do when you put your mind to it, but I don't see you doing a lot of studying."

I flinch.

"I've been studying." But I sound weak. I should be studying harder. Neve has been trying, and I've been focused on trying to draft this measure.

"This hasn't gone the way I hoped," he says softly. He reaches into his pocket and withdraws a ring. It's made of rose gold with a round, blue diamond in the center and four tiny white diamonds flanking its four sides.

"I'm going to ask you to wear this for your protection," he says, but he sounds a little sad. "It was my grandmother's. If you could keep it safe when you take it off —"

"Do you want me to take it off?" I ask softly. He blinks up at me. Then shakes his head.

"Marry me, Arden?" he asks.

A swell of a thousand emotions floods my head, blocking out everything except the two of us. He holds my hand and slips the ring onto my finger, but doesn't let go.

"I'll make the soil good. And I'll keep it strong and healthy. As long as you do the same?"

I look up at him, at this boy who has become a man in front of my eyes, asking me to do for him what he has done for me.

I nod.

"Yes," I say. He smiles, but it's sad. This isn't the proposal that he deserves. But maybe it's the right one for us. I push up onto my toes and kiss his cheek.

"Maybe we can return to Swendenland after we're married?" he says. My gut twists, and I can see in his expression that he knows how disappointing this is. Maybe there's some way to get Carmen word that I failed? Or find someone else to ignite the network from there?

I don't have the chance to respond, though, because just then, an alarm blares through the ship. One I know all too well.

We're under attack.

CHAPTER SEVEN

I run through the passageways, rocking with the sudden jerks and jolts of a ship under fire.

"Arden, stop!" Declan shouts from behind me. But I don't. Because I know what this is, and I know where we're likely headed.

I climb the steps to the bridge and push through.

The captain and first mate are poring over an ancient-looking map and turning north. Toward the Mittlesee.

"Do you know where you're going?" I ask.

They ignore me. I lurch forward with another knock.

"Miss, we're under fire. You need to return to your rooms," the first mate says.

"Arden, you need to go," Declan says, but I lean forward.

"Where are they?" I ask, looking through the glass windscreen. But all I can see is the dark desert of water and sandbars that is the Mittlesee at night. I move to the door to go out on the deck, and Declan tries to stop me.

"You can't go out there!"

"Watch me," I say, and I push through the door. He

doesn't follow. I look around the starboard deck and see nothing. Then I hear a crack and a splash. I run to the other side, picking up my skirt to move more easily. There's a larger boat in the distance, gaining on us, and below, there's a smaller ship that looks as though it's going to try to board us.

I run back inside.

"They're in a skiff, coming up portside fast."

The captain looks at me. The first mate steps between us and lifts his palms.

"Miss, you need to get to safety —"

"How fast are they coming?" the captain asks.

"Maybe twenty knots? They're pushing us toward the Albinedes Rift."

The captain leans forward, and the first mate at least has the good sense to consult his map.

"Shit," the mate says, then shoots me an apologetic glance.

"Arden," Declan says, his hands on my shoulders. "How do you know this?"

"I learned," I say, quickly. "We can't get shoved into it, there'll be no way out."

"Right," the captain says.

"What would you have us do?" the mate says.

"Let me see your maps," I say. The mate clears out, and I pore over them. They're outdated and don't account for at least six major sandbars and rifts that could wreck a ship like this.

"I think there's a rift that could get us north if we veer west," I say.

"They'll reach us even faster, board in no time," the mate says.

I keep staring at the maps, the hand-drawn rifts and lines and squiggles that only months ago meant absolutely nothing to me. Another crack rocks the night, and the ship tilts in the wake of the near miss.

"Are they getting closer?" Declan asks, a note of fear in his tone. Nobody answers, which is as good a confirmation as anything.

"Are you certain about west?" the captain asks.

I want to say yes. But I can't. Because now, I'm doubting everything. Everything I knew suddenly seems fuzzy and foggy and less certain.

I let out a sharp sigh and stamp my foot in frustration. There's one person who could fix this quickly. I turn to Declan.

"No," Alvin says, suddenly there, anticipating what I'm about to ask.

"We need him, Declan," I say. But Alvin stands firmly between us, as if that will stop the conversation.

"I said, no. If this gets out, that we let a prisoner steer a Nordanian ship—"

"If he doesn't help, none of us may get off this Nordanian ship—"

"Get him," Declan says. His voice is decisive. Authoritative.

"Sir," the nearest sailor says, then rushes out the door.

"Sir Declan," Alvin says, sputtering, "you can't be serious."

"I'm serious about the lives on this ship. He is the only person on the face of this earth who knows the Mittlesee like that."

"What makes you think he wouldn't just steer us into a sandbar?"

Declan's gaze flickers to me, then back to Alvin.

"He wouldn't."

Another crack splits the night, and this time, the ship jolts with a direct hit. I rush back out the door and look down. It's hit the railing of the deck. At first glance, it seems like it must've been a mistake. But then I see the skiff approaching and the grappling hook they're waving. It would be much easier to climb through an opening in the side of the ship.

"They're about to come up," I shout through the open door.

"Arden!" Declan says, his voice firm. "Get back in here." I glare at him with fire in my eyes, and he wilts. "Please. Just get back in here where you're at least protected from explosions a little bit more."

I huff and do as he asks. Just then, Beck launches through the door to the bridge. His green eyes are bright despite the grimy look of the rest of him.

"What do we have here? A skiff attack? Or a pajama party?" he asks.

"Is that a real question?" the first mate asks.

"Ah, I see. Going for a booze cruise up the Albinedes Rift?"

The first mate looks shell-shocked. "How did you — "

"Aw, it's okay, buddy. This part of the sea is a nook-shodden mess. And the lemon-suckers out there couldn't tell a toothpick from a tree."

"What is he talking about, miss?" the first mate says.

"They don't know where they're going either," I say.

"What's the plan?" Beck asks.

"We're currently heading north, northeast at eighteen degrees," the captain says.

"Great plan."

"Wonderful."

"Sorry. Something got caught in my throat. It's very dry in the brig. Could really use some more water down there — "

"Will you spit it out, you musty rat-catcher!" I yell. The

entire bridge freezes. Beck glares at me. But I swear the corner of his mouth quirks.

"What would you do, Miss Thatcher?" he asks. I don't like the way my title rolls off his tongue. But I suppose it's as much of an insult to call me by my real name as it is for me to actually insult him.

"West," I say.

"West?" he asks. "Run right into them?" He's infuriating. It bolsters my nerve and my confidence.

"They're not expecting it. Then we can slice right up the Shazzibadean Divide."

"The what?" the captain asks. He leans over the map alongside the first mate.

"You won't find it on that map," Beck says, approaching the deck. "May I?"

"I demand you step back at once!" Alvin says, stepping forward. His forehead is coated in a thin sheen of sweat.

"Oh, hey there, Uncle Al," Beck says. "Haven't seen you since you messed with my lunch."

Alvin sputters. "This is preposterous. To allow a criminal to steer us into the Mittlesee toward an avenue that doesn't actually exist on the map."

"Just because you can't see it doesn't mean it doesn't exist," Beck says. "Sometimes, you just have to clap your hands and click your heels and *believe* really hard."

Declan turns to me.

"Do you know what he's talking about? What is this Shazzy-whatsis Divide?"

I smile. Because I do know what he's talking about. "Shazzibadean Divide. It's real. And they're not going to see it coming." Declan looks between me and Beck and the captain. The captain shrugs.

"It's your call, sir," he says.

"You can't be serious," Alvin says.

"I trust you, Arden," Declan says, lifting my left hand to his lips and pressing them to my knuckles. I don't know if he meant to do it, but the ring he just gave me catches the dim light, and I'm pretty sure everyone in the bridge sees it. Alvin hisses under his breath. I press a quick kiss to his cheek and launch toward the deck.

"Where are we now?" I ask, looking for where the instruments might be. Beck's ship didn't have nearly this kind of technology. It was held in place by spit, superfluous slang, and superstition.

"Approaching thirty-two degrees south, one-hundred-twenty degrees east . . . one-hundred-twenty-one . . ."

"We need to go west," I say.

"I'd say about, oh, three-twenty degrees?" Beck says.

"Three-twenty?" I ask.

"You think I'm wrong?"

"You have been below sea level for a little while. Maybe your ears aren't adjusting."

"You've had your nose in the clouds for a little while. Maybe you're—"

"Play nice, kids," the captain says.

"I'd go three-ten," I say. "That'll put us on course."

"Sure. It's a lovely angle. It'll angle us right up Shazz's crack. But remember—" A large crack interrupts him, and we all look portside, as if we can see them. "We have party crashers."

"Right," I say, begrudgingly. "Three-twenty will crash that party for sure."

"Do we have a radio on this thing?" he asks.

"Why? You want to invite them to call back another time?" I ask.

"I just want to know who we're dealing with. Then I can predict how far they'll chase us up Shazz's crevice."

"Crevice? Crack? Divide?" Alvin says with disgust.

"This is sounding less and less like a real place and more and more like a trap."

"It's not on any maps because we only just found it a few months ago," I say quickly. "We named it after one of his crew members as a joke."

"Shazz's crack is no joke. It's a national treasure," Beck quips.

"It's a national something," I mutter.

"Ah," Declan says. There's a note of discomfort in his voice, but when another crack fills the air and the entire ship jerks right, there's no time to assuage him.

"What are we doing here? Waiting to ask the lady to dance?" Beck snaps.

"Right," I say. "Let me put eyes on the skiff."

"Stop," Declan says, grabbing my wrist again. From the corner of my eye, Beck stiffens, but steps up to the wheel. "There are at least three other people paid to do that."

"Right," I say. He lets go of me, but I don't move away from him. I don't want Beck to think Declan has done anything wrong. I don't know why I care, but I stay there, just the same.

"Tell your men on the deck to hold on to their conches," Beck says.

"Does anyone understand a thing he says?" Alvin wails as the ship pitches left. Declan grabs me around the waist, and I hold on to the railing against the instrument panel. A crackle of static fills the bridge, followed by unintelligible garble.

"Keep at it, man," Beck grumbles as he holds the helm tight to our course.

"You try picking up radio waves when you're on a ship commandeered by a criminal with the finesse of a drunk ox," the first mate says. Beck grins, as if he's pleased with this assessment. I snort under my breath, and I hear Declan do the same. He's pressed against my back, and I'm not sure whether he's holding me, or holding on to me. Then there's a strange, skittering sound and a loud splash outside. Then, cheers.

"What was that?" Alvin practically squeals.

"Sounds like we got them," Declan says into my ear. His breath is warm against the edge of my neck, and it sends a flush down my back. It's almost enough to distract me from the radio signal that comes in.

"They've countered — man overboard! Man overboard! Abort mission! The girl will have to wait. Shit! They're on our channel — " Then it cuts out.

The bridge is silent but for the crackle of radio static. We all heard it. The distinct accent of the voice on the other end is unmistakable.

"I've lost them. I can't find — "

"No need," Beck says, his tone sober and serious. As the ship rights itself into the calmer waters of the Shazzibadean Divide, the realization of what we just heard spreads through the bridge. Declan straightens, making sure I'm steady on my feet before he steps back. Though he keeps a firm hand pressed to the small of my back.

"Was that?" the first mate asks. Declan lets out a heavy sigh. Alvin is remarkably quiet.

"Yes," Declan says after a long moment. "They were Nordanian."

CHAPTER EIGHT

*T*he realization hits us all that the ship that just tried to attack us, the one that nearly shoved us into a dead end that would beach us and leave us stranded in the middle of the Mittlesee, was in fact controlled by Nordanians. And they were searching for me.

"Not to break up this fun-times jamboree," Beck says, "but in about twenty minutes, this trench splits in two. So, where do you want to go?"

"Where does it split to?" Declan asks, sounding like a commander.

"We can go west to northern Nordania," he says, the subtlest inflection in the way he says it. It'll put us out on the way to New Covington, the closest port to his family's home in northern Nordania.

"Or?" Declan asks.

"East-northeast to the North Sea. Closest port city would be Barth."

"Swendenland?" I ask. Beck nods.

Declan chews on his bottom lip. Something I've rarely

seen him do. His gaze is fixed to where my hand is pressed against the railing. He steps closer, turning his body to cut off my view of Beck.

"This isn't the landscape I was anticipating," he says softly. "I don't know who would've sent pirates or mercenaries or whatever those people were, but one thing is for certain, they were our own. I've always underestimated the danger you face. I wanted to believe that with me at your side, it would be neutralized. But here we are, again, and I feel the fool."

"You couldn't have known, Declan," I say, taking his hand in mine.

"I should have."

"Should you?" I ask, and I'm really curious. He's quiet for a long moment.

"It's your call."

"What is?"

"Nordania, or Swendenland?"

And just like that, he's given me command over a whole Nordanian ship. I blink rapidly, as if it will clear my vision, and then I'll see that it's all a ruse. Just a fun laugh until we turn west for Nordania.

"Arden?" He holds my gaze, and I see the sincerity in it.

"Swendenland," I say.

He nods.

"The trip from Swendenland to Nordania via the North Sea takes five days," he says softly. There it is. The consequences of our actions. I swallow thickly and nod.

"I know," I say. We'll go to Swendenland, and then we'll elope.

"We'll figure it out," he says, pressing a kiss to my temple. "You'll wear flowers in your hair." Then he steps back, decisively.

"Swendenland," Declan says, with confidence.

"Swendenland?" Alvin repeats with confusion. "Why in god's green earth are we going to Swendenland when you're due to—"

"Swendenland it is," Beck says.

CHAPTER NINE

I've never traveled so far north, and the wind has a bite I wasn't prepared for. But still, it's more comfortable to stand on the deck, letting the sharp chill burn my cheeks and nose, rather than to stay cooped up in my rooms with Neve, who has become a quiz factory.

And being on the bridge isn't an option anymore. The crew would welcome me, but they've also welcomed Beck. They've forgotten the fact that he's technically a criminal they're transporting. And honestly, as we've been navigating the northern part of the Mittlesee, an area I never traveled, it's prudent to have him on the bridge. But being in the same room with him like that is confusing and overwhelming.

And that doesn't even bring Declan into the picture. Declan has been quiet and distant since our lackluster engagement turned pirate attack. It's been two days of traversing the Mittlesee and now, the North Sea, and I've only seen him twice. The first time was when he asked where in Swendenland I wanted to go. The second time, he apologized for not being able to stop and visit because he was in a time crunch. I'm not sure who is crunching his time, since we've extended our travels so unexpectedly. But I don't know what to say to him either, so it's just as well.

Not that I ever really pictured myself getting engaged, but this isn't what I pictured it being like. I suppose I imagined it would be exciting, and I'd be feeling floaty and in love and adored. I do feel adored, but there's also an element of shame or discomfort behind it. And that adds to the overall claustrophobia.

"Miss Thatcher?" Alvin says. He doesn't have sea legs. I wonder if this is intentional. He still wobbles back and forth, despite doing his darnedest to walk with the posture and grace of a man befitting his station.

"Yes, Alvin?"

"I'm to inform you that you and Mr. Levington have been invited to visit with the Prefect of Parth."

I can't hide the smile that flirts with my lips. "Is that really his title?" I ask.

"Yes," he says, showing not a small amount of disdain. "That is really his title. A bit ridiculous if you ask me." Then he catches himself. I press my lips together.

"Go on," I say.

"It will be a formal dinner, so you'll want to be dressed by sundown."

"When will that be?" I ask, looking out at the already pinkening sky. This far north, the days are so much shorter. It feels like I only just had lunch.

"I would imagine within the hour." His expression is smug, and I wonder how long he's been waiting to tell me. As if hoping I won't be able to be presentable in such a short amount of time.

"Thank you," I say. "I'll be ready."

"See to it that you are," he says. "And no gaffes this time?"

He always has to have the last word. I decide a different tactic.

"Of course, Alvin," I say. "And might I say, you're looking rather fetching today?"

He flinches. Sputters. And then, pink-cheeked, remains stuck in place as I turn on my heel and return to my quarters.

"Have I mentioned how lovely you look tonight?" Declan says, patting my fingers that are tucked into his elbow.

"You have," I say, smoothing my free hand down the navy velvet dress I'm wearing. The best thing about it is the thick layers of underskirts that keep my legs warm in the frigid night temperatures. The dress has an off-the-shoulder neckline, and I've just given up the faux fur capelet the girls wrapped me in, but the entry hall is still filled with the winter wind from outside.

"You really do look perfect," he says with a sweet smile.

"I might say the same about you," I say. It feels awkward to speak this way, but I suppose these are the parts we've committed to playing and the more I practice, the more natural it will feel. Someday perhaps?

"Declan!" A tall, jovial man with pink cheeks and a gold bow tie approaches, arms widespread.

"Prefect Gordon," he says, approaching with his hand extended, leaving me behind him. This is the way it's done. They greet each other like they're old friends, although, for all I know, this could be their first time meeting. And then they introduce the women like we're their pets.

"Please, you're an adult now. Call me Phillip."

"Phillip, it's lovely to see you. Allow me to introduce Arden Thatcher, my fiancée."

Phillip blinks twice, as if in surprise, but it doesn't affect his posture or anything else.

"So the rumors are true?"

"It would seem so." Declan grins.

"Well, how about that," Phillip says, approaching me with the wide grin of a doting uncle. "This is the young woman who finally caught your eye? You must be something quite special."

"I don't know about that," I say, "but I think we see the world the same way."

"Yes," he says, slowly, then he leans in and kisses my cheek. "We will have to spend some time comparing experiences then."

My stomach tightens, but he and Declan continue chatting, as Declan meets his wife and daughter, Genevieve, who is thirteen years old and completely starstruck by him. It's almost adorable—except her being besotted with him makes me the enemy, and I spend most of dinner as the recipient of her glares, wondering whether she's tried to add anything extra to my plate.

It's only halfway through the meal, when Genevieve is talking about her schooling, that I realize we haven't met his son. I suppose, if his son is grown and married, he might not come home for dinners, but if one of the graduates married him, I guess I thought he would come up in conversation at some point. But he hasn't.

"I think I prefer linguistics to maths," Genevieve says.

"Ah, why is that?" Declan says, steepling his fingers and looking adorably interested.

"Because there are so many ways to say the same thing, and it can be interpreted so many different ways. There's only one way to do maths. And it's boring." We all laugh, though I wouldn't mind having learned a little bit of maths. That's not something included in training at the institute.

"Does your brother help you with your schooling?" I ask. The laughter stops, and I worry I've said the wrong thing.

"He's not home anymore," she says, as if it's the most obvious thing. I turn to the prefect, and he shakes his head.

"I forget you are young," he says, good-naturally, though it is a little patronizing. "He is married and has moved south."

"South?" I ask, trying to picture the world map from the library at the institute. South of here is Osterstan, I believe.

"He's a solicitor with a small but prestigious firm in Salisbury, a trading town along the southern border of our prefecture," Constance explains.

"You must be very proud," Declan says.

"Yes," she says, "very proud."

"And do you have grandchildren?" Declan asks. "Forgive me, I can't remember."

"Yes," Constance says, though her response is stilted. "One boy. His name is Peter." I don't know what this is about, but the way she's become so stiff sends chills down my spine.

"You see, this is not table talk, but as it has arisen, they have lost three children to God. All born asleep."

"Oh, no," I say, realizing that this woman who was Nordanian has been through something tremendous and terrible.

"Yes," Phillip says. "It is terrible, indeed. But we must give thanks for the blessings we do have. After all, we have all been blessed by the Lord in so many ways and must carry our mantle of service the best way we know how." I'm surprised at the sudden turn of tone to a religious tenor. He grins, and it seems decided: we will talk about pleasant things. Still, it means that the Ember I'm looking for isn't here in Parth. She's further south, in Salisbury. I wonder if Declan will let me go look for her.

"I understand you are recently engaged?" Constance says just before she takes a bite of minced lamb from inside the delicate squash blossoms. It seems far too cold to have fresh squash blossoms. But maybe they utilize greenhouses like Carmen's in Sudersberg.

"Yes," I say with what I hope is a demure smile.

"Congratulations," Phillip says, dabbing his mouth with his napkin. "Do you have a date set? Your father made it sound as if you couldn't wait."

The air in the room becomes thinner, and I swear Genevieve tosses some extra salt on my roasted yams. Or at least, I'm hoping it's just salt.

"We are quite excited," Declan says, giving the effect of the happy-in-love princeling that the world wants to see.

"He made it sound as if you might return already married? That hasn't already happened, has it?" Phillip asks.

"Phillip," Constance says, chiding him. "Leave them alone. Their business is their business."

"Oh, like our business was our business?" Phillip says, leaning in to press a kiss to his blushing wife's jaw.

"Ew, stop," Genevieve says, and for once, I couldn't agree with her more. It's uncomfortable to watch.

"I would never presume to keep such a big moment from my people," Declan says. "I am humbled to be their chosen servant and am blessed to earn their love and respect. A moment of such joy as a marriage would only bolster Nordanians." The way he says it surprises me. He's never expressed a devoutness in conversation, but that's the only word to describe it. The sense of duty and loyalty is at odds with the way we've talked about change. What surprises me even more is the way everyone at the table nods in agreement. I've never felt like such an outsider.

"So I suppose I can't talk you into eloping here in Parth?" Phillip says. He grins at me, and then winks.

Declan laughs, as if this is a lovely ruse and we're all in on it. But I'm not sure what the joke is.

"I could be your bridesmaid," Genevieve says, suddenly batting her eyelashes and looking angelic. The adults laugh again, but in a sweet, good-natured way that doesn't at all match the little devil I've been sitting next to all night.

"That's a very sweet offer," I say, "but we won't be getting married until I've finished my studies and graduated from the institute."

The room falls silent. Genevieve grins, as if she's won some game I didn't know we were playing. Constance frowns at me, and Phillip clears his throat, his smile spreading across his face.

"Of course, education and enrichment is important," he says, "but family is tantamount. Could you not marry, and then finish your coursework?"

"I suppose I could do the work," I say as Declan shoots me a look that I don't know how to interpret. "But then I wouldn't be able to vote."

"Vote?" Constance says, and then lets out a little laugh. "What would you want to be bothered with that for?"

A server removes my plate at that moment. As if it is his job to remind me that I've said the wrong thing and now, I should be on my way.

"It is important to be informed and to be able to participate in fair and free elections," I say, but once again, this is the wrong thing.

"But you will be married to the figurehead of your nation," Constance says. "And if my memory serves me correctly, you'll be the moral figurehead."

I consider this. Then I consider my glass of water. It looks slightly foggy. I decide it's better to be thirsty than risk whatever Genevieve might have done to it.

"I suppose that's true. But what better way to set an example than to demonstrate my passion for civic engagement."

"But you said so yourself earlier, that the two of you are of such similar mind. And you have the love of your people. If you side with one side or another, it presents you as political leaders, and political leaders are not meant to lead forever."

"Well, maybe no one is meant to lead forever," I say.

The room goes still. I think even the taper candles on the table stop flickering. Phillip clears his throat.

"Perhaps the lamb was a bit under seasoned. We could do with something sweet to lighten the mood," Phillip says. Constance flickers a hand, and I realize my mistake.

They are not elected officials. Neither is Declan's father. They have all inherited their positions and now, here I am, telling them that what they view as their calling from God is wrong. I don't need Alvin to tell me I've put my foot in my mouth.

"Tell me," Declan says, turning the subject, "where did you find squash blossoms this time of year?"

"Ah," Constance says, pleased to have a new subject. "We have a greenhouse that produces them all year. The autumnal light filters through in such a lovely way for a bright, clean flavor, though I do prefer the summertime ones we get outside. They're so much sweeter."

I'm beginning to realize I prefer the outdoors as well. Being in this cold weather is doing nothing for my own sweetness.

CHAPTER TEN

I can't sleep. Everything was just off enough at dinner, and it has my mind whirling. I didn't even fight off Neve as she made me wear some sort of goopy seaweed and mud concoction on my face to "reduce my massive pores," or fight off Meredith when she combed through my curls and applied some sort of creme. The way the prefect and his wife got stilted when talking about their son and his wife. She's had a child with this man, and they were weird talking about it. That doesn't sound like the happy, "family-first" people we had dinner with.

I walk the deck, my legs now used to absorbing far more than the little swells of this bay. It's cold, and the blanket I wrapped around my shoulders isn't really enough. But as I approach the prow, I see a familiar shape standing there. Declan is a silhouette of dark and silvery moonlight leaning over the railing of the prow. The set of his shoulders, the way his chin lifts into the night, he looks every bit the princely persona I first met.

"Declan?" I ask. He turns, surprise evident in his features.

"What are you doing out here?" He approaches, immediately moving to take off his jacket. I stop him.

"It's too cold for chivalry," I say. He offers a modest smile but drapes his jacket over my shoulders nevertheless. The lights of the towns along the coastline dot the darkness extending beyond. So many lives I know so little about, represented by nothing more than a point of electricity.

"We should probably talk about what happened at dinner," he says.

"I hoped you would say that," I say, wrapping my blanket tighter as a breeze gusts toward us from the north. "I can't stop thinking about it."

He looks surprised, and then sympathetic. "It wasn't that bad."

"Wasn't that bad?" I ask, frowning. "It's just so strange. The way we met their daughter but not their son. And for as much as they love family —"

"Wait," he says, raising a hand, "I don't think we're talking about the same thing."

I frown again. "What are you talking about?"

He hesitates. "The things you said at dinner, you offended them. You know that, right?"

I freeze. Yes, I suppose I did know that dinner hadn't really gone that well, and that I'd said a few things that led to some awkward pauses. But it was always in response to something offensive they'd said.

"You're out here, unable to sleep, because I offended the prefect and his wife?" I ask, taking it all in.

"It's my fault," he says, pinching the bridge of his nose. "I should have prepared you for them. They're very conservative."

"So, I'm not allowed to offend them, but when they tell me I shouldn't worry about having the right to vote —"

"They welcomed us into their home. They accepted you

as my official partner. We were on their turf, Arden. That's how it works. We pretend they're being gracious hosts, and they pretend to accept us as we appear to be."

"So, you don't have any concern about their daughter-in-law?"

"Who?" He frowns. I drop my jaw. "I'm sorry, I wasn't thinking about—yes, of course I have concerns. She wasn't there, and I would have felt better to see her and know she was well."

"Don't you think they would've wanted to show off a grandchild?" I ask.

"Children aren't really expected at these sorts of dinners."

"There was a child there tonight."

"She was fourteen," he says.

"Thirteen."

"Thirteen isn't a child. She could chew with her mouth closed and not dribble on her dress."

"You only say that because she was in love with you and you didn't have to sit next to her. That little bitch isn't to be trusted," I snap. He laughs. Actually laughs. And then I laugh, because we're literally fighting about a thirteen-year-old who over salted my food.

"Please don't take this the wrong way—"

"Well, now I know that I should definitely take this exactly the way it sounds—"

"Arden," he says, and I raise my palms in surrender. "I didn't realize your preparation was, shall we say, deficient in some areas that matter."

"Deficient?" I say, hating the way the word chokes in the back of my mouth.

"I'm sorry, that's the wrong word. I had spoken with Neve, and I'd asked her to make sure that you were up to speed on the local customs of the places we're traveling to.

That you're familiar with . . ." He trails off, and I realize with a heavy lump in my stomach exactly what the stakes are here. Neve hasn't just been quizzing me on things for the exam for the institute. She's been prepping me to be Declan's partner *now*. And I've been brushing it aside because it didn't seem important.

"She's been helpful," I say. "It's my fault." And it is. It's my fault that I've offended these people who might be the gatekeepers to the next Ember on the list.

"It's not your fault," he says.

"No, it is." I say. "She's been pushing me to study more, and it's just . . . well, it's a lot. It's so much information and—"

"And if you'd been properly trained before you arrived at the institute, this wouldn't be so much information."

I tighten the blanket around my body—the truth of his words hits hard—around the shiver of shame.

"It's not your fault, Arden," he says, rubbing his hands up and down my arms, trying to distill some warmth into me. "It's not your fault that you got a crappy education. That's on Conrad. And it shouldn't have happened."

I nod, slowly. I don't know where he's going with this. There's nowhere he can really go, because the bottom line is that I was the fool who accepted the hand I was dealt and didn't fight for more. I would laugh at someone who makes a wish on a star and is disappointed when they don't wake up to a purse full of gold on their doorstep, but am I really any different? There's nothing worse than being the fool. All it does is put a target on my back for others to aim at. A better person—like Neve—would use this feeling to fuel her into making up for her deficit. Hell, that's exactly what Neve did.

Despite what he says, it is my fault. I could've educated myself. I could've tried harder, and I didn't. I'm still not

79

putting all my effort into Neve's tutoring sessions. A mollymawk catches my eye in the sky, circling overhead as if it expects to find a late night snack churned up in our wake.

"It shouldn't have to come down to luck of the draw when it comes to beneficiaries getting education. Hell, it shouldn't come down to luck of birth when it comes to Nordanian girls getting a good education. You're right." He pauses, and I hold my breath. "I know it's going to be a big leap for some of the old guard in the North Wing, but if we're going to say that the women from the institute represent one fourth of governance, then we need to protect them. We need to protect all of them, from start to finish, if we want to represent Nordanian interests in the world."

I nod vehemently.

"So, what's the next step? You need to find this woman?"

"Yes," I say, surprise coating my voice. "Yes, we need to find her. Do you think that's something we have time for? That we could do next?"

Declan nods. "I'll have Alvin make arrangements in the morning. I don't see why we couldn't visit. If we go to their house in the southern prefecture, and she's not there, then we have cause for concern and could make inquiries. And if she's there, then you can take the next step." A swell of relief and elation fills me, and I want to wrap myself around him and squeeze. But he looks defeated, not triumphant.

"Is that okay?" I ask.

He sighs. "I don't know how to explain it, but it's disappointing. Just not for the reasons you're probably thinking."

"What reasons then?"

He turns and leans back against the railing, arms crossed over his chest.

"I've been raised to believe that I was born into my family and blessed with the God-ordained right to lead." I blink, surprised at his sudden turn of topic. His smile turns chagrined. "I know that must sound inane to a non-believer, but that's what I've been taught — it's what I believe. That, in exchange for my blessed birth and privilege, I owe a life of service to the country. It's my manifest duty and honor."

I listen, quietly. I don't know what to say, so I just listen.

"But now, as I'm about to come into my own, after having lived with this belief system my entire life, I realize that isn't exactly how the world works. That even my service and belief couldn't save people who are under my protection."

The wind picks up, whipping curls into my face and sending the scent of lilacs and mint along the wind.

"If it helps," I say, leaning into his arm, "I don't think anyone blames you."

He nods.

"It helps a little, I suppose."

"They might blame your parents," I say, and his gaze flickers up to mine, "but not you." He sputters a wry laugh.

"Thanks for that, that really helps," he says, shaking his head.

"Declan," I say, stepping in front of him. I hold his biceps and squeeze. They're firmer than I expect, hiding an inner strength that perhaps not even he is aware of. "You're learning. And you're adjusting the way you think. It's harder to change your beliefs than it is to keep doing the same thing, and you're committed to doing the right thing — the hard thing . . . right?"

"Yes," he says firmly.

"That takes strength of character, and having the moral fiber to admit that things aren't right for everyone, that you're willing to make a change, that says a lot. More than you know. People will respect that. And you're worthy of that respect."

"You believe that?" he asks. His voice is small.

"Yes," I say. "I really do."

He wraps his arms around me and pulls me into his chest. He's warm and solid, and I coil my arms around his back. We hold each other like that as the wind blows from every direction. And I wonder if perhaps this is all we need to weather the storm.

CHAPTER ELEVEN

"*D*enied?" I ask, my mouth practically flapping in the wind that comes off the North Sea in shock.

"Yes," Alvin says. "I'm sorry." He doesn't sound the slightest bit sorry about it. I turn to look for Declan, but he's nowhere to be found.

"I need to talk to Declan," I say, looking around the restaurant where I've been having tea and little almond cookies with Neve. I couldn't stand waiting around on the ship for the official word about when and how we'd be able to go see the next Ember. Ever since Beck has been given some freedoms—particularly the bridge of the ship—it feels smaller. I used to like going to the bridge to see what the captain sees and study the star maps. But now, it's too risky. It's too hard to be around him. It just makes me feel angry and confused, and all that anger and confusion gives me a headache.

"He's indisposed at the moment," Alvin says, reminding me of just why I dislike Alvin. I'd thought we were getting somewhere the other day with his joke about the prefect. But I guess I should've known better. I mean, who says *indisposed* like that? Like he knows something salacious, and he's not going to tell me. Even if it's just that Declan is using the bathroom, he makes it sound like I'm never going to be on the inside of this world.

"Of course he is," I mutter.

"I'm sure he would like to speak to Arden," Neve says, trying to help. "After all, Arden is his first priority when we are aground in a foreign state."

Alvin's eyes widen, as if having forgotten something. In this moment, I'm so happy that she's with me. And that she's memorized everything ever written about Nordania. But also, I need to ask her exactly what that means.

"Yes, of course," Alvin says, smoothly, "but he is in a meeting at the moment and is truly unavailable. He will be with you shortly." Then he turns on his heel and leaves.

It's not as if we're completely alone. We have two guards sitting on the opposite side of the restaurant from us, pretending to sip their chamomile tea and nibble their fig pastys. But Declan isn't here to explain exactly why it is that we were denied a meeting with the prefect's son, who is married to a Nordanian graduate — and Ember.

"Now what?" I ask Neve, sinking into my chair in the most unladylike fashion. She shoots me a sharp glare and floats down to her chair. She lifts her tea with two fingers and sips without slurping, then sets it down. She doesn't even dribble it on her matching emerald green jacket and skirt.

"Now, we do exactly what they expect of us. We sit, and chat, and finish our tea."

"How is that supposed to —"

"If you'd be quiet and drink your tea, you might learn something." The glare she shoots at me could kill, and I don't have the energy to fight her. So I do what she does. I practice lifting my teacup to my mouth in the Swendish style, and I sip the floral tea. It smells better than it tastes. The almond cookies are good, though—crisp on the edges, with a buttery-soft center.

"It's an interesting mix of people," Neve says, her voice almost whisper soft.

"Is it?" I ask, looking around the room. The tearoom is decorated in heavy fabrics—soft green and coppery damasks, benches and chairs with fluffy pillows, and stained glass lamps hanging over tables. It's cozy, and every piece has a note of elegance, and yet the overall effect is strangely eclectic. Or perhaps it's the clientele. Because, as I take them in, Neve is right. It's an odd mix.

There's a table of ladies in bold satin jacket-dress combinations, complete with sparkly brooches and large feathers. Then, another table of two old women with a young gentleman, all dressed in heavy fabrics that look clean and sharp, but wilted at the edges. As if they're wearing their finest, but their finest isn't all that fine. Then, there are our guards sitting toward the back. But that's when I realize there's another table of gentlemen about two tables away from ours. My back has been to them, and their voices are low.

They're dressed in a nondescript, nice enough style. Hair combed, trim beards, and mustaches in the local Swendish style, collared shirts, silk ties, and pressed slacks. But their tea is no longer steaming. The plate of almond cookies looks untouched. There's something odd about it, and I can't put my finger on it. That's when I hear the crack of broken ceramic.

"Oh goodness!" Neve says, leaping to her feet. Neve's teacup sits on the tile floor in pieces, tea spilt all over the mosaic tile. Remarkably, none of it landed on either of us. A waitress approaches us with towels and apologies, as if it was her fault.

"I'm so sorry, miss," Neve says, looking at me with the expression of a servant asking for forgiveness. "If you'd like to go . . ."

I'm confused. I don't understand what's happening. But then, Neve's gaze flickers to the table behind me. One closer to the suspicious men.

"No," I say, waving my hands at the panicked-looking shopkeeper. "Of course not. It was just an accident. We can just shift tables."

"Yes, of course, ma'am," the waitress says. There's a flurry of activity, and next thing I know, I'm sitting with my back adjacent to the gentleman behind me. A fresh teapot is delivered, and our new cups are steaming with the entrails of steeped chamomile, as well as a fresh plate of almond cookies.

"I don't know what they think they're doing," the man behind me says. Neve picks up a cookie and thoughtfully nibbles at it.

"Taking their . . . time of it . . ." the other one says. They're being so quiet, it's really hard to hear them.

"What are they saying?" Neve says so softly I only understand it because I read her lips.

I shake my head.

"—the last thing they want . . . spark the network . . ."

I sit up straighter.

"How much do they want?" the nearer man says.

"Will that be all, gentlemen?" the waitress interrupts. Her voice is so much louder that it makes me flinch. Neve's expression and renewed interest in her tea cup tells me everything I need to know: I am not being subtle. Then the men close out their check and get up to leave.

"I think they know something," I hiss at Neve.

"Like what?"

"About the network. The Embers."

"That's too much of a coincidence," she says. I shrug and shake my head. Maybe it is. Or maybe not. Declan sent word asking about seeing her today, and she's not available. Alvin says Declan is indisposed, and then I hear men talking about this. I repeat everything I heard, and Neve doesn't take her eyes off the men as they move toward and out the door.

"What if they know something?" I ask.

"What would they know?" she asks.

The door opens, letting in the light and noise from the street, and I see the chance leaving. It's probably irresponsible and unladylike and everything else I'd get shamed for, but I stand, knocking into the table.

"Arden!" Neve says. "What are you doing?"

"We have to follow them."

"We absolutely do not," she says.

"But what if—"

"Is everything all right, ladies?" Clem, one of the bodyguards, is standing next to me now.

"Yes," I say, then feign a blush. "I just realized I don't have my notes with me to pay. I'm so embarrassed."

He smiles, a patronizing thing, and reaches into his jacket pocket. "We'll handle this."

"Thank you, Clem," I say. "We have to rush now. You understand, lady issues." I take Neve's elbow and rush her toward the exit before Clem's blush recovers.

Out on the street, it's busier and brighter than I'm prepared for. The smells remind me of the peninsula: fish and brine and something vaguely spiced. But the air has a chill that never existed on the peninsula.

"Where did they go?" I ask, scanning the street for their green and blue jackets.

"There," Neve says, pointing to the left. They're walking along the opposite side of the pedestrian street. We cut through the cross traffic, weaving between fishmongers and craft-sellers, and I keep my eyes fixed on the green jacket. They move with purpose down the busy street, swerving between clusters of people. Then they veer right, and I lose sight of them. We approach the place where they turned right, and there's a narrow alleyway.

"Miss Arden," a voice calls. It's Clem, and he looks harried from in front of the tea shop.

"Arden," Neve says, sounding irritated but not uncomfortable. As if she's not afraid to follow these mysterious men.

"Come on," I say, "we have to."

"Fine," she says. She tugs my hand, and we veer down the alleyway. There's two doors and a dead end. One door appears to go into the side of a tavern. The other looks to be a residence.

"What do you think?" she asks. I reach for the handle of the residence, but it's cold. I don't know why this surprises me. It's cold outside. But when I reach for the handle of the tavern, it opens before I can touch it. The man in the green jacket stands right there.

"What do we have here, and why have you followed me?"

It feels dangerous now. The two of us in an alleyway with a dead end, essentially cornered by a man who is aware that we've followed him.

"Well? What is it?" he says.

"I overheard you in the tea room," I say, my voice sounding bolder than I feel. "I heard you talking about the network. Sparking the network."

Understanding colors his face.

"You know what that's all about, do yeh?" Suddenly, his polite Swendish affect is gone, and he sounds downright . . . well, Nordanian. It's surprising. And scary.

"Miss," Neve says, not revealing my name with purpose. "Perhaps we should go."

"Arden!" Clem's voice roars from the street. The green coat looks at me with recognition.

"I think you two had better come inside. Now."

CHAPTER TWELVE

"*Y*ou should know that if you plan to detain us, you're in for a bigger headache than —"

"Will you keep your voice down?" the man hisses at me. "I know exactly who you are. What I don't know is why you've followed me."

My cheeks flush, and the man, who isn't that old and isn't bad-looking, smiles as if even in the dark he can see it.

"We thought we heard something, that's all," Neve says. It's as if she's giving him an easy out — and us too — but still not admitting that we know nothing, in case he wants to tell us more. It's smart and savvy. I can't help but have the feeling that Neve has done this before, or something like this.

"You've followed me here. How do I know you won't send the authorities after us?" he says. He points at me and nods. "I know you were dining with Swendish royalty last night."

I snort. They were hardly royalty. And Swendenland doesn't actually have royalty, anyway. He grins, exposing a gap between his front teeth.

"Who are you?" I ask, having a strange feeling this isn't the first time I've seen this man before.

"You wouldn't know me," he says. Neve squints at him, and he looks away. "Look, we're not looking to get into any scuffles with anyone. We're trying to keep our heads down. And inviting the betrothed princess of Nordania into our back-alley business meeting isn't exactly keeping our heads down."

"I can see that," I say. "But if you don't give us a reason to make a scuffle, we won't . . . make a scuffle." I feel awkward in this position, and I can't help but think that Neve would handle this better than I would.

"Seems fair 'nuff." He leans back against the wall and stuffs his hands into his pockets.

"So, what are we doing here?"

"We? We're just chatting."

"You, then?"

"I'm sussing you out."

"What business do you have here?" Neve asks, her voice sharp enough to cut through the bullshit. He grins.

"We're an amnesty organization."

"Amnesty?" I ask. "Like, you help people in bad spots?"

"Something like that."

"From the back of a bar? And a tea room?"

"Business gets conducted in stranger spots. Believe you me."

"Oh, I know," Neve says bitterly. "You might have noticed we're women. Not allowed a lot of places." He nods, sagely, and that seems to be the deciding factor.

"We've been helping your graduates."

"Our graduates? How do you know —"

"I can read a newspaper."

"Oh, right."

"Helping them how?" Neve asks, squinting.

"Since you said you knew what the network was, it should come as no surprise to you that the institute graduates hold significant potential for power in the Nordanian government."

For a moment, I wonder if he's trying to trap me. If he's overheard me talking about this with Declan, or Neve, or even Meredith, and is somehow feeding into what it is that I'm trying to do, and now he's trapped us here and we're about to be kidnapped. But then, I see the glimmer of excitement in his gaze, and I realize that despite being from very different walks of life—or maybe not so different—we might be fighting on the same side of this battle.

"Yes, I was aware," I say.

"Well, you're not the only one who figured that out," he says.

"What is that supposed to mean?" Neve says, stepping closer. His gaze skims down her, assessing her as an adversary or lover, I'm not sure which—but I know he wouldn't survive either way.

"It means that just as their network has been triggered, just as they've started rallying their ranks, someone has offered up a bounty for their heads."

"Someone is paying a bounty to have them killed?"

He laughs and shakes his head, but I don't know what's so funny about this.

"No, I didn't mean their actual heads. But someone wants them rounded up, and they're paying mighty good for it."

"How much?" Neve asks. Her gaze is intense. He meets her intensity.

"Three thousand."

"Three thousand Nordanian dollars for a graduate? Is that—"

"Swendish kroner."

One Swendish kroner is worth about fifty Nordanian dollars. Which means—

"Who has that kind of money?" Neve asks.

"People who don't want these women to vote," I say. The man nods.

"So, you're doing what? And who are you?"

He presses his lips together tight, and then, as if making a decision, uses the momentum of his body to roll onto his feet and off the wall. He extends his hand.

"Name's Elm."

"I know you," Neve says, a mix of recognition and fear. He nods, but she doesn't take his hand.

"And I know you," he responds, his gaze haunted.

"How do you know him?"

"He's from Osterstan."

"I'm not from Osterstan."

"You were there."

He nods. "I was."

"During the explosion."

Explosion? What explosion, I want to ask, but I keep my mouth shut.

"Yes, ma'am."

"Don't call me ma'am," Neve says with a slight shiver. He nods. I could swear Neve's eyes go glassy, but as soon as I see them, they're gone.

"I don't know you," I say.

"No, but I know you, Arden," he says. There's a long pause, like a standoff between him and Neve, and then, with a sigh, he says, "You should know Carla is safe."

"Where is she?" Neve asks.

"Safe," he repeats. And it's all he says. If what he does is help people who need amnesty, maybe it's for the best that he's not telling us where she is. It could mean he's trustworthy.

"Why should we trust you?"

He shrugs one shoulder. "I guess you don't have a choice."

"What are you doing here?" I ask.

"Same thing you are," he says. "Helping an Ember at risk."

"It wouldn't happen to be the same one married to the prefect's son, would it?"

His brows lift, and he steps closer. Closer still. Neve holds her ground, but I step back. Elm reaches behind me and locks the door.

"You'll have to keep your voices down."

We follow him down a narrow, damp-smelling stairwell. At the bottom of the stairs is another door, and Neve hesitates.

"This feels like a trap."

"If it is, you're already in it," he says with a shrug. I look at Neve, and she shrugs with the same level of surrender and a spark of vital curiosity.

"Would you let us leave if we asked? Right now?" I ask. His eyes bore into mine. They're so dark blue that in this dim light they almost look black.

"How would I know you wouldn't go rat us out?"

"Rat you out?" Neve says with a huff.

"You'd have to take my word for it," I say. He leans his weight on one hip and looks at me. Really assesses. Then he shakes his head.

"You're not going anywhere."

A sluice of icy fear slithers down my spine.

"What makes you say that?" I ask.

He laughs, but it's not villainous. "Because you want to know what's behind door number one as much as she does." He jerks his head toward Neve. She glares at him. But I know that glare. She's not mad that he accused her of something. She's mad that he's read her like a book.

"I'm not the bad guy here," he says. And this time, I don't know why, but I believe him. I nod, motioning for him to go on and open the door. He does.

He waits for us to enter the chilled basement space. It's dim, but once we enter, we see there's a radiator pumping heat out from an above fireplace. And right next to it is a comfortable, if shabby-looking armchair. A girl is resting in the chair, a blanket over her lap, a cup of tea on a side table next to her.

CHAPTER THIRTEEN

"Simone?" Elm says, approaching her slowly. She sits up, slowly, and turns. And I remember her. She was considered the front-runner about five years ago—the first year I was at the Laarsworth plantation. The last time I really paid attention to who went to the institute.

"Simone Hartford?" Neve says with a gasp.

Simone looks at us, stilling in her chair. Her dark eyes glitter in the dark light, the whites of her eyes offsetting her dark brown skin. Her hair is pulled up into a neat coil of braids. She looks back and forth between Elm and us.

"Who are they?" she asks, fear in her voice.

"Friends," he says, kneeling next to her. He reaches into his green jacket and withdraws a small white package. I realize that it's the almond cookies that had been untouched on the table where he sat with the other man.

I'm only just now realizing that I don't know who that other man was, or where he went.

"Are you safe, ma'am?" Neve asks, thinking faster on her feet than me. I'm focused on cookies, and she has the common sense to ask after her health and safety.

Simone looks back to Elm, and Elm nods.

"For the moment," she says. "Don't call me ma'am. Who are you?"

I step forward, suppressing a smile. "My name is Arden Thatcher, and I'm —"

"I know who you are. I meant the other one."

I halt.

"This is Neve Ruiz. She is my friend," I say.

She frowns and studies Neve.

"I have been at the Port of Pleasure for the past months. I have a shop there."

"Makeup?" Simone asks. Neve nods, but I see the hint of satisfaction creeping into her features. "I love your lipstick." Simone touches her bare lips, perhaps thinking of something she's left behind. Because obviously, if she's hiding in this basement, with someone like Elm bringing her cookies, she's not brought everything from her trousseau with her.

"What is happening here?" I ask.

"I told you," Elm says, tucking the white paper bag back in his jacket, "we help people who need amnesty. Miss Hartford needs amnesty."

It's all coming together. She's left her husband and son. The memory of my mother pressing a kiss to my cheek and telling me to be good comes back, nearly knocking me over. One glance at Neve tells me she's having a similar feeling.

"I want to help," I say.

She doesn't react. Just sits where she is and takes a sip of her tea.

"I don't know how you would."

"I . . ." I begin, but then I remember why I'm here. "I've actually come looking for you."

At this, she lifts her eyebrows.

"And you knew to come to this basement?" She flickers an uneasy glance at Elm.

"No," I say. "That was a bit of luck. I had dinner last night with your in-laws — or whatever they are to you now . . ." I trail off, not sure if I've misspoken.

She stares at me for a long, quiet moment.

"I'm sorry."

Neve snorts. As if she understands this all too well. I still have so many questions to ask her about her time between the peninsula and the Port of Pleasure.

"We expected you and your . . . their son to be there. But you weren't. So we tried to arrange a meeting today."

"I imagine that was rather difficult."

"Declan's valet wasn't all that sorry to tell me our request was denied."

"Valets . . ." she says, setting her tea cup down on the table. "I always thought that was a world that I would love to be a part of. Now, I'd rather never meet another one." Neve snorts, and I let out a little laugh.

"I know what you mean," I say.

"I don't understand something," she says. She rises, and I realize she's tall. She's also curvy in a soft, maternal way, and carries a maturity in her posture that is both intimate and inspiring. "Why were you looking for me? Not just because I'm Nordanian and you were in the neighborhood?"

I smile and step closer.

"I was sent here. By Carmen."

Her eyes widen and understanding settles into her expression. She folds her hands against her stomach, but they're fidgety.

"Carmen?" Elm says, sensing the shift in the environment.

"It's the network," she says.

"Fuck," he says. He turns and paces away.

"What?" I ask. "What's wrong?"

"This timing couldn't be worse," she says.

"I understand there are bounties out there," I say, "but there must be a way. It's been activated, and this is our shot to change things for good."

"Change?" she asks, hesitating.

"I'm going to bring a measure before the legislature at the next assembly. It will outline changes to the institute, and to the beneficiary program to protect the beneficiaries. I'm also working on something to help the graduates."

"Something to help the graduates?" She stills. Looks at me in an odd way. "What is this something?"

I hesitate, fumble. "The particulars are still being ironed out."

She laughs. But it's not funny. "Are you serious?"

"Simone," Elm says, placing a placating hand on her arm, but she shoves him off.

"This is why the bounties are happening, isn't it? Because of a measure without particulars? This is why the network has been compromised? That network is meant for life-and-death situations."

"I think that some beneficiaries have found themselves in life-and-death situations," I say, a little sharper than I intend. She snaps to face me.

"You think I don't know that?" She approaches, and I realize that she really is tall. It's not just her confidence or presence, she's just tall. "I was disciplined every time I did something wrong in my benefactor's house. And those discipline sessions left marks. Marks that my husband then pointed out and called 'ugly' and 'disgusting' on our wedding night. The night that I thought would free me of my past only reinforced what I'd always feared: that I would never be enough, that I would never be free of what others thought of me.

"So don't tell me that I don't know that this is a life-or-death situation for some of the beneficiaries. I've seen some take their own lives."

I feel the warmth drain from the room, and Neve steps closer to me.

"I've seen it too. We both have. And I've seen what happens to the women who are taken from the institute prior to graduation. I know it doesn't get easier, and that it can feel as though their own country has abandoned them in exchange for favorable treaty terms."

I stare at Neve. Who is she talking about? Who does she know that was taken from the institute?

"And that is why this is so important. Right, Arden?" She lobbies the ball back to me, and I nod.

"Yes. We need to get this right. We need input from people like you. And I want to get you out of here if we can."

"If you can?" she asks. "That's not a plan. That's as good as 'thoughts and well-wishes.'"

"Well, what was your plan?" I ask, looking from her to Elm. He looks at Simone, and then she nods, resigned.

"There is an amnesty house in east Osterstan. We are scheduled to take the train tomorrow morning."

"In east Osterstan?" I frown. I think back to what I know about Osterstan, which isn't much. And none of it is good. But still, this doesn't sound right at all.

"Osterstan is more free than you would imagine," Neve says, as if in explanation. But it doesn't explain things to me at all. Once again, I'm realizing just how bereft my education has been.

"Would you come with us?" I ask. "I don't know what benefits there are to going to this amnesty house, but if you come with me, come onto our ship, I can promise you certain protections."

"What kind of protections?" she asks. I expect Elm to argue. But he's quiet.

"The kind that comes from Declan Levington."

She laughs. Then shakes her head.

"The last time I saw Declan, he was fifteen and chasing my skirt."

Neve snorts again, and I can't help but laugh at the image of a teenage Declan following a beautiful woman around the capital mansion.

Just then, the door flies open and the man in the blue jacket from the tea room enters.

"We have a problem," he says.

"Fantastic," Elm mutters.

"There's a Nordanian search force out there for—" Then he stops, his gaze landing on me. He sighs in a way that sounds a lot like a string of curses.

"I think our window to get you out of here, either way, just got a little tighter," Elm says.

"Please," I say, approaching Simone. I take her hands in mine and give them a gentle squeeze. "Please give this a chance. Whatever needs to be done to keep the network going, we have to at least try. But we can't do it if you're not safe."

She frowns. Deep in thought.

"Why me?"

"Because Carmen—"

"No, why me? You've found me, why not just move on?"

"Because every single woman who ever walked the halls of the institute, or applied to the institute, deserves our protection. If we're revered as the moral arm of Nordania, maybe it's about time they treated us like it. You're one person, yes, but isn't one person the most important thing?"

She considers me for a long time. The room is silent, and for a moment, I think I've lost her. Then she nods.

"I'll go with you," she says. "Under one condition."

"What's that?" I ask.

"I want to live in Nordania after this. Quietly. By myself."

"By yourself?"

"Perhaps someday, my son might come visit me. Or stay with me. I know it's unlikely, but . . . I can't come back here. It's not an option for me."

A sudden, intense wave of anger floods my senses. It makes sense to be angry at the situation, but I think I'm angry at her. It's as if I'm watching my own mother grapple with whether or not she should save me or sell me.

And I think I'm justified in feeling some anger. I know what her son must be feeling. Who gives up their child and leaves them in a situation where they don't feel safe? Or maybe I've got it all wrong. Maybe it was the only option, and a better person would have empathy here? But she's made her choice. She's asking for amnesty, for the option to live apart from her child indefinitely. And I will never sympathize with that.

She tugs on her necklace, and I recognize a silver locket, the same kind so many Nordanian mothers wear with a lock of their baby's hair inside. My mother wore one that had belonged to her own mother. As she rubs her thumb on the silver front, I know she'll never see him again. She'll have to live with that, and that's enough to abate my anger, at least for the moment.

"I understand that. I'll talk to Declan. I'll make him understand why this needs to happen."

She nods in thanks. "There's something else . . . I need

someone to go to the amnesty house. They're expecting me. And . . ."

"And what?" I ask.

"That's where the network is."

"What do you mean, that's where the network is?" Neve asks.

"That's where the next several levels of the network are. If you want your votes, someone will need to go to the amnesty house to make it work. Otherwise, it won't ever work."

I look at Neve. She doesn't look phased.

"Once we leave here, there will be no way we can get back."

"There are other access ports," Elm says. I nod.

"It's getting hot out there," the other man says, darting back in through the door. He's not talking about the weather. There's an odd sound from the street—almost like a knocking or scuffling.

"If we're going to go, it needs to be now," Elm says, his gaze flickering to the door.

"Yes," I say quickly. I can't lose this chance. "Yes, we'll make it happen."

"Thank you," she says.

CHAPTER FOURTEEN

*L*eaving the hideout is a kerfuffle of quick costume changes and activity. Simone puts on a hat and wraps a scarf over her shoulders. I realize the rest of her dress is unbefitting of a woman of her stature, and I'm sure that was intentional. I have no idea how long she's been gone, but it can't have been long.

"Ready?" Blue Coat says. We all nod, and then he motions for us to follow him up the stairs. When we reach the alleyway, he's right. The city is much louder, and people are rushing back and forth. There's an alarm bell ringing, and there are shouts for my name.

"You need to go," Elm says to me. "If they find you with us . . ."

He doesn't need to finish that sentence. They'll pin it on him, and then whatever it is that he's running will be destroyed. There will be no more amnesty rescue organization.

"Stay with them," I say to Neve.

I expect her to argue with me, but instead, there's a sort

of pride that flares in her eyes, and she nods. She coils her arm with Simone's, and they leave the alleyway first, splitting off to the right in the opposite direction of the ship. Elm follows them about ten paces later. Then, it's just me and the stranger with the blue jacket.

"If she's going with you," he says, his voice somehow both soft and strong, "you must be doing something sensational." I don't know about sensational, but I nod, because I have the feeling that anything less than sensational would leave him asking more questions.

He nods to the left, toward the ship.

"Fastest route to the ship is to take the next alleyway across to the right. Just watch your step." Then he splits off to the left, blending into the cacophony of the portside crowd. I wait another ten seconds or so, take a deep breath, and then plunge into the masses.

It's far more frantic than I expected. I don't know what all is going on, but it doesn't take long to realize it's not just the fact that the Nordanians are looking for me. Women are running in the opposite direction, clutching each other, or children as they pass. I spot the tea room ahead to the right and see George, my other guard, flattened on the sidewalk.

Without another thought, I run toward him.

"George!" I yell as I kneel next to him. His eye is already swollen purple, and I lean over him to listen for his breath. I can't hear a thing in this crowd, though I do finally see the slow rise and fall of his breath.

Just then, I feel the jerk of my arm — my bad arm — and I yell out.

"What's this now?" A grimy face comes into view, and it's clear that this man knows exactly who I am, and more likely than not, exactly what I'm worth.

"Let me go!" I spit into his face.

"Why would I do that?"

"Whatever you think you're getting paid, I can double it," I say, assuming Declan would support whatever it is I say. The truth is, I have no idea if he would. The man grins and lifts my arm slightly, making my shoulder tweak in a painful way. It's as if he knows this is the arm that was dislocated when the barn caught on fire back in Beck's family's hometown.

I'm instantly sent back to that moment with how much familiarity there is between this moment and that. I'd run from a dark shed into action to save a little girl then—this time, I ran from a dark basement in order to help Simone. There was chaos both times, the smell of fear on the wind, and now, a gruesome man threatening to hurt me for a payday.

But this time, there's no one to save me.

I swing my free arm back and punch the man in the jaw. It barely makes a dent, but it surprises him just enough that he loses his grip. I pull my arm from his grasp and run. I only make it about three steps before he grabs my skirt and I start to topple forward. He hoists me up, pressed against him, his foul breath hot against my ear. I swing my heel back, aiming for his instep, but he lifts me off the ground and I hit his shin.

"Feisty little bitch, ain't yeh?" he grunts. He drags me back toward the alleyway that the Blue Coat guy told me about, which confuses me. Until I realize he might have his own boat ready to take me somewhere.

"Let me go!" I scream. I reach back and grab at his hair and tug. He swings me around, but I don't let go. I fist his hair and tug harder and harder as he curses. He swings me forward, and I slam against the stone wall. My elbow takes the brunt. I groan at the impact, and he laughs as he tucks my other arm against my body.

"If you cooperate, nobody has to get hurt," he says. But this makes me madder. My shoulder throbs, my head pounds, and I try to think of the things Beck taught me: how to disarm your opponent. But the way he's holding me, he's in control. I just need something. My free arm aches, and there's a sharp pinch in my back that can't be normal, but I push past the pain and reach back, raking my fingernails down his face. He yells in pain, and I throw my head back, colliding with his nose.

He drops me on the ground, and I fall, landing on my knees and chest, slamming my chin against the wet stones. My teeth knock, and a sharp pain throbs through my head. Dazed and throbbing in pain, I push up to my hands and knees and crawl away from him, pushing through the pain in my knees, my arm—he grabs at my skirt with a roar.

"You fucking bitch, why can't you heel?" I hear fabric tear, and he yanks my legs back as I slam against the ground again. The air sucks from my lungs, and I suck in air, the sound pure animal.

A crack and a thud sound behind me, and when I turn, the man is laying on his side, eyes unblinking. Clem rushes toward me from the alleyway behind me.

"Are you all right?" he asks.

"Yes," I say, though as I say it, I can feel the trickle of blood down my chin. He helps me up, and I get to my feet without too much trouble, though I favor my good arm. He presses a cloth to my mouth.

"Can you hold this here?"

I nod.

"I'll spare the lecture until you've stopped bleeding, but I think we're in agreement that this is your fault and I was not inept as a guard?"

I laugh, even as it makes my side ache.

"I'll take the fall, Clem."

He nods, just as a police whistle sounds.

"This better be worth it, girl," he says. He wraps an arm over my shoulders, and we keep going down the alleyway. The entire way to the ship, I can't help but wonder how many more have to die because someone offers a bounty for my head?

CHAPTER FIFTEEN

"*O*uch!" I say as blood continues to drip into my mouth.

"Shoot, sorry," Meredith says, stuffing tissue beneath my nose. The official prognosis is a broken nose, bruised ribs, sprained shoulder, and a chipped tooth. Considering the blow I took to my chin, it's a wonder it's not worse.

"I still don't understand how this was allowed to happen," Alvin practically squeals. His usually dour expression has gone panicked, and his sweaty forehead is working overtime, leaving his thin eyebrows looking like two caterpillars that just got caught in a rainstorm.

"You left us in the tea room," I mutter, and then hiss as Meredith dabs at the underside of my nose a bit too egregiously.

"You're saying this is *my* fault?" he says. "You are not my responsibility, missy. This is *not* on my head."

"Nobody said it was," Declan says, his crisp baritone cutting through the sitting room. He's so still, it's as if he's sucking up all the sound. But there's nothing clam about him. He's practically vibrating with fury.

"Of course, nobody said it was," Neve says, carrying a tray of creams and ointments toward me. I can't smell much, and I'm breathing through my mouth, which makes my injured tooth hurt, but I'm pretty sure she's carrying enough minty camphor to knock out a platoon. "Why would you think it's your fault?" She blinks at him innocently, and he flushes bright red. I suppress a smile, mostly because I think it would hurt and might start up the bleeding again.

"How do you expect me to explain this to the press?" Alvin says, pointing at me. Apparently, I'm now a *this*.

"Explain what?" Declan asks, watching Neve and Meredith's pass off of the bloody tissues with mild interest. "That my fiancée was left in a foreign country without support and injured in a bloody attack?"

"That she looks like she lost a bar brawl!" Alvin snaps, as if he's the one being harassed. All of us turn our heads to him. I can hear Meredith sputter, and Neve looks like she's about to turn the business end of a mascara wand on him. Declan shifts his body so that he blocks me from Alvin's view completely. He moves so slowly, so deliberately, a shiver rushes down my spine.

"I would choose your next words very carefully, Alvin," Declan says. I can't see Alvin's face, but I know he's sputtering and stressing over this shift in dynamics.

"I—I mean, sir—a woman in her position should not be bleeding from her face. This will affect her appearance. What am I to say when people ask—"

"You will tell them that it is my fault."

"Sir?" Alvin sputters. Meredith presses a cold pack to my chin.

"You will tell them that as her fiancé, it is my duty to ensure Arden is safe while on foreign soil. I was *indisposed*, if you will, and failed to perform this task. As such, it is my fault, and I will bear the full weight of the penalty."

"But, sir," Alvin sputters, and Neve clucks her tongue.

"Sucker," she mumbles. I realize that if there's a fall man for this, it'll likely be Alvin.

"Of course," Declan says, "we could just not address it. But that is your call. You've taken on the role of my press secretary, after all. I'll leave you to it." Then he turns his back on Alvin. I can't even imagine what Alvin looks like as he backtracks out of my room.

"I think the bleeding has stopped," Meredith says. She motions for me to lower the cold compress, and when nothing drips into my mouth, I nod. Neve gently massages aloe and camphor into the skin around my nose, and if the goal was to make my breathing easier, mission accomplished.

"Ladies, may I have a minute alone with my fiancée?"

The girls give me a look, and when I nod, they take their supplies with them and leave. Declan stays where he is, arms crossed over his chest, looking down at me.

"Are you okay?" he asks. I nod.

"Sore, but okay."

"Good. Because I need you to hear what I'm about to say, and I don't want your injuries to cloud your ability to understand."

"Wow," I say, "that sounded positively condescending."

"Interpret it how you will," he says. But he doesn't make himself any less formal. "I understand you snuck away from your guards and brought this on yourself? Brought this on George?"

"Oh!" I say, gasping, and then I cringe, because that quick inhalation was far too painful. "Is George okay?"

"Yes," he says. "He's concussed, but otherwise fine." I

breathe out a deep sigh of relief. He doesn't look relieved, though. He looks livid. "As my wife, however, you can't do things like this. It's not appropriate, it's not safe, and I need—" His voice catches. "I need to know that you are always safe."

"Declan," I let out a long, exhausted sigh. "I'm never safe."

He shakes his head.

"If you slip your guards, of course you're not."

"Even with those guards, do you realize there's a bounty on my head?"

"Of course I do." I flinch, even as he shakes his head again. "There's a bounty on my head too. We're political leaders. There will always be a bounty on our heads."

"You're not understanding me. There's a bounty on my head, and the man who tried to attack me—he was Nordanian."

Declan frowns. "There are always bad apples."

"That man was Nordanian. The men on the skiff boat, you heard them. They were Nordanian." I sigh. "And it's not just me. There are bounties on all the graduates—all the Embers." I tell him what I learned from Elm and Simone. Simone, who is now resting in her own stateroom down the hall. When I finish telling him all the details, he shakes his head.

"It doesn't make sense."

"Of course it makes sense," I say.

"No, it doesn't. This can't be a Nordanian cause. Why would Nordanians try to kill the moral arm of our country?"

"Why do you think? As long as the institute runs the way it does, there will be an easy avenue to get deals done. Favorable trade terms and whatnot."

"No," Declan says, pacing as he shakes his head, insistent. "This doesn't make sense."

"People would pay a lot of money to make sure they don't lose their position, their status, their money, whatever. I mean, look at Fiona."

He stops, and his gaze sharpens, as if my feisty, red-headed colleague at the institute was suddenly standing in the room with us.

"What do you mean, 'look at Fiona'?"

"You don't think it was a coincidence that you were partnered up with her for so many of those formal dinners?"

"It just so happened that her family was visiting from Espancia. And then her parents visited."

"Declan, don't you think he already—"

He looks like he's about to argue with me, but then his face falls. His cheeks lose their flush, and it's as if a puzzle that was dormant in the back of his mind just snapped together. Still, he shakes his head.

"I can't believe . . ."

"You've never had to," I say. He paces again, and then slows and sinks down on the settee next to me. He slouches back against the back, and it's the worst, most defeated posture I've ever seen on him.

"I need to talk to my father."

"About what?" I ask, cautious.

"About this. He should know."

"Declan, if he doesn't already know—"

"You really think he knows about this and wouldn't tell me? Wouldn't caution me? This affects me too, you know."

I sigh, carefully. But the creases between his brows deepen, as if he's just remembered something.

"You can't tell him this, Declan. We don't know what he knows, or what he might tell to an advisor, or your mother, or—"

"What does my mother have to do with this?"

"Declan, really?" I stare at him. He lets out a heavy sigh and rubs his hand over his face, as if only now remembering what his mother was willing to pay to keep me out of the picture.

"I was only just talking to my father this morning. He is upset that we're not back. More girls have left."

"What?" I sit up straighter. If more girls have left, it means fewer will graduate.

"They've read the 'writing on the wall,' so to speak. They don't see any reason to stay if I'm not there."

"I thought they weren't supposed to be in it for a husband," I say.

"Says my fiancée," he says with a wry smirk. Touché. "He's insisting we elope sooner than later. There's been more bad press, and they think it would help."

"How would it help?" I ask, standing, before I realize my balance is off because of my bad arm. I tip toward him, and he catches me around the waist. He rights me, his hand lingering on my hip.

"Bring some hope to a country that is starting to see this institute as a joke."

"The institute is a joke," I say.

"Excuse me?" He steps back.

"It is, you can't deny it." I reach the wall and look out the window at the slowly disappearing shoreline. "We've talked about this thirty different ways. The girls don't get jobs, they get husbands. And the only ones who are seen as successful are the ones who marry into your family."

"That's not strictly true," he says.

"They're supposed to make up a quarter of the government, but nobody returns to carry out that role."

"Okay, okay," he says, rising and crossing the room to the window. "Let's not argue. Please." I nod. He continues,

"Fine, say you're right. What good is any of this if I can't bring you home in one piece?"

"I told you I'm sorry."

"I know you did, but I don't believe you."

I look at him. Really look at him. And it's as if he's starting to see me. Really see me — not the girl who needed his help at the estate, or the one who needed him to rescue her from a ship or an abusive boy. He sees me standing on my own feet, wanting to move headfirst into this challenge and make a difference.

"I'm not sorry I brought Simone here."

"I understand that."

"I am sorry about George. I will take full responsibility for that."

"No, you won't," he says, then pinches the bridge of his nose. "I wouldn't let you do that."

"That's not fair."

"Probably not," he says with a chuckle, "but if you took blame, it would be a speedy vote of no confidence."

We're quiet for a moment. I sense his hand rather than feel it as it wraps around my waist. It slips up my back and settles on my good shoulder. He doesn't pull me into him, acutely aware of my bad shoulder.

"Clem said you fought back." I nod. I half expect him to tell me I shouldn't have to fight, or that I shouldn't be fighting, that it's not ladylike. "Beck taught you to fight, didn't he?"

My stomach tightens. I don't want to talk about Beck. Especially not with Declan. I don't even want to think about the days when he taught me to fight — when he taught me how to stand up for myself and how to be brave enough to do that. To know I could if I had to.

But he's waiting for an answer. So I nod. He lets out a heavy sigh.

"I think he should start teaching you again."

"What?" I whip to face him, and it's a little too fast. My nose twinges and tears spring to my eyes. Declan mistakes them for something else and gently brushes his thumb across my cheeks.

"I hate the asshole, and if you don't want to see him again, we can forget I said anything. We could find you a different teacher."

I nod. Then I consider what he's suggesting. If he had to spend time with me, teaching me to defend myself, it might put him in a position to answer my questions. To admit all the things about what was real and what wasn't. Because I can't for the life of me figure that out. So much of it felt real. But then, ever since I found out that he'd been doing all of that to get a paycheck from Siobhan, it all made sense. The way he taught me to protect myself, to fight back, to run away . . .

But he'd been leading me on for money. He took me to his bed for coin. The hard truth is that the days when I was sparring with Beck were days when I felt more like myself than any other time. And returning to fighting form, as appealing as it is, makes me nervous. I fell for Beck once. What happens if I can't keep my heart shut to him again?

But also, I have questions. I don't understand why Beck did what he did. Why he went through all the trouble just for money. I met his family, for crying out loud. I know he wants them taken care of, but they take care of each other. They took care of me. And I let them . . . and liked it.

And the tattoo. I press my fingertips to my hip. When did he decide to work for Siobhan? Was it before or after he held my hand while a stranger covered the brand on my hip with mountains from the myth he told me? Was it before he ever met me? And which answer hurts less?

Maybe it would feel good to get answers. Or it might feel even better to punch Beck in the face.

I nod. He nods. Neither of us says anything else. But it feels like we're toeing into dangerous territory and neither of us wants to admit it.

CHAPTER SIXTEEN

When I wake up in the morning, it's quiet. Too quiet. The seas are calm, but more than that, Neve and Meredith aren't lurking around, prodding me to get started on my morning skincare routine.

I fix myself up in the way I'm most comfortable: hair pulled back in a ponytail, face fresh and clean—and wearing pants. I don't know what those girls have against pants, but I have to actually dig through this stupid wardrobe for a pair of lined wool pants. I tie on my boots and grab a coat before I make my way toward the galley.

But once I'm in the galley, it's very quiet there too. I help myself to a cup of coffee and a slice of orange tea bread. I should enjoy the peace and quiet of a solo breakfast. And yet . . . it's as if something is happening and no one has bothered to tell me. And the only reason that could happen is if someone is trying to keep me from knowing.

Except that doesn't seem right either—because, if they really wanted to keep me from knowing something, surely

Neve and Meredith would be sent to distract me, right? Which means I should go to the bridge and get to the bottom of whatever has happened.

Which is exactly where I find everyone I could possibly be looking for.

Simone is sitting in the captain's chair, surrounded by the others. Even Beck is there, setting off an obnoxious pang in my chest. I wonder when that will go away. He's focused on Simone, who is talking about eastern Osterstan.

"Where exactly is it?" the captain asks.

"It's in the border town of Ouracéu. There's a thriving community there, even beyond the graduates," Simone says. Her Nordanian accent has been affected by her time in Swendenland, adding a girlish lilt to it.

"And who are these people that were going to take you there?" Declan says, pinching the bridge of his nose. I can see how troubled he is by this. And I understand. He's seen the world one way his whole life, seeing his position as a birthright ordained from God. And now, it turns out there's a lot more going on in his world that he didn't know about.

"It's an amnesty group," Simone says. I notice she doesn't name Elm. Neve looks at me at that moment, as if she could sense I'd entered, and the expression on her face brokers no argument. I will not reveal his name either.

"How has this been allowed to happen?" the first mate says. The captain waves his hand.

"That's not for us to have an opinion on," the captain says. "It's up to you, sir," he says, turning to Declan.

"What's up to Declan?" I ask. I feel everyone's gaze, followed by their pity. But from the corner of my eye, I sense something much sharper, more violent.

"We didn't mean to wake you, love," he says, approaching and taking my hands in his. He presses my knuckles to his lips, and I swear I see Neve stiffen from the corner of my eyes.

"You didn't. Actually," I say with a small, slightly painful smile, "the quiet startled me. There was no one hounding me about Swendish conjugations or trying to exfoliate me."

Neve huffs, and Declan frowns.

"Should I know what that is?"

I shake my head.

"How are you, Simone?" I ask, feeling anxious under the sudden, intense scrutiny. I'm sure my face can't look great with the beating I took yesterday.

"I'm much better," she says, and the relief in her voice is evident. "Declan and your captain asked about my next move. They don't feel right not notifying my husband."

"You can't do that," I say, a little too sharply. I wince at the pain in my nose, but don't let it stop me. "She can't go back —"

"I agree," Declan says. "It wasn't actually my idea to notify her husband."

"It would only be proper," Alvin interjects. "Under international law, not notifying the next of kin could be viewed as an act of aggression." It all makes sense now. Alvin, the prim and proper hand of the old ways, has found a way to stick his nose where it doesn't belong.

"Would you send a lost child back into a burning building because it would only be proper to send them home?" I snap.

Alvin shakes his head, indulgently. "Of course not. You're not seeing the big picture."

"Alvin, I think we all see the big picture," Declan says, shaking his head. "Simone, what is it you'd like to do?"

"I'd like to go to Nordania," she says, glancing at me, "as we discussed."

"As you discussed?" Declan says. He frowns at me.

"We did discuss that," I say. "I just hadn't had a chance to relay that discussion to you yet."

"Aw, is this a lovers' spat?" Beck drawls.

"Well, I'm all ears." Declan's jaw ticks with impatience or irritation.

"I said that I would talk to you and make sure that she could safely return to Nordania, seeing as she was in an unsafe situation thanks to our institute and government."

"Thanks to our institute and government?" Alvin sputters, but Declan raises his hand.

"Is that all? Do you wish to send for your son as well?"

She hesitates. I can see the emotion fill her features.

"They will never allow that," she says, and for the first time, I see her tough demeanor falter. "But I do wish to send word to the amnesty house in east Osterstan."

"We were just talking about that," the captain says to me. "It's in Ouracéu, at least a day by train. And the best access point is Parth, which we would be fools to return to."

"That's not the only access point," Beck says. He's leaning against the instrument panel, chewing on an orange peel, ankles crossed with an almost ladylike precision.

"Where else, then?" Declan says crisply.

"We could go further east to the border town of Queensbridge."

The captain and first mate both start laughing, and Alvin sputters.

"I take it people have opinions on Queensbridge?" Declan says.

"It's a known haven for piracy," Alvin says.

"It's not the easiest bay to navigate. We might encounter some unsavory characters," the captain says.

"As it so happens, I have a unique expertise with

unsavory characters," Beck says, crossing his arms over his chest. "I'd be happy to help with the portside negotiations."

"Oh, I bet he would," Alvin mutters.

"But that's not the only problem," the captain says. "Once on land, it's a frontier town. There could be gangs of bandits and bounty hunters on the ground. There's no guarantee that it would be a safe passage to Ouracéu."

"But there is access to the train that goes there?" I ask.

The captain stares at me for a long moment, and then nods.

"You couldn't go," I say to Simone. "It would be too risky."

With a sigh, she nods. It's clear who needs to take this journey. I roll back my shoulders and meet Neve's gaze.

"So then, who —" Declan starts, and then his brows narrow as he looks between the two of us. "No. Absolutely not."

"It makes the most sense."

"You can not make this trek."

"Why not? Chances are, no one would recognize me. Put a wig on me, and they never would. Especially with the way I look right now — ask Alvin!"

Alvin's face turns red, and it's hard not to laugh. I'm pretty sure Neve turns away to mask hers.

"And who would accompany you?" he asks.

"Who says anyone needs to come with me?"

He points at my nose. "I don't think I need to answer that."

I frown and from the corner of my eye, Beck stands.

"I could take her," he says.

"Absolutely not," Declan says.

"Actually, that's not a bad idea," Neve says, to my surprise. "He's a scoundrel and knows how to navigate among the lowlifes of the world."

"Thank you," Beck says, eyes gone glassy.

"No," Declan says. He's standing taller, as if he can somehow grow taller than Beck by puffing up his chest.

"In all the time she was with me on my ship she never looked like that," he says. His tone is light, but his body is tense.

"We don't need Beck for that," Declan says.

"You can't send me with bodyguards," I say.

"Of course not," he says. Tension fills the room as the two men seem locked in some unspoken argument. I'm confused about what isn't being said, confused about why Beck thinks anyone would allow this, confused at why Declan is so angry. "I'll go with you."

"Sir!" Alvin says at the same time that Beck snort laughs and Clem steps forward and says:

"You can't be serious."

"Of course, I'm serious," he says.

Beck sputters. "That's like sending a Yorkie to a dog fight."

"I know how to defend myself. And we can take a day or two to let Arden heal—and for Beck to brush up on fighting with her." The last part, he barely chokes out.

"I'm gonna do what now?" Beck says.

"You taught her to defend herself once before?" Declan says. Beck puts his hands on his hips, as if he's going to come back with a real zinger. His mouth twists, he takes a deep breath, and then, as if winding up to launch a cannonball, he says:

"Uh, yeah."

Declan smiles. "Then you can do it again." He steps closer, and I've never realized how tall Declan is. In my head, Beck always seemed taller, but right now, maybe Beck is slouching or Declan is wearing different shoes. He has a commanding presence that startles me, though not in a bad way. "We discussed it yesterday, and despite the questionable actions you've taken over the past months, I believe you taught her self-defense with good intentions." Beck nods. "I would like you to continue teaching her."

I feel my cheeks flush hot. I didn't think Declan would actually ask Beck to teach me to throw a punch. I know he suggested it, but now that it's actually out there like this, it feels somehow humiliating. Even Neve won't meet my gaze.

"Is that what Arden wants?" Beck asks. His voice wobbles at the end. I don't think anyone else hears it. There's a question in his gaze. Despite his bored posture, his careless tone, and his obvious disinterest in this entire half-baked plan, he wants to know what I want.

Which is why I nod.

Because despite everything he's done to me, when he looks at me like that, I say yes.

And I hate myself a little bit.

"Then it's settled?" Declan says. He still looks bigger than Beck, though perhaps a bit deflated.

"Two days at sea, and then we port at Queensbridge," the captain says. Declan nods, decisively, and then presses a kiss to my cheek and leaves. Alvin stammers after him. Neve's expression is stony, and Meredith looks flustered.

Beck is frowning, staring at me. Then he turns toward the door.

"I assume you'll call for me when you're ready," Beck says over his shoulder with a sharpness I've become more accustomed to.

"Yes," I say again, feeling a wash of anger and humiliation and stupid longing.

"Find some real pants," he says. Then he's gone.

Oh, it's all anger now. All anger.

"Those look like real pants to me," Meredith says with a shrug. Neve just stares at me, as if she couldn't be bothered with anything as trivial as pants.

I shake my head at her and say, "I'll show him real pants."

CHAPTER SEVENTEEN

The sun comes and goes faster than I'm ready for it, and still, I haven't sent for Beck. I don't want to "send for him." I don't want to seem like I need him. Or want him. For anything. I used to just go find him when I needed him, and now, there are so many layers to the space between us that I don't know how to start without turning everything cockeyed.

Which is why, when Neve walks in and hisses, "Stop being a wimp about this," I realize she's right. It also helps that she sent for him so I wouldn't have to.

He's waiting for me on the front deck of the ship, dressed in loose pants and a sweater. It doesn't seem like nearly enough clothing given the cold wind blowing in, but I'm sure we'll both be sweating in no time.

"Your highness," he says with a little bow. "What should I call you? A pirate without a boat?" He smirks, his crooked nose twitching. I should knee him in that nose. It hasn't been broken in nearly long enough. He rises and scratches the side of his nose.

"You gonna be okay to do this?" he asks.

I shrug. "I've had worse."

He doesn't balk, but he doesn't look away either. "Fair enough. Get in defensive stance."

He takes me through a quick refresh of what we've worked on before, focusing on my feet. They're slower and clumsier on the ship, and it takes longer than I would like to find my footing. But then I do, and we get into a good rhythm of him coming at me and me dodging him.

"How's your shoulder?" he asks, nodding at my bad arm.

"It's been better," I say, sidestepping when he comes at me.

"Can you swing it?"

"I don't know."

Just then, he grabs the collar of my sweater and yanks. I stumble toward him, shutting my eyes. He stops me just before I can slam into his chest, but it's close enough that I'm enveloped in his familiar scent of orange and salt. It hits me harder than I expect it to, and my body doesn't know how to react. It tenses up, as if waiting for a brutal blow that's never going to come.

"What the hell was that?" he asks, not letting go of my collar. I look up at him and try to push him off, but he doesn't let go.

"You tell me," I say. He's close. Too close. I can see the gold flecks in his green eyes, the bump along the ridge of his nose from where it was most recently broken. "Let go," I say, trying to sound cold and detached.

"Make me," he says.

I swing my good arm at his head, and he dodges it. I push him off with both arms, though it's obvious just how weak my bad arm is right now. A twinge of pain shoots up the bad arm, though it's nothing compared to my nose as I suck in air faster than I should. My ribs hurt, and my chest feels like there's a weight on it.

"Breathe, Capo," he says. I blink at him, stunned. As if he's only just realized what he said, he blinks and releases me. I step away and take a deep breath of the north wind. When I turn back, he's watching me warily, hands on his hips.

"How the hell did that happen?" he asks, motioning at my face and arm.

"I wasn't paying attention to my surroundings. Someone grabbed me from behind. He was big." I shrug, not sure how else to explain it. Beck's expression is stony, and he shakes his head violently.

"Not good enough."

I'm not sure what he means, but it's clear he thinks I've failed. Obviously. I have a broken nose and a sprained elbow on top of the recovering shoulder situation.

"Come 'ere," he says, motioning for me to come close. I hesitate. "Come on. I can't do any worse than you've already had done."

His words hit me square in the chest, laying me bare and burning as if my trauma is an open wound in this salty air. As my eyes sting and my breath catches, I know this is wrong. I shouldn't feel badly for feeling vulnerable. He knows my secrets. I trusted him. I shouldn't have, but that's *his* fault. I should be strong enough to move on, and if anything, he's the one who should be ashamed. Anyone else in my position would feel angry. But he's seen me at my worst, and the way he says it, I don't know how else I'm supposed to feel.

He stays quiet. He doesn't say anything, just watches me with an unreadable expression on his face. His mother's voice fills my head, repeating a gentle refrain of "*Beck might never say.*" Right now, he's not saying anything, just looking at me like he can see through me. And it hurts. It's not fair that he can do that. This isn't the Beck she was talking about, though, when she made me think that he might feel something stronger, something sweeter. That Beck is gone.

But I'm still here. I let out a slow breath and approach him. Slowly, warily. He lets out a slow, sad breath.

He yanks my collar again. I flinch and stumble, shutting my eyes.

"What are you doing that for?" he asks.

"What am I supposed to do? You just grabbed my shirt."

"Don't shut your eyes. That's admitting defeat from the start." He lets go and backs up. "Reset."

I step back and try to hold my stance like we practiced. He reaches for my shirt, and I dodge. He nods, impressed. Then he lunges to my right, and I dodge again, but don't see his left hand coming. It grabs the bottom of my sweater and tugs me around so that he's trapped me against his body, my back to his chest.

He's trapped me tight, and his scent seeps into my pores, blinding me to everything I should be paying attention to. All I can smell is his sweat and orange peels. All I feel is his ropy forearms, calloused fingers on my arms. I can't see anything—I don't know when I shut my eyes . . .

"Arden," he says.

Fuck it all. I push back, and he lets me go. I don't turn around. I thought the worst had happened, but this here? Learning to defend myself in close proximity to someone whose bed I've shared? Who used me and broke me so completely? This is a terrible idea.

"I'm done," I say.

"No, you're not."

"I said I'm done," I snap.

"You're not done yet," he says. And his voice sounds

rickety. I don't look at him—I can't. It's too hard. "Turn around and face me." I've been dealing with him ever since we got on this Godforsaken ship, but now that it's just the two of us, doing the thing we used to do, touching each other, trusting each other . . . I feel like such an idiot for thinking I could do this.

"Arden." His voice is hard and low. As if he's *trying* to be cold.

I take a deep breath, and even though I know this is a terrible idea, I do. He looks exhausted. At least as exhausted as I feel. But still, he raises his hand and motions for me to approach him. I do. He grabs my shirt again but doesn't pull. Gently, he tugs me closer, closer, close enough to feel his warmth. Then he takes my good hand in his.

"My pinky is vulnerable," he says, his voice softer, less barking orders and more kindly instructor. I look down at his hand, and then back up at his face. Then he places my hand on top of his attacking hand.

"Grab it here," he says, curling my fingers around his. "Make sure you get the pinky."

I do as he says, tucking my fingers beneath his pinky finger. His hands are thick with callouses, but warm, just like I remember.

"Good," he says. "Now pull."

I yank on his hand, and it forces him to turn to the side.

"Now, push me away. Against my shoulder," he says. I do. I push him hard. Really hard. He isn't expecting it. He stumbles and catches himself against the railing.

He laughs. It's that raspy, barking thing I remember.

"Good. Really good. One more time."

I nod. He grabs my shirt, and I grab his hand, tug on it, and then push him by the shoulder.

"Is that all you've got?" I ask.

"Oh, don't worry, costermonger, I've got more where that came from."

He turns around and tries to go for my waist, but I dodge him and lift my knee just as he slips past me. It lands right in his stomach—not precisely where I was aiming, but it'll do. He stutter steps, stumbling forward, bent over in half. I laugh.

"You okay over there, sweetheart?" I say.

"*Sweetheart*?" he says, letting out a wheezing laugh. "Is that the best you've got?" But he stays bent over, and I wonder if my aim actually hit a little lower. I approach him.

"Are you ok—"

He spins and grabs my shirt. I reach for his hand to break the hold and don't even see his fist coming. It lands against my ear and rings through my head. My head jerks, snapping my neck, and he tugs harder on my collar.

"Come on, Capo, fight back," he whispers into my ear. Stars float in my vision, the world spins off its axis, and it takes me far too long to get my bearings. Then I feel the vomit come up. It shoots out and down my leg, landing on the deck with a splat. But still, he's holding on.

Except, he's not holding my collar. His arm is braced against my collarbone and a firm hand is pressed to my back.

"Shit," he says.

"What in god's name do you think you're doing?" Declan's voice comes from behind us. I'm still too wobbly to respond.

"The Tango," Beck says. "Obviously, she's out of practice."

"It looks like you're beating her up."

"She has to learn how to defend what's coming," Beck barks back. He hasn't let go of me. He's still holding on to me, and it's the sharp scent of citrus that finally snaps me out of it.

"I'm okay," I say, though my voice is wobbly.

"Arden," Declan says, much closer. His hands are on my shoulders, and then I'm pressed back against him. The cold breeze is a shock, and I shiver against him. "This was a bad idea, my love. I'm sorry I put you through this —"

"Tomorrow?" I say, looking up at Beck, who is no longer fuzzy. He looks at me, his green eyes round and contrite.

"Arden, this isn't what I meant when I said you should learn." Declan brushes hair off my sweaty forehead. "We can find other ways —"

"Same time tomorrow?" I ask again, forcing resolution into my voice. Beck nods.

"Don't throw up next time," he says. Then he walks away.

"You don't have anything to prove," Declan says, gently turning me to face him. I can feel the vomit seeping into my pants, chilled against my calf. Acid taste still coats my tongue. The bruise to my ear from his punch could've been much worse. He pulled that punch, otherwise I would be unconscious. Next time, I'll dodge so he can't do that. Next time, I'll get him back.

"I'm good," I say, and I can't help the smile that cuts into the corners of my cheeks. And for the first time in a long time, I mean it.

CHAPTER EIGHTEEN

The next session with Beck is closely monitored by Clem and George, who is feeling much better. In fact, well enough that he stands in for Beck a few times as my punching bag. Not that I punch that hard. I definitely hit Beck harder than I do the others. But it's also easier to stay on task with them as buffers. I'm not mad at them.

I think it makes Declan more comfortable too, not that we talk about it. Once the decision was made that I'm going to go to eastern Osterstan, it turned into negotiations over who would go with me. Though Declan originally insisted, things are different in the light of day, when everyone who cares about national security can see what a dangerous idea this is. Beck is the new front-runner, but nobody other than Beck thinks this is a good idea. The only reason he's the front-runner is that nobody else has volunteered—or seems worthy of the task.

But after two days at sea, the ship drops anchor about twenty miles north of the Bay of Kasqey. A Nordanian fleet in the bay, much less docked at Queensbridge, will draw too many eyes. So a small skiff will take me and my yet-to-be-determined partner through the bay to Queensbridge.

Neve has done her best to hide my features, emphasizing the bruising around my nose and temple. I look positively malnourished by the time she's done with me. Meanwhile, Simone has braided my hair in a similar style to hers, which she says is common among the middle class in Swendenland. The braids are so tight they make my scalp hurt. I already have a headache by the time we're finished. I don't look like myself at all, especially not in these wide-legged trousers, sweater, and oilcloth coat.

Even knowing that I look different doesn't prepare me for Beck waiting in the skiff. Or Declan sitting next to him.

"What's going on here?"

"Not happy to see me, princess?" Beck says.

"You can't be serious?" I say to Declan.

"I try not to, but right now, I'm just trying not to laugh," Beck says.

But then I look at Declan. Really look at him. His hair isn't golden anymore. It's been colored dark. Almost as dark as Beck's. And he hasn't shaved. His facial hair is darker than I would expect, and incredibly patchy, but not as dark as his hair. He looks . . . terrible. I press my lips together.

"I would appreciate quiet from the peanut gallery," Declan says.

"Touché, boy wonder," Beck says, scratching at his own beard.

"I couldn't let you have all the fun," Declan says, helping me sit across from him.

"Hold on to your hats," Beck says, and then starts the engine on the skiff, steering us toward the mouth of the bay. The waves aren't noticeable on the massive ship, but now, on this little boat, they're a beast to cross. I'm grateful for the oilcloth to wick off the water that splashes at my back.

Declan takes the brunt of it, and the closer we get to the bay, the greener he looks.

"If you need to heave, do it over the side," Beck says.

"I'm fine," Declan says.

"What's going on?" I ask.

"I'm going with you," he says, gripping the sides of the boat as yet another three-footer crashes over the prow.

"Are you sure that's a good idea? I thought—"

"What other option was there? You go by yourself? Or go with *him*?"

"I have feelings, you know," Beck says, steering us into the side of a wave so we don't take the full brunt. It knocks us side to side, and Declan looks like he might heave.

"Knock it off, crustmudgeon," I yell behind me. I swear I hear him laugh.

"You're getting better at that," he says. Fortunately, the waves start to abate the closer we get to the bay. Beck wasn't kidding—this place is like shifty sailor central. The bay is crowded with ships of all sizes bearing a litany of flags and unscrupulous-looking characters, and they're all watching us.

"Don't stare," Beck says. "Act like you belong here."

"But I don't belong here," Declan says.

"That's why you have to act like it. Come on, is this day one at your institute?"

"Leave him alone," I snap.

"It's fine, Arden—"

"They can read lips, wonder kid," Beck says.

"You're what? One year older than me?" Declan hisses.

"Is that all?" Beck asks, mock wonder in his expression.

"Really?" I ask. It's the wrong thing to say, but Declan doesn't seem to notice. Beck does seem so much older than Declan. Maybe I knew this, but for some reason, in this moment, with Beck steering us through pirate territory with the confidence he has, and Declan about to throw up with his bad dye job and terrible beard situation, it feels like I'm in a boat with someone play-acting at the part and another man who is a professional. I feel immediately guilty at the thought. But then we pull into the dock, and it feels so much more real.

A man at the dock shouts something at us in Swendish. To my surprise, Beck responds in fluid Swendish without missing a beat. His accent could rival Neve's in authenticity. Declan looks amused, if not frustrated. I wonder how much of it Declan understands.

"Up," Beck says after a particularly long back and forth.

"Up?" I ask.

"Up and out." Beck goes first, and then reaches down to help me. He pulls me up using my good arm, and then catches me with a firm hand to my back. Declan is left to scramble up on his own. At first, I think to help him, but as I watch how awkward Declan is getting out of the boat, I realize there is no way in hell anyone would ever look at this person and think he's the heir apparent to Nordania.

"Now what?" I ask, once Declan is on his feet, a small bag slung over his shoulder.

"We get you to the station."

"Excuse me," Declan says, offering me his arm. But Beck slings an arm over my shoulders and gives Declan a glare.

"What the hell do you think you're doing? Do you think someone who looks like you, walking through this port, would ever offer his arm to a woman like her?"

Declan's cheeks burn red.

"Look around, man," Beck says, waving his arm with the wobbly piratical effect I got used to seeing. "You gotta blend."

And just like that, Beck leans on me a little bit more, wobbling just enough to look drunk. Declan grunts, but follows the two of us. For as much of a pain in the ass as Beck is, I realize he's right. As we walk along the docks and toward the dusty promenade, nobody pays us any mind.

The town is unlike any town I've been to yet. There's a feeling of wildness that's both exciting and intimidating. Dusty clapboard buildings and rustic stands line a dirt and stone road. There aren't vehicles or even horses. I don't get the sense there's much reason for people to have them here. At the far end of the street, there's a rudimentary shelter with a sign for trains. Next to it, train tracks end about thirty feet before the ground gives way to boulders and then the sea.

The only standing buildings appear to be pubs of various repute. Two of them have women wearing far less clothing than seems ideal, given the brisk winter wind. I shudder as we pass one, and Beck leans into me a bit more and lets his head flop. I imagine he looks terribly drunk to passersby, but all he's done is shared a bit more of his warmth.

I don't understand this version of Beck. To be honest, I don't understand any version of Beck anymore. I thought I did once, but it was all a lie. And yet now, he's helping me. I don't understand why he's helping me. Unless maybe sending me to eastern Osterstan is another component of getting paid. Could this still be part of his job? For Siobhan? Sending me to Easternern Osterstan would certainly be an effective way to keep me out of the picture.

"Is there anything else I should know about where I'm going?" I ask softly.

"It's a shit hole," he mumbles into my shoulder. The warmth of his orange-scented breath and vibration of his voice against my shoulder sends another shiver down my spine.

"Am I going to die there?" I ask.

He stills. I've caught him off guard. Then he coughs and hocks up something onto the ground that I don't look for.

"Why would you ask that?"

"Because it would make Declan's mom very happy."

He's quiet for a long minute. We pass what looks like a produce stand, but all I see is wilted cabbage. The shopkeeper catches my eye and doesn't look away. I break the gaze and pretend to struggle under Beck's weight. But a feeling of unease spreads over me.

"I don't want you dead, Arden," he says.

"You just want to get paid."

"Fudging butter munch," he mumbles, or at least, I think that's what he says. "I already got paid."

"But you failed," I say.

"So what?"

"Wouldn't you get paid more if you — "

"And what would I do with it? I'm sort of in a rock and a soggy place now."

"You could run."

He huffs. And then laughs.

"When have you ever known me to run?" Of course, we did run once. He took me away from the institute for my safety. Or so he said.

He pretends to stumble, but it has the effect of stopping us in place. I look at him, and he's so close. Close enough I can see those gold flecks in his eyes, the ones that once mesmerized me.

"You should run," I say. I don't know why I say it. I shouldn't want to protect him. But there's a piece of me that still connects with a piece of him that maybe never existed but felt like it was once mine. Maybe that's enough of a reason to not want to see Alvin turn him in. Or maybe I want to prove something. He could run, but if he doesn't, what does that prove?

"You're here. You're off the ship. They let you take us here. There's nothing that says you couldn't."

"There's nowhere to go," he says.

But we both know it's a lie. He could get on this train with us. He's industrious. He could figure out a way to do it. As if he reads my mind, he shakes his head. "There's nothing but bandits and thieves in the steppe for fifty miles in every direction. And even if I did get on that train and go to Easternern Osterstan, what kind of life is that? Living in a war zone? Far from the water? It's no better than being trapped in a cell two floors beneath you."

My stomach tightens. I don't know this version of Beck. But there's something in his words, his tone, the protective arc of his arm over my shoulders, that reminds me of who he used to be to me. It would be all too easy in this subterfuge to fall into old habits. He's made a buck off me and my heart. Even if he says things occasionally that remind me of the version I fell for . . . that wasn't real. So why does this feel so real?

"What's going on here?" Declan interrupts. As if in answer, Beck coughs up something that lands on Declan's shoe. Declan's face goes green again, and he looks like he might gag. I elbow Beck in the kidney and he jerks slightly, but I swear I see him smirk.

"Nothing," I say, then pretend to hike him up on my shoulder. "I think we're almost there."

"Almost where?" Just behind Declan, the man from the produce stand is right there. And he's not alone. He has a friend who looks weaselly and like he recognizes at least one of us. Beck tenses, but doesn't change position from my shoulders.

"We're off to catch the train," I say before Declan can say anything else.

"The train?" Weasel says. "Yeah, I can help with that."

"No, thank you," Declan says, not masking his high brow accent in the slightest. Beck groans.

"Do I know you?" Weasel says to Declan.

Beck snorts, and I laugh. "Not unless you know my brother," I say. Beck snorts again.

"What's so funny?" Weasel asks.

"Man, you gave yourself away," Beck says.

"Wot that s'posed to mean?"

"My brother over here just got out. He's been away for six years."

Weasel flushes almost as red as Declan and steps back.

"You're lying."

"Is he?" I ask with a snort laugh. Declan opens his mouth to respond, but I swing my fist into his stomach and he bends over, coughing. "You been to Fillmire? Or Sanktown? This asshole's been to both."

Declan grumbles, and the Weasel seems to think twice.

"Yeah, whatever. Two in Fillmire. But it was years ago."

I stiffen. Because Fillmire is where the most dangerous prisoners in Swendenland are sent.

"Then we're practically friends," Declan spits out. He sounds less proper, but it's mostly because he's trying to catch his breath from when I punched him.

"Unless you're gonna tell us that you have train tickets for us, I suggest you leave us to it," Beck says.

"Yeah, whatever," Weasel says again. He and his friend step out of our way, and I don't hesitate to start walking. Beck drags a little bit more, as if for emphasis that he's not a threat—maybe so that he can surprise them if they don't let up. But Declan doesn't move.

"Come on, man," I call back to him. It snaps him out of

it, and for a moment, he walks just like he normally does. Upright and proper. A few passersby stare at him as Weasel and his buddy let us go. But I don't trust that we're through the worst of it yet.

As we approach the train station, it's apparent that the train isn't on time. For one, there are at least a hundred people standing around the station podium with bags, boxes, and crates. I'm shocked by just how many of them seem to be full of oranges. For another, the train isn't physically there. Beck grunts toward the till, and he leans on me a little bit more.

"Over actor," I grunt.

"Weakling," he grunts back. I elbow him in the side again but this time, he swerves it, putting more weight on my shoulders. I'm ready to kick him in a very tender spot.

The ticket salesman sits inside the booth, looking like he can't be bothered. His head is tilted down, showing me the shiny crown of his head. The fuzzy black hair around it looks like the corona of the sun. He's holding a book in his lap, and I watch him lick his finger, turn the page at a glacial pace.

"Hello," I say. He doesn't even look up from whatever it is he's reading. "Sir? We'd like two tickets."

"Tickets?" he says, and then coughs. And coughs. And keeps coughing. When he looks up, his eyes are bloodshot, and he looks as though there is something seriously wrong with him. Beck's grip tightens on me, confirming there's something wrong here.

"Yes," I say, cautiously. "Two tickets to Ouracéu please."

"You get those on board."

"But don't we need tickets to get on board to begin with?"

"Yes," he says, leaning back against the wall of the ticket

booth behind him. His hairline is sweaty—or whatever you call the top part of his head where he doesn't actually have hair but might have in his younger days. His skin looks waxy and almost gray. He looks sick and yet . . . not sick, not exactly. I remember seeing someone like this at the market with my mother when I was younger. It gives me the chills. Beck shifts slightly and pushes some bills across the counter to him. Then he reaches in and finds the tickets. The man inside the booth watches this all.

"You need to stamp these, man," he says. His voice is soft but commanding.

"Right," the man says. Slowly, lethargically, he lifts the stamp, and brings it down on each ticket. Then Beck takes them and tucks them into my pocket. We back away carefully, and then walk down the platform to the very end.

"What was that about?" I ask, though I think I have an idea. I'd seen people around the peninsula with that vacant expression, most of them living on the streets and the kindness of neighbors.

"You've never seen anyone coming down before?" he asks. It clicks. There was a severe opium problem in one of the places we lived when I was eight. It was around the time I first heard people talking about trade with Osterstan. I stay quiet. Mostly because there's nothing else to say.

We pass by people waiting for the train. Mostly men, but some women and children. I wonder what circumstances could possibly lead a family to bring children to a war zone. Then again, I'm taking the same trip.

"Thank you for your help," Declan says, placing a hand on the small of my back. "I think we can take it from here."

Beck stiffens against me. I realize I have two choices: pull away, or stay where I am. And the reality is, I'm not ready to be alone with Declan. Not here. I may not trust Beck, but he's gotten us this far. And I don't know who is protecting who once it's me and Declan. And yet, I don't understand what Beck's game is.

Has he really just done this because he can be helpful? The worst thing is that I want this to be true. And I hate myself for feeling that way.

"I don't think that's a good idea," Beck says. "Still time for things to go sour." Declan scowls, but then, off in the distance, a train whistle sounds. I squint my eyes and see the puff of smoke getting closer and closer. But then, behind us, there's a scuffle. And noise.

"Over there!" someone yells.

"There she is!"

CHAPTER NINETEEN

*M*y stomach drops. Beck shifts so that he's blocking me with his body. Declan looks confused. As if he doesn't understand what is happening to us. Meanwhile, my body tightens like a coil. I feel Beck do the same as footsteps thunder along the wooden planks of the platform.

"Just wait right there, missy," a familiar voice says behind us, and Declan's eyes widen. There's something about the word—*missy*? Who says that to people?

"I don't think it's her, Frank," the second voice says. A hand grabs my shoulder, but Beck's hand is already there. The hand jerks me around, and Beck moves fluidly with me, falling across me like a useless drunk. I look up, and it's the weasel from earlier, his buddy, and another larger man who is wearing all black and has a pistol at his hip.

"Look at her," Weasel's friend says. "Doesn't look like her at all."

"Doesn't matter if it looks like her," Frank says. "Just needs to look enough like her for the money."

"You didn't happen to come off that Nordanian ship that's sitting off the coast? Didja darlin'?" Weasel asks.

"What?" I ask, trying to lean into the elongated vowels of Simone's Swendish accent. But the man just laughs. Behind me, the train whistles again.

"Blue eyes, that part matches," Frank says. I blink as if trying to hide my eyes. I can't believe that's the part they would notice, what with my broken nose and black eyes and bruising on my temple.

"They don't like when you bring 'em the wrong ones," Weasel says.

"What exactly are you accusing us—" Declan says, but that only makes them grin and he stops talking.

"And who do we have here?" Frank asks, a grin creeping into his ugly face beneath his blond mustache like the cat who got the cream.

"Strong stance," Beck murmurs into my neck.

The train whistle is louder, and I can feel the vibrations beneath my feet.

"Why don't you come with us, darlin'? We'll take good care of you," Frank says.

"No, thank you," I say.

"I wasn't asking," he says.

"Just the same, I'll stay here," I say.

"Come on," Weasel says, stepping closer. "You don't really want to go on this train, do you?"

"Leave her alone," Beck grumbles.

"What's this now?" the little guy says, laughing. "The drunk can talk?"

"There's two ways out of this," Frank says, getting close enough that when he looks down at me, I can smell the tobacco on his breath. "You either come with us, or I take you with us." He reaches for my neck, but before he gets all the way there, I hook my fingers around his pinky and yank, then push as hard as I can. He's a big guy, and I'm not strong enough, but it catches him off guard just enough that he stumbles toward the tracks.

"What the feck?" he says. The passengers who had been waiting near us clear out. But as the train approaches, we have nowhere to run. "Grab her," he growls.

The little guy grabs at my sweater, and I cut his grip the same way Beck taught me and shove him aside. I don't see Weasel, but Beck does, and he socks him in the nose. Weasel squeals, turning around as blood rushes down his face. The little guy comes back at Beck, ramming his shoulder into his gut, but Beck is ready for him, slamming his elbow down on the back of his head and knocking him out.

I turn around, and Frank is right there, pistol pointed at Declan's temple.

"You think I don't know who this is?" he asks.

Just then, Beck grabs me around the waist and sticks something hard against my back. I gasp.

"You think I don't know who is worth money?" Beck growls. Frank's eyes widen. He didn't expect to have someone call his bluff. "How bout you take yours, and I'll take mine."

Frank doesn't like this. Which makes me wonder, am I really worth more than Declan? And if so, why?

Except of course, I know the answer. Someone wants all of the Embers and potential graduate voters incapacitated so that we can't do what we want to do.

Frank grunts as the train slows next to the tracks. The door opens, and the conductor gets out.

"Frank McVie, you'd better not bloody up my platform. You still owe me from last time," the conductor says. I press my lips together to stifle the laugh that bubbles up. It doesn't make sense. There are guns involved. Lives are at stake. But nervous laughter bursts out of me. Because this is funny. This is so stupidly, ridiculously funny.

Except that Declan has a gun pointed to his head, and when I look at his face and see that all the blood has drained from it, I realize that he does not think this is funny. This has never happened to him.

"This isn't your business, Gerry," Frank says.

"Does this man have a ticket?" he asks.

"Yes," I say.

Gerry, the conductor, looks at me, then back at Declan and Frank, and flicks his hand.

"Leave it, Frank."

Frank grumbles and lowers the gun, pushing Declan toward us. I catch him before he stumbles to his hands and knees. He's cold and sweaty.

"You come back through here, you're mine," Frank says.

"Yes, yes, we're all terrified," Gerry says, and this time, I don't stifle my laugh. I let it out. And so does Beck. "Come on, now. We have a schedule to keep."

This town is crazy. Literally crazy. But I sort of love it just a little if someone like Gerry can exist here.

I reach into my pocket and withdraw the tickets. I pass them to Gerry and nudge Declan to the door. He climbs up, slowly, his steps stilted. I'm about to follow him when Beck tugs on my wrist.

He doesn't say anything. Not for a long minute. His brow is furrowed, but he doesn't say anything. It's as if he's lost for words. Or like he knows what he wants to say but not how to say it. For a moment, I wonder if this is it. Is he about to make a run for it after all? Is this goodbye? *He might never say.* Is this an apology? My chest squeezes and despite everything, I shiver.

"Remember to watch your surroundings," is what he finally says.

"Oh," I say. "Right."

He looks frustrated.

"Don't let your guard down. He's not going to be able to protect you, so you're going to have to do it for both of you."

I should've known that Beck couldn't let us go without taking one last shot at Declan.

"I'll be fine," I say brusquely. But he doesn't let go of my wrist.

"Beck, I'm fine. I won't tell anyone how to find you or whatever it is you're worried about."

He leans in, tucks a braid behind my ear, and kisses my cheek. His lips linger, as if he's going to whisper something in my ear, and I shut my eyes on instinct. I inhale his leather and citrus scent. I open my eyes, and he's gone. It's as if he was never there.

My face flashes hot with anger and all the emotions I'd been keeping down. It's not fair that he did that. That he can just pull something like that, and then be gone.

"Are you in or out?" Gerry says. I look over my shoulder to where Declan is in our seats, looking out the window.

"In."

CHAPTER TWENTY

*T*he train ride is long, dusty, and uncomfortable. We have one bag packed between the two of us, which makes the ride easier. There aren't any stops, but that doesn't mean we don't see people. After the first two caravans that whip past us, I stop watching them and start watching Declan. He doesn't take his eyes off them, as if committing each face wrapped in cloth to memory. It's hard enough to make this journey on a train, let alone by foot. And some of those feet are significantly smaller than ours. We've been riding for about thirty minutes when a now-familiar green jacket appears.

"You?" I say, unable to hide the surprise in my voice at Elm's appearance on this train. But Declan doesn't look surprised. He looks like he expected this, which means I've been kept in the dark. Elm sits across from us, but doesn't respond more than a cursory nod.

We start slowing as the sun is dipping below the horizon. It looks red-orange and casts the desolate wasteland around us in deep umbers and oranges. I can imagine someone looking at this with a romantic gaze and thinking it's beautiful. But I look at it and wonder how anyone finds anything to eat or drink. I wonder what Declan is thinking as the train slows to a stop. I look out the other side of the train, but don't see a station.

"Screening," Elm says.

"Screening for what?" Declan says. I give him a meaningful glance, and he just says, "Oh."

When you're entering a war zone, everyone is suspect. As Swendish military members board our car from the one in front, they carry flashlights and large guns. I don't think I've ever seen a gun that large. But I sit still, back slouched, and nudge Declan to do the same.

"Tickets," the woman asks. Her blue eyes are all I see, since she's wearing a mask over the bottom half of her face, which seems like a pretty good idea right now, as I cough up more dust. The windows are all shut, and yet it still floats in the air, casting everything in a musty sepia tone. Elm passes our tickets to her, and she reads them all. She looks up at each of us. I make eye contact, and then look away, as I imagine most travelers would. But Declan doesn't do a thing.

"Sir, where is your final destination?"

"Ouracéu," Elm supplies. "I'm taking them to visit a sick aunt."

"I'd like the man to answer for himself," she says. Declan looks up at her, and I can feel the panic. I nudge him, hard, and he recoils.

"She's talking to you, *Clem*," I say. He frowns, and takes a moment too long to respond.

"Up," she says, motioning for him to stand. My heart races as everything of this day, everything of this journey to find the Embers comes crashing down to how effectively Declan can improvise. Slowly, he pushes to his feet, stands up straight, and then belches.

I don't think it's on purpose, but it serves its purpose. The female officer recoils.

"Sorry, miss," I say, trying to imitate Neve's accent. "I think he had some bad fish in Queensbridge."

"That'll teach him to eat ceviche out of season," Elm says with a chuffing laugh. The officer rolls her eyes and nudges him back toward his seat.

"Don't eat ceviche in Queensbridge, period," she says, passing our tickets back to Elm. The officers slowly move through the rest of our car, and then to the next. The occupants give out a collective sigh, and the tension fades.

"Is it always that tense?" I ask. Elm shakes his head.

"Only since the explosions."

"Explosions?" I ask, frowning. Declan tenses. "I heard about one in western Osterstan. Was there another?"

His face goes stony, and he nods. "Collapsed a tunnel between Sudersberg and Ouracéu." He doesn't say anything more. But he doesn't need to. Given the way his mouth tightens, I can imagine what that means.

"Monsters," I say. He flinches but doesn't say any more. I wonder who he lost in that explosion.

"Found what they were looking for," I hear a woman behind us say. I look out the window, and a man and woman are led away from the train. We start to move away as the guards question the man. We've picked up speed, and I turn around. Declan flinches.

"What?"

He's not looking at me. He's looking back to where the man and woman were being questioned. When I turn around, the woman is on the ground, the officer's weapon still raised over her limp body.

We enter a tunnel and are submerged in complete darkness. There are no lights on the train car, and the steam from the engine wafts back, flitting in through the cracks in the windows. It feels like it's going to choke us. Next to me, Declan breathes quickly. I reach for his hand, threading my fingers through his. It's possible he's never seen death before, much less watched it happen. I suppose I'm in good company now.

The station at Ouracéu is surprisingly busy, considering there's only one train a day that comes and goes. Elm stretches his legs, as if he's been crammed into the luggage compartment. Then leads us through the busy platform and the mess of people of different nationalities. It's a true melting pot of people here, and I wonder where they've all come from. Or where they're going. Though it doesn't seem like people are boarding the train.

We follow Elm through the station to the busy street outside, full of horses and a few automobiles. We turn down a wide avenue, and the sides are littered with stands selling unfamiliar-looking fruits and vegetables, scarves in rich colors, and carts selling roasted meat on a stick. The meat smells herbed and rich, and my stomach grumbles at the delicious aroma. But we keep walking.

As we wind through the streets, I'm shocked at how densely populated Ouracéu is. I'd always imagined it to be a small outpost in the middle of nowhere.

Elm stops at the corner of a quiet street. The houses stand in a row, three stories tall, and I wonder if once upon a time, this wasn't the wealthy part of town.

"About halfway down the street, you'll see the brown-painted house with a chipped cobalt front door. Knock four times, wait, then knock twice. If nobody answers after five minutes, try again." Then he turns as if to leave.

"Wait," I say, reaching for him, though he's already out of reach. "You're not coming with us?"

His face takes on a strange expression, something along the lines of regret. Then he shakes his head.

"I've gotten you where you need to go."

It's obvious there's a story there, but it's just as clear that he's not going to share it.

"Thank you," I say. He nods, then pulls a hat onto his head and adds a scarf around his neck. As if he's no longer the person that helped us, he's now someone else.

"Well?" I say to Declan. He nods, his eyes wide, and then I lead the way. The house is just where he said it would be, halfway down the street on the right. It's a three-story house, just like the others, not unique in any way except that the front door is a dingy dark blue compared to the others in bright corals, greens, and yellows. I knock, just as he said. And then we wait.

Declan fidgets, stretching and clenching his fingers. I've never seen him so uncomfortable, so out of his element. Just then, the door opens, and the man who answers is the last person I ever expected to see.

"Teddy?" I say, looking at the boy who was my only friend on the peninsula for all the years I was there. The boy who remained my friend, and stayed kind and loyal to me, even after CJ and his friends beat him up so badly that he had a limp afterward.

"Arden?" he says, his eyes wide with shock. "What are you doing here?"

I laugh. "What are *you* doing here?"

He motions for me to come inside, and then looks at Declan. He looks back at me, and then quickly motions Declan to come inside. I don't have to ask to know that he has recognized the prime minister's son on his doorstep.

"How are you here?" I ask.

"I think we both have a lot to tell each other," he says.

"Teddy? Who is it?" The voice that calls from behind him is familiar, from another life. I had once worried I would never hear it again. Teddy moves out of the way, and I blink fast to keep the sudden tears from my eyes as Zerah steps into the dim light.

I don't wait. I launch at her, wrapping my arms around her slight figure, and I squeeze her tight.

"Get it together, you weirdo," she says into my shoulder. But she's hugging me just as tight as I'm hugging her.

I pull back and cup her cheeks, looking at her as if she might slip through my fingers.

"How are you both here?" I ask.

"Zerah?" Declan says behind me. His voice is scratchy with disuse, and I realize it's the first thing he's said since the train. She looks over my shoulder at him and stiffens.

"It's okay," I say. "He's okay."

"I think we need to sit down," she says.

We find ourselves in a comfortable room in the back of the house, sitting on the floor around a low table. A handful of women fill the table with flatbreads, pitchers of a yellow-ish citrussy juice, and what looks like meatballs and some kind of white sauce.

"Lamb and a spiced yogurt dressing," Zerah explains, passing them toward me and Declan. He has been quiet ever since we arrived. I'm not sure how much of it is from overwhelm from a day of difficult travel, and how much is from seeing Zerah again. The last time he saw her, he sent her away to be married. And now, she's here, in a home for women in trouble. She pours us each a glass of the juice.

"And this is calamansi juice. Sort of like orange juice, but not."

I take a sip of the juice. It's different than I was expecting, and maybe it's just the fact that I haven't eaten anything all day, but I think it's delicious. We dig into our humble, but delicious meal, and Zerah just lets us.

"Does she know?" I hear Zerah say to Teddy.

"Not yet," he says. He makes a grim expression, and then nods and leaves.

"What don't I know?" I ask. Zerah nods and flaps her hand. She's dressed so differently from the last time I saw her. She's still wearing long sleeves—it's cold, after all. But her neck is exposed, and in the dark, I can make out a few scars that she's no longer afraid to hide.

"How are you here?" I ask as I finish chewing a piece of the buttery, light flatbread.

"This is my house," she says.

"Is Whitey here?" Declan asks.

"No," she says, and there's a strange glint to her eye. "He's gone." But she doesn't offer anything more.

"Is everything okay?" I ask.

"I'm housing women in a war zone. Do you think everything is okay?" she says, a little too quick for comfort. This is my chance.

"You're housing Embers, aren't you?" I say. Her pupils dilate, and it's enough confirmation for me. "That's why I'm here."

Then I explain to her what I'm doing. How I spoke with Emlyn, then Irina, then Carmen. How it led me to Simone, and she led me here. Then I mention Elm briefly, and I don't think I'm wrong when I see her eyes flicker to the door where Teddy disappeared through.

Then I wait for her to say something. She gets up and goes to a cabinet in the wall, pulling out a tall bottle of something that looks like liquor. She pours three short glasses and passes them to us. I hold up my hand to decline, and she nudges it toward me again.

"Trust me, you're gonna want this."

"Why do you say that?"

Just then, the door opens and Teddy limps through. But he is not alone. No, he's holding the door for someone. Nothing could have prepared me for the moment that the woman with the once bright smile and the no longer bright eyes and dark curls walks through that door.

"Carla?" I say, looking at my old roommate. The one who both Neve and I left behind at the plantation. She blinks at me, as if she isn't sure whether she's dreaming or not. I look at Zerah. She simply sips her drink, and then nods.

I jump to my feet, and Carla just blinks at me.

"Arden?"

I don't let her say anything else. I launch at her, wrapping my arms around her, squeezing her to me as tight as I can. I'm not sure when she starts crying, or when I start sobbing. But I don't let go for a long, long time. And neither does she.

CHAPTER TWENTY-ONE

*T*heir stories couldn't be more different.

Zerah's husband, William Whitey, took a position as an ambassador to Osterstan. Without going into specifics, Zerah explained that he died suddenly, but that, as his widow, she inherited his estate, which was much larger than anyone could have anticipated due to some illegal dealings. She took the money and went somewhere that nobody would look too carefully at a widow with that much money. Once here, she found the safe house that she'd been told about. It used to be located in a small squat, but she then bought this house and started running it the right way.

Carla arrived shortly after she did. Carla's story is harder to follow. She took a ship, then a train, and Teddy with her. It doesn't take much to realize that perhaps Elm was involved in her getting here—and that perhaps she's the reason he stayed away. It's a story she doesn't have much practice telling, one that has left its scars. When she cuts off abruptly, I wonder whether she'll ever be able to fully tell it.

To my great relief, she makes it clear that CJ never touched her, either before or after I left.

Then it's my turn. I fill Carla in, then tell them exactly what it is I want the Embers to do. Zerah leans back onto her hands and frowns, as if she's thinking hard.

"This isn't a place they can come and go."

"I understand that," I say, taking a small sip of the liqueur. It is sharp and bitter.

"They come here because they have nowhere else to go. The world out there isn't safe for them."

"I don't understand," Declan says, a frown deeply etched into the lines of his face. Up to this point, he's been listening attentively. "They're from the institute. How did it get this bad?"

Zerah stiffens, her chin raised.

"Most of them were never safe in the first place," Zerah says simply.

"Look at the two of us," I say, and then catch myself. "All three of us, actually."

"I didn't have it as bad as you did," Carla says, curling her feet beneath her on her cushion. "But I took the long route to get here, and I saw a lot of other people who were less fortunate than we were. It opened my eyes to how many other experiences there must be in the world, and maybe I was naive to think those experiences didn't exist in Nordania."

Declan looks up at her, his fingers tracing the rim of his glass. I wonder if this has never occurred to him. That the people we saw in Queensbridge, and the people we saw on the train and on the side of the road before the tunnel, might be experiencing the same things as the people in Nordania.

"What if I could guarantee their safety so long as they

come to the assembly?" Declan asks. Zerah considers this, running her tongue over her bottom lip.

"That's not a bad start, but that's only half the battle. Attending the assembly tells people where they are. It puts a target on their back."

"Then what if we write it into the legislation?" I ask. Zerah and Carla seem intrigued. "Whatever it would take to keep them safe both before and after the assembly. Simone asked for safe passage to a new home on Nordanian soil after she attends." She motions to the space around her. "Could you do something like this in Nordania?"

"Something like what?" Zerah asks.

"Build a home for graduates who need a safe place to go."

Her gaze flickers to Declan, and she shrugs.

"I think it depends on whether the institute thinks that's a good idea."

Declan rubs at his chin and shakes his head.

"I don't know," he says finally. "It seems that this is a necessary place." He sounds defeated as he says it. Just then, a woman enters the room. She is petite, with blonde hair and sunburned cheeks. But her eyes brighten when she takes in Declan.

"Declan? I thought I heard your voice," she says. Declan shoots to his feet, in shock, and then recognition seeps into his face.

"Camille?" He doesn't say anything else. It's as if he can't fathom that this woman is here.

"I thought I was going mad, hearing things." She crosses the small space and shakes his hand.

"What are you doing here?" he asks, his voice softer. She shrugs one shoulder.

"What are any of us doing here?"

Zerah stands and motions for me and Carla to do the same.

"Perhaps we should let the two of you"—she glances at the door and sees more women hovering there—"all of you catch up." Declan looks overwhelmed, and I squeeze his elbow.

"I'll stay, if you want," I say. He looks overwhelmed as he nods.

"Please."

So, I do. We sit for hours, deep into the night, as he catches up with no less than seven women who used to live in his house. They share their stories, and they all have one thing in common: they were taken advantage of and wronged by powerful men. Not all of them bear physical scars, but there are enough that Declan stops asking clarifying questions. One thing led to another, and they found their way here. Declan listens to each one, and throughout their stories, I gather that there are many more living here than have joined us. There are so many stories. I wonder what stories from this year the other girls like Fiona and Molly and Avery might tell. The oldest among them, a black woman called Francine, recalls Declan as a seven-year-old. She has some of the best stories, and we all laugh.

But Declan's laughter grows softer as the night wears on. His posture remains upright, solid. He's engaged, leaning forward throughout. But he looks exhausted, like he's going to fight through the tiredness so that these women can be heard. I thread my fingers through his and give him a squeeze. Then I raise his hand to my mouth and kiss his knuckles. I don't know why I do it, but it feels right. He lets out a deep breath and leans back in his chair, then presses my knuckles to his lips, his eyes shut tight. A shiver races up my arm, and I feel a warm fullness expand in my chest. He keeps my hand in his, squeezed tight beneath the table through the rest of the stories. This visit has clearly tilted the axis of his world, and I'm glad I can give him some strength to push through.

So I make my pitch. I tell them about my measure, what I hope can happen to the institute, to the benefactor system, and for them. I ask them to return to Nordania to vote. Some of them, sadly, aren't eligible to vote. But from what I'm able to gather, there are enough of them, here in the corridor, who are. Not all the women live here in Zerah's house. Some have found work, gotten their own flats. People aren't so judgmental about single women living alone or together here in the corridor.

We talk until I can hardly keep my eyes open, and then we're left to our own devices. Zerah makes her way back down and offers us a bedroom. I'm too tired to argue with her, and she promises to visit more in the morning.

It's a tiny room, with a twin bed pushed against an interior wall, a small window with a pretty linen curtain, and a stone floor. It's even smaller than the room I shared with Neve at the estate. But this one has one bed. The last time I shared a bed with a man, I was . . . well, it wasn't Declan I was thinking about.

"I'll take the floor," he says.

"Declan—"

"The floor is fine."

"The floor is stone."

"It's only proper," he insists.

"I think we're six hours past proper," I say. But he doesn't budge.

I sigh and sit on the small bed. It's a tiny room, and I can't help but wonder who else has slept in here. It makes me wonder if it's meant for new arrivals who need to feel safe. It's the sort of room I would have wanted if I'd had the courage to run away from the Laarsworth estate and CJ.

"How do you do this?" he asks.

"Do what?" I ask, fluffing a pillow behind my back.

"Know what to do." When I don't answer, he continues. "What to say, what to ask—when not to ask more. How . . ."

"I don't," I say. He stretches out his legs and leans against the wall.

"But on the train, at the station, with Elm before. How did you know what to do?"

"Oh," I say, and then I frown. I don't know how I knew what to do. In fact, I wouldn't say that I did. But I suppose I knew to keep my head down and make myself smaller, to not attract attention. And Declan only knew how to stand out. "I suppose I've become good at watching other people over the years and reading their moods."

"It helped you survive?" he guesses. I nod. "You're so much more capable than I am."

"I don't think that's true," I say. "I can barely answer the questions Neve gives me."

"That's not real," he says, shaking his head and pinching his nose. "This is real. Getting to a train station and riding it to a new destination. Moving through crowds, and making it through security checkpoints, and avoiding conflict. Finding food. That's real."

I shrug. "You've just been lucky."

"I've been coddled." His frown is so deep I can practically hear it. I consider arguing the point, but he shakes his head, as if he knows what I'm thinking. "I've been taught that it's God's will that I take over as prime minister of Nordania. That I was born into this, that it is my inherited destiny, and that I owe my life to both my Lord and savior, and the country who has put its faith in me.

"But now, listening to these women? Nordania is broken. It's so deeply broken. These women are supposed to represent the moral arm of our nation—the moral compass of my own existence is broken. What does that say about me?"

He slumps against the wall, not looking at me. He looks so young, even despite his dark scruff along his jaw. I slip off the bed and sink to my knees next to him. Gently, I lift his face to mine. His gray eyes are stormy and glassy with conflict.

"It doesn't say anything about you. It says that the country you were born into is complicated and fractured. It says that there is room for improvement, and there is need for someone like you, who feels so deeply and cares so much."

He blinks, and a tear rolls down his cheek. I want to wrap my arms around him and hold him together, but I know that's not what he needs right now. He's been coddled his whole life. Now, he's seen the way the world works.

"I don't know about God," I say, and he flinches. But I hold his face right where it belongs. "But I know you care about these women deeply. I could see it in the way you listened. I guarantee you that these women haven't experienced that in a man in . . . well, maybe never. You heard them. And it has moved you to action. If there is a God, then I have to believe that this is part of his plan. You being here and understanding what is actually happening. If you don't make it right, then that would be a failure. But I know you won't do that."

He nods, resolute. Then I wrap my arms around his neck, and he coils his arms around my back. He cries softly into my shoulder, and I fight back tears. This cry belongs to Declan. The least I can do is let him have that much. We sit on the hard stone like that until my shirt is no longer damp from his tears and our breath falls are synchronized. I press a kiss to his forehead, nudging the colored hair from his eyes. He catches my gaze and something passes between us. It's a spark of something, though I'm not sure what. I tug him to his feet, and without a word, we slip into the tiny bed together.

He curls around me, our foreheads close together, covered by a thick wool blanket. We sleep like that, my hand pressed to his chest and his coiled around me, as if holding me dear. Right now, as he's breaking apart, and I'm still finding all my pieces, so we just hold on to each other. And it feels right.

CHAPTER TWENTY-TWO

*M*orning comes too soon. We wake up the way we fell asleep, and stay where we are for a long moment. His eyelashes are dark and thick, and his eyes are so gray they look like pearls.

"Did you sleep well?" he asks, his eyes adorably groggy. I nod.

"Yeah. You?"

"I've never slept with another person." He shuts his eyes. As if it's suddenly too intimate to make these kinds of confessions. Then he sighs and opens his eyes again.

"I liked it," he says. It's such a naked confession. He pushes hair off my forehead, tucking it gently behind my ear. Even though we're fully clothed and as proper as could possibly be, given that we slept in a narrow bed together, I blush. And then the reality hits. I liked it too. I felt safe, and I slept well and sound. He's so honest and raw with me, I feel like I owe him the same.

"Me too," I say. A wash of relief floods his cheeks, and he cups my face. I don't stop him when he presses his lips to mine. There's a quiet confidence in the way he kisses me.

He strokes my cheek as he tastes my lips, breathes me in like it's the most important thing in the world. And I kiss him back. He sucks on my top lip as he deepens the kiss, as he threads his fingers through my hair, clinging onto me like I'm his lifeline. It feels good. It feels right. I curl my fingers around the back of his neck and hold him close to me. A soft sound hums in his throat as his fingers trace beneath the collar of my sweater, and his tongue presses hot and sweet against mine. I gasp at the delicious sensat—

There's a knock at the door.

We freeze.

"Time to wake up," Teddy says without opening the door. "Your train leaves in an hour."

"Right," I say. Declan shuts his eyes. Everything comes crashing down around us. Because we're not just two people who shared a bed and are getting to know each other in a new way. We have a heavy responsibility, and today is decision time. Today is when we find out how many of these women will trust us and come with us. And it's out of our hands.

"You go ahead," he says. I nod and slip out of the bed, then the room. Once the door is shut, I lean against the wall and shut my eyes, taking a deep breath.

"It's going well, is it?" Zerah's wry voice cuts into my brief reverie. I arch an eyebrow to match hers, and she laughs. "Come on, let's get some breakfast in you before you melt."

Declan joins about halfway through breakfast, and our meal goes down quickly. There must be thirty people sitting around the breakfast room—the same room where we sat last night and talked to the women. I didn't know a house this size could hold this many people. There are more women who remember Declan from various years of his life, and I give him the space to reconnect and relearn them. But he never goes for more than a few minutes without squeezing my hand or pressing a kiss to my knuckles.

Far too soon, Zerah claps her hands, and the room quiets.

"By now, I believe you all know what is being asked of you." She gives everyone a moment. Several heads nod. "I will not tell you what to do. I will only tell you that if you do leave, it will be very difficult for you to return. This is your decision, and yours alone." The room remains quiet. The nervous energy from before has evolved into a taut tension. "But I have decided it is of paramount importance that I attend."

I jerk my head in surprise. Judging by the few gasps, I'm not the only one.

"If I can create a home for women like this within Nordania, then I must. Carla will stay in my stead and run this home. This home will continue to function as it always has in my absence."

My gut tightens, and I look for Carla. She stands in the back of the room, hands tucked into the pockets of her wide-leg wool pants. She looks somehow harder, more grown up than even just last night. As if she's ready for this. But there's still something I'm missing. Teddy shifts next to her and gently leans his shoulder into hers. She leans into him just as subtly. I don't know what that relationship is, but I don't think it's what it looks like.

"Of course, you can't all just take the train. It would raise too many eyebrows. We have worked through the night to coordinate caravans for anyone who wishes to go."

"Caravans?" I ask, thinking of the trains of people

walking through the desert. I can't imagine how long that would take, but it definitely won't be short.

"We have transports. They will only be a little slower than the train. Of course, there is risk, as some of you well know," she says. I see a few nods, but nobody says a word. It makes sense that most of them would have arrived by whatever means they could.

"I have it on good authority that these caravans will function with as much safety as can be promised in a trip like this."

"Who has coordinated this?" I ask.

Zerah's gaze flickers to Carla, and Carla looks at the ground. Her jaw tightens, and her expression is unreadable. Teddy squeezes her shoulder.

"I believe you met our fixer already?" she says. When I frown, she leans closer. "He goes by the name Elm."

This gives me pause. If even mention of him makes Carla so uncomfortable, I don't know that I want to put all my eggs in his basket. True, he got us here, but it seems as if there's more to the story. Before I entrust him with these women's lives, I need to know more. Zerah raises a finger to me, as if to say that this conversation can wait. She turns her attention to the room full of nervous women.

"You will have enough time to pack a small bag. You may not be able to return here, so don't leave anything precious. The first transport will leave at noon."

Apparently, that's the end, and the women start to meander away from the room. I turn to Zerah, who motions for me and Declan to follow her to the front of the building. We walk down the hallway and stop at the front door.

"Should we be concerned that Carla has such a strong reaction to Elm?" I ask.

"That's something you'll have to ask her," she says, then

pauses. "All I can say is that I believe his new life's work is atonement. He got you here safely, didn't he?"

Atonement? What does that mean? It doesn't make sense. But as she presses two train tickets into Declan's hand, I realize there may not be time for that story. Not without abandoning the women who have chosen to believe in us.

"Should we say goodbye?" Declan asks, frowning at the tickets.

"Not if you want to make your train," she says. Panic rushes through me.

"But Carla—"

"Carla knows you're in a rush. She knows how to reach you. I assume a Nordanian ship at port in Queensbridge would raise a few red flags?"

Declan nods.

"Tell your captain to navigate east to one-hundred-and-eighteen degrees west. There's a tiny port there called Gimley. It's not on a map. It only exists for our purposes. One small dock. But it's out of radio contact of Queensbridge. Wait thirty knots offshore. Watch for a flare. Then come in for whoever comes. I will come with the first transport."

"That's it?" I ask.

"That's the best we can do," she says.

"How many transports—"

"That's the best I can tell you right now. You'll have more news when the transports arrive. Now, you need to leave before you miss today's train and this is all for naught."

I look down the hall, but Carla isn't in sight. I hesitate for just a moment. Zerah steps closer.

"Know that if she could, she would be right here alongside us. If she could handle a goodbye, she would. She loves you so dearly. Talks about you . . . I know this will be a regret she holds close for a long time. But I also know she . . ." Zerah's throat catches. I don't know what she's been through, either of them, and I can't believe this is happening. That I have to choose between the Embers and Carla. But if this is what Carla wants . . .

"Arden," Declan says, slipping his fingers through mine. A piece of my heart severs in that moment. It will stay here with Carla, I know. And with that, I turn and follow Declan out the door.

CHAPTER TWENTY-THREE

$\mathcal{T}$he train ride back is somehow even more tense than our arrival. Perhaps it is because we don't have Elm by our side to guide us. Or because the stakes are so much higher now, with the caravan of Embers making their way to an invisible port. The stop before and after the tunnel was long and tense, but Declan did better this time. The sun was brutal, the dust flitted in through the cracks between the windows, and by the time we got back to Queensbridge, we were covered in it.

When we reach the dock, I realize I've been holding my breath because I don't know who will meet us. Will it be Beck? Has he left? I see broad shoulders, dark hair, and we are surrounded by a rush of salty sea air. I pick up my pace, and as we approach, he turns—it's the first mate.

He escorts us to the dock in silence. The port is busy with activity, but it seems quieter somehow, like it's also holding its breath. Declan squeezes my hand tight, and I squeeze back. But it's not the same as last night. Something has shifted.

As we ride in the skiff back to the ship, my heart pounds

in my chest, and I swear Declan can feel it. He keeps casting nervous glances at me, and I don't think it has anything to do with the chop. When we finally reach the ship, Meredith and Neve are waiting for me, alongside Alvin. All three audibly sigh once we're safely on board.

Declan leaves with Alvin almost immediately, heading to the bridge to fill in the captain, and Meredith and Neve waste no time getting me cleaned up.

"Where to now?" Meredith asks as the engines on the ship shudder to life. She rinses my hair in the basin that substitutes for a proper bathtub on board, and I swear I can smell the muddy mess it must make of the dust in my hair.

"East," I say.

"That doesn't seem wise," she says.

"How's that?"

"Doesn't the weather get nasty east the further you get from the Mittlesee?" As if on cue, the ship rocks violently, causing the basin to splash all over Meredith's sleeves.

The door opens, and Neve tumbles in, bearing a jug of water.

"What is that captain doing?" she asks.

"We're going to meet the caravans in a tiny port to the east."

"What happened?" Meredith asks. "Was it as awful as it sounds?"

Instinctively, I look to Neve, who holds my gaze. I have to tell her about Carla. But I don't know how to explain that I found her and then left her behind.

"Just say it," Neve says. Her shoulders are stiff, and the air goes cold. I can't keep this from her. Not even if I wanted to.

"I saw Carla."

Her complexion pales, and she sits on the edge of the bed.

"What?"

"Who's Carla?" Meredith interjects.

This is not what Neve was expecting. Which begs the question—just how much does she know?

"Is she one of the girls coming on the caravan?" Meredith asks.

I sigh. And shake my head. Her jaw tenses.

"Why not?"

"She refused. I couldn't . . . Teddy is with her. She isn't—"

"Teddy?" Neve barks a harsh laugh, and I don't know what it means. She shakes her head and stares off toward the window, as if the answer to everything she's puzzling out is somewhere out there.

"What did you think I was going to say?" I ask.

She sighs. And then rigid resolution fills her face.

"I was married."

Meredith gasps. I keep my face measured, but I swear I feel the bottom of my stomach fall out. Because the only reason a girl like Neve, Unchosen, would get married, is if Conrad wanted the money for her contract paid.

"Who?" I ask, feeling hot anger replace that emptiness. The idea of who would marry an Unchosen girl and pay off that big of a contract makes me sick.

"I was married to a nice man. I promise, he was . . . and we lived in Osterstan."

Meredith presses a hand to her chest, and it starts to make sense. I'm about to ask more questions when I realize that Neve's eyes have gone shiny, and her bottom lip is trembling. I sit up from the basin, water probably dripping everywhere, and I go to her side. Meridith flanks her other side, and we each hold a hand.

"Tell me what happened," she says, as if asking for a reprieve from what is clearly an emotional memory. So I do.

I fill them in on the details without giving away too much. I don't know why, but I feel protective of these women. And if they want Neve and Meredith to know who they are, then I assume they'll show up on the caravans in Gimley. I just hope there's enough of them.

The girls help me finish cleaning up, and Meredith pins back my hair as Neve applies tonics and creams to my face. Finally, the ship seems to slow down, and I pull on my boots and go to the bridge. I pause. Nobody has told me anything about whether Beck returned. He's either here, or he's not. With a fortifying breath, I open the door and enter —just as Alvin thunders past. He bumps into my shoulder with some heft. But he doesn't stop, not to apologize or anything. Declan is standing there, with the captain, first mate, and in the corner, binoculars to his eyes, is Beck.

The sight of him in his element makes my stomach flip. Even though I should still be angry with him, there's a sense of rightness about it. I swear I breathe easier. Though maybe I shouldn't.

"I felt us slowing down," I say as I enter. Everyone turns to see me. Declan hasn't left since arriving, judging by the dust in his hair.

"We're holding for their signal," Declan says, approaching and kissing my knuckles.

"What's the plan?" I ask.

"You heard her," Declan says, his voice low. "We need to wait for the flare, then we can send the skiff to collect them."

"Who is going on the skiff?" I ask.

He nods toward the first mate.

"I do love a good firework show close up," Beck says, the binoculars practically glued to his eyes. "If you can't taste the sulfur, you're not doing it right."

"Is he going?" I ask.

"We thought it would be wise to have another body on board," the captain says, tactfully.

Beck snorts and finally lowers the binoculars. "What he means is he wants some muscle on board. Just in case."

"Can I look?" I ask, nodding to the binoculars. Beck hesitates, then shrugs and passes them to me. My fingers brush his, just briefly, and then I take the binoculars and approach the instrument panel. It takes a moment to focus the lenses, but when I do, I see what Zerah described. There's a single wooden pier that extends into the choppy waters. There's not even a single booth or stand anywhere near the pier. I can't imagine who would use this pier except for us.

I try to imagine the women arriving to the pier after their long journey through the cold, dusty desert. They'll arrive, and the skiff will be waiting — with the first mate and Beck aboard.

"I'll go too," I say.

"What now?" Beck says at the same time Declan says, "No."

"I'll go," I say. I look back through the lenses, then pass them to him. "Have you looked at that place?"

"Yes, of course. It's dangerous, and the chop is severe. We need trained mariners out there."

I shrug. "I'm a trained mariner. I can handle it."

"Arden, this isn't a joke."

"Do I sound like I'm joking?" I ask, looking him square in the eye.

"This is dangerous."

"Yes, it is. And these women will be doing the journey. They're going to arrive, hungry and tired, and they're going to find two *men* waiting for them with a meager boat," I say. "I shouldn't ask them to do something I wouldn't do."

Declan pinches the bridge of his nose. "I'm not going to talk you down from this, am I?"

"No." He sighs and kisses my knuckles again. Beck looks away. I don't know why I notice.

"Don't be reckless," he says. I kiss his cheek.

"I promise."

And that's how I end up throwing up over the side of the skiff ten knots from the ship.

"Easy there, girl," the first mate says as he tries to steer the ship into the side of another seven foot wave. The water splashes, and the fishy smell is almost too much.

Beck leans in close enough so that only I can hear. "Come on, Capo, you've faced worse than this."

"Don't call me that," I hiss.

"I'll call you what fits," he says, his voice a little stiff.

"Right back atcha," I say.

"What's that supposed to mean?"

"It means, I'm going to start calling you Donkey Face."

"Oh, ouch," he deadpans. "You've done me in with that one."

"I don't know why, Donkey Face."

"Will you two stop flirting and pay attention?" the first mate says, just as another wave splashes into the side of the skiff. My face heats, even as I realize that we're much closer to the shore now and about to hit the breakers. Beck is suddenly fixated on the shoreline, his expression hard. It's almost as if he was trying to distract me until we could reach safer waters.

The first caravan of women is waiting for us, and I climb out of the skiff and onto the pier. As promised, Zerah is there with them. She looks tense but ready.

"How did it go?"

"It was touch and go at times, but we're here." She nods to the women as Beck and the first mate help them aboard.

The skiff can fit ten, including the men, and the first mate gets ready to go.

"You're staying here?" Beck says to me, hanging on to the pier.

"That's the plan," I say.

"Be good," he says. Then they're off.

"Be good? What the hell is that supposed to mean?" I say to no one. When I look at Zerah, her head is tilted, and she looks like she's puzzling something out.

"Wasn't he at that first dinner?" she asks.

"Drunk off his gourd? Yes."

She chuckles and shakes her head. "He wasn't drunk."

"Of course he was," I say, as she keeps shaking her head. I turn into the wind to watch for the next caravan.

"What makes you so sure he was drunk?"

"He was drinking."

She scoffs. "You and I both know there's a big difference between the two."

"Don't worry, there's a twist. Siobhan paid him to get rid of me."

Zerah is quiet for a long moment, staring off into the distance.

"Well, clearly he's done a fine job of that."

Just over the horizon, I see a transport crest the hill. It looks rough and tumble, and I can't imagine it made for a comfortable ride.

"How many in that one?" I ask.

"Eight."

I nod, doing the math. This isn't what I was hoping for, but having seventeen women, even if they're not all voting eligible, is a lot. It's a big number of women who can testify as to the conditions they've experienced. It's meaningful.

"Then another seven on the third."

I look at her. "Three transports?"

"They were moved by your words. They believe you can make a difference." She holds my gaze steady, and it's humbling. "Don't squander this."

"I won't."

The caravan approaches as close as it dares, and the women file out. They look harried and afraid, but they're here. Elm follows them.

"Things got a little tense about an hour ago. I think we're okay, but I'll feel better once the last transport arrives," he says.

"Tense how?" Zerah asks.

"Mercenaries. And not the good kind."

"There's a good kind?" I ask.

"There's the kind that takes you alive, and there's the kind that takes whatever they can get." A shiver shuttles down the back of my neck.

The wind picks up, and the women huddle together. As I watch them tighten into a circle, their scarves and blankets a poor defense against the brutal wind and dust, I feel like I've already let them down. I should have thought to bring better blankets, or food, or at least hot beverages. Some little comfort to make them feel more safe.

We wait for what seems like an hour until, finally, the skiff arrives. The sky darkens, and far in the distance, dark clouds threaten. They're able to fit all the women from the second transport on the skiff, and they're about to turn back. Beck waves for me to come over. I half expect some sort of joke. But he motions for me to come close enough that only I can hear.

"We haven't seen the third flare," Beck says.

"When did you see the second?"

"On the way back with the first group."

"Elm says that they ran into a little trouble about an hour back," I say.

Beck's expression hardens, and before I can object, he motions to the first mate and climbs out of the skiff.

"What are you doing?"

"I can't leave you here."

I stare at him. He doesn't say anything for a long moment. The wind whips cold and sharp between us, and I feel shame creep in. I should've known better. Old me might've read his words to mean that he cares about me and doesn't want me to be afraid or in danger. But it's the way he says it. It's not that he won't leave me here—he *can't*.

"Right," I say, putting it together. I swallow thickly, realizing that in spite of everything, there is still part of me that was hoping there was a small part of him—of us—that was real.

But there isn't.

I nod and let out a sardonic chuckle. "You need to get paid."

"Fuck, Arden," he says, scraping his knuckles against his stubble. He turns his back on me and approaches Elm. They stand and talk with their backs to us, and I realize they both have a similar stance, their legs slightly bandied and their posture tense, as if they've gotten used to needing to split at a moment's notice.

"You sure let him have it," Zerah says. When I don't respond, she slips her hand in mine. I stare at our hands together for a long moment, at the oddness of it. Zerah, who doesn't like to be touched, is holding my hand. Right now. As if she sees something the others don't. I should tell her everything. She would understand. She wouldn't judge me. But she doesn't ask questions. And as she holds my hand, I feel her support, her strength. This woman who just traveled in a rickety caravan across a dangerous country is giving *me* support.

"Thank you," I whisper.

She doesn't look at me, simply hums in response.

Instead, we stand with our backs to the waves, taking the full brunt of the wind and the dust, facing the crest of the hills, watching for the others. Beck turns and jogs back toward us.

"We're going to go up the rise, see if we can see anything from there."

I nod, and he and Elm go. Zerah and I hold tight to each other in the frigid wind, waiting for the skiff, for news, for the girls. After what feels like far too long, as the dark clouds shift and the wind picks up to a low, steady growl, the skiff finally approaches the breakers.

"Maybe they've seen something?" I say, feeling dread edge into my bones.

"I don't think so," she says. It really does seem like it's speeding over the waves, if possible, more recklessly than before.

That's when we hear the blast.

It shakes the ground beneath our feet. We turn around and see the flames and smoke shoot into the sky. It's not that far from here, and it's definitely not a flare. We stare at the rise where Beck and Elm disappeared not twenty minutes ago, and there's no sign of them.

"Beck?" I call. There's no answer. I step closer. "Elm?" My voice is shaky. Zerah's hands are on my biceps, firm and solid. We wait, both of us holding our breath.

I smell the smoke first. It's sharp and acrid. I shouldn't be able to smell it. The wind should be blowing it away. Zerah is shaking in my arms, and her gaze is faraway. She's next to me, but she's worlds away, and I can't even begin to imagine where.

"Where are they?" I ask. She shakes her head but doesn't say anything. I stare at the horizon, waiting . . . watching . . . wishing . . .

The men crest the hill, running toward us, shouting. I can't make it out and move toward them, even as they wave their arms. Zerah tugs on my arm, but they're still yelling, and it seems important. I keep moving closer as they come back, and just as I hear the motor of the skiff, I make out the words.

"Run!" Beck yells at me. He takes my hand and tugs me back toward the pier. The skiff is still about twenty yards out, and we're helpless until it arrives. A second explosion rattles the pier and I trip, falling on my hands and knees. Strong arms wrap around my waist and pull me to my feet. Then the skiff is there. The first mate and Elm help Zerah into the skiff first, then me. Then Beck gets in, and we look up at Elm. He hesitates.

"Get in, man!" Beck yells.

Elm hesitates. Then he steps back. His decision is made.

"Elm," Zerah says, rising to her feet.

"I'll send a flare if there are survivors."

If there are survivors . . . I know, when I smelled the cloud, felt the explosion . . . but to hear it from Elm . . .

There will be no survivors. A caravan full of Nordanian women are dead. Because of me.

The men nod. As if they know what he's saying. As if they believe it is impossible that anyone would survive.

"Elm!" I shout over the noise.

"Get in the boat," Beck says.

Elm shakes his head. "I have to . . ."

Zerah just nods. She understands something I don't. Lets him go back toward the mess, toward the danger.

"Go," Elm says. Zerah motions for the first mate to leave, and I don't understand what just happened.

"Elm!" I scream. I'm leaning toward the rail as we buck into a breaker. Strong arms grab me around the waist and hoist me back into something—someone—solid, just as the railing dips dangerously close to the waves. Not that I have time to ask questions, because then the first mate and Beck turn the skiff, and we're off. It's much less rocky this direction, or maybe it's just the fact that we're terrified of whatever just happened. It's not until we're a solid twenty knots out from shore that I can see over the rise, to where the charred remains of a transport sit.

Zerah stares at it, her face numb, her eyes glassy.

"Someone killed them?" I ask. "Someone is trying to kill all of them?"

Nobody answers. Beck lowers his chin.

This is on me. This is my fault. I'm the one who set this up. Who convinced them to come. And now, seven women and their driver are dead.

CHAPTER TWENTY-FOUR

*T*he rest of the ride back to the ship is quiet and wet. A storm has started blowing in, and the chop is foamy. My feet are wet and cold, my hands are stiff with the chill as they grip onto the edge of the skiff, but I don't dare let go. When I turn my head to look back, I swear I can smell the burning fuel and the blistering skin. As long as I look ahead, all I smell is brine and seaweed.

Zerah climbs the ladder first, and it takes her a few minutes to find purchase before she ascends in earnest. I'm barely aware of it. Not the moment she nearly slips, and not the moment she reaches the zenith and boards the ship.

"Arden," the first mate says, nodding at the ladder. I've done this before. Though usually only on the way down. That first time was terrifying, in the midst of the storm, watching Kern get caught and then dive into the churning seawater. I wonder where he and Beck's crew are now.

I approach the ladder with more confidence this time and grip it. My hand slips on the wet rope immediately, a burn carving into my palm. A warm, calloused hand folds around mine, squeezing onto the rope. I look up and meet

Beck's gaze. This close to the water, his eyes so green it's cruel.

"Breathe, Capo," he whispers. I do as he says, and only once I've taken three good breaths does he let go. Then he guides me onto the ladder. His hand stays on my back until he can't reach any further.

I climb the ladder faster than I should be able to. By the time I'm at the top, Declan is already there and the captain and three other sailors are heaving ropes over the side to hoist the skiff. Declan hugs me tight. I don't fight it.

"I saw that explosion and . . ." He doesn't finish the thought he whispers into my hair. I don't respond. The wind whips across the deck, and he turns so that his back takes the brunt of it.

"Let's get the ladies inside," Beck calls from the top of the ladder. The first mate is already up, and they're securing the exit as the others hoist the skiff on board. I look for Zerah, and she's shivering.

"Zerah," I call, and Declan lets me go to her. I show her the way inside and lead her up to my room.

"Meredith!" I call as soon as we're inside. "We need warm clothes."

"I'm coming," she calls back.

"I can only imagine what your skin looks like after —" Neve stops in her tracks. She looks from me to Zerah and back again. Then back at Zerah.

"Neve," Zerah exhales. My chest expands at the way she says it. And then again at the way Neve's bottom lip quivers in the lamplight. It's all I can do to let go of Zerah just as Neve approaches and coils her arms around her. They hold each other close, Neve not caring that Zerah is covered in dust and salt and mud. She kisses her temples and holds her closer, and when Meredith returns with blankets, I wave at her to stop.

I don't know how they know each other or what has happened between them. But I know this isn't a moment for others.

"What happened?" Declan asks. We're all on the bridge. Simone is there, as are Zerah and Neve, who hasn't left her side since she arrived. Beck is focused on the horizon, helping the captain navigate the storming seas. The dark, unholy skies have split open in our retreat, and we're thrashed by waves taller than should be possible.

"I assume there are no survivors," Simone says solemnly.

"Not with an explosion that size," Beck says.

"Elm said the second caravan hit trouble about an hour before they reached the shore. Mercenaries—the bad kind, he said," I explain.

"The bad kind?" Declan says.

"The killing kind."

"But why would someone want a transport full of our graduates dead? How are these women more valuable dead"—Declan swallows hard—"than alive?"

Nobody answers. They just look at him.

"What?" he asks.

"We've had to hide for a reason," Zerah says. Neve rubs her back.

"But who would be paying these mercenaries for an exploded truck full of dead women?" the captain asks. Simone flinches, and he mutters an apology.

I look at Declan. Beck is ignoring all of us, brow tense as he remains focused on the still darkening horizon.

"I think we all already know," Neve says with a targeted glance at Declan.

"What? You think this is Nordania?" Declan says, flustered. "No. Absolutely not. Impossible."

"A few days ago, you thought it was impossible that the graduates had been mistreated," I point out.

"That's different."

"And your mother paid men to take two different women away from you," I say. Declan's gaze flickers to Beck, but to Beck's credit, he doesn't engage.

"My mother may be many things," he says, his voice low and steady, "but she is not a murderer."

"She's also not here," Beck says. Declan lifts his eyebrows. I can't think of a time when he has ever taken Declan's side. Maybe it's just Declan's darker than usual hair, but there's something so similar about the two of them in this moment.

"What's that supposed to mean?"

"How would she have known there was a caravan of women on their way to our ship? It's not like she followed you to Ouracéu."

Declan's face drains of color. He looks toward the door. The door that is shut and devoid of the presence of a certain sweaty-foreheaded valet.

"You don't think . . ." I say.

"I don't know," Declan says, looking more troubled than ever before.

"If Alvin—"

"I'm not sure that anyone did anything."

But it makes sense. The only other person who could've done something was Elm. He knew the plan too. But the way Zerah said he was fighting for his salvation? One look at his face after that explosion—hell, when we arrived at the safe house, and I believe that. Alvin, on the other hand, has hated me ever since I met him.

"Somebody told those mercenaries to explode that

transport," the captain says. His voice is rational and mellow, and he stands at the helm, not taking his eyes off the horizon or the pounding surf. "I saw it. I stood there, not half a mile from it, and I watched it explode. Nobody was chasing them, nobody tried to stop them. It was intentional, it was targeted, and it was horrific."

We're quiet, but for the sound of the instrument panel and the pounding waves against the hull.

"Seven Nordanian women died today. Plus their driver."

I press my hand to the compass at my chest, focusing my breathing on that spot that carries warmth.

"Who was the driver?" Neve asks.

"A volunteer," Zerah says. She shakes her head, shame creasing her forehead. "I don't remember his name."

The tragedy of this death sucks the air from my lungs. I press the compass harder into my sternum. We're all standing here, dry and warm, arguing over whether Declan's mother is capable of ordering a hit, and women died. A nameless volunteer, braver than the rest of us, gave his life to help those women. To help us. All so that my bill, the one I still haven't finished writing much less polishing, has a chance at passing.

"Before, in Queensbridge," I say. Something gets caught in my throat, and I clear it. "The mercenary there said they wanted me alive. What changed between then and now? It's only been two days."

"I think," Zerah says, "you returning from Ouracéu with three cabs full of women happened. I don't think it's that hard to follow the line of logic."

Declan shuts his eyes. Pinches the bridge of his nose. Then lowers his head.

"Clem," he calls, and the door opens, revealing my favorite security guard.

"Sir?"

"I need you to take Alvin to the brig for questioning."

"Where am I supposed to sleep?" Beck asks. Declan arches an eyebrow. Beck retreats and waves him off. "You know what? Never mind. I'll figure it out."

"We need to get back to Nordania and fast," Declan says to the captain. My stomach flips. I swear Beck tenses, but then he nods at the captain, and with that, our course is set. This is what we've been working toward. This is what I've wanted. So why does it feel like I'm running with my tail between my legs?

CHAPTER TWENTY-FIVE

"The best course of action will be to go through the Mittlesee," Declan says. We're in his sitting room, and while we've paced, circled, and shifted through the space, we're still here.

"I disagree," I say.

We've been at this for at least an hour now. We both agree that we need to do whatever it takes to keep the women on board safe. But we disagree on how to do that. It's been a full day since we left the tiny port where we picked them up—where we watched some of their friends and adopted family burn to death. Because of me. I will not let it happen again. And fighting about it is keeping my mind off the guilt that threatens to suffocate me at every turn.

"They will be safer where we have control over security measures," he says.

"Forgive me if I laugh," I say with an artificially elaborate guffaw. He leans back, arms crossed.

"What, pray tell, love, was that?"

"It was my laugh."

"It sounded like you were choking on a snail."

"Why would I eat a snail?"

"Have you seriously never had snails in garlic butter before? They're divine," he says.

"I forget sometimes that we grew up very differently."

He pinches the bridge of his nose. We keep getting derailed like this. It shouldn't be a difficult decision. He should see the danger the women could find themselves in, arriving at the capital without any security in place, given the fact that mercenaries are looking for them, dead or alive. And from what we've been gathering from our intel—and from Clem's interrogation of Alvin—the preference is dead.

Alvin doesn't know who issued the edict. Though he wouldn't admit it if he did. He has to have been involved. There's just no other way. It doesn't make any sense that someone with that kind of ammunition would have been able to track them like that. There can't be.

"Arden, enough is enough. The institute is still running, and you're missing it all. The longer we're gone, the better the argument that you not be allowed to sit for the test will be."

I flinch. "Is that on the table again? I thought my option was to marry you or else?"

Now, he flinches. "Is that really how you see this going?"

I sigh and slump back into the chair where I started this conversation. I lean into my elbows on the table in his sitting room and sigh again, just for good measure.

"I don't want to fight."

"I don't either."

"But I want to vote."

"I could vote for you," he says.

"I could vote for you," I say.

He sputters and shakes his head. "Don't be absurd."

"What?" I ask.

"That doesn't make any sense."

"Why not?"

"Because I'm going to be the prime minister. I need to establish my voting record."

"And if things go the way we've planned, I'm to be your wife. Is it any less ridiculous that I rely on you to vote for me?"

He sighs and slumps into his chair. It's the same fight, in the same figure eights, over and over again.

"We need a plan for when we return."

"I agree," I say.

"You should sit for the exam," he says decisively.

"I agree."

"And then we should be married at the assembly."

It's a concession. It's not an elopement like the capital seems to want. It's public and cost-effective, and there's still an element of occasion. I should take it and run. But there's something in my chest that holds me back. I can't put a name to it, but it's as if something is clinging to my ribs, tugging and yelling and begging me to slow down.

He shifts to the chair next to me and takes my hands in his.

"We agree that we want to be together, don't we?"

I look at the way his hands engulf mine. They're soft and warm, and they feel safe. Safe is good. I look up and meet his gray eyes. They're so full of kindness. Why wouldn't I want to face that every day of my life?

"Yes," I concede. "But I don't see what the rush is?"

"It's not that it's a rush," he says. I tilt my head, and he scoffs. "Okay, some people might want to push us a little faster than we might otherwise go. But it's more about appearances at this point."

"Appearances schmappearances," I mumble.

"Arden, we have to take this seriously."

I sigh and nod. But there's an odd expression on his face. As if he knows something I don't.

"What is it? Out with it."

He sighs. "It's probably nothing. Just a gossip magazine."

"So, why did you make that face?"

"What face?"

"The squirrel face."

"I do not make a squirrel face," he says. Then he shakes his head and laughs. I smile. "There's a Swendish gossip magazine that printed a story that we were spotted entering a bedroom together and didn't emerge until morning."

I feel my cheeks heat.

"Oh."

"Right."

"Well, where did they get that information?"

"It doesn't really matter," he says.

"Of course it does. Did they see us inside the safe home? I can't believe any of these women . . . well, it doesn't add up. But that could lead us to our leak."

"It's enough that when I told you, you blushed like a child who stole candy."

My face still feels hot.

"The fact is, we have shared a bed," he says. He leans in and looks a little nervous. "And if I'm being honest, I wouldn't mind doing it again." He looks at me with a sheepish grin. I squeeze his hands to set him at ease. The truth is, I wouldn't mind it either. I slept well when we shared a bed. My mind was calm. I don't know what would have happened if we hadn't been interrupted in the morning. We might have kissed more. We might have crossed another line, though I don't think it would have come to that, to be honest.

"Okay, so what then? If it's out there, it's out there, and we can't avoid it in Nordania."

"Then we go back, and we have a plan in place to get married after the assembly. And in the meantime"—he holds up a hand as if anticipating that I'm going to argue with him, which I want to—"while you're studying and taking the exam, we spend the rest of our time together, courting the old guard. If they can meet you and hear you out, they'll find it impossible not to respect what you're trying to do. Maybe you can even win some of them over."

"Or," I say, raising my hand in the same way he did, "hear me out. We don't do that, and instead, we round up a few more Embers and take our time going back, keeping everyone safe on the way?"

He looks frustrated.

I know I look frustrated.

There's a knock at the door. Clem steps inside. He takes one look at us and steps back out.

"Clem," Declan calls. Clem returns, but only his head. He literally sticks it in the open door space and looks at us as if he'd rather be anywhere else.

"Sir?"

"Tell the captain to route us for Nordania via the Mittlesee."

My chest tightens, and I curl my hands into fists on the tabletop.

"Yes, sir," he says.

"So, that's it?" I say.

"I would rather have your support, but at the end of the day, it's on me to make these kinds of decisions. I believe that everyone will remain safest if we return to Nordania as directly as possible."

"I thought you were going to be a different kind of leader," I say. I know it's a low blow. He stiffens—his shoulders, his forehead, his mouth tighten.

"I have listened," he says. Folding his hands on the table, he leans closer. "I have listened, and I have considered, and I have given you far more leeway to find the other women than I think anyone previously in my position would have."

"So, you coddled me?"

"No, not at all. I listened, and I believe in what you're doing. But enough is enough. We have to do the safest thing."

"Sailing through the Mittlesee?" I say. "Really? You want to talk about safety, and you're going to let that buffoon take us through the Mittlesee? Why not admit what it's really about? Keeping up appearances."

"Arden," he says, pinching his nose. Then he pauses and looks up. "Clem? Is there more?"

"Yes, sir," he says. Then he passes a folded paper to Declan. He reads the paper, poker-faced, and doesn't indicate what it's about. Is this a glimpse of how our future will look? The Arden at the institute might have been okay with this, but now? Being consulted for my opinion, and then summarily ignored when it's inconvenient? I don't have the patience for whatever this is.

"I'll leave you to it then," I say. "Why don't you let me know what you've decided I should do tomorrow so I know how to dress."

I'm out the door before anyone can stop me.

CHAPTER TWENTY-SIX

I didn't actually mean it when I told Declan to let me know what we'd be doing next. But that's what happens.

Actually, what happens is Meredith arrives with a navy ball gown, and Neve is behind her with a makeup kit. I can't think of the last time I saw Neve. She and Zerah have kept to themselves since Zerah arrived, and I haven't had a moment to ask a question edgewise, but it turns out, there's not much point in asking the questions, because Neve doesn't share very much.

Apparently, Zerah and William Whitey were the first people she met in Osterstan. They became friends. They helped each other through their complicated marriages. And that's all she'll say.

They powder and prod and squeeze me into place until I look almost unrecognizable.

Then a bag is packed—not just for me, for Neve as well. But no more details. Just that I'm to be ready by tea time. Which is impossible to tell these days, as the sun has started dipping below the horizon earlier and earlier each day.

That, and we're winding through the Mittlesee like a drunk duck. Or perhaps a drunk duck is in charge of the navigation. I keep losing track of south and north. If not for my compass, I'd have no idea that we've been on a southern trajectory. Which doesn't quite align with Declan's plans to return to Nordania as fast as possible.

There's a knock at the door that sounds like a beer barrel polka, and I can't take it any more. I yank the door open and gasp. Beck is standing there, dressed in a suit, neatly shaven. I've never seen him neatly shaven. His jaw is crooked, his nose is wonky, his lips are chapped . . . and despite it all, he looks unfairly handsome. His eyes burn as he takes me in, and then a cough behind me seems to nudge him out of whatever stupor he'd been caught in.

"I'm your tail tonight."

"You're my *what*?" My cheeks flush hot.

He grins. "I thought you'd like that."

"What is happening? Where are we?"

He frowns at this. "Isn't this the Orange Top Circus Galavant? I could have sworn they'd have told you. So odd they didn't —"

"Beck," I snap. He flinches.

"We're in Sudersberg. State dinner, apparently."

My chest tightens, and I feel a little lightheaded. Then I feel the panic pour in. This is a big deal. Why wouldn't Declan have told me himself?

Then it clicks.

"Ah," I say, looking over my shoulder at Meredith. "If he'd told me what was going on, then he'd have to admit that we're not going straight back to Nordania."

"He didn't tell you?" Meredith asks. "I thought you knew. Why else would we have put you in that dress — those jewels?"

Neve looks amused as she exits the changing room in a

simple black sheath. She looks like she could attend a state dinner or rob a museum.

"You knew too?" I ask her.

She shrugs. "I didn't know you didn't. You're going to a state dinner. And staying the night."

I gasp, looking at the bags.

"Then what's he doing?" I ask, nodding at Beck.

"I'm your tail for the night." He grins.

"Will you stop saying that?" I snap.

"He's your security detail."

"How does that make any sense?" I ask.

"They don't know who he is. And wouldn't the future wife of the prime minister have her own security detail? I mean, if it was legit . . ."

"Is this some kind of a joke?"

"I had the same thought," he mumbles.

I push out the door past him. I walk down the hallway, realizing we must be in port, as it's not rocking at all. When I reach Declan's rooms, I don't even bother to knock.

"What's this about a state dinner?" I ask. Declan is buttoning his shirt, a sliver of his tanned chest still visible.

"Clem? Are you just letting anyone in here?" Declan says. His tone is biting. I immediately feel a presence at my back, and when I look, I see Beck standing there, taller and sturdier than before. Declan's gaze flickers to Beck, and a frown settles into his forehead.

"Ah, right. Stand down, man," Declan says, flicking his hand at Beck. For some reason, this careless motion angers me more than anything. But he turns quickly, and mumbles an apology.

"Why didn't you tell me about this?"

"I figured you'd be pleased, and that someone would mention it while you were putting on my grandmother's jewelry."

I touch the three-stranded sapphire necklace around my neck, which is layered over my compass pendant, having not realized what it was. These jewels are incredibly precious and are practically national emblems as much as the four-pointed star is.

"Nobody did," I say.

He sighs and gives up on the bow tie he's currently strangling himself with. "I'm sorry," he says. "I only found out about it a few hours ago. They asked my parents, and when my parents mentioned that we were so close—"

"So close to Sudersberg? Were we actually 'so close' to Sudersberg?"

"Closer than them, anyway," he says, then continues. "They agreed that we should attend in their stead. *We*. As in you would be recognized as a representative of the state."

He approaches, and his meaning sinks in.

"I thought this would be a step in the right direction," he says, but frowns at my expression. "But I can see that I've misjudged you yet again. Can we just . . . get through the night? We'll stay in separate rooms. It'll be good for publicity. Put those rumors to rest so that it won't muddy our reputations any more than they already have been."

"What does that mean?" I say, recoiling at his tone.

He exhales and pinches the bridge over his nose.

"Arden, it's been a long day. I don't have the energy to fight with you over semantics."

"I'm full of energy," Beck says cheerfully.

Declan glares at Beck, and I'm suddenly feeling like I'm in Beck's corner for the first time in a long time.

"Can I meet you on the deck?" he asks.

"Fine," I say.

Neve and Beck follow me to the deck, and we wait, tense and silent. The breeze is chilly, but not even the cold air can stifle the fire inside me. I don't know what is going on here, but I don't like it. It feels off, and the fact that Beck is following me and Declan and I are fighting doesn't help things. I just need to get through this night, and then we can figure it out tomorrow. One step at a time. As long as I take one step at a time, what's the worst that can happen?

CHAPTER TWENTY-SEVEN

*J*uulstern is a sparkling port city along the Brandeissland border with Sudersberg. Thankfully, they aren't nearly as attached to tea as some other places in the country. Perhaps it's their location along the Mittlesee and the Brandeiss border that gives it more of a cosmopolitan feel.

The dinner isn't just a lineup of Sudersberg's greatest hits. It of course features a litany of spices that I still can't name, and ends with their piece de resistance: the Sudersbergian *riisi* pie. It's an even better version of the one I first sampled in the capital kitchen months ago, a pastry filled with dates, milky sweet rice, and cinnamon.

By the time the meal is over, I'm stuffed and exhausted. Because not only have I eaten everything placed before me for fear of offending someone, but Declan hasn't spoken a word to me the entire meal.

I would break the awkwardness between us, but I don't know how. Also, he's the one in the wrong. I thought we were going to be equal partners in this relationship. But he just pulled the trump card, and even though we're not in

Nordania yet, that's where we're headed. Regardless of what I think.

As glasses of a thick, syrupy liqueur are poured and passed around, he laughs, mid-conversation with the man to his right. I pretend to listen in, as if I might contribute anything. The thing that maybe I should find odd in this whole night is that nobody has noticed that he's not talking to me. Or that we're not in sync. They invited us here, to a state dinner, as an official representation of Nordania. They've recognized me as his partner. And yet nobody has made an attempt to talk to me, or to ask about us or our plans. I'd been dreading talking about wedding plans, but it hasn't been an issue. Nobody cares.

"A toast!" Harold Herrsmith lifts a goblet at the head of the table. He's the governor of this province, and our host for the evening. I suppose I would have expected the governor to be more centrally situated, like Capital City is in Nordania. But this is the most important part of the province because of trade, so this is where the governor's seat is.

"To our esteemed guests for the evening." He directs his glass toward me and Declan. I lift the glass, prepared to pretend to sip when the time is right. "Thank you for making us a part of your procession. We wish nothing but the best for your future. And the future of our two great nations. May we both find ourselves aflame with good fortune and prosperity."

Declan nods, and then leans in to kiss my cheek. It feels so forced, but I have learned enough to know I'm supposed to smile demurely. So I do that, but honestly? I'm confused. It's clear that ours is not his natural language, but it's such an odd turn of phrase.

"And to you," Declan says, lifting his glass. "Thank you for extending your hospitality. I can't remember the last time I ate so well or was greeted with such warmth. We," he corrects as he reaches for my hand and presses my knuckles to his lips. Cold ripples down my arm, and I duck my head, feigning overwhelm. In reality, I feel tears pricking at my eyes. Which is ridiculous and embarrassing. I never wanted any of this in the first place, but over the past weeks, I thought that at least some of what we had between us was genuine. The glances, the stolen kisses, the sweet touches? Apparently, that meant more to me than I realized. Because here he is, using this little act of affection for his own purpose. And it's worked all too well.

"We are honored to be here and are grateful that this could be our first official state dinner as representatives of Nordania."

Glasses clink, and I feign taking a sip. I lick my lips, and my cheeks pucker at the cloying bitterness of the dessert wine.

"And now," Harold says, rising from his chair and extending his hand to his wife, a dour woman with a flat smile, "won't you be so kind as to join us for the first dance of the evening?"

Declan grins that politician's grin and rises. He takes my hand, and I go with him to the dance floor, nearly tripping over the layers of sheer navy fabric that make up my skirt. I'm reminded of that first dinner at the institute, when he danced with Fiona. Was that all it was between them as well?

Declan takes my waist and my hand, and when the music begins, he leads. It's a light, lilting waltz that I recognize from our lessons on Sudersbergian culture. It's not their national anthem, but it may as well be. It's a lovely song about travelers or tea or something like that. I can't remember, but as Declan holds me through the dance, I feel his gaze getting more and more intense.

"What?" I ask.

"Are you giving me the silent treatment?"

"Me?" I say, a little surprised. "You haven't said a word to me all night."

"I thought you wanted some space," he says, stepping back and leading me in a circle around him like I'm sure he's been taught to do since he was old enough to walk. When I return to his hold, he's frowning.

"I would have said something—"

"I just assumed that if you wanted me to speak to you, you would have told me. You're so good at that, after all," I say with what I hope looks like a demure smile to those not within earshot. He stiffens, then spins me. His movements are just as smooth as ever, but his expression is anything but.

"Is this how it's going to be?"

"I don't know what you're talking about."

"Someone has to be the adult here," he says, still smiling through gritted teeth.

"And apparently, it was never going to be me."

"Of course not, not when you're still unwilling to make adult decisions about our future."

"So this is my fault? I'm hesitant to marry someone who is technically still dating other women? And that makes me immature?"

"You knew what this was when you applied."

"I never applied," I say tersely. As if he needs reminding.

"I don't want to do this, not here." He tucks a hair behind my ear.

"Then when? When would be most convenient to give input on our relationship?"

"Arden . . ."

"Follow up question: when can I expect you to throw

out my input and make a unilateral decision? Will I receive prior notification?"

He steps back, and the room is silent. I realize the dance has ended. He bows, and I realize I'm meant to curtsy. There is applause, and then the dance floor fills with other couples eager to join us. I smile as I've been trained to do, and then, with another small bow, I join Declan, the governor, and his wife in motioning for everyone to join us. Declan resumes his hold on me and pulls me a little closer.

To anyone on the outside, listening to the romantic, slow song that has just started, we might look like a couple in love. But I know this is so we can keep our voices down.

"You know I've made my decision. You have to stop crucifying me for something out of my control."

"You're right," I say. "But are you really asking me to have empathy for your lack of control when you're actively taking mine from me?"

"Is that really what you think is happening here? That I'm just, what? Oppressing you? Willy nilly?"

"Willy nilly?" I say, with a laugh.

"Oh, of course. That's the part you take issue with, and then you poke fun at me because I'm not as quick and witty as some other men who have given you everything you want—except, oh right. He gave you what you wanted because my mom paid him.

"Pardon me, if I don't feel too bad about making decisions that impact the safety of my crew, my citizens, and the women you've insisted we pick up and carry with us as chattel."

I recoil, and there's no masking it. Murmurs fill the space around us, and he smiles and presses a kiss to my temple, as if that will fix it. This is not okay. Not in the least. But I don't want to make a scene. I don't want everyone staring at me, and I don't want to read about our "lovers' tiff" in the Sudersbergian newspapers tomorrow.

"Chattel?" I hiss. "Is that how you see them?"

His face is pink. "Of course not. It seems like you do, though. It doesn't matter to you who they are, or how they're living on board. It's about numbers to you. Is that true? Is that what it seems like?"

"You can't be serious."

"Besides Simone, can you even tell me the names of three of those women? Where they're from? What they love in life?"

"That's not fair," I say. People are staring. Declan continues spinning us around the dance floor. "I didn't spend my childhood living with them, keeping them as pets."

"There you go again, referring to them as animals." He tsks his tongue, and it's so upsetting, so infuriating, I want to slap him. "And that's why one of us needs to be the adult here. I'm making the hard decisions. Would I like to find all the graduates that are in harm's way? Yes. Of course I would. Is it safe or prudent to do that? Right now? Absolutely not."

"Then when?" I say between gritted teeth.

"I don't know."

"That's the easy way out."

"That's the truth. And it takes maturity to admit when you don't know something."

"Oh, would you like a pat on the back? Because I'll give you —"

A bell rings. Then another. And another and another until the room is filled with the tinkling of tiny bells. I look around and realize all the people in the hall are holding tiny little bells. Declan drops his head to my shoulder and lets out a mirthless laugh.

"What's this?" I ask.

"Sudersbergian tradition," he mumbles.

"Great explanation."

He lifts his head and cups my cheeks with both hands. I stiffen.

"They want us to kiss."

"What?"

"Engaged couples are celebrated with the tinkling of bells, and it's said that if they're really in love, if their love is true, they'll kiss through the end of the last tinkling bell, unaware of when it's done, because they're so in love with each other."

"You've got to be kidd—"

But I don't get to finish my question, because his mouth is on mine, and he's holding my face to his. Slowly, people start cheering, clapping, and whistling. It makes it harder to hear the bells. But they're still there.

Then, Declan slips his fingers into my hair. He palms the back of my head, tilts my neck so that I gasp. His tongue slips between my lips, tasting mine, and when I try to pull away, he holds me in place. His other hand is coiled around my back, holding me tight to him. He's kissing me, tongue in my mouth, and I can taste the bitterness of the liqueur that he drank and the salt from his dinner and something else that makes me feel queasy.

I tug at his hair, to try to get him to ease off, but that makes people cheer louder. It's too much. He's all over me, and he's holding me too tight, and I can't breathe. I can't breathe. I gag, and I can't—

"Give her some room to breathe, sir," Harold says, clapping Declan on the back. Declan, perhaps in surprise, releases me. I'm shaky, and everyone laughs it off. It's as if they think I enjoyed that kiss. My body trembles, my lips buzz, and I can taste sour bile on the back of my tongue.

Declan did that. Sweet, kind Declan, who I thought would never hurt me. It was a kiss. It was only a kiss. But I didn't want it. He did it because it suited him, but he humiliated me. I didn't want him to hold me in place and put his tongue in my mouth—I wanted him to stop. He had to know. I pushed. I tried—he didn't stop. He didn't stop, he didn't stop, he—

"This love is real and true," Harold declares, clapping Declan on the back again. Then someone mumbles something about getting me some water, and Declan guides me to a table. I pick up the water and I drink it. When I look up, I see Neve and Beck standing in the corner. Neve's expression is unreadable. Beck's eyes are hard, his jaw like granite.

"I need to go," I whisper. Declan's face falls, and then turns stony.

"I'll walk you."

"It's fine. I need air."

"I can take you."

"Declan, please. I—"

"I'll escort you both," Beck says. I don't know when he arrived, but Neve is right behind him.

"We don't need an escort," Declan says.

"I believe you do," Beck says, tapping the guard pin on his lapel, as if goading him. "Sir."

Declan's jaw feathers, and then he nods. He makes our apologies, and then we're on our way.

I'm hardly even paying attention to where we are as we weave through the fortress turned governor's mansion. The halls echo with the clack of our shoes, and finally, we end up in a hall that ends in a doorway.

"If you'll wait here for a moment," Declan says, nodding to the hall.

"If you think I'm leaving you alone with her right now, you're mad," Beck says, his voice razor sharp.

"After the local tradition? I'll beg you to watch your tone and remember who you're dealing with."

"Oh, I know who I'm dealing with, sonny. And you should know who *you're* dealing with." Beck steps closer, and even though he's shorter than Declan by a few inches, you'd never know it. An unspoken threat passes between them. A cough from down the hall startles us, and after a tense moment, Declan lifts his palms in surrender.

"Fine. Whatever."

Beck opens the door, and I find that we've ended up in a round bedroom. There is one large set of windows on the opposite side that open to a balcony. It looks as though this must be one of the turrets.

"This is for me?" My mouth feels numb. I tuck my hands into my skirt to hide the shaking.

"Yes," Declan says. "As much as they accept us as a couple, they thought it best to split us. I agreed."

"I'm sure you did," Beck mumbles.

"What is your problem?" Declan turns on Beck.

"I have so many. Would you like an alphabetical list? Because you know, guys like me, I always struggled with that elemeno-p section . . . or I could just chuck them out there?" He scratches the side of his nose with his middle finger.

"Spit it out. I don't have all night," Declan hisses, pinching the bridge of his nose.

"That little stunt downstairs. I have a problem with it."

"Really?" Declan says, looking amused and irritated. "You have a problem with the local tradition? Or is it that you have a problem with me kissing my fiancée?"

"Nah, junior, you can kiss your fiancée however you

want. As long as she likes it. I have a problem with the fact that she didn't like it."

Declan's complexion blazes red. "You've overstepped."

"I don't think I have," he says. "She looked like she wanted you to stop."

"I don't think you have the first clue what she wants."

Beck grins, but there's no joy. He steps closer.

"Anyone with two eyes could see that. Everyone, in fact. And you're no dummy. Not like me and my elemeno-ps. Which leads me to think that you're either blind or the worst kind of man."

Declan blazes, stepping closer. "I think it's time for you to leave."

"Or what?"

"Oh, my god, just whip them out and get it over with," Neve mumbles. I didn't realize she'd followed us. Judging by the expression on Declan and Beck's faces, neither did they. I step between them.

"Enough," I yell. A shiver rushes through me, and I realize I've pressed one hand to each man's chest. I try not to think too hard about which direction that shiver came from.

"That's what she said on the dance floor," Beck says.

"Will you stop already?" I ask. "I can handle myself."

"Clearly not."

I narrow my eyes at Beck, and then turn on Declan.

"And you," I say.

"Couldn't this wait until we have some privacy?" he says, keeping his voice low, as if Neve and Beck don't already know all of our dirty laundry.

"We have no privacy," I say. "But the next time you want to use our 'love' as an example in some sort of pissing contest I'm not aware of, I'd appreciate it if you'd ask my permission." I'm shaking. I keep my face hard and angry. If I'm shaking with anger, then I stay in control.

"See what I mean, man?" Beck says with a shit-eating grin. "Didn't like it. I could give you a few tips —"

I don't think. I swing my fist, and I hear the crack more than feel the connection. Beck doesn't fall over, but blood drips down his mouth. The bruise around his nose seeps in fast.

"You broke my nose?" he mumbles. Declan laughs. Neve nods, appraising.

"And you?" I turn on Declan, whose face quickly pales in surprise. "Out."

CHAPTER TWENTY-EIGHT

$\mathcal{N}$eve is quiet as she helps me strip the layers of makeup and hair pins and under layers meant to make me passable as Declan's other half. She wordlessly ices my knuckles, and then presses a pack of ice to my sternum. I gasp in a breath, and it slows my breathing. Not that I have much to say, but she doesn't let out so much as a disapproving grunt. I've never known Neve to be quiet about anything.

"What?" I finally ask.

"What?" she repeats.

"You've been quiet."

"So?"

"You're never quiet."

"I don't have anything to say."

"Since when?"

She shrugs and takes the binder that kept my waist pinched into the perfect proportions to a standing chest that was unloaded sometime between when I arrived and now.

"Ever since Zerah arrived, you've been—"

"This has nothing to do with Zerah," she says. But even

the way she says Zerah's name is different. There's something there she's not telling me.

I can see it. I can see how someone like Zerah, tough and soft in equal spades, would be a match for Neve.

"What is going on between you and Zerah?" I ask. She stills, and studies me for a long moment. Then continues with her ministrations.

"We're not talking about this."

"Why not?"

"Because it's my private business."

"Fine. That is fine. But then, don't hound me about my private life like it's everyone's business."

"It's not your private business. It's everyone's business," she snaps. "You gave up that right the second you applied to the institute."

"*I* didn't apply," I snap. "You know that I didn't apply. CJ did it as a—"

"As a joke," she finishes. "Well, it wasn't a joke to me."

"Do you want to trade positions? Because I'm pretty sure this getup would look better on you, anyway."

"Of course not," she snaps. "But you've made your bed. Now, you have to lie in it."

A wash of exhaustion fills my veins. "Why do people say that? I would love to lie in my bed right now."

"And as for Beck," she says as she lowers a nightgown over my head and tugs a little too hard.

"What about Beck?" I challenge, feeling the anger seep back in. She quirks an eyebrow.

"You know *what* about Beck," she says.

"I don't think I do," I mumble. She glares at me, and I sigh. I haven't talked to anyone about him. And not talking hasn't made it any easier. "You weren't here for all of this, but I thought he was . . . my friend."

"Oh, I know what you thought of him," she says. "Those walls at Irina's aren't nearly as thick as you think."

A blush fills my cheeks.

"It doesn't matter. It wasn't real. I might've thought it was, but it wasn't. It wasn't . . . anything. So, there's nothing to talk about."

Neve's expression softens. "You have to forget about him."

"I don't know what you're talking about."

"Stop the bullshit, Arden," she snaps. And her eyes are blazing. She's pissed.

"What are you so upset about?"

"You're unfocused and lazy. You have this opportunity in your lap, literally, and you're doing nothing about it. You're squandering it, and you're dragging him down with you."

"What in the world are you talking about? He used me! He *used*—" My voice cracks. "He literally used me to make money. How the hell am I bringing him down?"

"You know what you're doing."

"Oh my god, Neve. Could you be any more cryptic?"

"Declan loves you. That's the goal. You marry him, you get to write your own ticket. Your own future. Not just that, but you have the power to rewrite the future of all those women on that boat. The girls growing up like we did? You could save them. And instead, you're out there sulking in half a million dollars of sapphires and punching a man who just defended you."

She shakes her head as if she's disgusted. As if she has some sort of attachment to Beck. Some kind of friendship. A flash of something hot and ugly washes through me.

"What do you know about him?" I ask.

"I know you're going to be the death of him."

Her words—Irina's words—hit me like a ton of bricks.

"Why is he still here?" I ask.

"Because he's a prisoner," she says.

"He could leave. Now. He could have left at the port in Swendenland. He could have—"

"But he didn't," she snaps. "He could have, but he didn't. Doesn't that tell you everything you need to know?"

I stand there, nearly naked, in nothing but a nightgown.

"Declan isn't stupid," she says, stepping closer. She pushes me down to sit on the bed and starts braiding my hair. She's not gentle. "He can see that you're using him."

"I'm not using him."

"You are. At least have the integrity to be honest about it."

She yanks too hard, and I protest, but she continues as if my scalp means nothing to her.

"I don't mean to," I say. My throat is raw. I feel dizzy and breathless from this whiplash.

"Yes, you do. You have plans. You have a mandate. You're doing the big, bad thing, and he supports you. Hell, Arden, he's supporting you *despite* his family and the rest of the country telling him not to. He's doing it because it's the right thing to do. And then he makes a decision that you don't like, and you, what? Pout? During a state dinner? What the hell is wrong with you?"

"Ow!" I squeal as she tugs too hard on my hair. She doesn't apologize.

"Do you know how many people would kill to be in your shoes?"

"They're welcome to them," I say.

"Stop being a child," she says, tying off the first braid. "If you want to play in the adult sandbox, then it's time to put on your big girl panties and braid your own damn hair."

And with that, she leaves.

I sit on the edge of my bed, twisting the other half of my hair into a braid with shaky hands before I realize what just happened. I've literally alienated myself. Have I been a child? Is Neve right? Do I need to grow up?

Declan was wrong tonight. He shouldn't have forced himself on me like that. Does he know that? I don't even know. Because I didn't talk to him about it. Instead, I punched Beck.

What is wrong with me?

I had to grow up so fast. Too fast. And now, I've let people take care of me, baby me. I gave Declan the silent treatment during a state dinner. I didn't attempt to talk to anyone else, didn't try to be a good representative of Nordania. I even let Beck and Neve fight my battles tonight.

I'm pacing the room, and I can't calm down. I can't remember the last time I was this agitated. Back at the institute? On Beck's ship? The air feels thin, and it's hard to take a full breath. It's dry and crackly as it goes into my nose and burns down into my lungs. Where does Neve get off telling me to stop using Declan? We had an agreement, or so I thought. And that stuff about Beck? She couldn't be more wrong.

Okay, so it is weird that he didn't leave in Swendenland, but it's not that complicated. He'd be no better off than his brother Ammon: on the run and in hiding. He took the money from Siobhan to seduce me. That's the cold hard fact. It's so simple. So why is it suddenly so hard to breathe?

I'm so panicked, so upset, that it takes me far too long to realize it's not the air that's hard to breathe.

It's the smoke.

CHAPTER TWENTY-NINE

*I*t's spilling beneath the door in thick, dark wisps. I run to the balcony and throw open the glass doors. It's bone cold outside, and it does nothing to spark a chill in the room. I didn't realize the room had grown so hot. When had that happened?

Maybe the smoke isn't what I think? Maybe it's just a grease fire or a snuffed candle. I cross the room and reach for the handle. As soon as I touch it, I jerk my hand back. The metal is blisteringly hot. The skin on my palm is already bright red.

I'm stuck. This room is literally at the end of a long hall on the top of this turret. It's like a fairy story: I'm stuck at the top of the tallest tower with nowhere to go but down. But there is no handsome prince to rescue me.

I go back to the balcony and look outside. The smoke pours out from the room around me, but the cold night air is a blessing to my starved lungs. The perch juts out over the cliffs, ever so slightly, to the frothy, angry waves below. The chill finally reaches me. I wrap my arms around myself, and when I turn to go back into the room, it's unrecognizable. It's filled with black, angry smoke. I grab a robe from the standing wardrobe and wrap it tight around my body. Then I go back to the balcony and look down.

It's a long way down. And that's assuming I can dodge the rocky outcropping at the top of the cliff. I look left and right. The stone walls are smooth and slick, as if designed to avoid someone climbing them. That's probably exactly what they were designed for. To keep people out. But in this case, it's keeping me in.

Where is the port from here? Why can't I see it? That's when I realize I'm in the southwestern tower, and the port is on the northeastern side of town. If I were able to send up some sort of flare, I doubt anyone on the ship would even see it.

My options are to choke to death on smoke, wait for the fire to reach me and burn me to death, or wait out here and possibly freeze to death, while also choking on smoke. Because there's no way I would survive a fall. So, it's come to this. My life — pitiful though it may be — has come to this? My eyes fill with tears, though maybe it's just the sting from the smoke. Nonetheless, I let myself feel the sadness. I feel the heave of regret — that I couldn't do more for the Embers, that I couldn't make things better for Carla or Zerah. That I couldn't make things up to Neve. That I left things on such a sour note with Declan. And Beck . . . I don't know what to think. But I think of him.

With a final, coughing shiver, I shut the glass doors and watch as they blacken over with smoke. The smoke starts to spill out through the spaces between the glass and the hinges. My eyes burn, and I shiver in the battering cold wind. I turn around and look down again. It's at least seven stories up from the surface of the water. Water that can't be much more than about thirty-five degrees. A whimper escapes my lips, and I hug myself tight. But no more tears slip from my dry, burning eyes. All there is to do now is wait.

Behind me, I hear a crack and a crash. The fire must be reaching the ceiling beams overhead. It reminds me of the barn fire in Beck's hometown. The moment that overhead beam came crashing down, and my heart nearly gave out, afraid I wouldn't get that poor little girl out of there. If those supports are giving out, what does that mean about the balcony supports? My stomach lurches, and I feel like I might be sick as I turn back to the water. It might be my best chance. My only chance.

A rattling snaps me out of my decision-making process.

Someone is at the door.

The smoke is so thick I can't see through the glass. I turn the handle, but the doors are stuck. From the heat? I jerk and push at them, and the other person pulls, and finally, they break free. The doors open, the smoke clears, and a large man stumbles through, coughing and half folded over the balcony ledge. He kicks the door behind him, but it's too much against the smoke and the heat. The glass shatters. I wince, and the distraction makes it so I almost don't realize who it is.

"What are you doing out here?" Beck asks.

The smoke clouds my vision and fills my lungs, and I cough. Hard. He pats my back, and I lean over the stone railing toward the cleaner air. We're both folded over the ledge, hacking against the heat at our backs. And he just ran through fire to get here.

"What are *you* doing out here?"

"Nice night for a view?" he asks.

"Oh, you know me. I can't resist an ocean view," I say.

"Yeah," he says, his pats turning into slow circles on my back. "You okay?"

My throat clears, and I nod. "What are you doing? How did you—"

"I know you like your questions and all, but right now, we need to go."

"Right," I say, turning toward the room. It's like a wall of smoke and flame, the smell of the fabric, the stains on the furniture, mixing to create a chemical-tinged piquant odor. I have no idea how he made it through that room, much less that hallway, but it's not passable now. He tugs on my elbow.

"Not that way."

"Then what—" I look at him, then look at where he's looking. Down. As in, way down where I had just been picturing my head cracking on the rocks. "No. No, there's no—"

"It's the only way."

He coughs and something occurs to me.

"Where were you?"

"Not the time for questions, sweetheart."

"But you—"

"Arden," he says, taking my face in his hands. "I will answer your questions later. I promise. But right now, there's a rather serious fire, and it doesn't care that you're naturally curious. I need you to forget that I've been an unforgivable butthead and take my hand and jump with me."

"Jump?" My voice comes out like a squeak. He hoists himself up on the stone wall with far more balance and confidence than anyone should feel standing on a ten-inch ledge. He turns and reaches his hand down. His eyes flare gold with determination.

"Come on, Capo. You can do this."

Something swells in my chest. Just then, something cracks and pops behind me, and with a massive puff of black smoke, it gets hotter. I could take my chances waiting here. I could try to go back inside and hope someone else comes to my rescue. But for some reason I don't understand, I put my hand in his.

I swear something shifts in his expression. He tugs me up onto the railing in one smooth movement. It's so smooth that I almost miss the railing completely, and my foot slips. He wraps an arm around my waist and pulls me into his side.

"Not yet," he says. Then he steps away from me, just slightly, but grips my hand. Then he changes the grip. He threads his fingers between mine. I look at our hands, then up at him. He's looking at me. Just looking.

"Do you trust me?" he asks.

I shake my head. "No."

He nods.

"Can you trust that I don't want to die right now?"

Something aches in my chest.

"Yes."

He nods again.

"On three." I wait, looking down. "Jump as far forward as you can. Don't try to go up. Don't lean forward. Keep your feet down and push forward."

I don't have anything to add to this, so I just nod. The fire behind us is getting hotter and louder. The smell of melting fabrics and paper is so strong, it stings my throat. I'm no longer cold.

"Three!" he shouts, and it catches me by surprise, so much so that I lunge forward. He doesn't let go of my hand.

We fall so fast. It feels like my heart is in my throat, and my stomach is right behind it. I kick my legs on instinct as sea spray stings my eyes. I barely register that the rocks pass in a blur—we didn't hit them. I smack against the water, sucking in a breath too late. I swallow salt water as I sink.

And then I keep sinking.

Because until that moment, I'd forgotten that I can't swim.

CHAPTER THIRTY

$\mathcal{T}$he water is so cold, it stings my limbs like a million tiny needles. I'm struggling for air in my water-soaked lungs, and I can't stop myself from coughing. Then I accidentally suck in more water as I sink further and further into the black.

It's so dark that I can't see anything. The saltwater burns my eyes even as I strain for a sight of something, anything. My thin nightgown and robe twist and coil around my legs, binding them tighter and tighter, pulling me deeper and deeper. But the deeper I go, the less shocking the cold. My lungs stop fighting, and it's almost peaceful beneath the waves. I shut my eyes, though I hardly feel the stinging anymore.

My arm jerks, a sharp pain in my shoulder jolting me back to reality. I look up, as if I'll suddenly have underwater night vision. My legs are numb, and so are my hands, so I barely register Beck's fingers squeezing mine. He tugs upward as my lungs burn, screaming for air. My hand breaks the surface before I do. When I finally break the frothy surface, I hear a guttural, feral screech that sends adrenaline pumping through my body. But it was me. The horrible animal sound was me sucking in air. Beck is talking, telling me something, but I can't hear over the roar of the ocean or the hammering pulse between my ears. I'm still sucking in air when another wave hits me in the face, and I take in more water. He coils an arm around my chest as I cough, choking on brine and blood. But he holds me tight to his side as he moves us through the water. I don't know where we're going. There's no beach beneath the cliffs.

My feet are the first to stop moving. Not that they're much use anyway, all coiled up in my nightgown. But he moves us alongside the waves, moving with the current. I let my head drop back on his shoulder, and he's only barely warmer than the water.

"Stay with me," he whispers. Though maybe it's not a whisper. The waves are so damn loud. I shut my eyes to block out the stinging saltwater. The only thing keeping me awake is the splash of water and the saltwater I keep coughing up. He swims, and I cough and sputter, and he says something I can sort of hear before I shut my eyes again. We do this long enough that I'm not sure how he can still be moving. When he stands, I'm not prepared for it.

He pulls me to my feet, and my knees buckle. My legs are useless in the cold, and my jaw aches with how hard my teeth chatter. As cold as it was in the water, it's somehow colder out here, where the wind is bitter and brutal. With each wave comes another breeze and another round of chills.

"You with me, Capo?" he asks, as we step into a copse of trees that all lean away from the water. In the moonlight, they look like their barks are made of broken silver and crystallized onyx.

"Yeah," I think I say between my chattering teeth. *Fuck it all.* I accidentally bite my tongue, and Beck laughs.

"Forgot you had that mouth."

"What mouth?"

"Let's get somewhere warmer," he says, nodding to the right. All I see is darkness ahead, but I'm too cold and tired to object. Walking uphill feels impossible with how stiff my limbs are, but moving through the underbrush forces some friction into them, and the burn isn't unpleasant. The gradient gets steeper, and my footing is clumsy and slippery. He helps me up the hill and into another thicket. At the base of the thicket is a tall rock wall.

"Wait here a minute," he says, once he's sure I'm not going to move from where I'm leaning. I watch as he moves further along the rocky outcropping, and then disappears into the inky blackness. A gust of wind hits, roaring through the trees like a ghoul. It's not nearly so cold here as it was along the waterfront. But it's spooky here. Seems like a good place for a death.

"Come on," he says, looping my arm over his shoulders. My hips don't move. He picks me up, swinging my legs over his arm like I weigh nothing. I have no idea when he returned, or how long he was gone.

"Where are we going?"

"There you are," he says with a little chuckle. "I wasn't sure you were really in there without the incessant questions."

"Cute," I say in at least eight syllables from my shivering. He chuckles as he carries me into the darkness. We approach a split in the wall. It's not a proper cave, but it's protected on three sides. Trees tower overhead and around in a thick barrier between the entrance and the walls above. I shudder again, and he squeezes me before setting me down.

"Stay here. I'll find some dry brush so we can warm up."

"I can help," I say through chattering teeth. He laughs.

"You'll just get it wet."

"I won't—"

"You're dripping with all that fabric. Just stay put. I'll be quick."

He scuttles around the cave and collects dozens of little bits and bobs of dry brush. And then he sits down and creates some sort of little device with a stick and a long, thin fiber from another stick. And soon enough, there's a spark of fire.

If I never saw another fire again, it would be too soon. And yet this fire might be the thing that keeps me alive.

"Take off your clothes," he says.

"What?" But it's barely audible through the chattering. He takes off his jacket and shirt at that moment, and I feel a warmth creep in.

"You're going hypothermic. You need to warm up."

He's right. I know he's right. But this is ridiculous. Another shiver wracks me, the suddenness pulling a sharp ache in my back, but I do it anyway, wrestling my way out of my robe. It's the heavier of the two items. I peel it off, parsing it from my nightgown, and then shiver as the night air meets my bare arms. He looks up at me at that moment. His eyes go wide, and he immediately looks at the ground.

"You don't need to take that one off."

I look down at the nightgown. The wet, white nightgown that is completely see-through to the nothing I'm wearing beneath it.

"Oh, for fuck's sake," I mumble. "It's nothing you haven't seen before." I wrap my arms over my chest, and he mumbles something under his breath as he adds bigger sticks to the fire.

When he finally looks at me, his gaze is intense.

"None of it is going to matter if we can't get you warmed up."

None of it will matter? As in us being embarrassed? Or the money he won't get paid? I don't even know if he's still getting paid. My brain is foggy, and a dull, throbbing ache pulses behind my temple. I sit down next to the fire, sliding my wet nightgown up my legs so that they can get more of the heat.

He starts stacking more dry wood in a pile next to where he sits opposite the fire and takes off his boots.

Looking at his boots, his wet jacket and shirt, it all hits me.

"What were you doing?"

"I'm making a fire, Arden."

"Earlier, I mean. Why did you run into my room?"

He looks up at me, frustrated.

"Because it was on fire."

"People usually don't run into burning rooms."

"You ran into that barn when it was on fire."

"Yeah, because I heard a child."

"Well, you were in that room."

"And I'm a child?" I ask.

"You know that's not what I'm saying," he says, scratching the side of his nose. "I'm supposed to be your guard. It would've looked suspect if I hadn't."

"Oh."

That makes sense. He was there to play a part. To protect me. So he did.

"What if I hadn't been in there?" I ask.

"You were."

"Yes, but what if I hadn't been?"

"Then I would've gotten to shore a lot faster."

I recoil. Disappointment stings my eyes. But why? He's

money motivated. I know this. Why would this time be any different? What was I hoping he would say? No. That's a pointless exercise. I shiver violently, and he scoffs.

"This is a stupid game," he says, breaking a stick in half and tossing both pieces onto the fire. The fire sparks where it burns sap. "You were trapped. I got in. We jumped. Now, we're building a fire."

It's all so logical, so simple with him.

Except, something isn't adding up. Something I've been considering in one way or another for a long time. And it clicks.

"You could go."

He stops what he's doing with the pile of sticks and looks at me. But he doesn't say anything.

"You've done your good deed. I'm alive and sitting next to a fire. There's no one here to watch you. You could just leave."

"Why would I do that?" he asks.

"Because you've already been paid. You don't want to be a prisoner. If you leave, you don't have to put up with me. With any of this."

He looks at me warily.

"I'm not actually a prisoner. Am I?"

"No." I know that. Declan knows that. But nobody else knows that.

"Maybe I'd like my name cleared."

"Is that what you want?" I ask. The firelight glints in his eyes, and I have no idea what he wants. A light breeze flickers the fire, and a shiver coasts over my shoulders. He gets up and toes the pile closer to my side.

Is he going to leave? Is he actually going to go? Leave me with this pile of sticks to keep warm until someone finds me? Panic skitters down my spine, and I blink furiously. Is this really how it ends? With him leaving me in a cavern next to a pile of wood? Not saying things I want to say but don't have the courage to? So many things unanswered . . .

But he doesn't leave. He walks around the fire and sits behind me.

"Come here," he says.

"What?" I whisper.

"I'm half dry," he says. I look back at him and see he's right. His chest is dry, and even from where I'm sitting, I can practically feel the heat radiating off of him.

"But I'm not," I say, motioning to my nightgown.

"I'm aware. You're going to freeze to death if you don't warm up." His expression is neutral but intense. Another shiver rolls in bumps over my arms and legs. It's not a simple decision—it's heavy with complication and nuance and hurt. But in the end, I'm cold. He's warm. And that wins out.

I scoot back and wait for instructions. It's awkward. Until he places a hand at my waist and tugs me into him. He's soft and warm, and suddenly, it's the most natural thing in the world to lean back.

"Turn around," he says. I frown as I turn to face him. He smiles and shakes his head. "No, like this." He somehow picks me up and rotates me so that I'm stretched alongside him on our sides, with my back to the fire. He wraps an arm around me and lifts my hair off my neck. I tense, half expecting him to press his nose to the curve of my neck.

"Is that better?" he asks. I look up at him. His head is propped on his fist as he looks down at me. The fire is hot, and warms the back of my nightgown, my neck. Between that and the warmth of his body, the shivers subside.

"Yeah," I say, though it sounds like a sigh. Exhaustion hits me like a body hits water when jumping out a seven-story window.

"Go to sleep, Capo," he says.

My eyelids are far too heavy to fight, and as they shut, something pops into my head.

"Why do you call me that?" I whisper. He's quiet for a long moment. I can't open my eyes. The world fades; the sound of his breath and my pulse and the crackle of the fire blend into a hypnotic lullaby. I swear I feel him press a kiss to my forehead, though I can't be sure.

"I'll tell you later."

Then I fall asleep.

CHAPTER THIRTY-ONE

*I*t's the cold that wakes me.

But that doesn't seem right. I can hear the fire crackling behind me, feel the flare of heat from a fresh log. I open my eyes just as Beck sits in front of me. He pauses, catching my gaze.

"You okay?" His voice is rough.

"Yeah," I say, pushing up.

"Don't," he says, pressing his hands into my shoulders. "Slow, okay?" He helps me up, and as I rise, the blood rushes to my head and I feel myself wobble. Then it all seems to rush to my cheeks as I realize I'm in nothing but my thin nightgown in front of him. But at least it's mostly dry. Not nearly as sheer. He helps me turn to face the fire, and it's hot against my face.

"Easy," he says, shifting behind me. He straddles his legs and pulls me back against him. I'm too dizzy to argue, and it feels good. But it's not okay. None of this is okay.

"Beck, we can't—"

"We're not," he says into the top of my head. He rests his hands on the tops of his thighs, and his arms brush the sides of mine. "I think you hit your head in the dive last night. You fell asleep really fast. That's when I noticed the blood."

"Blood?" I ask. He touches a spot on my scalp. I wince.

"Sorry," he says, brushing my hair out of the way.

"I can sit on my own," I say. It's the right thing to say.

"I know."

But neither of us moves. We stay right there, just like that, my head on his shoulder, his cheek to mine, facing the fire. I look toward the cavern opening and the glimpses of sky I can see are a dark blue. Not black.

"Is the sun coming up?" I ask.

"Should be soon," he says. "The cavern should funnel the smoke straight up. Lead a search party here. If they know what they're looking for."

He lets his head fall back against the wall, and that little shift sends me back with him, my head tilted so that my cheek is against his warm chest.

I can't imagine he's comfortable leaning against the cold stone, but if he isn't, he doesn't say anything. How many times has he sacrificed his comfort for mine? We're on opposite sides right now, and yet here he is, doing this for me again.

"Why are you still here?" I ask.

He's quiet for a long moment. The fire pops and sizzles, a particularly large hold of sap sending smoke gusting up into the sky.

"Where would I go?"

"You could find your way home. I know you could."

He shrugs.

"I made a promise," he says. My stomach turns leaden, and I shift, uncomfortably. He's talking about Siobhan. He promised her something about me. Keeping me from Declan, at the very least. Though, if that's what he's trying to do . . . he's doing a very good job of it at the moment, actually.

As if he can sense what I'm thinking, he shakes his head, leaning forward so that his forehead brushes against my ear.

"Fuck Siobhan," he whispers. "Have you forgotten what I said so quickly?"

His gaze is intense and sad.

What did he say?

I slapped him, and he said he didn't see my slap coming.

No, it's something else. That I packed a punch. No, not that. . . . What did he say? What have I forgotten?

His eyes are dark and sad, like he's been laid bare, and he's exhausted. He presses his lips to my shoulder and my entire body goes warm. What is happening? My eyes go hot. I've missed something.

"Arden!" a voice yells from beyond the cave entrance. I freeze. Beck's gaze is so sad, but suddenly fierce. Almost ferocious in its fight.

"There's another way," he says.

"What?" I whisper.

"There's a back way out of the cave. You say the word and—"

"Arden!" The voice is closer.

It's Declan. It's not whoever he would have sent to look for me. He's looking. The sky overhead is a deep cerulean. They'll be able to see the smoke soon enough.

"If this isn't what you want—if he isn't what you want —just say the word, and we can be gone." Beck's words are simple and matter of fact. As if I haven't just spent the past weeks reeling from his betrayal. But now—what is he saying? It's another layer of confusion on top of this terrifying night, and I can't see up from down. Worse still, there's a small swell of something warm and delicious in my belly that feels an awful lot like hope. Hope that this is real.

But what do I want?

Do I want to run away from a man who doesn't understand me, who possibly doesn't respect me in the way I want to be respected, but who represents possibility? Not just my own potential, but the potential of women throughout Nordania? For this man who used me? Who is holding me right now, having saved my life—again—and is offering me a way out?

Maybe it's what I wanted once. Only a month ago, maybe I would have taken his offer. I would have let him lead me into the night and followed him wherever. But now? I don't trust anyone but myself. If I'm going to back out of something, it needs to be on my terms.

"Declan!" I yell back.

Beck stilts. His jaw tenses.

But he nods, imperceptibly. He places his hands on my hips and pushes me to my feet. I rush to where he's somehow rigged my robe on a wall. It's mostly dry, and I wrap it around my body.

"Arden!" Declan's voice bounces off the cave wall, and I turn around just as he enters.

Then he freezes. His gaze falls on Beck. When I turn, I realize what this must look like. Beck, still shirtless, and me tying my robe.

I don't give him a moment to say anything. I run across the cavern toward him and throw my arms around him. He wraps his arms around me, and if there was any doubt in how he felt about me, it's erased by the way he holds me, shaking ever so slightly.

"Are you okay?" he says into my hair. I nod, shaking as I do. He leans back, holding each side of my face and looking me over. He frowns, his gaze settling on the crown of my head.

"Are you cut?"

"I hit my head."

He frowns and looks past me again, as if only just remembering that Beck is there. He takes in the scene behind him. Really takes it in. His eyes land on the fire, and I can only imagine what he must be thinking. Finding me in my nightgown with Beck, who is only just now pulling his jacket on over his untucked shirt.

"You did all of this?" Declan says to Beck. Beck raises an eyebrow, and only then do I realize just how tired he looks. It's more than tired. It's exhaustion on a level I've never seen on him. Perhaps it's from our polar plunge. Perhaps it's from making sure I didn't die from my head injury. Or perhaps it's something else, something that has my bones aching to stay right here in this cavern.

"Yeah. I can rub two sticks together."

Declan doesn't respond, so Beck narrows his eyes.

"If you're asking about the knock on her head, then you'd better think again—"

"Of course not," Declan says, fumbling with his words in a way I don't think I've ever heard. He sounds uncomfortable and awkward. Like he doesn't know what to say. He crosses the cavern toward Beck, and then slowly extends his hand.

"Thank you," Declan says.

Beck looks at his hand, then at the guards that are hanging out at the entrance of the cavern. Then at me. I nod toward Declan's hand. Beck suppresses a smirk, and then nods and shakes his hand.

"Yeah, sure, man. It's not like I did anything—"

"Don't make this a thing. Just let me thank you for saving Arden's life."

Beck's nostrils flare, and this time, his gaze doesn't flicker from mine.

"It's nothing. I'd do it again."

My chest tightens, and I have to look away.

"If there's anything we can do—"

"You can hold up your end of the bargain," Beck says, his voice a little gruffer. "The sooner I can get back to my ship and away from all of this, the better." His words sting, though I can't fault them.

"Of course," Declan says, lowering his voice. He returns to my side, wrapping an arm around my shoulders and giving my opposite shoulder a little squeeze. "We promised. We'll keep it."

"Of course," I say, echoing Declan. Though it still feels like we're on tenuous ground. As if I still have to ask him for permission to protect Beck or to keep our bargain with him.

We are all standing there, awkwardly. As if waiting for the next thing to happen. But nobody says anything and nobody moves. Beck starts kicking dirt on the fire and breaking it down. Declan doesn't move.

"Should we—" I start to say.

"Would you mind giving us a moment?" Declan asks.

Beck stops mid-kick and looks up at us, almost lazily.

"I think the girl is plenty warm, man," Beck says. It's like a punch to the gut. Like I'm back on the dance floor, and Declan is kissing me for show. But it's just the three of us here. So why does it sting?

"I'd like a moment alone with my fiancée, and I don't think it would be proper to leave you here, unguarded," Declan says. I tense. I don't like the way he said that. Beck's jaw feathers. He doesn't like it either. Declan raises an appeasing palm and says, "Merely keeping up appearances. You understand, don't you?"

Beck arches an eyebrow, and then breaks out a wry grin.

"Sure. Of course I do." He approaches until he's standing right in front of us. He looks me right in the eye and crosses his arms over his chest. "I'll leave, if Arden says it's okay."

Declan sputters a laugh, and I feel my face burn.

"What is that supposed to mean?"

"It means, you left her to burn last night, and I helped her escape, and then brought her back from the dead. Forgive me if I don't want to assume that she feels safe alone with you."

Declan is burning next to me. He doesn't even look at me. He grinds his teeth and forces a polite smile. Beck smiles back. Declan steps away from me and turns me to face him.

"Arden," he says, his tone soft, "will you please tell him that he should leave us alone for just a few moments?"

It's not the way I would have wanted him to ask the question. And when I look at Beck, his expression is hard. As if he knew this is exactly what would happen. That he would put Declan on the spot, and Declan would disappoint me. Or maybe, perhaps, he wants me to make a choice. Maybe this is just another mind game. Or maybe it's real, and there's something I'm forgetting, and he's looking at me like I'm not just asking him for the room — like I hold his salvation in my palm. But I've done this dance before, and I know how that ended. I can't—won't let myself go through that again if this is just a pissing contest. And that's why I lean in and kiss Declan's cheek, then turn to Beck.

"Thank you, Beck. But I'm fine. You can go."

Beck flinches. Whatever tension he was holding in his posture is gone. He nods. And then he's gone.

"Are you really okay?" Declan asks. But there's a new hardness to his expression.

"I'm fine," I say.

"What happened between the two of you needs to stay here," he says quietly.

I jerk back. "What exactly do you think happened between the two of us here?"

"I don't know—and that's what I'm saying. I don't need to know." His words hover like I'm missing something. Who is he? So quick to forgive whatever imagined transgression I've committed? Especially when he and Beck hate each other so much.

"Nothing happened," I say, sharply. He visibly relaxes. But it pisses me off. So I step closer. "No, you know what? Let me tell you what happened. You forced yourself on me in front of people who already think I'm not good enough for you."

"Arden—"

"You showed them that you think the same, that you can just use me the way you want to, when you want, in front of whoever. That's what happened. And then you delivered me to my tower for the night, where a fire 'suddenly' broke out in the hallway, and I was trapped. And you know what happened next? Beck walked through the fire to help me."

His nostrils flare. I can't tell if he's angry or jealous. I can't tell where I fall between the two.

"He literally walked through fire, and then he helped me jump from the window into the water below. I nearly drowned, and he saved me from drowning. Then he helped me get to shelter, and he built a fire, and he helped me warm up and dry off, and the only reason I am here right now is because of him.

"So if you want to keep that here, and not talk about it

again, then fine. But you need to accept that I would be dead if I'd been left to rely on you."

He flinches like he's been slapped. I've had enough of relying on him—on men in general, to keep me safe, to keep me alive. Much less to get what I want.

"I'm—I'm sorry, Arden," he says. His eyes are glassy. He reaches for my hand, and then hesitates, doesn't touch me. "I'm sorry. I wish I hadn't—I haven't been . . ."

I don't say anything. I don't help him find his words. And he can't find them.

"Sir?" Alvin is standing behind us, looking at me curiously. I narrow my eyes on him, but he doesn't look concerned.

Declan turns around.

"Clem?" Declan says. Clem enters the cavern.

"Sir?"

"Will you please stay behind? Alvin, we need to have a talk."

"Sir?" Alvin asks, looking troubled.

"Would you like us to take Arden back?" Clem asks.

Declan hesitates. Then nods.

"Make sure she stays with you and Beck. Take her straight back to the ship."

Alvin frowns. "Declan, you can't be ser—"

"That's enough from you," Declan snaps.

Declan reaches for my hand, his touch ghosting my fingertips as I pass, and I pause.

"Get some rest. I'd like to talk with you at dinner." He hesitates, his eyes softening. "If you're open to that?"

It's his ship. What else can I say? Then he gently presses my index finger between his.

"You can say no, you know?"

I consider this for a long moment. Then I nod.

CHAPTER THIRTY-TWO

We're on the water faster than I'm ready. My legs are so tired of the rocking of the Mittlesee—not to mention just tired from fighting for my life the night before—but it's not safe for me to be anywhere else, apparently. Things tend to burn down.

Neve is quiet all day, but Meredith is emotional. She makes it known how much she worried about me when she saw the flames from the ship. Neve has to intervene so that I can get some rest, but I spend all day in bed, unable to fall asleep.

I don't examine that too closely.

The day oscillates between gasps and naps until it's time to dress for dinner. Declan's request hasn't changed, and I request that Meredith let me dress myself tonight. I'm nearly ready to go when there's a knock at my door.

"Come in," I say. Neve enters, hands folded in front of her. She doesn't shut the door, just stands there.

"Can we talk?" she asks.

"Okay," I say. I turn and wait for her to approach. She closes the door and crosses the space. She watches me for a long moment, her green, almond-shaped eyes narrowing on the way I've left my curls down and messy.

"Are you really okay?" she finally asks.

"Yes," I say. "Does my hair look bad?"

"It doesn't look good," she mutters. But that's all. She doesn't tell me how to fix it, and she doesn't tell me how bad it looks.

"I'm really okay," I say, softly.

"Good."

"Are you okay?"

She flinches. Then, without notice, she throws her arms around me and buries her head into my shoulder. I fold my arms around her, and I hold her to me, feeling the way she shakes against me. I've never seen Neve cry, and this is on a different level.

"Neve, what's wrong?"

"You almost died," she says, still buried into my shoulder.

"But I didn't."

"But you almost did, and I said things—I was angry and frustrated and jealous. And I said cruel things I couldn't take back. I never want to . . ." She tapers off, and then steps back. She looks up at me, her eyes wide, the whites making her irises look even more green.

"My husband, Rafi. He died. In an explosion."

"Oh my god," I say, touching my lips. I knew she'd been through something, it was all over her face, but I had no idea, could have never guessed she'd been through so much. "I'm so sorry," I say.

"I'll never get to say the things . . ." She doesn't finish her sentence. She shakes her head and wipes at her cheeks. "I was accused of causing his death."

"But you didn't," I say, though I don't say it as surely as I wish I could.

She doesn't look angry. She shakes her head. "Of course not."

"I'm so sorry," I say again. "I'm so sorry you had to go through that alone."

"Zerah helped me," she says, shaking her head. "She was there for me when nobody else was. Zerah and Irina."

"Irina?" I repeat. Her name makes my blood go cold. Even if she helped me in the end, there's no love lost between us.

Neve takes my hands in hers, and I can see this is not the time for this part of the story.

"I wasn't wrong in what I said to you."

"Oh."

"You have an extraordinary opportunity to lift women and girls from all over Nordania out of poverty and abuse. You need to keep your eye on the ball and persevere."

"Right." My chest falls.

"I perhaps could have phrased it differently."

"Perhaps?" I say, feeling a smile quirk the corner of my mouth.

"I know wishes are worth nothing in this world, but I do wish things were different."

"Different how?"

"Declan does adore you. You can see that, right?"

"Yes," I say, though it sounds less certain than it probably should.

"I wish you would just—"

There's another knock at the door, and it clicks open. Clem peeks inside.

"Miss? Are you ready?"

"Just about," I say. I squeeze Neve's hands again. "We'll continue this talk later, yes?"

She doesn't respond. Maybe I already know everything I need to.

Declan's rooms were most likely never meant to be his. They're cramped, and a little dingy and threadbare.

And yet, here we are. Eating fish. Covered in some sort of citrus glaze. Exactly the dish I swore I would never eat again after leaving the peninsula. We drink our water and eat our fish and greens and make polite conversation. It seems that deep talks are not meant for the fish course.

"Will you excuse us?" Declan says once we've been served a plate of chocolate truffles that were gifted to us by the Swendish delegation. The kitchen boy leaves with a nervous smile, and then it truly is just the two of us.

"I want to apologize."

"For what?" I ask. He looks surprised. But he rolls with it.

"For not listening to you. For not treating you as an equal and coming to a mutual understanding about our next steps."

"Thank you," I say, accepting his apology without forgiving him. I don't know why I do that. It wouldn't cost me anything to say I forgive him. But I can't bring myself to do it when he was definitely in the wrong.

"You mean more to me than I ever thought someone could." His expression softens. His hair flops in his eyes and makes him look younger.

"Oh?"

"Don't be coy," he says, his fluster fluffing his hair. I smile. It's so quintessential Declan.

"I'm not being coy. I appreciate your forthrightness."

He smiles and lowers his chin. "I only want you to be safe and happy. And I can see, now, that you are neither."

My chest tightens. But I can't dispute that. As much as I want to, I can't.

"I'm sorry," I say.

He shakes his head. "Don't be." He sighs and reaches for his water glass. I've noticed over the course of our travels that he has shifted from drinking wine to water. "It's not my fault either," he says, then nods. "Not completely."

"You're not doing anything wrong . . . most of the time."

He winces, and it makes me laugh.

"I can strive to make you happy, but that will take work, and that will take time. I want that for both of us. Do you believe me when I say that?" He winces again, but this time, it's a twisty expression. The ship rocks left to right, and my stomach roils with it.

"I do believe that."

"Thank you," he says, reaching for my hand and brushing the tops of my fingertips gently. Then he sighs. "The thing is, I only have so much control over the other thing."

"The other thing?"

"Your safety."

"Oh."

"The only place I can control your safety is in Nordania."

I open my mouth to disagree, but he raises his hand.

"Please, let me finish," he says. I close my mouth and nod, urging him to continue. "I know you're not completely safe anywhere, and the reason we left was because I couldn't control your safety there. But now, it's different. Now, you're my fiancée. That entitles you to different security measures. It will be different this time.

"One of the reasons it will be different is because, when we return, we will have a plan."

"A plan?

"Yes," he says, then leans in, raising my fingertips to his

mouth. But he doesn't kiss them. He looks at me. "We will have a plan for your legislation, a plan for your graduation, and a plan for our lives after that."

"Our lives?"

"Women's education is important to both of us. Why else would I have lingered for so long around the institute if it wasn't?"

"I can think of a few reasons. Some on this ship . . ." I say with a teasing laugh. He laughs too.

"Hogwash," he says, shaking his head. But he's grinning. "Let's do this the right way. Let's get back, announce our formal engagement, and then announce your graduation plans and our plans to introduce legislation. This is our story. It's about time we start writing it ourselves."

His words are beautiful, and they ignite something in me. I feel inspired.

"That sounds good," I say.

He smiles and presses his lips to my fingertips. Not my knuckles. It feels like an important distinction, something he's put thought into. Then he presses my palm to his cheek. And I look at him. Really look at him. This is a man who knows his mind. He knows what he wants, and he's willing to do the work to get it. Not just that, but he was wrong, and he admitted it. He apologized. That's more than I can say for any other man I've ever met.

And I believe him. I believe he is sorry. I believe he will do everything in his power to protect me, and to make sure the Embers are safe and cared for. He's everything I could ever want and more.

And yet, as I change into my nightgown that night and tuck myself beneath the covers, unable to sleep, there's a chill where a lying, good-for-nothing pirate kept me warm only one night ago.

CHAPTER THIRTY-THREE

*W*e're having lunch in my room. And by "we," I mean me, Meredith, Neve, and Zerah. It's the first time I've convinced Meredith to join me for anything, and also the first time I've gotten Neve and Zerah to sit down and talk to me in the same place.

"I need to know," I say, swirling tea in my cup as Meredith finishes her creme patisserie, "how exactly did the two of you meet?" Neve looks annoyed. We've already had one iteration of this conversation. "I know you met in Osterstan. But . . . *how*? How did that . . . just *how*?"

They look at each other a little uncomfortably, like they're trying to decide whether to let me into their secret club. I expect Neve to tell me it's their business and not mine, but it's Zerah who leans forward as Neve yields to her. It's not the way I know them. Neve is always the confident one, and Zerah leaned back into the background. I don't mind it.

"You remember Whitey?" she says.

I shudder to remember the cringey man who was seated

between us at the first hosted dinner we attended at the institute.

"And his mudflats full of clams?" I say. Neve makes a face, but I can't read her expression.

"They were not full of clams, as fate would have it," Zerah says, amusement tilting her lips. She lifts her teacup to her mouth and takes a delicate sip. She looks relaxed telling this story. I even notice that she's been wearing tops with relaxed collars and pushing her sleeves up her arms. Her scars from her benefactor are fading.

"So, I take it you didn't stick around to see if they would return?"

"We did not. In fact, he received some sort of post in Osterstan, which wasn't entirely legitimate. In any case, almost immediately after the wedding"—she gives a little shudder, and I straighten my spine—"we left for Osterstan with thirty emus in tow."

"Thirty emus?" I say. Then I remember that Beck called him the emu guy.

"They hated him," Neve says, laughing.

"Seriously?"

"I don't blame them. He would pluck their feathers—and add them to my clothes." She exchanges a glance with Neve, and they both muffle a laugh.

"You must be joking?"

"I wish I was," she says, shaking her head. "Their aggressive disdain didn't stop him from embracing his reputation as the purveyor of fine emu goods, however, and forcing me to wear emu feathers on all of my outfits. It was awful."

"It wasn't that bad. You looked adorable," Neve says, gently stroking Zerah's wrist. Zerah's cheeks flush, but she rolls her eyes.

"I did not. Don't lie. It's unbecoming."

"Fine, you looked ridiculous. But it was a cute ridiculous."

"Emu feathers are massive, aren't they?" Meredith says, crinkling her nose.

"And riddled with mites," Zerah says. Meredith shudders, and we all laugh.

"So, what happened to Whitey?" I ask. Neve snort-laughs, and Zerah shoots her a look. "What?" I ask again.

"He died at sea," Zerah says.

"Oh, my," Meredith says.

"His emus attacked him on a boat," Neve says.

We're all quiet for a moment. I look from Neve to Zerah. Then back again.

Zerah laughs first. Then Neve, and then Meredith and I join in.

"You can't be serious," Meredith says, snorting around a giggle.

"Excuse me, I am a grieving widow," Zerah says. But she can't keep a straight face. None of us can. Perhaps it says more about us than I ever realized that we find ourselves laughing at gallows humor. Literally. Just then, there's an assertive knock at the door.

"Yes?" I call.

"Miss? Are you decent?" Clem calls through the door.

"Never!" Zerah calls back, which has us laughing all over again. He opens the door and peeks inside, but when I see the hard expression on his face, I stand, immediately sober.

"What is it?" I ask.

"We've been intercepted," he says. "Nordanian navy. The party's over."

I join Declan in the bridge. He watches the Nordanian naval ship that blocks our access to the Mittlesee with a somber gaze. If we try to go around it, we'll run aground.

"What's going on?" I ask. The captain looks from me to Declan, as if asking permission. Declan waves him off.

"They want to board," Declan says.

"Who is they?" I ask.

"My father's naval general."

"Why?"

"They're concerned after the security risk we faced in Sudersberg. They received some intelligence that concerned them."

"It would have been nice of them to have shared that with us before I nearly got burned up," I say.

"You don't have to tell me," Declan says under his breath. His hand settles on the nape of my neck. I smile, liking this side of him.

"You threw a party, and no one thought to invite me?" Beck says, standing in the doorway. His voice is mercurial, but his gaze is stony. I feel it down to my marrow.

"Not exactly a party, friend," Declan says.

"Looks like the party's over," Beck says, repeating what Clem said below.

"Why do they want to board?" I ask. Declan looks frustrated. "I mean, why not just escort us back to Nordania?"

"That would be the question of the day, wouldn't it, kiddo?" Beck says. He's leaning over the instrument panel, eyes on the horizon.

"What do they know?" I ask.

"Like I said, they have intelligence that there was a threat to us in Sudersberg. They probably want to put eyes on us, make sure we're all right."

"Eyes on us?" Beck quips.

"Do they know who we're carrying? That it's not just us?"

Declan hesitates. Then he nods.

I don't know what to think of this. He was right yesterday when he said that he couldn't keep me safe anywhere but in Nordania. But I still don't trust that his father's military can keep the Embers safe. Or that they have good intentions.

"They're concerned that something could happen to the ship. With us carrying citizens of other countries on board. Some of them have been reported missing from those other countries, and an attack on this ship could constitute a declaration of war."

"That doesn't even make sense," I say. Beck casts a glance in my direction, and he's thinking exactly the same thing. It's just an excuse. But an excuse for what, I don't know.

The phone rings, and the captain picks it up. I can't make out what the other side is saying through the receiver, but the captain responds with short, terse responses. When he hangs up, he presses some buttons, and the ship slows.

"What's going on?" I ask.

"We're slowing so they can board."

"So, this is happening?" I ask. Declan sighs. He looks defeated. As if he's just lost a battle.

"Come on," he says, tucking my hand in the crook of his elbow. "The least we can do is pretend it was our idea and greet them."

It's almost funny to watch the large men crossing the temporary bridge between our ships. Theirs is so much larger than ours, but we hit the waves at different times, so they have to course correct their steps to make sure they don't fall overboard and get smashed between the ships. They're in full military regalia, but have the balance of baby giraffes. Once boarded, the four of them salute Declan.

The interesting thing is that three of them are men, and one is a woman. I've never seen a woman military officer before. I wonder if it's intended to be a peace offering. Which would be a strange peace offering, but then, everything about this experience has been strange.

Declan introduces me to them as his fiancée, and I see one of them visibly flinch. The woman casts me a grim expression, and I don't know what it means. Then he takes them on a brief tour of the ship, ending in the bridge.

"They know what you're trying to do," the woman says. I look at her, and up close, I realize she's older than I thought. At least Dean Edina's age. Her eyes crinkle in the corners, and she has deep lines stretching from her nose to the corners of her mouth. Her fair hair is tucked back into a low bun, and up close, I see streaks of gray woven through the blonde.

"What am I trying to do?"

"It depends on who you ask," she says, looking away, as if she's pretending not to talk to me. "The consensus is that you're turning Declan against his own country."

"Is that what you think?" I ask.

She smirks. "I'm not paid enough to have an opinion. But you should watch your back when you return."

It sends a chill down my spine. Of course, I knew this. I knew that taking on the establishment would be dangerous, but receiving this confirmation from a member of the military carries a different sort of weight.

The door opens, and Clem enters with Simone. My heart races as the officers approach.

"Simone Hartford?" the shorter one, with steely gray hair, asks.

"Yes?"

"You have been reported missing by your family in Swendenland. We are glad to have found you safe and will be happy to transport you back."

She takes a step back.

I look at Declan, and he looks stunned.

"You can't — " I say at the same time Simone says,

"No."

The general looks unimpressed and unmoved.

"You have surely endured a traumatic experience. We will see to it that you receive appropriate medical care and receive the treatment you need before returning you to your home."

"That's not my home," she says.

"That's not what your husband says," he says through gritted teeth.

Declan steps forward, shoulders back, chin up.

"Simone," he says, stepping between the general and the woman, "do you feel that your safety is at risk if you were to return home?"

"What is — " the general says, but Declan silences him with a glance.

"Well?" he asks Simone.

"Yes," she says decisively.

"I don't see what — "

"Then under Section Five of the charter for the institute, which, as you know, falls under the Fourth Subsection of our constitution, ensuring that we protect all members of the institute from mortal peril, I must intercede and insist we offer amnesty."

"You can't be serious," the general says. "That is meant for refugees from war-torn countries."

"Would you argue that a woman who finds her life in mortal peril is different from a refugee fleeing a war-torn country?"

The general looks ready to argue, but the woman next to me steps forward.

"I would side with Mr. Levington in this case," she says. The general clenches his fists and looks ready to go to battle over this, but lets it go.

"In any case, we will need to evacuate this ship, save for your captain and first mate, and any other essential workers."

Declan nods and motions for Clem to inform the others on board. The general steps closer to Declan.

"One more thing," the woman says, approaching. Declan flinches at the sight of her, and I don't know why. He steps closer to me and places a protective hand at my back. Only a moment ago, she had seemed a savior on our side of this conflict. Now, it's as if he's trying to protect me from her.

"Photos have made their way back to Nordanian gossip papers."

"Photos of what?" he asks. She reaches into her pocket and passes him a folded-up newspaper. He opens it, and his cheeks flush bright red. I lean over and feel the heat drain from my face.

It's a picture of the two of us, in my bedroom in the tower, looking . . . passionate. Of course, I know that we were angry. But with the bed in the background, and a robe and nightgown hanging next to it, and my shoulders exposed . . . well, it doesn't look good. The only other people who were there were Beck and Neve . . . or at least, I think so. I suppose someone was able to set the room on fire without anyone noticing, so it's probably anyone's guess who took the picture.

"Well, that's that," he says, a tone of finality in his voice.

"There have been others. From the ship, dancing in Sudersberg, and so on. Those have a new context in light of this one."

There's a question in his gaze. I know what the solution is without him saying anything. I think about Neve, pleading with me to stay the course; Declan arguing over who was capable of making adult decisions; Beck willing to run, but staying. We've come too far to turn back now. I nod, and the expression on his face is truly sorry.

"You can tell my mother," he says, pronouncing her moniker with the sharpest angles his tongue is capable of, "that we'll be married post haste."

CHAPTER THIRTY-FOUR

*M*y return to the capital is very different from my departure. For one, I don't cling for my life in a tiny rowboat, going over river rapids. Instead, I ride in a long, shiny car with Declan at my side. There's no rush, but lots of pomp. People wait alongside the route and wave, trying to peer inside the car.

Meredith and Neve ride in the car behind me, or so I'm told. It's all very slow and fast at the same time. Our progress is slow, and yet before I realize it, we're beneath the storied cupola. When we arrive, Declan exits first, and then helps me out with a gentle hand, and we enter the famed foyer of the capital building. When my heels click on the black-and-white marble tile, it's under the watchful eye of everyone in the capital.

And I mean everyone.

As Declan's father and mother approach, I notice everyone lining the double stairway that splits up the center of the multi-storied foyer. Cooks, assistants, guards, and yes, my classmates. Although, there are far fewer of them. They stand in a neat line at the top of the stairs, hands folded delicately in front of them. Avery, Fiona, Molly, and two others remain. And they don't look happy to see me.

But I don't have time to consider this, because the prime minister is kissing my cheeks.

"We are so relieved to see you returned, healthy and safe," he says. The smile that matches Declan's reaches his eyes, crinkling the corners like a good-natured elf. I smile and nod, saying nothing, because it's so jarring to see this man who, the last time I saw him, had been far more distant and shrewd, in a room full of other men judging my fate.

He steps back, and then Siobhan, Declan's mother, steps forward. Her blue eyes are icy, offset by her dark, nearly ebony hair slicked back into a low chignon. She kisses one cheek, then the other, though her lips ghost the air around my cheeks.

There's no faking with her. She isn't happy to see me. Though I'm not sure why. I've never known why. I suppose I always thought it had something to do with the fact that I couldn't do anything for her, or for her so-called reign. But the same could be said of her husband, and he seems genuinely happy that I'm back.

"I'm so grateful you and my son have found your way back to us," she says, her eyes fixed on Declan. Declan smiles, and I don't have the heart to say anything to interrupt this moment. Despite the fact that she and I don't have the warmest regard for one another, she is still his mother, and that holds credence. If I was returning to my own mother, I would like to think she would be genuinely happy to see me as well. The thought leaves an empty ache in my chest, and I try to conceal it with a bigger smile.

"We'll have a dinner tonight, to formally receive you and Ms. Thatcher, returned from your travels," the prime minister says. "In the meantime," he says, stepping closer to the two of us, "the arrangements you've requested have been made."

Arrangements? I give Declan a quizzical look, and he just smiles broadly, though I recognize it as the political mask.

"The plans I mentioned earlier," he whispers in my ear, "when we had dinner. The increased security." A rush of relief settles me. And I feel guilty—why should I be so relieved that he's not talking about wedding plans? I smile and nod, then giggle for good measure, in case there are any nosy eavesdroppers in the room. Wait. Who am I kidding? Of course, there are.

"Until then, we'll leave you to get resettled," the prime minister says. We both nod, and Declan offers his elbow again. I'm about to take it when his mother steps closer, curling her long, cold fingers around my elbow.

"Why don't I show you to your rooms, dear? It'll give us a chance for a little girl talk."

My smile freezes on my face, and I glance at Declan. His expression is much softer, but I swear I see his anxiety. A rustle of whispers rolls up the balcony, and then people start to move about their business. But I still feel eyes—ten of them—watching me and Siobhan.

"Girl talk?" I ask, trying to keep things light.

"Well, although it's not official yet, my understanding is that you're going to be joining the family." I feel my heart in my chest. I swear I see someone shift at the top of the steps, as if reacting to what Siobhan has just said.

"That's my understanding as well," I say, not sure what else to add.

"Come," she says, fully looping her arm through mine and turning me toward the right hall, toward the back staircase to my old room. "Let's have a little chat."

I cast a backward glance at Declan, but he's looking up

the staircase, and there's an unreadable expression on his face. The other girls descend the steps. He surely has some explaining to do if they've stuck around this long thinking they had a shot, and then he returns with me, wearing the family ring.

Which I just realized I forgot to take off.

So, it wasn't just lip reading that was happening back there.

"I think you'll find your rooms more comfortable this time around," Siobhan says, soft enough to seem discreet, but loud enough that passersby can hear.

"They were perfectly comfortable last time," I say.

"Not so comfortable that you wanted to stay," she says. I don't have anything to respond to that with, because I might accidentally say something that would give me away. I'm still only allowed back because everyone thinks I was kidnapped by Beck. If I had truly been kidnapped, meaning I left against my will, then I can return, graduate, and vote. But if I left of my own free will, then I can't. I forfeit my right to the education, and I have to leave immediately. Of course, that doesn't mean that Declan and I couldn't marry just the same, but as I reach the door to the stairwell with the First Family on my arm, I'm not sure that's enough for me.

"After you," she says, yielding the staircase to me.

It's silent in the stairwell except for our steps and the swish of our day dresses. Hers is tea-length and silvery-blue. Mine is a little shorter, a shift that Neve encouraged, and slate-blue. We both have coordinating jackets. Both are wearing our makeup neutral and our hair back and pinned for diplomacy. Different iterations of the same role.

And yet, I can't help but feel like I've somehow walked into a cobra's nest. This would be the perfect place to push me down the stairs.

ERIN RIHA

At the top of the steps, I hold the door for her and she waits for me on the other side. She doesn't play at being a bosom buddy, just starts walking.

"I'm going to be honest, as I don't see the point in making pretenses," she says, not slowing down, not turning to meet my gaze. "I don't think you're going to last."

"I'm sorry you feel that way."

"It's not a feeling, dear," she says, and I hate the way she calls me that. It sounds so belittling. "You forget, I know my son better than he knows himself."

"He might disagree."

"He might. But he would be wrong. I've seen him over nearly twenty-one years. So many birthdays and holidays, so many gifts received. The ones that were new and unique caught his attention. But the ones that nurtured him kept his attention, helped him grow, and groomed him into the man, the leader he was destined to be.

"You, dear, are a fun, exciting toy for the moment, and he will tire of that. Oh, he will marry you," she says, looking back at me. I can't hide the surprise on my face, and she laughs. It's not kind. "I'll see to it that you're married. And then, when he does tire of you, you will become the scourge of the nation. The harlot who stole his attention from the woman he was always meant to be with."

"You're saying there's another woman?"

"Does it matter?"

"You just said—"

"We control the narrative here, Arden. I thought you would have realized that by now. Or didn't you wonder about why the fact that you killed your benefactor's son in cold blood never gained traction with the media?"

My blood runs cold.

"Oh yes," she says, a pitying expression turning her frown into something almost gleeful. "You don't think we didn't know about that, do you? Our eyes and ears extend far from the capital. Including into contested Osterstani territory."

"You leaked that photo?" I ask.

"You've seen it?" she says. Then she huffs and continues down the hall, leaving me bumbling. "It's not the most flattering image, but it did the job."

"What job?"

"It told the public exactly what sort of relationship the two of you have developed."

"They're going to think we're . . ." I trail off.

"That you're sleeping together, no doubt," she finishes, reaching my room and turning on her heel. "And then, they'll draw their own conclusions about what kind of woman that makes you. Because you know, and I know, that this country, as great and powerful as it may be, will never believe that it was their golden political savior that lured a ruined girl into a bed."

I'm angry. I'm so angry, and I can feel my face getting hotter and hotter. But I can't argue. Because of course, she's right. And I feel stupid for never having considered it before this moment.

"So, there are already people who hate me? Because they think . . ."

"Of course there are, dear."

She opens the door and steps inside. Her heels sink into the plush area rug, her back to me, and I stare at her. The sun hits her hair, strands of red flashing in the field of ebony. Beyond her, I can see that the window that was broken the night I left has been replaced. Everything looks as if it never went through that ordeal. As if it has always been that way. But of course, it hasn't. And looking at her standing there, it's like a dark mark against it all.

I step inside and look around. The room really does look

exactly the same. Except, I can see a few changes. For one, the closet has been bricked over. A wardrobe stands in the corner. She catches me staring at it. The place where I hid from my attackers with Beck. Where Beck first kissed me.

"Some oversights were corrected. We couldn't have a secret room hiding in plain sight where anyone could sneak in and hide, waiting to attack you. That wouldn't do."

My cheeks flush again, and I step toward the bathroom. Fortunately, the bathroom looks mostly the same: clean, pristine, and beautiful. I eye the deep tub greedily.

"Why are you telling me all of this?" I ask.

"Because you need to understand who is in charge here. You may think it's my husband. You might think it's Declan, or even Edina." She crinkles her nose in distaste. "But you would be wrong, and you would be foolish to forget."

"What do you want?"

"Well, ideally, I'd like you to leave. Go somewhere we'll never see you again. But I don't think you're going to do that."

"I can't do that. I couldn't do that . . . to Declan, I mean."

Her eyes flash with something. I know I've misspoken.

"I may not know exactly what it is you're after, but trust that if you mean my son anything but good, I will suss you out like a rat in a tunnel."

I should say something back. Something cutting to tell her that I'm not the weak girl who left before, who ran when things got too hard. But by the time I get my head around my thoughts, she's already pulling the door shut.

"Oh," she says, leaning back into the doorway, "and welcome home, *dear*."

With that, she's gone, and I'm left alone in the room I once considered a prison.

CHAPTER THIRTY-FIVE

*T*he room is exactly as I remember it. The green wallpaper is just as lush and luxurious as it was the first time I laid eyes on it. There are fewer tables — six, to be exact — and I recall when I first shared one with Avery, then Molly.

I'm the first one in the classroom this time, and I have a moment to take it all in. I remember when the space seemed so big, the notion that I would ever be able to take up room in this space insurmountable. Now, it's so much smaller than I remember. But then, I've seen so much in such a short span of time. I'm not the same girl who walked into this space with trepidation and a hole in the bodice of her dress.

"Watch out," a snarky voice says behind me as a flash of red hair bumps into my shoulder and passes, dead set on the front left table.

"Miss Thatcher," Edina's contra-alto voice rings out behind me, and I turn, taking her in. She too appears smaller than I recall. She had always seemed so tall, so magnificent. Now, her posture looks slightly hunched.

She approaches and bends over, hugging me. She doesn't even ask, doesn't look ashamed or embarrassed at the show of affection. I feel the gaze of the other girls on me as I gently pat her back.

"I'm glad to see you returned to us safely. We worried after you."

"Thank you," I say simply. The tables fill, and I try to catch Molly's gaze—the one person who I actually looked forward to seeing. But she averts her gaze beneath her bangs that look like they've grown into a flattering length, brushing her copper eyebrows.

She sits front and center, with Avery on the other side of her. Avery looks rigid, but as pretty as always. The first two tables in the back row fill in, and it's clear that I'm meant for the last table in the right corner.

"You understand, of course," Edina says, directing me toward the last-place spot. "You've been gone."

"Of course," I say with a nod, and I take my place. It's as it should be. Fair is fair.

"We are all, of course, glad to have our colleague returned. And there couldn't be a better time. We're in the midst of reviewing for the final exam, upon which your graduation hinges."

Of course, I knew there was a final exam. But her talking about it reminds me of the last time I spoke to her about an exam: my entry exam. When she reassured me there would be no more exams. Did she not expect me to make it to graduation?

"Today, we will be doing a sort of round-robin quiz. I understand you've been studying on your way back to Nordania. Of course, we understand there may be gaps, and this will be a good opportunity to highlight where those gaps are, so that you can brush up in those areas."

"Thank you, ma'am," I say. Fiona looks over her

shoulder at me with a smirk, and as irritating as it is, it feels good to be back in the midst of these women again. Even if she hates me, we're in the same room, and I can talk to them.

We rearrange our chairs so that we're sitting in a circle, and Edina starts with her rapid-fire questions.

"Fiona, what sweet delicacy does Swendenland claim?"

"Chocolate."

"Excellent. Molly, what product does Espancia trade to Sudersberg in higher quantities than anywhere else?"

"Cotton and spiced peppers."

"Correct. Avery, what group of people lives in the Osterstani corridor?"

"Ostracized followers of the Orthodox Lightbringer faith."

I frown. Is that correct?

"Very good," Edina says, then points the corner of the card at Avery. "Bonus round: who polices the corridor?"

"A coalition of Sudersbergian and Swendish peace forces."

I frown again. There was nothing peaceful about the officers who raided the train we took into the corridor.

"Correct again."

Edina catches my expression and tilts her head.

"Is everything all right, Arden?"

I consider correcting her, but before I can, Fiona clears her throat.

"It might just be a little fast for her. She's not used to this, after all. Having been away for so long." She draws out those last two words, and it makes me realize that I've been gone for half the time they've been here, learning all of this. Of course, I knew the answers to all of these questions from having traveled and been there, but I would have given the wrong answer, according to Edina, on that last question.

"She'll catch up. It'll take some time," Edina says with a gracious smile.

"Or she won't," Avery says. Fiona bats her unnaturally long eyelashes at me, and Edina continues with the next questions. They're about Espancia and the Mittlesee peace accord.

"Arden," she says, frowning at the card, "what is the unique custom service given after a formal meal in Swendenland?"

"Tea service," I say. The other girls titter, and I frown, wondering what they could be talking about.

"Ladies, anyone want to steal?" Edina says. Avery raises her hand, and Edina points to her.

"It's a brandy service for men, chocolate liqueur for women."

"Very good. Okay, back to Fiona—"

"I'm sorry, Dean Edina, but that's incorrect," I say. She looks at me, startled. Then she chuckles.

"I'm sorry if you've been misinformed, Arden, but that is the correct answer."

I shake my head, feeling the buzz of confidence. "When we had a formal dinner at the prefect's house in Swendenland, and then again at the state dinner we were invited to, and after each meal, there was a formal tea service. I know this for a fact because, at the first dinner, I wasn't aware that tea is considered a national point of pride in Swendenland, and I declined a cup. It was considered a slight, and we had to undo my unintentional error.

"After that, the men and women went to different rooms for libations and a salon, but the only formal service given after the meal was the tea service."

Edina stares at me. The rest of the room is quiet. Then Edina blinks.

"This is true, that they do take pride in their tea, but to say you offended them by declining —"

"If you don't believe me, you should take it up with Alvin. He had to undo the damage. And I had to endure no less than three lectures about it."

Someone suppresses a laugh. Molly's stoic face softens, and I swear I feel her quietly cheering me on. Perhaps there is a chance to reignite our friendship after all.

"Well, we can all learn from experience and from being wrong from time to time, and I would be a fool to assert that I am never wrong. I will follow up on this and come back to you with my findings."

"But what about the chocolate liqueur service we had with the First Family and the dignitary from Swendenland?" Avery asks.

"I think it is safe to say that Arden has attended a state dinner in Swendenland more recently than either of those women," Edina says, considering her words carefully. "Let's move on. Fiona, your next question."

She continues with the questioning, and I don't think I'm the only one that feels the shift in the room. I've been gone for half the time they've been studying, but I was learning firsthand about the world and the way Nordania interacts with it. I'm not someone to be cast aside. I've got a fighting chance.

⸙

Perhaps the strangest thing about being back at the estate is how little I see Declan. Even stranger, perhaps, is how little I think of him. I'm literally in his home, and yet it takes me two days to seek him out. And when I do, he's not alone.

He's sitting on a bench, alongside the capital, overlooking the lawn, talking with Avery. She looks upset, her chin downturned. It looks like a private conversation that I don't have anything to gain from interrupting. So I wander the grounds a bit. It's not nearly as cold here in the Capital City as it was along the Mittlesee, and while it's infinitely more comfortable, I find that I miss that fresh saltwater scent.

Which is possibly how I find myself standing outside the cabin in the woods. For half a second, I wonder if Beck is inside. But of course he's not. I don't know where he is, but they wouldn't send him back to this cabin.

The door opens, and a man exits, looking grizzled and beefy, and old.

"Can I help you, miss?" he asks.

"No, thank you," I say, backing away slowly. Then I turn with purpose toward the mansion and make my way back inside. It's nearly dinnertime anyway, and I'll be expected there to sit among the other women.

It's funny how, when I was here the first time, I thought of them, and myself, as girls. This time around feels different. When I reach the dining room, I'm not prepared for the mass of women milling around a dozen tables.

The Embers.

Of course they wouldn't just hide them away somewhere. They would invite them to dinner and treat them well to remind them that the government cares about them. And of course, when I look, Siobhan is milling among them, hugging them and asking questions with an expression that makes her look like the mother hen.

"This is quite the gathering," Zerah mumbles. Neve is standing next to her, a little closer than the other women stand next to each other. But it looks right.

"They have to eat, so why shouldn't the First Family try to kiss their asses and regain their favors?" Neve says.

"You two are super fun," I say with a smirk.

"Oh, wait till you see where we're sitting," Zerah says with a wry grin. I laugh, because I can guess. I wander to the back table in the corner and find my name tag exactly where I expect it to be—hidden away in the back, where nobody will see or think of me.

"Ah, memories," I say, nudging Zerah's shoulder. She snorts, but Neve just watches us and takes in the room with curiosity. Her gaze fixes on the opposite corner, and I see Declan enter, still talking with Avery. It makes me uncomfortable, but not in any urgent way. I wonder at it, though.

He addresses his mother and a few of the women standing around the lead table.

"I'm sure she has a good reason for it," Molly says, just then. Neve folds her arms over her chest, plumping her bust in a way that Molly notices. She then looks at her own flat chest and deflates a bit.

"Can you give us a minute?" I ask. Neve rolls her eyes, but Zerah leans in and whispers something to her that makes her blush. I don't know what's going on between them, but I like it. I like it very much.

"Who is that?" Molly asks. She's wearing a pretty blue dress with puffy sleeves.

"Neve," I say. I don't explain any more. She doesn't ask.

"I'm sorry about earlier," she says.

"You didn't do anything wrong," I say.

"I didn't exactly welcome you."

"I didn't really do anything to deserve a warm welcome. I came back engaged to the guy you're all here for."

Her eyes widen, and then she nods.

"We heard rumors, of course, but it sounds like it's official?" she says, her gaze tracking to my left ring finger. I shrug, but don't lift the hand. If I do, it might attract even more attention, and if Declan isn't ready for that, I don't want to be the one to start the whole thing.

"Pretty official," I say. "We haven't settled on a date . . ." Of course, there's more to it than that, but I leave it at that.

"Well, congratulations," she says, with a small, sad, yet genuine smile.

"Thank you," I say, sounding just as sad. I look around the room and realize Declan has moved, though I don't immediately see where he is. "Where are you sitting?" I ask.

She laughs, and then reaches for the name card at the spot next to mine. "Apparently, they thought I'd love to catch up with my old friend. Which is a pretty good punishment."

I laugh, and then shake my head. "I'm sorry. If you need to stop talking to me for a while to help your prospects—"

"Forget that," she says, her voice sharp. "I'm so over this. I don't want to just get married off. After you left, and then Declan left, it was like they panicked. Everyone else got married off in about two days. We're the only ones who stuck it out. And it's not for their lack of trying. I've had proposals. Fiona has turned down six."

"Six proposals? Damn, girl. When she knows what she wants—"

"I don't think she wants what you think she does."

"What does she want, then?" I ask.

She starts to answer, and then stops, and a mischievous smile sneaks across her lips.

"Arden," Declan says. I turn around, and he takes my hands in his.

"Hi there," I say. I forgot how warm his touch is, how nice it is.

"It's been far too long since we spent any time together," he says, kissing my cheek and lingering. It doesn't feel bad.

Not bad at all. Especially when I catch Siobhan's darkening gaze.

"I agree," I say.

"Then we're in agreement," he says, pulling back and holding up his name card.

"About what?"

"That we should spend time together. You don't mind if we squish another seat in here, do you, Molly?"

"Not at all," she says with a wide grin. Somehow, a chair arrives, and he sits in the darkest corner with me just as the prime minister arrives. He makes a toast—and then a joke about how his son has found the darkest corner to enjoy dinner with his fiancée—and then dinner commences.

There are toasts in congratulations to us. I get to have a nice meal with Declan and Molly and Zerah, and even Neve. Molly regales us with tales of how well I did in the round-robin quiz today. And after the meal, as a small musical trio plays classics, I get a chance to talk to some of the Embers. I tell them what we're trying to do with this measure. And Neve and Zerah do the same. Declan stays at my side through every conversation. It's all as it should be.

But something feels off. Like it's missing.

It's not until late that night, long after Declan kisses me goodnight, long after Meredith helps me out of my gown, and long after I tuck myself into bed, that I realize what was off.

Declan was sitting in Beck's chair.

CHAPTER THIRTY-SIX

The exam isn't nearly as difficult as Neve had me believing it would be. Which is probably a sign that Neve overprepared me for the exam. It's not a bad feeling. I'm the second to finish, behind Avery, and it feels good.

Later that afternoon, I find Molly having lunch with Neve. They seem to be on good footing, and I'm not surprised that they would get along. Actually, I'm not surprised that Neve would get along with anyone here. She was always meant for this life. I wasn't.

I'm about to fix myself a plate at the luncheon table when I see a streak of red out of the corner of my eye. Fiona darts through the door into the kitchen before I even see her face. I can't imagine what she's doing in the kitchen, but when I look at Molly, she looks concerned as well. She shrugs.

I don't know why, but I follow her.

The kitchen is quiet, the workers, having already done their job for the moment, taking a coffee break. I don't see anyone in here, actually. It looks so different from when we stuffed ourselves in here to try to figure out how to cook famous dishes from around the world. At the time, it had seemed like such a strange challenge. Now, I understand: they were trying to prepare us to be wives. Because that's the best most of us could expect or ask for.

I notice the door to the larder is swinging gently, and I make my way back. When I push it open, I see her. She's leaning over a shelf, shaking with muffled sobs. She turns around and looks at me, and hisses.

"Are you okay?" I ask.

"Leave me alone."

"You don't look okay."

"Wow. Thanks. How nice of you to come back here, corner me, and tell me how shitty I look."

"That's not what I meant, and you know it," I say. She flinches. As if she didn't expect me to bite back. Hell, I didn't expect me to bite back. It feels good. Until her face crumples and it feels terrible.

"Fiona, I know we're not friends, but what's wrong?"

"Are you fucking joking?" She laughs. But it's a sputtery, spitty thing. She's crying as she's laughing, and despite looking so completely unhinged, she also looks really pretty. Like, I can see through her makeup and her facade to who she is beneath. She's sensitive and vulnerable.

"I don't know anything you don't tell me," I say.

"You took it all. You took everything from me."

"I don't think —"

"Of course, you don't think. You don't know how this works. I was literally born to marry Declan. Our mothers planned it. And then you showed up here, and did whatever it was you did, and now you're wearing the gods damned ring that's been fitted to *my* finger, and I'm being set up with a second cousin."

I frown.

"Is that legal?"

"Is what legal?" she snaps.

"Can you legally marry your second cousin?"

She flinches, and then frowns. "I don't know. Things are different across country lines . . ."

Then I laugh. It's the worst-timed laugh of all time, and yet I can't stop it. I still can't stop it. It keeps coming out of me as Fiona frowns.

"You're being a real jerk about this. I mean, you should see my cousin. He's . . ." She trails off, and then she laughs. She clamps her hand over her mouth.

"You're not going to marry your cousin, Fiona. Declan won't let that happen."

"Declan doesn't really have a say in it," she says.

"Have you talked to him?" I ask.

"Why would I talk to him about this?"

I am about to answer, to tell her that he's going to be taking over for his father, and he is entrusted with protecting the moral wing of the government. But then I realize that's not how she sees him. She sees him as a guy she was supposed to marry.

"I'm sorry, Fiona," I say. "I didn't know."

She sighs. "I know you didn't know. Nobody did. Not even Declan, apparently."

"I don't think you should have to marry anybody you don't want to."

"Yeah, well, try telling that to my parents."

"That's not a bad idea," I say, testing the waters. Perhaps I could get her on my side here. And if I could get Fiona on my side, I bet I could get all of the other girls on my side too. I'm still not sure how many Embers are going to make it in time for the final assembly, or even whether Carmen and Irina and Emlyn are doing anything behind the scenes, but every vote counts. Our latest counts are too close for comfort. We might have enough, just by one or two votes. But it's going to be really close.

"What's not a bad idea?"

"What if we actually stood up for ourselves? Got the government to protect us the way they're supposed to?"

"Supposed to?" She frowns. Then her eyes light up, as if she's catching wind of what I'm saying.

"We're supposed to represent an entire wing of the government. Four-pronged star and all, right? But they're hanging us out to dry. We all get a vote —"

"— so long as we graduate," Fiona says. "But so many of us don't graduate."

"I know. And I can't help but wonder if that's done on purpose."

"Those filthy pigs," she says. It's the nastiest thing I've heard her say, and I laugh again. "What?"

"I just never thought I'd see the day when you said something I would say."

She laughs.

"So, how do we make this work?"

I fill her in on what I've been doing, why the Embers are here, and how there are others coming. She says she's going to think about whether there's any way for her to contact others in Espancia, given her contacts. And in the meantime, she's going to make friends with some of the other Embers here. See what she can do within the estate walls.

When we leave the kitchen, the dining hall is empty. But I feel more full than I have in a long time.

CHAPTER THIRTY-SEVEN

*I*t takes a lot to calm down after the exam, after talking with Fiona. As we get closer and closer to the assembly, more and more of the peerage and regional representatives arrive. And with them, comes the media.

Whether it's Siobhan's work, or the effects of me and Declan being not on the same page, I don't know, but I haven't seen him much lately. Every time we find a moment together, he is suddenly called away. And it doesn't feel safe to wander the grounds alone right now. Not when a quick photo snapped by a journalist could be misconstrued in whatever way they want.

Which is how I find myself wandering the estate. I'm about to walk up a stairwell toward the third floor when I hear voices. Voices I recognize.

"—you promised . . ." The feminine voice is wobbly and tear-soaked. It's uncomfortable to listen in, and I start to turn the other way, when I hear a familiar voice.

"Avery, you know how I feel."

It's Declan. I freeze. Why are Declan and Avery in a

stairwell, and she's crying . . . my stomach flips, and I lean into the wall, going nowhere.

"I don't understand why . . ." She tapers off, and I don't know what he says next, but they're both quiet. Too quiet.

This is the moment where Fiona would walk up the stairs with confidence and interrupt the interaction. Or where Neve would listen until all had been revealed, and then confront Avery and Declan separately to get what she wants. Or where Siobhan would listen closer until she'd heard everything worth listening to, and then make plans for whatever it is she wanted to happen.

"I think it's for the best that you accept his proposal," Declan says. And for some reason, my heart twinges. I turn and start down the stairs. I don't want to hear the rest of this. It's not fair to Avery, and it's not fair to Declan. If he wanted me to know about this, whatever this is, then he would tell me.

At the bottom of the stairwell, there is a door, and I push through it, not thinking too hard about where I am until I'm on the other side of the door. Then, I know exactly where I am.

The prison.

There are four barred cells lining the hall, two on each side, and at the end of the hall, there's a short desk with a large man sitting behind it. I don't recognize him. But judging by the way he flinches, he recognizes me.

"Miss? Are you lost?" He stands, looking concerned. As if he's been found out.

I approach slowly. The first two cells are empty; the doors are wide open. The last cell on the left is wide open as well, but the one opposite to it is occupied.

"No, I don't think I am," I say softly. Beck doesn't react. As if he expected me. But that can't be the case. He's sitting on a cot, leaning against the wall, one leg crooked, his arm dangling across it.

"Could you give us a minute?" I ask. The guard frowns.

"I don't think I'm permitted."

I tilt my head. And look at him.

"How about you give us five minutes to go get a cup of coffee, and I won't tell anyone?"

He hesitates. But I can see, even as he considers my offer, how his head droops just a little.

"Five minutes," he says.

"You can lock that door, if you want."

He sucks in a breath, and then goes. I hear the key turn the bolt, and then I'm left alone, in the basement jail, only metal bars between me and Beck.

"That was some top-shelf negotiation," he says. He's chewing on an orange peel, and I wonder where he got it.

"Are you comfortable?" I ask. I'm not sure what else to say. The last time I saw him, he'd just saved my life. He'd held me through the night, keeping me warm, and then let me go back to Declan. And now, here he is, looking pale and patchy and unbathed.

"Can't complain. I get three square meals a day, and all the orange peels I can eat. Since they're not shipping them anywhere else."

"What is it about the orange peels?" I ask. "I've never seen you eat an orange. But you always chew the peels."

"Keeps away the scurvy," he says. As if it's the most obvious thing.

"Why don't you just eat an orange?"

"Have you eaten the oranges? They're inedible."

I frown. "Of course, I've had the oranges . . ." But then I think. Have I ever eaten a raw orange? Or have I only ever had them reduced to some kind of sauce? "Huh."

"It's a thinker," he says, tapping his temple.

"And these people think that's our biggest export."

"They're not digging into the crates, are they?"

I don't know what he's talking about, but it's not why I'm here. Which is when I wonder if part of me knew I was always going to end up here.

"Why did you call me that?"

"What?"

"Capo? What does it mean?"

She shakes his head and shuts his eyes. "Not yet."

"Not yet? Then when?"

"You'll know when."

"You do realize you've been arrested."

"I'm aware, yes."

"You're behind bars."

"I've noticed."

"I could hold the key to your freedom."

"Got it."

"Maybe you should just tell me."

"Patience."

"So, when then?"

"So impatient."

"I don't know why I even . . ." I say, trailing off as I pace in front of his cell. "I might not see you again, you know." My voice wobbles as the words come out, and I have to bite down on the side of my tongue. I look down, embarrassed that I'm upset about this. This man doesn't deserve my tears. Or my pity or sympathy. Not after what he's done to me . . . but what exactly did he do? Because everything feels so muddled. He's watching me, his eyes gone glassy.

"What are you doing?" I ask. "I don't understand."

"I'm letting you call the shots."

"What does that mean?" I wave my arms in frustration. "I'm not the one calling anything."

"You are," he says. "You always have."

"You're infuriating," I say, frustration spilling over as tears and a sharp laugh. He smiles too. But it's sad.

"You still mad at me, princess?"

"Don't call me that," I hiss.

"Understood."

"I'm not going to renege on our agreement, if that's what you mean," I say.

"I never thought you would."

"You're the most confounding person I've ever met."

"Right back atcha, Capo."

I narrow my eyes at him, and in that moment, it's as if we aren't standing in a jail with bars between us. It's as if we're standing in the woods, sparring; or riding horses across the Nordanian steppe, arguing; or darting through a warren of tunnels in the walls of the Port of Pleasure, trying to get out alive. It's as if he's saying it to me all over again: *"Whatever happens, Capo, promise you'll remember."*

Was that real? Did that really happen? Right now, he's looking at me the way he did in that moment.

"You still with me?" he asks, leaning onto his elbows over his knees.

He's a liar. Such a good liar. But what if I was fooled by the wrong lies?

"Yeah," I say, and it's like I'm answering another question entirely. "I . . . yeah. I'm here."

He frowns, then leans back, resuming his relaxed posture, just as the door opens. The guard enters, a large, steaming coffee mug in hand, and seems almost surprised to still see me here.

"It's probably time you were on your way, miss," he says, approaching the tiny desk.

"Right," I say. I nod at him, and I'm about to leave when something niggles at the back of my mind. I look at Beck, who is watching me in wait, as if expecting this.

"Do you think I can do this?"

He cocks his head. "No doubt."

It's that simple. It's so simple it stuns me. Because yes, of course he thinks I can do this. Why wouldn't he?

"Of course," I say. I swear I see the flicker of a smile. Then I turn, and I'm on my way. The stairwell is quiet as I climb up to my floor.

CHAPTER THIRTY-EIGHT

*D*eclan isn't at dinner. Neither is Avery. I have a hard time keeping track of the conversation, but I'm distinctly aware that Neve and Simone are doing my politicking for me. I don't have the hang of it yet, and thank goodness they're on board. Fiona and Neve are in deep conversation, and I see Fiona nodding more than shaking her head no. I'm still not sure if Fiona will cross the line to join my side, or if she'll stay firmly within the side of the aisle that has kept her so comfortably clothed all these years. But she appears to be listening to Neve—and Neve to her. Zerah watches with a bemused, puzzled expression. Which is almost just as fun to watch as it is to watch the actual interaction.

But Avery being missing is bothering me. Especially since I heard them talking in the stairwell. She sounded upset in a way that only happens when someone's heart is at stake. Not just someone's position in the world. Thinking back on the way her voice hiccupped around her words makes me think of the first few nights on the ship after Beck said what he did. When his words made me so angry that I slapped him, and he said, *"You really pack a punch, Capo. I never saw it coming."*

My heart speeds up at the memory of those words, words that felt so flimsy and meaningless, but now take on a different resonance in light of his certainty that I can do this. That I could change the world.

But thinking about Beck isn't what I need to be doing right now. Right now, I need to talk to Declan. I need to make sure his head is in the game, and that he's ready to fight alongside me. That he believes in this, and that . . . that I'm not ruining his life by wearing his ring.

It's on the roof that I find Declan. Even though all the herbs and tomato vines are dead and de-headed, he's wandering the rows, plucking weeds, pruning his plants like a clockmaker fixing a watch. His forehead is creased as if it carries all his troubles. But his shoulders are loose and relaxed.

"I wondered where you are," I say, and he starts, as if he didn't know I was here. "And now, I feel foolish."

"Foolish? Why?"

"Because I should have looked here first."

He smiles and puts down his pruning shears.

"It's off season. Only a fool gardens when there's nothing to grow."

"Or someone who sees potential a long way off."

He considers this, and then approaches.

"Are you ready for tomorrow?" he asks.

"Am I ready?" I say, approaching him and leaning back against a planter box next to where he's stopped. He faces the opposite direction, leaning over the box slightly. "I suppose I'm as ready as I'll ever be."

"Do you think you have the votes?"

"Neve and Simone seem confident we can get them."

"You're not down there, working the room?" He looks puzzled.

"I've talked to everyone. They need to talk amongst themselves and come to their own decisions."

"That's not very assertive," he says.

"I don't want to have to convince someone that I know what's best for them. I want them to know that basic human rights and respect are what's best for them. And then be able to offer it to them when they vote for it. Other politicians will argue harder for things that aren't in their best interests. I think they know that."

He winces, as if taking it personally. But he doesn't say anything . . . and neither do I. A chill is in the air, and the wind smells like snow. I don't know if it ever snows here. It never did on the peninsula, though sometimes we had splashes of slush that made a horrible mess. Maybe that's on the horizon.

"Do you think I can do this?" I ask. He's quiet for a long moment as a breeze swishes over the roof. A shudder rolls down my back, and he removes the long coat he's wearing and sets it on my shoulders. It blocks the wind, but does nothing to warm me.

"I think that if everything goes the way we hope, then it will be hard to imagine a defeat."

He doesn't look at me when he says it. It's not the assured answer I was looking for. It wasn't Beck's, *"Of course."* I don't know what to make of it, in fact. And it makes me wonder how invested he is in all of this—in me.

He shifts as if he's going to go inside, and I lift my hand to stop him.

"I have to ask—I was in the stairwell earlier. You were talking to Avery, I think?"

His eyes widen, and then he looks away. And he looks . . . ashamed.

"I'm sorry you heard that."

"I didn't hear very much. When I realized what it was, I—"

"It wasn't what you think."

"I don't think it was—I mean, I hadn't come to any conclusions . . ." I trail off, awkwardly. "Of course you have other relationships, and I don't mean to—"

He steps closer and presses his lips to mine. They're soft, and he smells like mint, and yet, they don't warm me. But I kiss him back, just the same. I try. I really try, and just as I think I'm doing a good job at trying, I open my eyes—and see his eyes are open as well. As if he's trying too. Really trying.

We separate, and laugh, embarrassed.

"Do you really want this?" He motions to the rooftop.

"Your dead plants?"

"No," he says with a sheepish smile. "All of this. This life? Do you really want to marry me?" His voice is so fragile at the end that I don't know how to answer without shattering him. "You don't have to marry me. I don't want you to if it's not what you want."

"I know," I say, reaching for his hand and squeezing it. "I've never felt like you would force me into this."

"Good."

"But," I say, licking my lips, as if that will make it easier to say this, "if your heart is elsewhere, then I don't want to be the roadblock in your way."

His eyes go wide, and for a moment, I think he's going to deny it. But then, he just lowers his head. My stomach drops, but it doesn't wind me.

"I don't—" He stops himself, and then shakes his head. "I don't know what I feel. I know that my feelings for you are strong. Strong enough that I want you to keep wearing that ring."

I feel my cheeks blush even as my stomach drops. Because it's really Fiona's ring.

"But . . . ?"

"But . . . when you were gone, I had some time to spend with the other women. And I knew you were safe, so I wasn't preoccupied, thinking about you all the time. And I got to know some of them a little bit differently. They knew where my interest was, and so there wasn't the pressure. You know?"

I nod. Because I do know. I know what it's like to spend time with someone whose interests align with yours, without the pressure of so many eyes looking for you to get married. He frowns a little, but doesn't say anything.

"I don't know what I feel. I do know that I was happy to see Molly and Avery." His inclusion of Molly in that surprises me, but maybe it shouldn't. Molly is bright and sensitive and funny and can tick all the boxes he needs.

"Then, maybe you should consider that?" I say.

"Is that what you want?"

"I don't want to be the reason you are unhappy."

"Never," he says, leaning in and pressing his lips to my cheek. This time, his embrace does warm me. "You could never be the reason I am unhappy."

The first smacks of icy rain fall around us, and he lifts his coat over my head, protecting me. Once we're inside the door, we stop for a moment. He cups my cheek and presses a sweet kiss to my lips. It would be a perfect first kiss if it didn't feel like a goodbye.

"Sleep well," he says. And then he's gone. And I don't know what to think, or what tomorrow will bring. Only that I had better be prepared for anything and everything.

CHAPTER THIRTY-NINE

I passed.

Once I hear those words, everything else tunes out. It takes a long minute for it to sink in. The thing that makes it sink in is seeing Neve's eyes glaze over. Then watching Zerah kiss her. It seems to take Neve by surprise, but then she kisses her right back, and I leave them in my room to work out whatever is happening.

When I arrive in the breakfast room, I find Molly, Fiona, Avery, and Ophelia, one of the two remaining girls whose names I couldn't remember. They're all wearing wide smiles.

"Where's Gracie Beth?" I ask of the only one not with us. Fiona cringes, and Molly shakes her head. How I passed and she didn't—someone who had been here the entire time—is beyond me. But I don't question it. I don't want to go digging around too deeply into whether there were grading errors, because I *passed*.

I look at Molly, and she grins, and we hug each other. I realize I haven't hugged her, or maybe any of the other girls, ever. And next thing I know, Ophelia is hugging the two of us, and then Fiona joins, which shocks the hell out of me, but I don't say a word. Surprisingly, Avery stays back, just smiling at us.

Or maybe not surprisingly, considering how she apparently feels about Declan. I can't imagine this is easy for her, and I realize after a long, quiet beat that she's staring at me. No, not me—at my hand. At my ring. I tuck it into the folds of my cerulean day dress, and then Dean Edina is there, rallying us into fighting form for the assembly.

She's as flustered as I've ever seen her, and I exchange nostalgic looks with the other girls. Despite everything else, we all know what it's like to have worked with her in a way no one else does. Especially the other girls.

"Are you even listening? Get your heads out of the clouds, ladies," she says, clapping her hands. Avery looks suddenly calmer, which surprises me.

"I'm sorry, Dean," I say.

"Well, I understand there's a lot of excitement, and everyone is all a twitter," Edina says, brushing the wrinkles out of her skirt.

Molly looks at me and mouths the word "twitter," and we muffle our laughter.

"There has been a sudden and astonishing interest in this year's assembly—or perhaps, in our graduates," she says, letting her eyes fall on me, not so subtly. "There has been quite the influx of arrivals this morning."

A wash of warmth floods my chest, and I realize, we've done it. It's happening.

"What sort of arrivals?" Avery asks.

"Assembly members coming in to vote. And so, we've had to rearrange some of the seating. It's going to be quite compact. There might be some spillover into our quadrant of the assembly . . ."

Something clicks in the back of my head, and I'm confused.

"Spillover?" I say, not even sorry that I've interrupted her.

"Are you listening to anything I'm saying, Arden? Or is your head in wedding-planning mode?"

My entire face flushes red. She lifts a hand, as if in apology.

"In any given year, about sixty percent of our voting members attend."

"That's including graduates of the institute?" I ask.

She frowns. "Oh, most of the graduates don't attend. This year is the exception." She waves it off as if it's not a troubling thought. "It seems we have near one hundred percent of our voters upstairs, waiting to be seated."

"That many came?" I ask, thinking of all the women who have come out of the woodwork. "That's amazing. So many graduates to come —"

"You're not listening, Arden," Edina snaps. She looks flustered and angry. "Yes, the women you brought with you have arrived, but the other three arms of the general assembly are at capacity. We will have to make adjustments to the way we practiced your entry."

My stomach drops. There are that many more people who have come out of the woodwork to vote — and they're not women? Not graduates? That means, there are that many more votes to counteract. And if there aren't any more women than the ones who arrived with me on Declan's ship . . . I can't focus on Edina's instructions, but Molly squeezes my hand as if to tell me that she's got this covered.

I'm in a daze the entire way through our rehearsal. I get my first glimpse of the assembly room, and it's massive and resplendent in all its glory. The tile floor is blue marble with gold veining, and the windows behind the dais are swathed in three stories of blue satin with gold cording. We walk up the center aisle, and Edina shows us where to stand, then where to sit in the massive room. There are two large sections of chairs crammed together on either side of the center aisle, and then two more sections shooting off the sides of the dais. One for each arm of the legislature.

The smallest section by far, the one we're standing in front of, is currently having chairs removed to fill out the one to the left. My heart races as I realize that all that we've done, everything we've worked for, it might not be enough.

Neve and Meredith dress me in a blur. They know. I don't tell them anything about what the assembly room looks like, but somehow, they know. Meredith tries to change the subject, asking Neve about Zerah. She's tight-lipped, but the blush on her cheeks is unmistakable. I force happiness as Meredith teases her. And I am happy for her. She and Zerah deserve happiness, and if they have found it in each other, that's beyond wonderful. But I can't stay focused.

Not as Neve applies layer upon layer of "natural-looking" makeup. Not as Meredith dresses me in my navy floor-length gown and matching blazer. And not as a knock comes at the door, and Siobhan enters.

"May we have a moment please, ladies?" she asks, as if someone might tell her no. Meredith and Neve file out of the room, leaving me with my future mother-in-law, alone.

"You look lovely, Arden," she says.

"Thank you," I say, as if I believe her. It seems the right thing to do.

"These walls are not as thick as you might believe," she says.

"I've never given any thought to the thickness of these walls," I say.

She huffs. "It's nearly impossible to do anything within my *home* without my knowing. Including trying to persuade your colleagues to vote for a measure you think you have the right to pass?" Her eyebrow arches high and elegant, as if she's spent years sitting in front of a mirror, practicing exactly this look.

I don't say anything in response. I won't lie to her.

"Hmm," she says, with a nod. "This thing"—she points at me, flicking her wrist as if I'm a gnat—"is far from over. And despite what I choose to believe are your good intentions, you will fail."

"You don't know that," I say.

She laughs. Actually laughs. "Oh, sweetheart. You don't understand politics. You don't understand how this all works. This whole system"—she waves at the room as if indicating the larger estate—"only works because it is a finely tuned machine. It only works because everything and everyone has its place. And as soon as one piece doesn't work, like in a clock, the entire thing will fall apart. There are many people who would be very unhappy if it fell apart."

"And there are a lot of people who have to suffer so that those people can be comfortable," I say.

Her nose scrunches, and she looks as if she's snarling.

"I believe your situation has been resolved, no? I mean, you killed the man you accused of assaulting you. It's hard to argue that you're still in danger."

"Of course, it's only a non-issue as long as we say it's a non-issue. If you were to step out of line, though, upset the apple cart, so to speak, it might become a bigger issue."

"Are you threatening me?" I ask.

"Of course not," she says, stepping closer. She reaches

for a curl that sits on my shoulder and gives it a slow tug. I feel the pain at my scalp. "But I also know that you haven't been completely honest with my son."

"He knows everything there is to know about me. Right down to the tattoo on my hip," I say. If she's surprised by this, she doesn't show it. Which makes me think she knows everything.

"Oh dear, that's not what I'm talking about." She shakes her head, but slips her finger around my curl, rolling it around the hair until it's tight around her finger. "I'm talking about the fact that you're hardly a virgin."

"He knows that," I say, feeling embarrassed. But not for me. For her. This grown woman, picking on me because I was abused.

"That's not what I'm talking about," she says. Her gaze is fixed on my curl. "I'm thinking of a night at a certain pleasure palace with a certain sailor."

I gasp. It's out before I can stop it. She looks up at me in triumph and tugs her finger out of my curl. The hair yanks at my scalp, and I jerk in her direction. She's in control. She's just showed me that. Not just of my emotions, but literally of what I do. The only thing that hits me harder is that I don't know who would have told her. The only person here who could have known just applied my makeup.

"I don't know how he would feel about that," she says.

I try to calm down. But she's right. He doesn't know about that. He knows that I developed feelings for Beck. We had that conversation. But I never told him everything that happened between us. At first because it didn't matter. I was never going to talk to Beck again after what he did to me. But then, after everything else that happened. After he saved my life again. After I spoke with him yesterday in the basement. It just feels different.

I roll back my shoulders and lift my chin.

"Tell him," I say.

This surprises her.

"Oh, I don't think you want me to do that."

"Fine," I say, stepping back and moving toward the door. "I'll tell him. You're right. He should know."

"You damn foolish girl," she hisses. And I can see that I've called her bluff. She's never going to tell him. It would hurt him. And despite being a truly horrible woman, she doesn't want to hurt her son.

"I don't understand you," I say, shaking my head, reaching for the door handle.

"You don't need to understand me," she says. "But you should know that you're messing with fire."

"I've played with fire before and made it out alive. Forgive me if you don't intimidate me."

"Do you have any idea how many strings I've had to pull and fix and rethread to keep this institute open?"

It's the first admission of something she really wants. And it surprises me.

"There's too much money involved in the institute to shut it down."

"Yes," she says, folding her hands over her waist. "It's too big to fail. Right? Who do you think made sure it was set up that way?"

I frown. "You're saying that you are responsible for making the young women of Nordania commodities."

"And I would do it all over again."

"I don't understand you. Don't you see the effects this has? On people like me? I'm not alone. For every one of me who makes it here, there are a thousand others—girls like Tatiana, who was also with my benefactor—who don't make it. Who are stuck beholden to their benefactors and forced into bad situations."

"But at least they had a chance. Would you really be

better off if you'd never been given this opportunity? What if you hadn't been chosen by a benefactor? And instead, you'd stayed with your mother and lived in squalor? Never to lift yourself out of poverty?"

"How do you know I wouldn't have?"

"Oh, please. Do you know how hard it is for those people to lift themselves up to do an honest day's work?"

I recoil.

"That's most of the country, madame. *Your* constituents," I hiss. "And why do you get to decide that for me? So what if I had stayed with my mother and lived in poverty? And what if I had found my way to school and a living? Or what if I hadn't? Then that would've been my life, and I wouldn't know any different. You could say that's a terrible burden.

"But instead, I was bought and sold. To a man with a son who did terrible things to me. And I had no way out. Because I became indebted to my abuser's father."

"Not every benefactor is like yours."

"True," I say, thinking of some of the other girls here. "But too many are. And no matter what you do, under this current system? You can't possibly weed them out. Things need to change."

"Change doesn't happen overnight."

"You sound like Declan," I say with a grumble. I see the corner of her mouth quirk with a smile that looks remarkably like his.

"You will fail," she says. "And then it will be even harder down the road when you want to try again."

"You don't know that," I say.

"I do." She steps closer, and she adjusts the lapels of my jacket. "Even if you win, you will fail. You will bring down this entire system on your head, and you will have no one to blame but yourself. You will become a cautionary tale for why Nordanians shouldn't trust women."

There's a knock at the door, and Meredith pokes her head in.

"I'm sorry to interrupt. Arden? It's time."

I let out a deep breath.

"I'll let you go," Siobhan says. She nods at Meredith, as if showing gratitude for the reminder. But there's nothing but anger and panic left in her wake. What if she's right?

"Are you ready?" Meredith asks.

I shake my head. But I don't have much of a choice.

I step through the door and go to seek my fate.

CHAPTER FORTY

*M*y gut twists into knots, and I feel like I might vomit at any moment. The other graduates stand next to me. The only one who doesn't look nervous is Avery. Which makes me even more nervous.

"Good evening, ladies," Declan says. He strides toward us with a confident swagger in a navy blue suit. A four-pointed star is pinned to his tie, just like his father's behind him.

"Good evening," his father says, with Siobhan on his arm. She smiles at us, blandly, and if anything, she looks bored. She greets us each with an air kiss to our cheeks, murmuring praise about how lovely each of us looks. She pauses, taking a little longer with Avery, and I can't help but look at Declan. He's watching the two of them, a vacant smile on his face.

When she approaches me, she takes my hands in hers and affects an air kiss to both cheeks. But she says nothing. Neither do I.

Then the prime minister approaches. He takes my

hands in his and presses a kiss to my knuckles. I don't have to wonder where Declan got this show of affection from.

"It will be lovely to have a voting member in the family."

Siobhan flinches. And I just smile. Behind him, Declan grins, as if he's just received some sort of confirmation.

"That said," he says, stepping a little closer and turning us away from the group, "I understand you have a measure you're planning to bring before the assembly?"

I don't dare look behind me. I don't know who told him, between a beaming Declan and a conniving Siobhan. There's no point in denying it. So I nod.

"Yes, sir."

He smiles, and it's a well-meaning, kind thing. "Once you have graduated and been sworn in as a voting member of the assembly, you are, of course, free to bring measures before the assembly to vote. But until then, you will have to wait."

"Wait?" I frown. What does he mean?

"We conduct the assembly as we always have. We first bring new business for the general secretary to create the schedule, and then we open the assembly as we always have. Then you will be graduated and admitted as a voting member. You will be able to vote, of course, today. But you won't be able to bring any new measures until such time."

How did I miss this? How am I only now realizing that this is the way this goes? All of these women are here. All of them have come from so far, risking so much, to vote on a measure that—well, for nothing.

Unless . . .

I turn around, looking for Declan.

"Before you ask," the prime minister says, "as members of the First Family, we have always observed a quiet role when it comes to legislative measures. We vote with the favored party, and we do not introduce legislation of our own. We wouldn't want to look as if we're using our position to selfish ends."

"But there's nothing selfish about this . . ." I start to say, and then I stop. He looks sorry. Truly sorry. "I'm not a member of the family . . . yet."

He frowns. As if he hasn't considered this. And then he looks sad. As if he's disappointed that I would bring this up.

"Hopefully, that won't be the case for very much longer," he says. And then he winks.

And that wink sends the world crashing down around me. What the hell does that wink mean?

"Ladies!" Edina barks. Maybe it's not actually a bark, but it's so out of the context of what I'm expecting to hear at that moment that it surprises me, and I jolt. "Arden," she says with a good-natured laugh. "You're going to have to calm your nerves, dear."

"Yes, dear," Siobhan says, with a false smile. "If you're going to get used to this life, you're going to have to hone those nerves of steel." There's a round of soft chuckles, and I don't think anyone means anything by it, but I'm rattled. A hand is pressed against my back. It is soft and kind and cold, and I look up at Declan.

"You're going to be okay," he says.

"But the measure," I mumble.

"What about it?" he says, looking at me quizzically.

"Your father just said—"

"In line, ladies. Now!" Edina hisses. And before I can say anything more, I'm pulled away from Declan and am standing at the back of a line of women who took the same test I did and passed.

The lilting, triumphant melody of the Nordanian national anthem spills out the thick walnut double doors that are now opened wide. It fills the atrium, and I'm glad that I'm not Avery, stuck going first. In fact, I'm last. And it doesn't disappoint me at all.

This is a mess. I spent way too much time focusing on the Embers and sparring with Beck and . . . Beck. Where is he? Is he still downstairs in the jail cell? It feels wrong to have him down there when all he did was help me to safety, when that's the only reason I'm here. Because he helped me escape, and then helped me lie about it. He didn't kidnap me, but he's paying the price for it, living in a jail cell while I parade in front of a full house.

Wow. There are a lot of people here.

Mostly men.

Why are there so many men?

The section to my left is full of men, all the way to the back of the room, where there is standing room only. Legislators who look bored and leer at us in equal measure. I'm fully covered from neck to toe, and yet I feel like I'm being examined, as if a hundred men are all staring at my rear end.

We file down the center aisle, and Avery splits to the left, Molly to the right, Fiona to the left, and so on, until I'm about to take my place at the center of them.

Just then, I feel Declan's hand on mine. He tugs me back, gently.

"Just a sec," Declan says, turning me toward him. He leans in and whispers, "Good luck," and then presses a kiss to my lips.

In front of the whole damn assembly.

There's a tittering of good-natured chuckles, and even a few catcalls to the effect of "it's about damn time," and "finally!" I feign a smile, but mostly I'm so nervous that I can't help what my face does.

I stand there, front and center, as we wait for the First Family to do a lap from far right to left, shaking hands, and exchanging short words with the people lucky enough to stand at the front of the group. It gives me a moment to look at the section of women. The Embers.

When I turn around and look, my heart sinks.

There are a lot of them. Enough to fill about half of the section. But judging by the sheer number of voting members who came out of the woodwork at the last minute, there's not enough. It doesn't matter.

"Please, have a seat," the prime minister says from his podium at the front of the dais. "Today, we gather for a number of reasons. Some are purely business, and some are worth the celebration and the distance you've crossed to gather today. We meet once a year as a full assembly to consider the direction the country is going, and to reflect on that. And we are granted with the opportunity, the great pleasure," he says, smiling down at me, "to graduate our next class of institute members. This year, we have five women who have completed the rigorous coursework and endured. No, not just endured, thrived.

"And as many of you may have read in the papers," he says with an indulgent smile, which is returned with a round of tittering and kind chuckles, "it would seem we have more cause for celebration. It would seem that my son, Declan, has been quite captivated by one of these bright young women, and I will be gaining a daughter."

There is a round of raucous applause. More shouts of "finally!" and "took you long enough!" The prime minister raises his hands as if to quiet the crowd. Fiona snorts to my left and mutters,

"Bright and captivating, huh?"

I snort back, surprised at her words, but not disagreeing. Avery doesn't react. And to my far right, I notice that Molly is dabbing at her eyes. I don't recall her being prone to emotional outbursts. Maybe she's just overwhelmed by the success of the journey?

"But first, business must be attended to. Secretary General? Will you do the honors?"

An old man stands from near the center back of the legislative arm of the room and pushes through the crowd. It's not easy going and people have to shift out of his way.

I turn around and find Neve. She's sitting near the back, smirking as Zerah whispers something in her ear.

A knock at the back doors thunders through the hall. Everyone turns as a security guard enters, looking harried, and then looks around, as if looking for someone specific. He rushes along the back wall, winding through the standing-room-only legislative members, and then winds up the aisle the secretary general is slowly walking up, passing him and nearly knocking him over. He approaches the guard standing to the left of the dais and whispers something in his ear. That guard looks stunned, and a ripple of murmurs goes through the room.

The second guard approaches the prime minister, who leans in, listening. Siobhan is right there, listening in. As soon as I see her brow tighten, I know it's something good. The prime minister stands, and Siobhan grabs his hand and shakes her head. But he kisses her brow and stands.

In that moment, I feel sorry for her. She clearly has an opinion, a strong voice, and he's just diminished it, treating her like a child. The prime minister waves at the first guard, who then rushes to the back of the room.

"It would appear we have more voting members who were caught in weather and have only just arrived. While we wait for our secretary general to get settled, we will allow them entry as well."

The doors open, and standing right there, dead center, is Carmen.

And behind her, a mass of women.

I don't even try to hide my shock, turning around completely as she motions for the women to enter. Commotion breaks out across the arcade, echoing off the walls from floor to the thirty-foot ceiling. The women file in, one after the next, some of them young, only a few years older than me — but some of them older than even the prime minister. As they file in, like a long snake of women, it becomes clear that there will not be enough chairs for them. Some of the men in the legislative section stand, offering them their chairs, but at the end, it becomes a standing-room-only situation.

I look at Neve, and she's busy counting heads. I hadn't even thought to do that.

"Attention, attention," the secretary general coughs into the microphone, and the crowd is slow to silence. Neve looks at me and slowly, slowly, a smile creeps across her full red lips. I smile back. But then my smile falls.

I can't bring the measure.

"At this time, I call for new measures for consideration to be added to the agenda," the secretary general says. Then he coughs. And keeps coughing. I wonder if this has been the secretary general since the first meeting.

Nobody approaches. Nobody raises a hand. Nothing.

"This is the second call for new measures for consideration to be added to the agenda," he says. My eyes flicker to Siobhan behind the podium. She's watching me, a look of triumph giving her a placid, calm look.

Just then, her expression tightens. Falls into something almost angry.

"Do you have the measure in writing?" I turn around and see Carmen.

Carmen. Who knows how this works.

"Ye-es. Yes, I—" I fumble, reaching into my pocket for

the paper that I've read so many times that the creases are almost as soft as linen. I pass it to her, and she smiles. And approaches the dais.

"Sir, please," she says, "I have a measure I'd like to bring before the assembly."

"Very well," the secretary general says, looking annoyed. "What is its title?"

"The Beneficiary Protection Act."

A wave of commotion moves across the room, and the secretary general coughs into the microphone. Then keeps coughing. Then nods, as if he didn't notice the commotion at all.

"It is entered into the agenda for consideration, thank you."

One challenge down. Now, to win the war.

CHAPTER FORTY-ONE

*T*he measure is slated for a vote after commencement and other "housekeeping" measures. I don't know what housekeeping means, but I don't have time to dwell on it, because commencement begins right away.

"Ladies," Edina says, "gentlemen, members of the assembly." She motions to each, and then nods. "It is my singular pleasure to present before you the members of this year's graduating class of the Nordanian Institute for Women."

There is a round of applause, and it is loud enough that I almost miss the door behind the judiciary wing opening. Two bodies move through it, one tall and one hunched over. And unkempt. And I swear I get the faintest whiff of oranges.

"While this year's class has experienced some unprecedented times," she says with an indulgent chuckle, looking at me, and the rest of the room joins her. I suppress a frown. Because, to their knowledge, I was kidnapped. Are we laughing about kidnappings?

But before I can dwell on it, I hear a grunt and look to the front row of the judiciary, where Beck is sitting in handcuffs. He is wearing an ill-fitting suit. Which almost makes me laugh. Except instead, it makes me think of the last time I saw him in a suit—the night he helped me escape the first time. He wore it willingly that night. The suit he's wearing right now looks remarkably similar. Did Siobhan provide the suit he wore that night? Are suits so similar that I wouldn't know one from the other?

"We of course would not be here, if it were not for the generous donations from our system of benefactors," Edina chimes in. She lifts her palms. "Let's give them a round of applause, as there was a record number of candidates this year coming from benefactorial homes."

I clap once. Twice. Then I stop. Because it feels so freaking wrong to clap for the benefactors when we've just introduced legislation to guard against the bad ones out there and protect girls from them. But also because the man who saved me from a predatory benefactor situation is literally sitting catty-corner from me, in handcuffs.

"When our founding fathers got together to discuss the founding of our great nation, they were guided by the great southern star, Liberius. Liberius, of course, means freedom. And it was freedom from tyranny that they sought to establish in this new nation. But they also sought to establish balance. They felt strongly that there should not be a unicameral government. Executive, judicial, and legislative branches would create some balance. But it wasn't enough.

"The philosopher among them, Credence Monkstrum, reminded them of the myth of Liberius, and it has become a tradition that at this point, before we welcome this new class of assembly members, we read it."

There's something off about all of this. I don't know

what. Siobhan looks far too relaxed. Declan looks uncomfortable. And Beck is here. Why is Beck here? He's already been imprisoned for his false crime. His head is down, his posture slumped. Our plan was and has always been that once Declan and I are married, we would have the power to pardon him of his alleged crime. But why is he here?

He looks up at that moment and meets my gaze. He looks like he's ready to surrender. And the confusion and chaos within me calms for just a moment.

"Liberius was a fisherman, earthbound as any mere mortal might be," Edina begins, and something is wrong. This story is familiar, but I don't know why, or what is happening. Beck doesn't so much as blink, and when I look at Declan, he's staring at his hands.

"He fell in love, and he fell in love hard. He was fishing one day to provide for his beloved, to prove he might be enough for her. While he was gone, Alijord, the God of the In-Between, penetrated the veil of the living. He caught sight of Liberius's beloved, the beautiful Capoleia. Alijord had been lost in his land of not quite here, not quite there. But one look at Capoleia, and he was beside himself.

"He appeared to her in the form of a handsome mariner and offered her everything. She demurred, waiting for Liberius to return. Alijord was enraged and persuaded his sister, Nordania, the Goddess of the Wind and the Tides, to intervene. She sent a massive gust of wind that turned into a swirling gale, and Liberius became lost at sea.

"Days turned to weeks and weeks to months, and Capoleia remained constant, waiting for her beloved Liberius. She became desperate and hungry and when, at long last, the creditors came calling, she feared the worst. She was certain she would be arrested or die. She knew that once she died, once she went to the land of the dead, she would never see Liberius again.

"Alijord appeared again and offered her a life of comfort in the land in-between. He promised that in the in-between, she could always return when he did, and she wouldn't be separated from Liberius forever. Desperate to survive, if only to see her beloved once more, she agreed.

"Liberius returned the next day and was met by the goddess Nordania. She was guilt-stricken and told him what had happened. Liberius was beside himself, desperate to get to the in-between and find his beloved. Nothing would stop him from reaching Capoleia, he said, not even death. Nordania was so sorry for her role in their demise, and she could already sense the imbalance in the world that had resulted from Capoleia's abduction. She wanted to set things right.

"But no one could go to the in-between without being called. Not even Nordania. But there was a place in the south seas where the veil between the realms was thin enough to peek through. And so, Liberius set sail, fueled by Nordania's wind, searching the south seas, never giving up hope that he might one day see his beloved again. Nordania continued to manipulate the tides until finally, they found the veil.

"When they arrived, Alijord was furious. But Nordania persuaded him to see the imbalance and allow Capoleia the chance to see Liberius again. He agreed, but he told Capoleia that in order for a mortal to see through the veil, she would have to receive his kiss. Only those who have faced the kiss of death could look back through either of the veils. She did, accepting the risk so that she might see her beloved.

"She didn't know that it was a trick. Because, once received, the kiss of death may not be returned, and the recipient may no longer pass through the veil into the land of the living. Capoleia was stuck.

"When she looked through the veil, she saw Liberius, free and handsome and strong—and grief-stricken that his love could not move through the veil. But as she and Alijord looked through the veil, they saw that the world had become wrong. It was unbalanced and chaotic, and needed to be remedied, if just for the moment.

"While he couldn't take back the kiss he'd given, Alijord allowed Capoleia to stand in the veil, and Liberius met her there. They held each other and wept and breathed each other in. This temporary ceasefire was enough to right the imbalance and bring goodness to the world.

"Each year, Liberius roams the stars, moving in a circle over the southern sky, fueled by Nordania's steady winds, searching tirelessly for his beloved. While Capoleia remains constant, due south, always waiting for her beloved's embrace, until the time when they can be reunited once a year, and burn three times as bright together as they do apart."

There's a round of applause, but I can barely hear it.

I can barely breathe.

I look at Beck.

Capo.

As in Capoleia.

He called me Capo the first time we met. It surprised him. I remember that as clear as yesterday, the way he looked almost stunned when he realized what he'd said. But he never stopped.

"It was with this in mind, that our founders recognized the importance of a softer touch, a sense of rightness and morality, and that they settled on the fourth prong of our national star."

There is more clapping, but I barely notice it. Or what

anyone else is saying. Because I'm staring at Beck, who is looking back at me, and there's no facade. He's not hiding anything. He's not denying it. He's not rolling his eyes or shaking his head or doing anything to make me think that this story has nothing to do with my nickname. Just yesterday, he called me Capo.

It all comes flooding back. Beck saying, *"Whatever happens, Capo, promise you'll remember."* His mother, washing dishes in their family kitchen, telling me, *"Beck might never say."* The expression on his brother's face when he called me Capo in front of the family. His crew's reactions when they heard it. They knew

They all knew.

Beck never said. I didn't know the story. He always followed the south star.

Capoleia is the south star. And to him, I am Capoleia.

"Arden Thatcher," Edina says. Fiona nudges me, and I realize it's my turn to step forward and say the oath. Edina prompts me, and I repeat the oath as practiced. But I barely hear the words. They're just words. And the tears that fill my eyes, for the time lost, for the sacrifice Beck made—the sacrifices he's continuing to make, sitting over there in handcuffs as I recite an insipid oath to a broken school and wear a ring meant for another woman, given to me by a perfectly nice man—these tears are not the joyous pride the assembly assumes them to be. Edina smiles down at me and cups my cheek, as if she's moved by my tears. Then I step back.

One by one, she places a medal around our necks. This medal is shaped like a diamond, with the top shorter than the bottom, and the top sides concave, as if it could fit together with similar shapes and form a four-pointed star. The four-pointed star that emulates Capoleia.

"Congratulations," Edina says, and applause fills the

room. But I can't stay here. I can't keep sitting here while he's chained up. He didn't do anything wrong. I look at him once more, and he smiles at me. It's soft and sad, and it breaks my heart. He knows I figured it out. He told me I would understand when the time was right. He told me to be patient. He said that he'd been letting me call the shots, that he always had. I feel confused, and I feel angry. Because I see it now, too clearly. But what if it's already too late?

A voice clears its throat at the front of the room, and I recognize the head jurist.

"Before we proceed with the rest of the assembly," he says, clearing his throat again, "we have a judicial matter to settle. It's a simple matter of sentencing for a capital crime. As all capital crimes carry with it the maximum penalty of death, it must go before the assembly."

"What's going on?" I say, looking at Fiona. She shakes her head and tsks her tongue.

"Your kidnapper," she says. "He's up for the death penalty."

CHAPTER FORTY-TWO

"*A*rden," Neve says. But I don't know how many times she's said it, or what she's trying to tell me, because the entire room has narrowed down to one person with green eyes and a foul mouth and a pair of handcuffs.

Siobhan threatened me earlier. I knew she wouldn't let things go between us, but I never thought it would go this far. I don't understand what's happening. How did this happen?

"Mr. Levington?" the assembly clerk says. "Are you all right?"

"Is this really the most appropriate forum for this? There should be a trial first."

Siobhan reaches for Declan's arm and tugs him back, but he jerks his arm away. There's a murmuring through the chamber.

The clerk looks awkward, glancing between Siobhan and the prime minister.

"He's already been tried, son," the prime minister says gently. "This morning. Your mother and I thought it would be best to have all loose ends tied before the ceremony."

Ceremony? What ceremony? I've never heard this called a ceremony before . . . the graduation was a ceremony, but why bring this up now, once graduation has happened? I'm missing something.

Declan looks at me, pale. And it sinks in. He's in a suit. I'm in a gown. Everyone who is anyone is here. Everyone here would be invited anyway.

There's another rumble of murmurs across the hall. The prime minister and Declan exchange soft words, and then Mr. Levington grins broadly at the room and shrugs.

"I suppose the cat is out of the bag. Once we're done with the formalities of this event, Declan and Miss Thatcher are to be married."

The blood drains from my hands and face. Everything is falling into place at the same time it's falling apart. Molly nudges me, and I realize there are more eyes on me than ever before, and I probably look shellshocked.

But I can't pretend. Not now. Not when there's about to be a vote on Beck's life. Like he's some common criminal, and not a man who risked his life to whisk me to safety— who we promised that we would pardon as soon as we were married and had the authority to do that.

We can't pardon him if he's dead.

Siobhan looks angry. Maybe this is a surprise to her as well. Or maybe she's angry that I wouldn't be thrilled to marry her son. But this isn't what we talked about.

"One thing at a time," the prime minister says, waving his arms in an authoritative way that pulls attention from me. As if he realizes I'm not in the loop about this wedding business, and that my reaction isn't exactly helpful.

"First, we'll need to vote on this matter. When it comes to sentencing, we refer to the leader of our moral wing of Nordania. Dean Edina, would you do the honor?"

Dean Edina looks shaky. I don't think she expected this either. But she rises from her seat and ascends to the podium, shaking hands with Mr. Levington with the class that only she could. She calls for a vote from each sector, and slowly, each member rises, walks to the front, and casts his vote.

"Arden," Molly says, pushing something into my hand. I don't know how long it's been there. It's crumpled and damp from my sweaty palms. "We're close, but I think we have the numbers."

"To save him?" I ask.

Molly frowns and shakes her head. "For your measure. This is from Neve."

I open the paper and read Neve's impeccable script: SHOULD PASS BY 2 VOTES.

I crumple it back up and press it into my skirt. I can't think about it. I know I should be elated. This is what I've been working toward. This is why we hauled ourselves all over the Mittlesee, why we put ourselves at risk of dying in fire and being attacked by pirates. If this doesn't pass, then those women who died in the Swendish desert will have died for nothing.

But Beck's head remains down as an entire gallery of people who have no idea that he's kind and confusing and deeply good decide his fate. They don't know that he loves his parents, that every dime he makes sailing across the most dangerous passage that exists goes back to his community, or that he treats his crew like family. He's being tried for a crime he didn't commit. And the women around me, they look at him, and they think he's guilty as well. Because of the lie I'm living.

I could stop this with a word. That's all it would take. But it would undo everything I've worked for. As we all rise and vote, I know, without reservation, that mine is probably the only ballot that will say not guilty. But as I reach to drop it in the box, Dean Edina stops me.

"Arden, you needn't do that," she says. She takes my slip and discards it.

"Why not?"

"You've been through too much already. You can trust that this chamber will have your best interest at heart and this will be taken care of properly." She squeezes my shoulder and sends me back to where I was sitting in the front row of our quadrant of the chamber, and I feel completely numb. I should speak up. Or do something. Beck would. He would pretend to be drunk and cause a diversion, and then be heroic.

But I'm not heroic. I'm numb.

Edina opens the polished wooden box, and with the help of the secretary, they tally up the slips. I'm numb as Molly squeezes my hand and tells me it'll all be over soon. I'm numb as Fiona makes a snide remark about my getting married in my graduation robes.

And when Dean Edina reads the verdict, I feel as if I've left my body completely. I'm not here. It's as if I can see myself from outside my body, and I look nervous and upset —like someone facing her captor. But that's not what is happening. That's not the problem.

"Very well," the prime minister says, accepting the verdict. He clears his throat. "This leads to the next, unfortunate matter of business. For certain, particularly egregious verdicts, including those committed against the First Family and the natural extension of itself"—he nods at me, as if acknowledging that I'm as good as family—"public execution is the appropriate remedy."

"What?" I say, louder than I anticipate. But nobody

seems to notice, because the doors at the back of the chamber have slammed open, and a man dressed in black approaches with a tray. As he approaches closer and closer, I see that there are two items on the tray: a syringe, and a rope.

This can't be happening.

Beck is confusing. He's been confusing and confounding me for as long as I've known him. He hurt me and lied to me, and despite it all, I now know, without reservation, that he played the villain to protect me. How could he call me Capo if he didn't have feelings for me?

"Molly," I say softly.

She looks at me, and confusion mars her brow. Like she doesn't understand what I'm saying. I don't expect she would.

"You don't have to watch this," she says, squeezing my hand.

"No. This can't . . . they can't . . ."

We're so close. We have a margin of two votes. We need my vote. But I can't do this. We're past the point of reason. Beck would never let it get this far if the roles were reversed. He would be brave. He would stand up and yell —

"Stop!" It takes a moment for me to realize that I'm on my feet, and it was my voice that echoed throughout the chamber.

Beck doesn't move. Declan rises to his feet, and Siobhan does as well.

The prime minister raises a hand, and the man with the tray stops.

"You can't do this," I say.

"Arden," Declan says, moving forward, but Siobhan holds him back.

"Stop this. He's not—"

"Arden," Declan says.

"What is this about?" Mr. Levington says.

"Can't you see this is upsetting her?" Declan says, pointing at me. "Can't this wait for a more appropriate . . ."

There's a rumbling in the chamber.

"Kill the scoundrel!" someone shouts from the gallery above. Someone else shouts out, and then the entire rotunda fills with the shouts of a mob of people who want to watch someone die. I blink furiously as tears flood my eyes.

"I can't do this," I say. I don't think I say it very loudly, but Siobhan's mouth turns up at the corners, triumphantly.

"Arden." Declan pushes away from his mother and hops off the dais toward me. He takes my hands in his. "We can delay this. Reverse the charges. We can do this."

"Listen to them," I say. "It's too late. We've played this too long."

"But we don't have to . . ." Declan cups my cheek, and I recoil. There's a gasp from my right. In the direction of Avery. But she's not the only one. So much for looking like a couple in love.

"Leave it," Beck says. His voice cuts through the murmuring. He looks at me out of the corner of his eyes, his head still lowered. "It'll be worth it."

But that's the thing. It won't. It couldn't possibly.

"You're an idiot," I say. He shrugs a shoulder.

"You graduated."

I swallow hard. And that's it. I look at Declan, and he shakes his head. He knows what I have to do.

"Arden, what are you doing?" Molly says, squeezing my hand.

"I have a confession to make," I say, loudly and clearly. There's a rumble through the rotunda, and the prime minister raises his hands.

"What is this about?"

"Let's take a recess," Declan says, frantic in his tone and movements.

"No," I say. "I have to confess that . . . Beck didn't kidnap me."

There's a gasp throughout the room and more chatter behind it.

"My dear," Mr. Levington says, "I know that the life of a man being taken is upsetting, but you need not feel guilty for it when he—"

"He rescued me. He didn't kidnap me. I went with him freely and willingly."

I look at Declan and wait for him to corroborate. I'm not going to force his hand. I won't reveal his part in this plan, not if he doesn't want it revealed. But part of me hopes that he's the man I thought he was. That he's the kind of man who will take responsibility for his part.

He sighs, and looks at me sadly, and then lets go of my hands and steps back.

I feel a lurch of sadness in my stomach. But I understand. He can't look as though he thinks the institute is unsafe. If he admits that this was his idea, then it would bring all sorts of other problems. I'm disappointed in him, but that's something I'll have to deal with another time.

"Beck is innocent," I say. "He is innocent."

The prime minister looks shocked, and angry, and then, finally, tired. He sighs and looks at Beck.

"Is this true?" he says.

Beck doesn't say anything.

"I will swear on it," I say. "Make a statement, whatever you need. I swear to you that this isn't his fault. The last night that I was here, someone did try to kidnap me. I was walking to my room and just as I approached it, someone put a black bag over my head and tried to take me from the building."

There are gasps, and the assembly clerk tries to retain order, but I've started talking and I can't stop.

"Beck came around the corner and saw what happened, and he rescued me. That's when the lockdown started. We hid in the safe room in my closet until Declan found us. My room had been destroyed by whoever attempted to take me."

"That's hogwash," Siobhan interrupts. "We investigated that and determined that the girl destroyed her own room in an attempt to cover up her indiscretions."

"That's not true," I hiss, "and Declan will corroborate that."

The chamber goes silent, as if everyone is staring, waiting for confirmation. Declan nods, sadly. Siobhan keeps her mouth shut, but looks furious. "That's when I . . . there had been other incidents . . ."

"What kind of incidents?" the prime minister asks. He looks confused.

"Things stolen, dresses ruined, dead animals placed in my room." There's a wave of disgust through the space, and I clear my throat. "I asked Beck if he would help me escape. I didn't feel safe here. Declan tried to keep me safe, but he couldn't. So I decided to leave. That's what happened. I wasn't kidnapped.

"And if my confession means that this man lives, then it's worth it. I understand the repercussions of this. Because, if I leave the institute willingly, then I'm no longer a student. Even though I've passed the graduation exam and done everything asked of me despite being gone for the time I was, I understand what I'm forfeiting. But I beg you, please consider what my experience means. Please remember that there are more girls in this institute, training for this institute, and who have graduated from or left this institute whose stories are not so dissimilar to mine.

"I've been injured, mutilated, kidnapped, fired upon, and even trapped in a burning building all because of what I represent. And what I represent is the moral arm of this great nation. If the institute is the moral wing of this country, then the very heart of Nordania is under threat. And I beg you to do whatever you can to protect the girls and women who make up that wing.

"If not for Beck, I might not be alive. If not for Declan, I might have suffered severe burns here at the institute. As much as we need strong, kind women with strong character to fill these halls, we need strong men with good character to support those women.

"I would argue that, as a graduate, I should be allowed to vote on this bill. I shouldn't have to justify that the only reason I left was to save my life. But here we are. And I regret that this is where we are, seven steps away from killing an innocent man."

The room is silent for a long moment.

"He's hardly innocent," Siobhan says, her tone sharp. "And neither are you."

"Siobhan!" the prime minister shouts.

"They've been sneaking off together behind Declan's back ever since he first arrived. I have proof."

"You mean your payments?" I ask.

She blanches.

"I've heard enough," the prime minister says, pinching the bridge of his nose, so much like Declan. "I need a moment." He motions for Dean Edina and the two other heads of the wings of government to convene at the back of the chamber.

Molly is talking to me, the other girls are trying to ask me questions, but right now, I can only look at Beck. He's staring at me, like he doesn't understand what has just happened. But in that look, I see everything I need to see. He's a man laid bare, and I know without a doubt that I love him as much as he loves me.

Dean Edina is tapping on the microphone when I tear my focus from his green eyes.

"Arden Thatcher," she says, and I rise to my feet.

"We agree that you should not have to choose between your life and staying at the institute," she says. I feel a wave of relief spread into my limbs. "But the fact remains that you left. Willingly. You caused an innocent man to be tried for a capital crime. You caused the navy to launch a full-scale search for you. You cost the Nordanian government hundreds of thousands of dollars in a futile goose chase."

I gulp. I hadn't considered it in those terms. It sounds awful. Beyond redemption. I feel the weight of hundreds of angry stares.

"We will not rescind your graduation. You completed the requirements, and in fact, finished at the top of your class." A wash of pride covers me, and Molly nudges me. "But until such a time as a formal inquiry can be scheduled and the board can discuss this in more detail, your voting rights must be suspended."

It's like the floor has been pulled out from beneath my feet.

But as quickly as I feel that, I watch the bailiff unlock Beck's handcuffs. Quietly, and without a backward glance, he's led from the chamber.

"Miss Thatcher," Dean Edina says, pulling my gaze from Beck.

"Yes, ma'am?"

"You are excused from the gallery."

I nod. And on trembling legs, I walk down the center aisle toward the doors. I've just upended my whole life. I've set my life's work on fire. Everything I've been working toward is up in smoke.

But Beck is safe. He's okay.

My entire body is shaking when I push through the heavy double doors into the hallway.

The empty hallway.

CHAPTER FORTY-THREE

J have no idea where he went. He should be here. I wasn't that far behind him. Was he taken?

"Arden." Neve is standing there, at the bottom of the stairs that wind up to the gallery.

"Where's Beck?"

"I don't know," Neve says with a frown. "He was released—that's not the point. They're voting."

"What?"

She motions for me to follow, and when I don't, instead wondering whether I should run down the hall looking for him, she grabs my wrist and tugs.

"He was released. He's very capable. And I guarantee you'll find him later. This can't wait."

With a sigh, I follow her. We race up the shallow marble steps until we reach the balcony overhanging the rotunda. One at a time, everyone below approaches the ballot box for the second item within an hour. There are different camps of people across the rotunda gathering and chatting. Molly is wrangling one group, of which Fiona and Avery look skeptical. I felt like I'd had good conversations with both of them, but now that I look at their expressions, I'm not sure.

Elsewhere, Carmen and Simone work different circles of men and women alike. Carmen is animated, Simone is reserved, and they all chat with passion in their eyes.

"You did this," Neve says. Her voice is soft, and I don't think I'm wrong that I hear a note of admiration in her tone. Zerah sits quietly next to her, chin tense and eyes gleaming.

"I haven't done anything yet," I say. The reality is that, while I saved Beck's life, we were counting on my vote, and now, it's gone. I wouldn't change that for anything, but nothing is certain.

"Of course you have," Neve says. "Look at what's happening down there." She points, but I'm not sure what she's seeing that I'm not. "They're talking about us. Not just us, but the girls who are like us. They're forced to confront the fact that the system is broken and discuss whether there might be a way to change things.

"You did that."

I look at the floor again, and notice that the groups aren't quite as segregated as they first appeared. Fiona's father is off to one side with some older-looking men—two of whom were in the room the day I was granted independent status. But two of the other men from that day are in a group with two of the girls from Zerah's safe house, as well as Simone. Molly is talking to two gentlemen wearing the traditional cardinal and gold colors from the Southeastern district, as well as a girl that arrived with Carmen.

"They're talking," Neve says, her voice insistent. "Not just amongst their ranks, but across boundaries and partition lines and party lines. They're having a discussion.

Even if this doesn't pass today, they're having the conversation. And you did that."

Neve blinks quickly as her eyes glisten. The secretary calls for last ballots, and Fiona approaches, casting hers.

"I didn't do it alone," I say.

"Arden," Neve snaps, "take the compliment. You don't know when the next one might come."

I laugh. It feels light and free. I can't remember the last time I laughed. Even with the things that have gone wrong today, there's something light about this moment.

"Take it," Zerah echoes, and she reaches across Neve to squeeze my hand.

As the secretary and Dean Edina tally the ballots, we sit there, the three of us holding hands crisscrossed over Neve's lap. My pulse picks up the lower and lower the tallies get in the pile, and soon enough, it's empty.

"There's one more," Declan says. I look to the floor to see who the straggler might be, but that's when I realize that Siobhan and the prime minister are standing, looking incensed and surprised, respectively.

"Declan?" I whisper. He casts his ballot, pressing it into the ballot box, and then steps back.

"I thought he couldn't —" I start to say, but Neve shakes her head.

"The prime minister and First Family are only supposed to cast votes in a ceremonial capacity. Or, rarely, as a tiebreaker. But Declan is neither. He is also a member of the central tenet of the government, and since he's of age, his vote will count."

"Did we factor that in?" I ask.

Zerah shakes her head. I feel his gaze and look to him. He presses a kiss to his fingertips, and I know that no matter where things lie between us, he doesn't hate me. I think it's safe to assume we're beyond a surprise wedding ceremony today, but right now, I feel more certain than ever that he is on my side.

Dean Edina begins to read the votes. Of course, they've already tallied them in advance, but for formal records, she reads them, and the secretary records them.

"Carmen Delarosa . . . in favor. Simone Hartford . . . in favor . . ."

With every name I recognize, I try to make eye contact with the woman and nod my appreciation. Neve and Zerah are keeping track of the tally, and it's incredibly close. We knew it would be, but the tension is killing me.

"Molly Freed . . . in favor. Avery Ashford . . . opposed."

My heart drops, and Zerah stills.

"We didn't have her in the —"

"We did," Zerah says simply as she counts the next vote in favor. Neve frowns, and I look for Avery. She sits facing forward, shoulders back, chin lifted. Siobhan smiles sweetly at her. I can't help but wonder what Avery has been told in exchange for her vote. Or perhaps this is just who Avery is. She benefited from this system, after all. Maybe I can't begrudge her that.

"Ophelia Norris . . . in favor. Justine Ngobe . . . in favor."

"Where are we?" I ask, as the stack of tallies grows smaller and smaller.

"Dead even," Zerah mumbles. I press my hands into my eyes.

"We're down to the final votes," Dean Edina says. I swear her fingers tremble. I don't know if she would vote in favor of or against. As the head of the institute, she's supposed to abstain from voting, but I wonder whether she hopes everything stays as it is. It would mean job security. Or if she truly does want what's best for all the women, which I can't help but believe to be the truth.

"Leopold Abramson . . . in opposition."

"Can't be surprised by that one," Zerah mumbles. I suppose she's right, but as I realize we're now down one vote, I feel my stomach tighten and twist.

"Declan Levington . . . in favor."

There's a little smattering of applause below, and I swear I see a smile on Dean Edina's lips. Siobhan, however, looks like she's ready to shout.

"I can't think of the last time a measure has come down to the last vote, but here we are," Dean Edina says.

"Who hasn't voted yet?" Neve asks. I look through the rows of girls, trying to remember who I made eye contact with. As I scan the rows, my gaze snags on a head of bright red hair.

And my stomach drops.

Because I know who cast the final vote. And if her best friend here is any indication of how she voted, it's not in our favor.

"Shit," Zerah says, figuring it out.

"Fiona," I say.

"Redhead bitch?" Neve says, and I nod. We squeeze hands tighter as Dean Edina opens the paper. I swear I can hear it uncrease. I can hear the way Edina's fingers slip over the paper, the way she inhales to project.

"Fiona Abramson . . . in favor."

I can't bring myself to say anything, and I don't need to. The entire gallery erupts into cheers, and the floor below is full of people—women and men alike, jumping, cheering, shaking hands. They're hugging each other and celebrating, and nobody looks at me, but it's okay. Because this is as much their victory as it is anyone else's. They made it happen. They took my idea and put it into action. And as the prime minister rises, I realize it's about to be signed into law.

"It appears that this measure has the necessary votes and will pass."

There are more cheers and clapping. He raises his hands and lifts a ballot slip.

"What's he doing?" Zerah asks.

"No, he can't . . ." Neve mumbles.

"What?" I ask.

"Sometimes, when a populist measure passes, the prime minister passes a vote to nullify it."

"He wouldn't . . ." I say, but would he? Declan frowns as Siobhan presses her lips together in what can only be considered a smug expression.

"There are moments in time where potentially watershed motions could upset the tilt of the world. This has all the makings of one of those moments."

As if everyone on the floor recognizes what is happening, they freeze, silenced.

"We must always move ahead, always move forward, but with caution and thoughtful intention. Which is why today . . ." He scratches something onto the paper and folds it, then passes it to Dean Edina. "I feel compelled to cast my own ballot."

He looks at Edina, who stares at the paper in stunned silence.

"Dean Edina, will you please read my ballot for the official record?"

She looks down at it, slowly. She nods, and the secretary picks up his pen. She steps toward the podium as the prime minister steps aside, hands folded over one another at his waist.

She opens the paper, and her hands tremble. She presses her lips together.

"Prime Minister Levington . . ." She swallows hard, and I swear I see a tear trickle down her cheek. My heart is in my throat, and I swear you could hear a rose petal fall. "Prime Minister Levington has cast his vote . . . in favor."

There's a beat of stunned silence.

What follows is a resounding chorus of applause and cheers. I'm crying, and so are Neve and Zerah. Everything we've done, everything we've worked for has been affirmed.

We watch as he signs it into law, a program that effectively ends the unmonitored benefactorship program, that makes abuse reporting mandatory and sets up channels for reporting among beneficiaries. A program that keeps the institute running, but with lines of employment directly into the Nordanian government, and follow-up programs for graduates.

This will change everything. As I hug Neve and Zerah, Declan grins, and Molly cheers, and even Fiona laughs as she applauds the prime minister. I have no idea what comes next, but right now, I know that I'm exactly where I'm meant to be.

CHAPTER FORTY-FOUR

There's a knock at my door, and Declan pokes his head in. I smile. I wondered when I'd get to see him again—if I'd get to see him again—before I left. After the watershed vote, it became clear that we were all expected to move on. As graduates, we were given the night, naturally, but there was packing to do. Goodbyes to say.

I don't have that much to pack, but there are still things I feel sentimental about. If not for me, then for Meredith. I want to make sure that if she decides to return and gets another diamond in the rough, that she has the best arsenal of tools at her disposal.

"You look like you've barely started," Declan says, eyeing my sparse suitcase. I shrug.

"I'm almost done. I travel light."

He nods, as if seeing the difference. He's done so much for me, and even though it's clear we're not meant to be, romantically speaking, I have a lot of respect for him. And so much gratitude.

"I should thank you," I say, but he raises his palms before I continue.

"Let's not do that."

"Please," I say, reaching for his hand without thinking twice. He looks at the way my fingers fold over his, and I realize, with a thump in my chest, that he's looking at the engagement ring I'm still wearing.

"I just want to say thank you for your vote," I say. I swear I see a bit of disappointment mar his features, but it's gone as quickly as I thought it appeared. "You've been a source of friendship and support ever since the very beginning, and I couldn't have done this without you. Any of it."

Then, because I know I must, I give him his ring.

"You should keep that," he says.

I shake my head. "Isn't it your grandmother's ring? Fitted to Fiona?"

"Fiona?" He wrinkles his nose, and then shakes his head. "Honestly, you're probably right. I suppose it's pure luck that you and Fiona wear the same ring size."

Fiona has always seemed larger than life to me. The idea that we're alike in more ways than I ever thought is enough to make me smile.

"Are you sure I can't convince you to stay?" he asks.

"Declan, you are so sweet and kind and —"

He laughs, and it's a sweet sound. "I'm not going to convince you to fall in love with me. I know we're not a match that way. I think we both wanted it to be true for a bit, but it's just not."

"What did you mean, then?"

"I think you could do so much. But so much of the work to be done needs a seat here, in the capital."

"What did you have in mind?" I ask, because I'm not

sure what else I should say. I can't imagine he's offering me a job. I also can't imagine staying here in the capital. Not since I've seen the world.

"Well, Edina has expressed interest in retiring."

"She's retiring?" I say with a gasp.

"Not yet," he says with a smile. "She's expressed interest. Which I think means she's got about five to seven years. We need someone to train as her replacement. It would be good timing, fresh blood and all."

"It's tempting . . ." I say, and I do consider it. The idea of reshaping the institute into something that I can only dream of would be a dream job for anyone. It would be mine to mold and build, for all women, not just affluent or well-connected ones.

"But?"

I sigh. "I've had another offer."

"Already? I thought I'd beaten everyone up here."

"Well, it's not recent. But if it's still available, I'm going to see about taking it."

"You're not going to tell me what this offer is?"

I shrug. "Does it matter?"

He shakes his head. "I've really enjoyed knowing you, Arden. And I want you to know, I don't regret any of it."

My sigh is shaky. After everything we've been through, all the times I've wronged him and led him on and brought trouble to his doorstep, I can't believe it's come down to this. That we can part as friends.

"Goodbye, Declan."

"Goodbye, Arden."

He slips from my room, and I take a moment to collect myself. He's been as good to me as someone can be. I wonder whether, in another life, I could have loved him. But I suppose that's for a different version of me to ponder.

When I return to packing, I notice there's a little tissue-wrapped package. I unwrap it, and inside is a posey of mint and basil flowers tied with blue ribbon. I take in a deep, sweet breath, and tuck it away. It's time to close the door on this part of my story.

CHAPTER FORTY-FIVE

I open the door before I hear a response and instantly regret it. Neve and Zerah are on Zerah's bed, wrapped up in each other, kissing like their lives depend on it.

"I'll come back later," I mumble. Zerah squeals and flies backward, but Neve grins.

"Argh, just come in," she says. She tugs her sweater back up onto her shoulder and sits up.

"Isn't there some kind of code you could've used to warn me? Or just lock the door?" I say.

"Isn't that what a closed door is for?" Neve says as she saunters around to the dressing table and uses a tissue to touch up her lipstick.

"I didn't hear you," Zerah says. She looks flustered and wears a pretty pink flush on her cheeks. Her color has improved overall, and I realize she's become a little curvier over the past weeks. I think Neve has been good for her.

"I'm getting ready to leave," I say. "I wanted to make sure I saw you before I did."

"Where are you going?" Zerah asks. Neve looks at me with mild interest, but doesn't say anything.

"I'm still figuring that out," I say, trying to hide the uncertainty in my voice. The truth is, I don't know exactly what my next steps are. I have an idea of where Beck has gone, but I need to find him before I decide for certain. And I don't really want their input on that.

"What about you?" I ask.

"Oh, we'll go back to Osterstan," Zerah says.

"Are you allowed to do that?" I ask Neve.

Neve shrugs. "As long as they don't know it's me."

"When I was at the safe house, I operated under the name Shideh Chione."

"Chione means snow," Neve says with a soft smile. "Same as Neve." She touches Zerah's cheek, and I wonder whether I should be watching such an intimate moment.

"So Neve is going to go by Sorcha Chione," Zerah says softly.

"Sorcha means bright, just like Zerah," Neve says. Which means her name will mean *bright snow*. I press my lips together, but I can't stop the laugh from coming out.

"What?" Neve snaps, as Zerah smirks in the background.

"Nothing," I say, sharing a glance with Zerah. I never thought I'd see the day Neve found someone who softened her edges.

Neve returns to touching up her makeup, and when I look at Zerah, she looks amused as well. I'm not clear if someone lost a bet here, and this is how it's playing out, but Neve doesn't seem the slightest bit perturbed about her chosen name.

"Are you sure you want to return to the corridor? Hopefully, there won't be nearly as much need for it," I say.

"There will always be need for it," Zerah says. Neve

nods, and there's nothing more to be said. Yes, things are about to change in Nordania. But change moves in fits and spurts. Sometimes, it boomerangs. Apparently, there was a revolt in the Southeast region in response to the bill last night. They've started calling it Arden's Law. It feels both humbling and vulnerable to have a bill like this named after me.

"Knock knock," Molly says, poking her head around the door. But she's covering her eyes. "Safe to peek?"

"How did you get to be so smart?" I ask. She spreads two of her fingers to peek through, and then grins.

"You live, you learn."

"Are you ready?" Neve asks, rising from the bench and tugging a mid-sized trunk shut. Neve didn't arrive with very much, and what Zerah brought with her wasn't much either, but together, they've got enough to require luggage.

"Ready?" I ask, frowning.

"I'm going with them," Molly says.

"To Osterstan?" I ask.

She nods. "I could use a little adventure in my life."

It doesn't seem like the right way to look at it. People in eastern Osterstan are struggling. They're dying and suffering. But they're also telling stories and singing songs and eating incredible street food. Molly hasn't seen much of the world. Maybe that's all that matters?

"Wow, should I be offended that I'm the odd woman out?" I ask.

Neve snorts as she coils an arm around Zerah's waist and tucks her chin on Zerah's shoulder.

"Do you want to come with us?" Zerah asks, skeptical eyebrow raised. I make a show of considering it. To be honest, if it wasn't for everything else, I might consider it. There's good work to be done there. I could be useful. But I shake my head.

"I need to see a guy about a job."

"Is that what they're calling it?" Molly asks.

I gasp at her crude joke, and the other two laugh. Molly laughs and mumbles an unconvincing apology as she sweeps me into a hug.

"Don't be a stranger," she says. I kiss her cheek, and then move on to Zerah.

"Make sure she knows you're in charge," I say as I hug her.

"Oh, she knows," Zerah says with an extra squeeze.

Then it's me and Neve. We've been through so much. I've known her as long as I've known anyone. I stole all of this from her without meaning to. I doomed her to a life where she became widowed, banned from one country, and left to sell her wares to survive.

And before I can say a word, she's wrapped her arms around me.

"I forgive you, Arden. You know that, right?"

I think I knew it. But the way the tension melts from every muscle in my body, leaving me with a sense of lightness tells me everything I need to know. I feel the tears settling in.

"Take care of Carla, okay?"

Zerah laughs. We both look at her.

"What's that supposed to mean?" Neve asks.

She cocks her head. "Carla can take care of herself."

Of everything we've said, I think this is the thing that makes me feel ready to really let go. I hug them all one last time, and then leave them to their plans.

There's one place left I need to stop. And I walk out the front door of the building and climb the grassy hill, headed, perhaps for the last time, toward the trees.

CHAPTER FORTY-SIX

eck's cabin in the woods looks the same. I'm inundated with memories of the first time I came here, the subsequent times I came here to learn how to defend myself, and the last time I was here, when Beck wasn't.

I don't know why I feel so certain that this must be where he is. But as I approach the door and knock, I have the sudden feeling that I might be horribly wrong. I wait. And wait. And wait. There's no answer. I knock again, and the door shifts inward. I lean in and peek around the corner.

"Hello?" I call inside.

It's dark, though I can smell the remnants of a fire from the previous night. Someone has been here recently, but I don't see any sign of a current occupant. Not that Beck would have luggage with him, but there's nothing here.

I step inside, and even though he hasn't been here for months, there's still something about this space that smells like him. It's not just the leather and woodsmoke, I swear I can smell orange peels and sea salt. I approach the fireplace

335

and look at the little figurines on the end of the mantle. One is a little ship, another is a mountain. They look like Beck. Or maybe they look like Beck because they were here when I first came to visit—when it was Beck's cabin.

I was wrong. He's not here. I don't know why I took my time, why I was so certain he'd still be here, that he'd wait for me. He'd watched me get engaged to Declan and rub it in his face every chance I got. Yes, he used a nickname from the myth that made it very clear that he'd fallen in love with me. But I'd nearly had him killed. Why would he stick around for someone like that?

I pick up the little ship and look at it. It's carved out of light wood. I'm not sure what type, but it feels like it could float.

"Careful," a deep voice says. "You break it, you buy it."

I turn and find him standing in the doorway. He's clean. That's the first thing I notice. His hair has been trimmed, and while his beard is patchy, it's nearly grown back. He looks thinner, but good.

"Promise?" I ask.

He smirks. But doesn't move any closer. "What are you doing here?"

My stomach falls.

"I came looking for you."

"Hmm."

"I'm . . . I'm so relieved you're . . ." I take a breath, but it's no use. I can't hide the way my breath shakes. He's here. Right in front of me, but he may as well be miles away.

"I'm so sorry," I say, and I cup my hand over my mouth to catch the sob that escapes. No sooner have I caught it, than he's right there, wrapping his arms around me, holding my head to his chest and shushing into my ear. He smells warm and solid, like a strong breeze on a sunny day.

"I'm here," he says. "I'm fine. You're fine. It's all fine."

"Fine?" I warble. And he laughs.

"I'd rather not have had that whole life-flashing-before-my-eyes death sentence thing, but it's all turned out okay."

The weight of his words crashes down on me, and it's almost unbearable. "I don't know how you can forgive me," I say.

"Arden," he whispers, stroking his fingers through my hair, somehow not catching any knots.

But it's exactly how I feel. I've been reckless. I've done all of these things in pursuit of a bigger goal, and yes, we achieved it. But it nearly cost him his life. It cost seven women from Osterstan their lives—no, not from Osterstan, from Nordania. And that doesn't even include Kern's mollymawk bird.

"I'm just so sorry," I say. He leans back, cupping my face.

"I'm sorry," he says. "I didn't want to ever say those things, or do those things, or make you feel . . . make you believe . . ." He sighs, and I realize I've never seen him cry. And that's exactly what he's doing.

"You called me Capo," I say.

"Yeah."

"The first time I met you, you called me Capo."

He sighs. It's big, and heavy, and then slowly, he nods.

"I did."

"How did you—"

That's when he kisses me. And it's like I've been holding my breath for months, and I've suddenly just had all the air pumped back into my lungs. He presses his lips to mine, and then his hands are on my back, my chin, in my hair—I feel his biceps flex, his chest go taut, his arms tighten around me. It's not enough, and it's too much, and—no, it's definitely never going to be enough.

He breaks the kiss, and his breath is fast and unsteady as he looks at me.

"I knew so fast it's embarrassing," he says, and he laughs. I laugh too, because this gruff sailor is anything but tough right now in my arms.

"This whole time?" I ask, thinking of all the times he's called me Capo, his other half. When we were running from the fire in Sudersberg, when we were sparring on the deck of the Nordanian ship, when we were racing horseback across the northern Nordanian steppe, and hiding in plain sight from mercenaries in taverns, and stuck in hedge mazes during a thunderstorm, and all the way back to when I first met a drunk pirate at a formal dinner.

"Of course," he says. "You?" And he looks vulnerable. His gaze softens, and his muscles tense, and I think about all the time we weren't together, the time I was trying to piece myself back together, whether on a dance floor with Declan, or talking to Embers in Osterstan—how he was always in the back of my mind. The way thinking he'd used me destroyed me.

"I love you so much it hurts," I say. His laughter sounds like a weird sob-sneeze, and that makes me laugh.

"I love you, Arden. Capo. So much."

We kiss for a long time. Long enough to have the presence of mind to shut the door and switch the lock.

But not so long that I forget why I came looking for him in the first place.

"I need to ask you something," I say, dipping my fingertips along his neck just beneath the collar. I like the way it makes him shiver.

"Anything."

"You once offered me a job . . ."

He looks at me for a long moment, and then tilts his head back and barks out a laugh.

"Is it still good?" I ask.

"You want to be my second mate?"

"A job's a job. I've got some skills."

"Yeah? I bet you do," he says, pressing his mouth to my neck. I nudge him back.

"I'm serious. I need a job. Can I have it?"

He studies me for a long moment, and then sits up.

"Well, sure, it's still available."

"Great."

"Of course, you'll need to go through the standard hiring practice. I wouldn't want anyone to accuse me of nepotism."

"Oh, right," I say, a little confused. "I wouldn't want that."

"So, you'll need to get in touch with Shazblister. Since he's the first mate, he'll conduct your interview."

"Sounds like . . . fun," I manage to get out.

"And of course, there's your skills test."

"Right," I say. He threads his fingers through mine and studies them for a long moment.

"Of course, there's another option."

"Another option?"

"I've been informed that you've had a counteroffer of employment."

"Wait, isn't a counteroffer something the employee would—"

"Shush." He presses his fingers to my lips. "I'm trying to do the right thing here."

"Oh," I say. I push his fingers away and turn them to an awkward angle. "And also: don't ever shush me again."

He grins. "I love when you sweet talk me."

My chest flushes hot, and the space between us closes. I am absolutely gone for this man, and it would be far too easy to fall into him right now. The way his eyes smolder

ERIN RIHA

and flicker to my mouth, I'm pretty sure he's having the same thought. I press my fingers to his lips.

"So, what's this other offer?"

He grimaces.

"I should probably just show you."

CHAPTER FORTY-SEVEN

*W*hen he said he needed to show me something, I didn't expect a two-hour cab ride. But once we're there, it's familiar in both the worst and the best ways possible. Rocky Point is where I first met Beck's crew, where I faced down CJ, and where I turned my scar into something beautiful. I touch my hip, and, as if he knows what I'm thinking, Beck slips behind me, pressing his hands overtop mine. He presses a kiss to my jaw and waits for my cue, then he leads me toward the docks.

"Arden!" Kern's voice carries over the bustle of the busy port. He runs toward me, and I'm so happy to see him. He looks strong, healthy, and maybe even a bit tanned. I thought everywhere was cold this time of year, but he seems to have found some sun.

"I'm so happy to see you!" I say, flinging my arms around Kern's shoulders as he lifts me off the ground.

"I'm so glad you're here. I want to be the first to congratulate you."

"Congratulate me?" I say. I know news spread about my

measure, but I didn't think it was the kind of thing Kern and the other guys would keep up on.

"Wait a sec," Beck says, stepping between us.

"Is she here?" a higher voice calls. I look past Beck and see a pretty woman with long dark waves and rosy cheeks speed walking toward me.

"Emlyn?" I say with a big grin. I hug her as soon as I get to her, and something nearly knocks us over, as if we've lost our balance.

"Easy there," Ammon says, catching his wife from behind, just as I feel hands catch me around the waist. "Remember, you're more toppley these days."

"Toppley?" I ask. Then I look at her. She's positively glowing in a red sweater dress and tan coat that is buttoned at the top—but not the bottom. As if it can't button at the bottom.

"Are you having a baby?" I ask. She grins and nods, and I hug her again. Ammon props her up, helping her stay balanced again.

"So, are you up for it?" Ammon asks when we've slowed down.

"The measure? For beneficiaries?" I ask with a frown. "Am I up for what?"

He looks at Beck, and after a long moment where they seem to have an unspoken argument, he shakes his head.

"Are you kidding? You didn't tell her?"

"I haven't had the chance."

"Oh, you've had the chance. Just maybe had your head on something else?" Beck shrugs and grins, and Ammon smacks the back of his head. "Moron."

"Don't give me a lecture about having my head in the wrong place. I'm not the one with the knocked-up wife."

"You take that back," Ammon says, rounding on him.

"Ammon, it's fine. I am knocked-up," Emlyn says with a shrug.

"Boys, knock it off," I say. But no sooner have I said it, than Ammon has Beck in a headlock.

"Are you being a chicken?" Ammon says.

"Knock it off. I can't tell her if I can't breathe."

"Sounds like you can breathe just fine."

Beck swings his fist and hits Ammon in the kidneys, but he doesn't budge. If anything, he just locks his hold on Beck tighter.

"Go on, tell Arden you think she's pretty."

Emlyn rolls her eyes, but laughs. It's like when we were on the ranch and they fought—but this time, Beck doesn't storm off. He looks right up at me and smiles.

"Arden, you're really pretty."

My cheeks flush hot. "Thank you."

"And tell her the rest."

"Not while I'm in a head—aowww!" Ammon scrubs his knuckles on Beck's head.

"Tell her that we're giving her the ship."

"What?" I ask. Ammon realizes what he's said and releases pressure. Which gives Beck just enough time to charge him and flatten him to the pier, his head hanging off the side.

"Sobeck Hermeston, do not drown the father of my child," Emlyn says.

"He can swim," Beck says, pressing his forearm into Ammon's sternum.

"Oh," she says, as if she's never considered this. "That's right. Carry on." But I can't focus on whatever Beck is about to do to Ammon, because I'm pretty sure Ammon just said he's giving me a ship.

"What did you say?" I ask.

"Ammon isn't really in the position to be sailing much

anymore," Emlyn says, rubbing her belly. "As much as he's wanted to get back on the water, he doesn't have the stomach for it anymore."

"Seasick?" Kern asks with a frown.

"No," Ammon says around Beck, who sticks a wet finger in Ammon's ear. Ammon squeals and darts out of Beck's grip.

"We've got a family on the way, you know?" Emlyn says, coasting her hand over her small belly. "He won't say it," she says softer, "but I think he's lost his edge. Too much to lose, you know?"

I understand, and I nod.

"So, there's this whole ship, and Kern told us about how you're as good a sailor as Beck, maybe even better, because you have more than two brain cells to rub together."

"You said that about me?" Beck says, staring at Kern with a hurt expression.

"Never, boss," Kern says, just as Ammon knocks Beck onto his back.

"That's enough!" Emlyn says. Her voice brokers no argument, and the boys stand, rubbing their respective bruises.

"She sounds like Mom," Beck says, rubbing at the back of his neck.

"I know," Ammon says, looking at Emlyn like he wants to carry her off the deck to somewhere more private. She flushes.

"Beck," I say, tilting my head, "were you supposed to tell me something?"

He at least has the sense to look a little ashamed.

"Ammon wants to give you his ship."

I look at Beck for a long moment, and then I look at Ammon and Emlyn.

"Why?"

"Someone should have it. I think you'd be good to it," Ammon says.

"And you'll need a fresh start," Emlyn says. "I've got what I need. So many of the other girls you've helped will have new opportunities. But you need something. Somewhere to land that's completely your own."

"If I'm being honest," Ammon says, "I wasn't sure what I was going to do with it. But then, when Beck had the idea, I—" Beck is shaking his head and glaring at his brother. Ammon stops talking and shrugs.

I look at Beck.

"This was your idea?"

He meets my gaze for a long moment, and there's something vulnerable in there. He wanted me to have something of my own. A place of my own to land, so that I didn't have to—what? Rely on him? Because that was my plan. To come sail with him and work with him.

"You don't want me to sail with you?" I ask.

"Of course I do," he says, taking my hands in his. "But if you sail with me, I want it to be a choice. Not a best-of-two-bad-options decision."

"Best of two bad options?"

"You know, like you could sail with me or be homeless? That's not a good choice. But if you decide to sail with me, and you have your own ship, then . . ."

My chest feels as if it completely melts apart. From the first time we met, he chose me. He had options—he could have left, or not stayed at the capital in the cabin in the woods, or not taken Siobhan's money, or any of it. But he stayed. He chose me because he wanted to.

Now, Beck is standing in front of me, giving me something that nobody has ever given me: something that is truly my own, without strings, something I can build a life on. And he's asking me to choose him, anyway.

"You . . ." I say, and I kiss him. I coil my arms around his neck and hold him tight, and he holds me tight, and when I kiss his cheek, he buries his face in my neck, and I know that, without a doubt, I would choose this man every single time.

"Thank you," I say when I turn around. Ammon is blushing as he nods, and Emlyn nudges him.

"Just one other thing," he says. "I'm not putting my wife and future child on that nutjob's ship."

"Hey!"

"Could you give us a ride back to New Covington?"

Kern helps load everything onto the ship that's been in dry dock for far too long. Ammon and Kern have been checking it out to make sure it's in good condition, while Slick, Shazzer, and Perlman have been hovering about a mile and a half into the Mittlesee on Beck's ship. They only just docked today, and have been missing in action.

We're planning to set sail as soon as everyone is ready to go, but Beck lingers.

"Any chance you'll need a first mate on that ship?" Beck asks with a flirty smile. He kisses my jaw and wraps his arms around my waist. We stand there and admire the ship, which is at least twenty feet bigger than Beck's.

"An incredible first mate is a must," I say.

"I'd love to put in my resume for consideration," Beck says, pressing a kiss to the slope of my neck.

"Oh, I've already got one."

"You do?" he says, kissing my earlobe.

"Kern is going to be great," I say. I step forward, and Kern waves at us from the ship.

"Kern?"

"We worked it out already. The second time you wrestled your brother."

"Are you kidding?"

"I would never kid about my first mate." I pretend to consider this seriously. "But if you want, I could put in a good word with him for you as second mate."

"Oh, really?"

I shrug. "I mean, you'd still need to apply. There's an interview process, and then a skills test. I wouldn't want anyone to think you were hired by nepotism."

"Oh, of course not," he says.

"We gotta go, Cap'n," Shazzer says, running down the pier from out of nowhere. Slick is right behind him, and up the hill, with his pants still around his knees, is Perlman.

"Hey Arden!" Slick says as he runs past. They both run up onto the ship.

"What the hell?" Beck says.

"Arden! You look good!" Perlman says. There's an angry yell from on top of the hill, and three women stand up there, one with a frying pan and another with a gun.

"Guess now is better than ever," I say. Beck pulls a face. "Get ready to set sail," I yell to Kern.

"Aye aye, Captain!" Kern calls back. He grins so wide that it makes me smile.

"See you soon?" Beck says, squeezing my hand. I nod. And hesitate. Is this where I'm supposed to choose him? I promised I'd sail Emlyn home. That needs to come first. I guess we'll meet in New Covington?

"Yeah, see you soon," I say. He kisses me, holding me in place a moment longer than necessary, and then I shuffle off to the gangway.

Kern and Ammon handle final checks while I get my bearings on the much larger ship.

The shouting from the hill is getting louder, and I see

Beck's ship start to pull out of moor. This is really happening. It's going to be an adventure, and I can't wait to start.

I look back at port, taking in the commotion coming down the hill, the fishermen paying no attention as they moor their own crafts, the clouds over it all, turning pink in the fading sun.

"Ready, Captain?" Kern says.

Am I ready? I look to my passengers. Ammon nods his approval, and Emlyn smiles at me encouragingly.

"You've got this," Emlyn says.

Something feels off. Not quite right, though I can't put my finger on it. Everything seems ready to go, and with Beck already moving out to sea, there's nothing left for me here. So I nod as well.

I look around at my ship—my ship. I don't know what I'll do once we've taken Emlyn and Ammon to New Covington. I can't imagine missing the birth of their baby, watching their little family grow. I could go visit Zerah and Neve in Osterstan, check in on Carla. Molly is going to be busy, and there's nothing that says I can't return to Nordania. Declan isn't going to be my husband, but I'm sure I'll want to visit him once his garden is thriving for some mint and basil and other herbs.

The point is that I have my own ship. I have my own way in the world, and I can write my own story. I look to my right, to where Beck is standing on his ship, looking at me. And I know what's missing.

"Beck!" I shout.

"You miss me already, Capo?" Beck calls from his ship. I want to respond with something quick or witty. But nothing comes to mind.

"Can you climb a rope?"

He grins and comes to the railing of his ship.

"I thought you'd never ask."

Ammon helps me unmangle a thick rope and toss it over the side. It takes us three tries to pitch it close enough for him and Shazzer to catch it.

He doesn't have finesse. He climbs like a cat trying not to drown, and his crew launches barbs and jokes at him with as much ferocity as Ammon. But when he finally reaches the railing and tosses a leg over, I grin.

"Permission to board . . . Captain?" he says. Oh. I really like the way he says "captain."

"Permission granted."

Then he hops onto the deck, takes my face in his hands, and kisses me.

"Setting sail north by northwest, Captain?" Kern says.

"Affirmative," I say. Beck takes my hands and presses his lips into my palms.

"Why don't you take a moment, Captain?" Ammon says. "I can stand in one last time."

"Thanks," I say, and Beck and I go to the back of the ship. He stands close behind me, his arms coiled around my waist. To the west, the sun is setting over Nordania, and the first stars of the night flicker over the distant mountains. They're close to each other, growing closer, blinking in the southern sky.

"That's us," Beck says, pointing at the stars, Capoleia and Liberius.

"They're bright," I say as he leans in closer and presses a kiss to the curve of my neck.

"And getting brighter."

ACKNOWLEDGMENTS

Thank you, as always, to Kisa Whipkey, editor extraordinaire. Thank you for seeing the spark at the beginning of Arden's story and standing next to me as I navigated a stormy story. REUTS was always the right home for this series, and I'm so glad that you were the person to bring her story to the world.

To Ash Rugirello for yet another killer cover. I don't know how you do it, but somehow you take my scrap of an idea and mold it into something so beautiful.

To my writing community. I will undoubtedly leave someone out, but Wingnuts, Gale Force, Roaring 20's, and Lit Squad, your support has been invaluable. In particular, Mari Hotchkiss, you're a rockstar storyteller and my favorite sounding board for ideas (mostly terrible, but some good). Cathleen Barnhart, your constant support has helped me keep my sanity throughout this season. Jefna, Heather, and Desiree, you've been there from book one, and I'm so grateful you're still here.

To Chris, for all the things. I'm never short for words, but when it comes to you, there aren't enough. I love you.

To Elliott and Walt, you probably don't even know how much you've supported me through the years. Maybe when you're older, my weird job will make more sense. Or maybe not. But you're the absolute best, and I love you forever.

To the readers who made this possible. To say it's been a bumpy road is an understatement. But you're still here, and I will always hold you in my heart for believing in Arden.